FANTASY

O.Z.R. KEELEY

Resistance

Chaos-Tol's Bane

Book One

When the eternal struggle sweeps a world
can a child's accident determine that world's future

Table of Contents

About the Author

SHAUN KEELEY IS A DEBUT fantasy author whose first novel, Resistance, showcases his deep passion for the genre. As an avid reader and father of three daughters (his Gargoyles), Shaun draws inspiration from his family, infusing his female characters with their strength and spirit. Beyond his literary pursuits, Shaun is a dedicated motor racing participant with a background in the motorsport industry. This unique blend of interests enriches his storytelling, combining the excitement of racing with the imaginative worlds of fantasy. Shaun's diverse experiences and interests shape his writing, promising readers engaging and dynamic adventures.

NORDINIUM

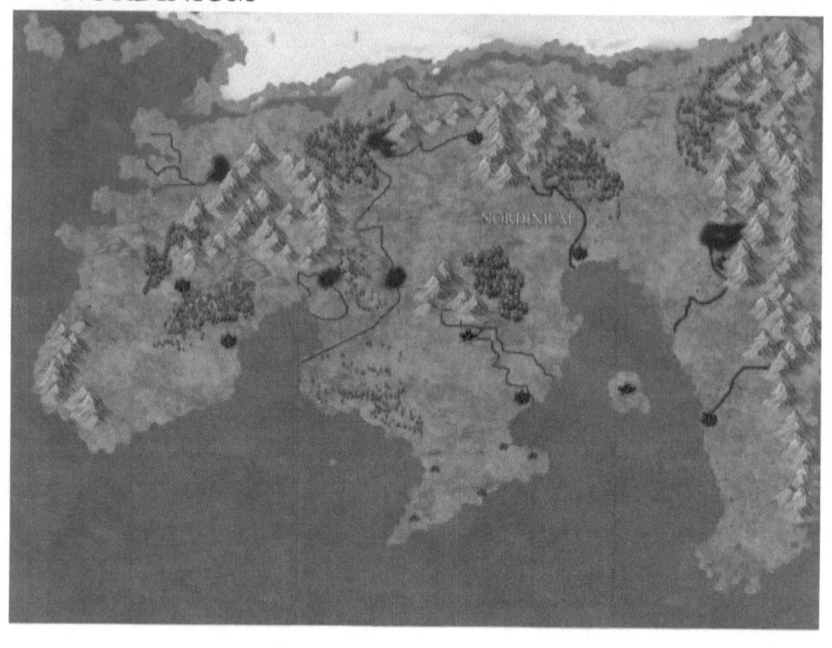

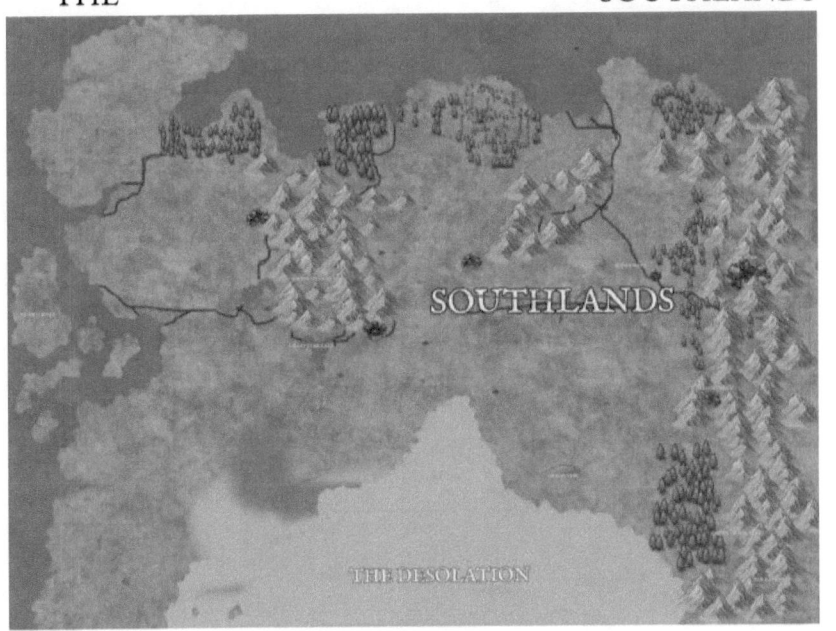

ISBN: 978-0-6458837-3-2 (pback)
ISBN: 978-0-6458837-2-5 (ebook)
Published by Shaun Keeley

Dedication

Dad (Martyn) Mum (Winnie)

Who gave us a life of Music, Imagination and Adventures.

3 Brothers and 3 Sisters

Who pushed, prodded and challenged at every turn.

3 Beautiful Daughters

Who pushed, prodded and challenged even harder.

	C	S	R	Keeley
The Team	Charlotte	Stephanie	Rachael	
		Shaun	Robbyn	
			Ross	

Dear Reader,

Although my name appears on the cover of this book, I am merely the chronicler of this story. The characters you will meet control the narrative of their part in the eternal battle of light against dark or good versus evil. Themes spread throughout the tale may offend some readers. Torture, murder, assassination, slavery and assaults against women are interwoven throughout. Some of the more genteel and educated characters may couch these themes in a more palatable way but some of those less refined do not have the luxury of an education and call a spade exactly what it is. Please join them in their quest to save their world and bring balance to their existence.

C.S.R. Keeley.

CHAPTER ONE
Occupation

In deep gloaming, chaos takes form
As blackness creeps, light will cease.

PERRIN OMHOLT SAT OUTSIDE the lean-to shelter gazing down the high mountain valley. His hands idly shredding long stalks of the alpine grass, releasing the rich aroma of a freshly scythed meadow. His thoughts meandered to the subdued solstice celebrations that neared, and particularly the lack of any eligible girls in the village. Dancing with a matron or young one was just not the same. The travel restrictions forced upon them by the invaders meant no visitors again this turn.

Looking over the valley, his eyes wandered the almost-circular rim of the old volcano crater. The steep walls of the remnant created a perfect barrier to keep sheep and goats safe and secure. Swaying green grasses spotted with patches of wildflowers provided the stock with rich grazing. Its bounty was nourished by the volcanic soil and plenty of seasonal rains.

Behind him, the incline steepened and connected the valley to the range of ancient mountains that reached with grandeur to snowy heights. The sun was falling towards the peak of the valley's rim. The chill Perrin felt was a result of the winds flowing off the mountain slopes.

As the shadows crept across the valley floor, Perrin suddenly realised the time. *Where was Bren*? His younger cousin should have arrived by now. Easily distracted by a covey of grouse or a deer sighting, his short attention span was always a worry. Perrin dare not be late for roll call again. That bloody-minded Brocken sergeant may just take it upon himself to make his life even more miserable.

Soon, the goats and sheep under Perrin's charge would head for the safety of the pens. The deepening twilight in the valley would fool them into thinking night was falling. Perrin knew that on the western side of the valley walls, the village would still have sunlight and was looking forward to a jack or two of ale and one of Gram's suppers after compulsory basic drill.

A local ballad echoing off the hills announced his cousin's arrival. Perrin collected his backpack, hat, staff, and the very precious axe and he bounded straight down the slope to meet him. Bren came through the small pass that hid the valley, well above the small village of Hightop.

'Bren, where have you been?' Perrin asked. 'You know I have to be in the square before the bells have rung.'

Perrin loved his cousin, but it was always a gamble on whether he would be punctual or pay attention to detail. The boy would reach manhood at the next solstice but he was still considered just a lad by all in the village. Hightop nestled in the elm, oak, and ash forests of the foothills in the shadow of the imposing Red Range mountains. Although only four or five suns travel from the capital of the Duchy of Sudhem the village was largely self-sufficient and well off any major trading route.

Perrin studied the boy he often wondered how he and his cousin could be related. Bren was willowy and long of limb with light hair that hung beyond his collar in waves. His slightly pointed chin and green, almond-shaped eyes contrasted with Perrin's own square jaw and round, brown eyes. Perrin was the stockier of the two and wide shoulders made him very powerful. In his fading memories of his mother and father, they had called him their 'little bull'.

'Now, Bren, here is the axe. Please take good care of it, and don't leave it out overnight,' Perrin instructed. 'Have you got your supper and a loaf for breakfast?' Perrin asked, secretly checking Bren's pack to ensure nothing had been forgotten. Perrin received a nod in answer. 'Good. Now, I will be back just after sunrise. You make sure you keep a close watch on the stock tonight. I heard a pack hunting up beyond the snow line last night, so be extra careful.'

Bren nodded and hugged his cousin. He picked his song up in mid-verse, shouldered the axe, and trudged towards the stout shelter they used while on herding duties.

Not one for words, Perrin thought. *Unless it was a song he had learned by repetition.*

The Omholts had never been considered a leading family in the small village. Their cabin set apart under the eaves of the forest had always been there, even if the resident was absent for periods. No villager could accurately determine the family's lineage in the history of Hightop. Normally not a difficult task as every other resident could be traced back to a dozen or so ancestors. The village forgave the obscurity as the Omholts held the important position of herders, but their real skills and vocation lay in the art of herb law and healing that they shared graciously with all in need.

Perrin broke into an easy loping run he knew he could keep up for easily half a sun. He had to be on time. The scenery seemed to flow past as he steadied his breathing to ensure his endurance. His stocky frame and strong legs made the downhill run easy. Just as Perrin reached the garden plots on the fringe of the village, he heard the first of five bell tolls. It indicated the end of the working sun to all residents and the start of a gruelling drill session for the young men of the village. The drill was overseen by the resident squad of occupation soldiers. Perrin made it to muster just as the last toll peeled away, echoing into the mountains.

'That was close, Per,' a squad mate whispered. 'Here comes that bloody Brocken three striper.'

Their sergeant marched to the stump he used as a podium. While he mounted the stump, his corporal marched up and down the rank of young men, counting heads and checking off the roll. He occasionally cracked one or another of those in line with his baton for no apparent reason or for fidgeting while standing at attention. After being presented with the roll, the sergeant nodded to his man, pulled himself up to his full height, took a breath, and began to bellow.

'A sorrier-looking squad of soldiers of the empire I have never seen. You will all be pulling double drills for the next week until I am satisfied with your performance. Corporal, begin!'

The entire squad groaned, giving the corporal another excuse to liberally use his baton upon those unfortunate enough to be within his reach. During the mind-numbing drill, Perrin thought that this increased effort and added cruelty by the occupiers could only mean one thing: a forced recruitment muster was near at hand.

That evening, as the men gathered in the village inn, the main topic of discussion was the recruitment muster and which of the young men would be taken away to the north. Every turn since the occupation, a large squad of regular soldiers would tour the controlled lands and net up any lad who had reached the age of sixteen. They would be marched north for basic training and assimilation instruction. Those such as Perrin—who had already undergone the pain of the full-turn-long torture—knew it was nothing more than a poor excuse to provide the Nordinium Empire with a free company of forced labourers.

RESISTANCE

Of the ten boys taken from Hightop over the last five turns, only Perrin and six others had returned. Each of the families in the village had suffered the anguish of a son or cousin being forcefully recruited. Of the others, no word had ever been heard again. Their parents had received notification from the Brocken, congratulating them for raising a son who had chosen to join the empire's regular forces.

Perrin knew this was a falsehood, as he had witnessed young men dying from beatings or thinly veiled accidents. In his nightmares, he still relived and suffered the pain endured at the hands of the instructors, whose beatings and sadism broke many a young man. Scars on his back from the whips were nothing compared to the scars in his memories. Perrin's mind wandered back to that time as he randomly doodled spirals on the tabletop, using the spilled froth of the group's ale as his medium.

'Perrin, does not your cousin turn sixteen at the next solstice celebration?' Belen asked. The smith was the head of the village council. 'They cannot possibly consider taking him as a recruit.'

'Bren can't be considered a candidate. I know he's coming of age, but I always think of him as younger with his singing and child-like wonder,' said Mitchum, the tavern keeper, delivering a round of tankards and taking up tokens in payment.

Perrin was shocked back to the present and considered the implications of their discussion. Like the others, he had forgotten Bren's eligibility due to his cousin's simplistic outlook on life. The villagers had considered Bren a little touched since he arrived to live with Perrin and his grandmother over four turns earlier.

'By Tyr,' Perrin said. 'I best be off and let Grams know about the muster. She will know what to do with Bren. Maybe we just leave him up at the top meadows when the soldiers come and hope that out of sight is out of mind.'

Those at the table nodded their agreement. All in the village respected the views of the old woman, who was known to all as

Gram. This was an honorific to a lady who had done so much for each of them. Either as midwives to their mothers or wives or directly dispensing remedies and nursing injuries.

Perrin downed his ale, gathered his gear, and rushed out the door, followed by the words of the smith.

'Arf ya luck,' Belen called.

Perrin wandered through the village, deep in thought as the light bled from the skies. Bren was as close to his heart as any brother would be. Many of the inhabitants of the occupied lands had suffered badly during the invasion and continued to be hampered by the ever-increasing tithes levied by the empire. Perrin and Bren had both lost their respective parents, and Perrin had also suffered the disappearance of his older brother. At the time, Perrin had not understood how or why his life suffered such a gut-wrenching upheaval.

When he considered the treatment Bren would endure at the hands of the assimilation officers, he was almost physically sick. Chills crept up his backbone as his own memories rushed to the fore. By the time he came in sight of his grandmother's humble cabin, he had determined that the soldiers could not be allowed to take his cousin.

'Gram, where are you?' Perrin called.

He stooped under the thatch and through the low doorway. Perrin looked about the sparse cabin and figured his grandmother must still be tending her herb beds in the garden behind the cabin. 'Gram?' Perrin called, slipping out the back door. 'What are you still doing out here?'

'Per, there you are. Come and help me with these. Gather those bunches. You know that senna root is best harvested at dusk to enhance its properties. We must set these to dry in the racks,' replied a small, wizened woman. Perrin surveyed the herb beds and wondered yet again how the old woman produced such an abundance and variety of vegetables and herbs enough to feed the whole village if it ever came to that. Yet there never seemed to be more than what was needed.

No one knew how long Gram had lived in Hightop, and she certainly wasn't letting anyone in on her secrets. The old lady only came up to Perrin's chest, but throughout the surrounding hills, she was highly regarded as a healer and midwife. She tended not only the citizens but all manner of beasts as well. Her most startling feature was that her long, still-brown hair, which she wore in a bun, was only marred with one or two strands of grey, which many younger grey-haired mothers envied. Her unlined features and strong hands belied her age.

Perrin collected the large baskets of foliage his Gram had prepared and took them into the drying shed he had built for her in the previous season of the long moon. The chill, winds and snows of that season were a time when most of Hightop's residents were kept close to home.

As she shuffled in behind him, she asked, 'Now what has got you all riled up that you come home with not even a kiss for your old Gram?'

Perrin hugged the dear old lady and apologised for his distraction. 'Gram, the Brocken are coming, and I am afraid for Bren.' he said. Perrin used the term the citizens of the south had coined for the occupation soldiers. 'The local squad are prancing around the village, puffing out their chests, and making life even more difficult.'

Those suffering under the yoke of occupation had named the regular soldiers of the northern invaders the Brocken based on the grey colour of their uniforms and the fact they fashioned their strategies on early morning attacks. Their raids were often aided by the mists and fogs yet to be burnt off by the sun.

'Well, that's certainly an indication that something is afoot,' Gram said. The old lady led Perrin into the neat one-roomed cabin. 'Sit down, and I will brew some tea, and we can decide on the implications of these latest happenings.'

Gram's answer to any problem was a cup of tea and careful dissection of the facts. As she pottered about with the kettle and tea fixings, Perrin's grandmother muttered to herself while taking sidelong glances at the grandson she so loved.

'Gram, something smells good. What have you got brewing over the coals?'

'You will know soon enough. Set the table for supper.'

He carefully placed his Gram's favourite cups on the table and took his place at the head of the table. This position was always insisted upon as his right as the oldest male of the household. Gram always adhered to the old ways and had drilled manners into Perrin and Bren, although the latter seemed a lost cause when it came to the correct etiquette for teatime.

'Bren would never survive the march north, let alone the punishment meted out by those sadistic bastards and their assimilation lessons. We can't let them have Bren,' Perrin said.

Gram continued carefully preparing the tea while she ruminated over the news Perrin had brought her. They had known this sun was coming, yet they had hoped to have more time to enjoy raising the young cousin who was taken in during the invasion and the resistance that followed. While Gram served the meal and poured the tea, she questioned Perrin about Bren's arrival at the high meadows.

'Did you make sure Bren had his supper and the mushroom nut loaf for his breakfast?'

Perrin was exasperated that Gram did not seem as concerned as he was over the danger the muster posed to his cousin. Did she not remember the scars, both physical and mental, he carried from his own experiences, from which he had returned almost two full turns ago in the season of the birth and growth?

'Yes, Gram. Bren had his pannikin and the loaf wrapped in one of your red napkins. What about the muster?' Perrin insisted.

Gram sat and sipped her tea while taking a good, long look at her boy. 'Per,' she began, 'Hightop is fortunate that it is far from the centre of the empire's influences and the depredations inflicted on the plains people. We deliver our tithes on time and are seen to follow the empire's directives without undue complaint. We do not draw attention to ourselves for a very good reason. If we cause no trouble, we are not scrutinized too closely. We will have Bren stay in the high meadow and hope whoever they send does not look too closely into the records or that the local squad does not consider that Bren is old enough for muster.'

'But, Gram, we must prepare for the worst. We must not take the chance.'

'Well, boy, I suppose there can be no harm in making some preparations.' Grams paused in consideration. 'We can stockpile some supplies in your lean-to and map out an escape in case it becomes necessary. Now, why don't you finish up your supper and get to bed? You need to leave early if you are to get back to Bren by sunrise. While you rest, I will gather some things you can take with you.'

He dutifully prepared for bed, all the while amazed at the old woman. She never seemed to sleep, always took charge, and had all the answers once she had carefully considered the options. Perrin had learned a great deal from his Gram, as she had always insisted on teaching him the ways of their mountain home. Her lessons also included the plants and animals that were most useful to him and the pre-invasion history of the Southlands. Perrin could barely read or write, but he could recite the lineages of the ruling families of both the people of the south and the elfin folk to the far west. He lay back on his bunk and began to recite in his mind the lists of herbs and their benefits that he had spent countless evenings memorising. It was an exercise that had served him well while he had undergone assimilation and training in the North. It now helped him relax and lessen the severity of the nightmares from that time that still plagued him.

Perrin was woken by the kettle rattling as it came to the boil on the hob and his grandmother's gentle muttering as she pottered about the cabin, picking out various items and packing them into his large hunting pack. As Perrin stretched through a mighty yawn, he noticed several packages sitting on their rickety dining table. All were labelled and tied with a bark twist.

'The monster arises,' Gram said. 'Why don't you prepare the tea while I finish up with this packing?'

Perrin was taken aback and thought things must be more serious than they seemed. Gram never let anyone else make the tea unless she was completely immersed in a difficult healing or birth. He knew better than to question her until the tea was ready. It was best to concentrate on the task at hand to guarantee that Gram would have no complaints and be free to answer the questions that had suddenly crowded his thoughts.

'I know we decided to be careful and make some preparations, but you seem to be getting ready for a full-on expedition. A pack that full will take some lugging to get it up to the high meadows,' Perrin said.

'I never thought my Per would shy at a bit of hard work,' Gram said. 'You know full well that if a job's to be done, it is to be done well. At this early time, you shouldn't be noticed, so I thought it best to get most of what you may need up to the meadows on this trip. Any further supplies we can smuggle up later. The Brocken will only become more vigilant as we get closer to the visit from their superiors.'

Once again, Perrin marvelled at the extent of understanding displayed by this woman who, to his knowledge, had not left these mountains in many turns. As he sipped his tea, he studied the packets on the table. There were agrimony, alder bark, basil, boneset, comfrey, snail root, dock, and other remedies he had spent many lessons memorising. The packet that really drew his eye was wrapped in a rich blue cloth and looked like it was sealed with stitches of gold wire. The Omholt family had never been one to covet riches, yet this packet appeared to contain something of great value.

'Gram, what is this packet? I know some of your remedies are rare and precious, but this seems to be solid,' he said. He hefted the packet in the palm of his hand.

'Now, Perrin, that is something we need to discuss in some greater detail than time allows at present. For the moment, just be aware that along with young Bren, that single package must be kept out of the empire's hands even at the greatest of costs. You must never reveal you possess this single packet, not even to someone you have the greatest trust in. Now finish your tea and get yourself gone before the village stirs,' the old woman said.

'But, Gram,' Perrin started.

'Not now, Perrin,' his grandmother said. 'We will discuss all this on the morrow when you and Bren come down from the valley. In the meantime, you just make sure that your cousin has his mushrooms for dinner. I have made you a small venison tart for your own supper. Now be gone.'

Perrin knew better than to question Gram when she had given concise instructions. As he pulled on his boots and collected his things, he wondered at her intensity but also realised she was right about the time. After hugging the old woman, Perrin shouldered the now full pack and slipped from the cabin. Fortunately, the need to grow herbs and forage in the forests for other ingredients meant that the Omholt cabin was set right under the forest fringe. Perrin did not have to travel far before being completely hidden by the underbrush. He had little chance of being spotted by any of the citizens of Hightop, let alone the Brocken soldiers.

In the gloom of the pre-dawn, Perrin trudged along the pathways he knew so well and allowed his mind to wander. He thought about the great upheaval in the simplistic lives of his friends that had been caused by the invasion and displacement of so many people. His parents had died fighting for the freedom of the Southlands, and although he understood the sacrifice, it was not easy to forget the pain of their loss.

Before he came to join his Gram in Hightop, his parents had owned a mildly profitable farm on the plains, ten suns' travel away from the village. Perrin's father had been the magistrate on very rare occasion that a dispute could not be judged by the local council. He was also a sometime advisor to the Duke of Sudhem and had even visited the duke's capital at Sudhemere. When the invasion came, Perrin had been too young to be considered a full farmhand. He had spent his suns working in his mother's vegetable patches, and running water and messages to his father and older brother in the fields.

Perrin's brother was the elder by five turns and had always been his idol. When not at his duties, Perrin would search out his brother and beg lessons from him. These focussed on farming and the care of animals, but the lessons he most wished for were those of bushcraft and hunting. His brother's lessons always centred around the care of the land, and the sustainability of the herds and creatures they shared the land with. Perrin was taught how to recognise the less dominant male and the mature female, who would no longer be a breeder.

Inattentiveness caused him to trip over a root, and his heavy pack drove him into the ground, causing a twisted ankle. He wondered at the irony that while thinking of his lost brother; he had forgotten the first lesson he had ever been taught: *when in the forest always concentrate and expect the unexpected.* Perrin bore the injury as a reminder and strove to remember his lessons as he made up for lost time, planning to reach the high meadows just after sunrise. As his mind had wandered, he had forgotten that Bren was his major concern.

With the pack as an extra burden, Perrin attacked the slope with renewed effort as a penance for his neglect. The sun was beginning to bathe the meadows in morning light as he breasted the pass. He saw a sight that gladdened his heart and reinforced his determination to save his cousin from the muster and the agony of the lessons of the Brocken instructors. Bren was sitting among a patch of new season's grass with the newborn lambs and kids gambolling about him as he grabbed handfuls and fed whichever beast came to him. Bren had always had an affinity with animals, and it was apparently reciprocated. This natural attraction was another reason Bren was left to follow the Omholt tradition as a herder rather than be apprenticed to any of the guilds in the village.

'Yo, Bren,' Perrin called. 'Come, give me a hand with this pack.'

Bren jumped up. Even from a distance, Perrin could see the smile that spread across his features. Bren's sudden move scattered the young stock, and he dashed across the meadow. Perrin had wearily divested himself of the heavy pack. Watching Bren, he wondered how the boy could move so fast yet barely part the grasses or leave an imprint in his wake.

'Perrin back.' The young man embraced his cousin.

'Yes, Bren, I'm back. Now, let's get this pack up to the lean-to and get this stuff safely stowed. We will have to make the store waterproof, as I have some of Gram's remedies. You know she would have my guts for garters if they got wet or mouldy,' Perrin said.

The cousins each grabbed a strap and, between them, lugged the pack towards the small copse of alder where the shelter was situated.

As they began to unpack, Perrin noticed the axe was not hanging from the rack that had been made especially for it.

'Bren, where is the axe? It should be right here.'

Preferring to show rather than tell, Bren grabbed Perrin's arm, pulled him out of the shelter, and began to drag him further up the mountainside.

'Where are you taking me?' Perrin asked.

Bren only pointed in response. After a time, they began to pass patches of ice and slush as they neared the permanent snow line. Perrin felt a strange sensation, and his gut began to churn. Bren stopped and pointed further up and across the slope at a jumble of rocks that formed a small cave or den. He would go no closer.

Perrin wondered at his cousin's reluctance, but saw the axe leaning against the rock pile. As he moved forward, Perrin felt a definite wrongness in this pristine environment. The closer he came to the rocks, the more powerful the feeling became. His skin crawled and shivered and all moisture in his mouth and throat disappeared. Only pure brute force kept him from expelling everything in his stomach. As he reached for the axe, he saw and smelled that Bren had not managed to keep the contents of his guts down. The acrid odour of the vomit nearly broke through Perrin's resolve.

Perrin peered under the small overhang of rock and spied a grisly scene. Two warf lay on the ground, and a gutted lamb, their kill, was jammed into a cleft in the boulders. The warf, thought to be a far-off kin to wolves, were one-third the size of the larger predators with little intelligence and were predominantly scavengers. They were known to take the young or sick from herds and usually hunted in related packs. This pair had obviously broken away from their pack to breed.

Only just managing to control his rebelling innards and fight off the waves of nausea and the terrible feeling of evil, Perrin wondered at the condition of the warf. Each was shrivelled, and their hides looked paper thin, only just managing to hold their bones together. The skin was stretched taut, and their skeletons were clearly outlined. Perrin could tell from the desiccated condition of the creatures that their internal organs were also devoid of moisture and blood. The scavengers lay in a patch of blackness that emanated evil, where nothing grew or lived. The stench of sulphur caught in the back of his throat, causing Perrin to cough and gag in an attempt to take a clear breath. Oddly, the body of the dead lamb seemed untouched apart from the treatment it had received from the warf.

This was an incident that would normally be reported to the Pathfinders so that, in their travels, they could pass on the news or learn of other similar happenings and investigate. The Pathfinders had been the messengers and right arm of the sovereign until they were outlawed by the Brocken. Now, Perrin's only option was to advise his grandmother because she somehow had some limited lines of communication throughout the foothills and forest. The familiar feeling of the axe's handle comforted Perrin as the wrongness of the scene threatened to overwhelm him. He turned his back on the scene and walked back down the slope to his cousin, every step bringing relief. Looking down into the valley reassured him that there was still some little beauty and good in the world. He could not bring himself to scold his cousin. Perrin knew the anguish Bren would have suffered after losing one of his young charges and seeing the warf. He took a long pull from the water flask Bren held out to him.

'Come on, let's head back.'

The axe's edge was blunt, and rust had started to spot the head. Since the occupation, weapons were strictly controlled. All had been handed into the Brocken squad and were stored in the village armoury. Only those who could justify the need for a weapon could requisition one. Perrin and Bren were only allowed one axe to protect the herds. A bow would be more useful, but they were only released to hunters and woe betide anyone who returned from a hunt without the full complement of arrows.

Climbing the slopes had inflamed Perrin's damaged ankle, and it was with some relief that he could ease the burden by shifting the weight to his good leg during the downhill stroll. He used the haft of the axe to brace the other. Once back, Perrin set Bren to storing the pack's contents while he sat to sharpen and clean the axe and oil the hand-and-a-half shaft. When he was nearly finished, Bren approached with the two wooden dowels they often used for sparring. Neither cousin had fought with a real blade, but from Perrin's experience and advice from some of the older villagers, they had developed their own training program and spent many afternoons maintaining their fitness and speed. If the occupying soldiers discovered they were honing their skills with weapons, they would be arrested and sold into slavery.

'If there are warf about, I think we start with axe drill,' Perrin said.

Using an axe, particularly in close-quarter fighting, often required facing more than one opponent. Perrin handed the axe to Bren and led him to the clearing they used as a fencing piste. Bren began a slow warm-up that soon developed into a blurring dance that had Perrin astounded once again at his cousin's speed and lightness of foot. Perrin's own practice was centred around form and footwork while favouring his good leg, and although not as elegant as Bren, it was nonetheless effective and produced a welcoming weariness in his muscles.

'Stretch out those legs and your back, Bren, before we move to sword drill. We don't want to cramp up tonight.'

The cousins had become evenly matched with the sword, as Bren had filled out and matured. They often pretended to be battling Brocken soldiers and took turns to be the Pathfinder, fighting for freedom in the south. Lately, Perrin had ceded the role of a resistance fighter to Bren. It was apparent that the boy was becoming the superior swordsman. They battled backwards and forwards with steadily increasing thrusts and parries. Only Perrin's greater experience blunted Bren's attacks until his weak ankle caused Perrin to stumble. Bren managed to breach Perrin's defences with a high thrust and score a bruising touch on his shoulder.

'Enough,' Perrin said. 'Once again, the Pathfinder has defeated the Brocken.'

Bren's broad grin lightened his face, which had been creased with concentration during the sparring match, and he reached out to help Perrin to his feet.

'Perrin's hurt,' Bren said. Bren had only now noticed his cousin's limp.

'My fault entirely. I stumbled on a root on the way up. I was being foolish and forgot the first lesson in woods craft.' Perrin answered.

After they made their way to the shelter and had refreshed themselves with cold water, Perrin took off his boot and inspected the sprain.

'Bren, hand me the burdock leaves from the pack, and I will prepare a poultice to bind my ankle while you check and pen the herds. We need an early supper and a good night's sleep. It is Sixth Sun tomorrow, and we can both go down to the village.'

Bren handed Perrin the packet, then headed off on the rounds of the valley to do a quick count of the stock and round up the odd stray. If the stock foraged too high up on the mountainside, they could attract predators. The sun was near to setting on the high meadows, and the stock would soon gather for warmth and protection. Although it was still the Season of the Sun, the valley just below the permanent snow line maintained a chilly night-time temperature. When Bren returned to the shelter, Perrin had their suppers warming over a small cookfire. As Bren seated himself, Perrin handed him the pot of mushroom and vegetable stew their grandmother had prepared for him. Perrin shuddered at the thought of not eating meat and bit into his venison tart with relish.

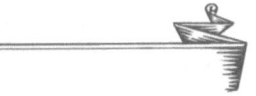

CHAPTER TWO
Recruitment

Creatures stretch, stir, rumble, swarm.
Time is nigh for dread's release.

THE EXERTION OF THEIR training and the work involved in securing the stock ensured a very deep night's sleep. Perrin and Bren woke to another pristine morning in the mountain valley. With a background of birdsong and the sun sparkling in the early morning dew, one could almost imagine that all was well in the world.

'Bren, can you fetch me some large rocks? We need to make sure these stores are neatly packed away. I will use the rocks to hold down the cover of the store. I want to make sure they can survive a shower of rain or any inquisitive birds or mammals that might explore the lean-to while we are away,' Perrin said.

When Bren was ensuring the fire was well out, Perrin took the strange blue package and hid it away in a far corner of the shelter, not even risking letting Bren know about Gram's special package.

'Come on, Bren, let's do a round of the valley to check the stock. Then we can head down the mountain.'

Every Sixth Sun, residents of Hightop were to present themselves before the local Brocken sergeant and have their names checked against his list. This was another example of the oppressive rules dictated by the Northern Empire, as it restricted people's movements. If anyone was not checked off the list, their family would suffer from closer scrutiny and higher taxes, if not direct beatings and imprisonment.

These threats against one's family were the most useful deterrent against resistance and disobedience the local Brocken squad used. Their menaces and intimidations pervaded most aspects of what used to be a rustic and peaceful lifestyle. Many residents had not left Hightop in turns, not even to visit relatives in other villages or on the plains. Passes to travel or relocate could only be obtained by completing onerous applications. The much-prized travel passes were only occasionally awarded to hunters or licensed traders.

The taxes levied by the Northern Empire left much of the Southlands short of many food products. Citizens in the farmlands were often at subsistence level as the Northern Empire increased the tithes every turn without considering crop yields or seasonal variations. The residents of Hightop and other mountain villages could at least rely on the bounty the mountains and forests provided as an extra source of provisions. Hightop was also grateful that it was far from the centre of the empire's occupation, so the resident squad of Brocken soldiers was lazy and easily appeased by the village council's concerted effort to appear to obey all rules with little complaint or resistance.

At least after presenting themselves, the rest of the sixth sun could be spent with friends and family. Sixth Sun was traditionally market time, where villagers displayed their produce and goods for barter. Many of the offerings were homemade crafts and preserves. The village had little contact with travelling traders or tinkers anymore, and visits from members of one of the south's other races—the Wolf Riders of the deep forests or Elves of the Sunset Islands—were even rarer. Gram was always available to dispense a remedy or advice in exchange for fruit, baked goods, a rustic woven basket, or a crude homemade clay pot.

Perrin and Bren looked forward to what the market brought, as there was usually a sweet tart or small cake to be had. With no visiting families and craftsmen from other villages, the offerings were limited. This did not stop the villagers from making the most of this small freedom, and each family put out their best produce for sharing and sale.

In the mid season the weather was warm and muggy, and the surrounding forests awoke early with myriad sounds and movements. The paths they trod were speckled with the sun's rays bursting through the ever-changing leaf patterns. Perrin hurried along as his cousin softly sang one of his many ditties. Bren sang most of the learning songs taught to the village children, although many had now been banned by the Northern Empire, and teaching the old songs was outlawed.

'Bren, I think it best you stay with Gram at the cottage when we get home. I don't want you to go near the village square.'

Bren usually did as he was asked. Perrin hoped that he could convince the sergeant with a little misdirection so that Bren could avoid going into the village and stay under the watchful eye of their grandmother.

As they approached the village, the usual clatter and bang of market stall preparation could be heard. It would not be long before the bell tolled to call the villagers to present themselves. Perrin pushed Bren in the direction of their grandmother's cabin and headed towards the village square to present himself. Perhaps by being early, he could later confuse the sergeant regarding Bren. Perrin was fortunate enough to be third in line when the corporal opened the squad room doors and directed the first villager to the sergeant's office. When Perrin's turn came, he stood at attention and announced his name. After the man looked him over and checked his name off the list, Perrin coughed to gain the man's attention.

'If you will excuse me, Sergeant, my cousin Bren Omholt is currently abed with a heavy flux. I was wondering if I could present in his place.' Perrin asked.

'That is the simpleton boy, is it not?' the sergeant said.

Perrin nodded the affirmative, and the man continued.

'I will accept your assurance this time, but you will pull double training duties and excel at your drills henceforth. You have attended the assimilation training, so I expect you to set an example to the young ones,' the sergeant said.

The man never let a chance go by to add further duties or responsibilities to any villager who may ask a favour or make a request of him. Perrin nodded, executed his best about-face, and hurried from the room. With great relief, Perrin rushed to his grandmother's cabin and saw her and Bren setting out the dining table and chairs she used to dispense her advice and remedies on this sun.

'Gram, I convinced the sergeant that Bren was ill in bed and was unable to present himself. We will have to keep him out of sight from the market and hope that none of the Brocken seek you out this sun for boils or flatulence,' Perrin said.

'Once again, you forget the important, young Per,' Gram said.

She presented her cheek to him. Perrin laughed as he kissed the cheek and then proceeded to wrap the small woman in a huge bear hug.

'You monster!' his grandmother said.

Perrin smiled as she slapped at his chest until he released her.

'That was good thinking. We have heard that the muster squad is sweeping through the villages and will be here soon. I think that after this sun, we must keep Bren up in the high meadows. We will discuss this later. Now help me with these baskets, and then go set the kettle to boil.'

'Gram. I have something bothering me. When I got to the valley, Bren showed me a pair of dead warf. The strange thing was that they were completely dried out. More than that, I had the most gut-wrenching feeling. My body battled between a mind-spinning faint or completely emptying my stomach. The feeling had the undertone of wrongness about it. Everything from the sight to the smell and how my body tingled and shivered was completely out of place and evil.'

Perrin knew this old woman was the only one in the village to whom he could tell his problem. She was regarded by all in Hightop and the surrounding areas as the wisest of the elders.

'Per, that is a conundrum, I will ponder. I will put the word out to see if there are any other reports of a similar nature. For now, we had better focus on the most immediate issue. The kettle will not boil itself.'

Perrin loved this woman and shook his head while smiling at the admonishment. Only Gram could make his problems dissipate with the understanding that she had fully comprehended the report.

After Gram made tea and they had completed the preparations on their market stall, she set off to present herself to the Brocken and to wander the family stalls. She was always looking for useful trinkets or herbs others may have collected in the forest. Sixth Sun proceeded as it had for turns, with families dropping by to exchange goods or produce for services and remedies. The main topic of conversation remained the recruitment muster and the agony of the families with eligible sons. Perrin realised Bren was hard done by with the ban to not join the only entertainment the villagers were free to indulge in. However, both lads were well aware that when Gram gave instructions, one was wise to follow orders.

Late in the sun, the village bell rang with the sequence that was a call for all residents to assemble in the village square. This was an odd event, as it was usually reserved to call up searches for children lost in the forest. When the residents rushed to the village centre, they were greeted by a new squad of Brocken warriors, some mounted on warhorses, behind a robed and hooded man. Although of indeterminate age, the robed man was clearly an authority. When the villagers had assembled, the robed figure spoke in a soft tone that carried to all.

'Males having reached manhood will assemble at the bell toll tomorrow for interview and recruitment,' he said.

This announcement sent a shiver through the gathered crowd. It was the practice in the Southlands that adulthood was attained if a child reached their sixteenth turn before the sun solstice. The empire chose to forcibly recruit all males for assimilation and basic training in the hope it would deter resistance and give their inquisitors a chance to program informers and identify the family members of known Pathfinder leaders. They could then hold hostages and forment discord in the resistance's ranks. The most surprising feature of the announcement was that the solstice was still ten suns hence.

After supper that evening, as the Omholts were tidying the cabin, there came a call and mad knocking on the door.

'Gram, Gram. You must come quick! Ernst the potter has been beaten. His entire family has been arrested and thrown into the cells under the Brocken barracks,' Belen cried. 'The soldiers have patrols out in the forest and caught Ernst trying to smuggle his son out of the village. They beat him and the boy, then took the womenfolk, too. We must hurry!'

'Per gather my medicinal bag and a waterskin,' Gram said. Her next words were said under her breath, 'Pack your belongings and be prepared to go. I will have instructions for you on my return.'

'Lead on, Belen,' Gram said. She crooked her basket on one arm and took Belen's elbow. 'We must hurry. I fear this visit from the Brocken is more than it seems.'

Perrin was deeply worried for his grandmother and was torn between joining her and his responsibility to his young cousin. After standing transfixed while watching her disappear, he suddenly shivered and burst into action. Praising his Gram for her previous preparations, the boys packed their remaining clothes and belongings. They searched the cabin for any item that may be of use. Perrin had a terrible foreboding that this may be the last he would see of the cosy cabin set on the fringe of the forest. After ensuring their preparations were complete, Perrin sat a rather bemused Bren down and tried to explain the implications of the sun's events and the need for them to escape. Bren nodded his understanding. The lad could grasp most instructions when spoken to directly.

'I had best put the kettle to boil. Grams will need a good cup of tea when she returns. We will also need some to fortify us during the night,' Perrin said.

As though by prescience, the cabin door opened just as the kettle rattled on the stove.

'Perrin, you have always been the most thoughtful boy. A cup of tea is just what is needed after the deeds done tonight,' Gram said.

She wearily sank into her chair. Perrin and Bren hastily set the tea things on the table. They knew Gram would not be prepared to talk without a cup in her hand. She smelled the steam rising from the cup, carrying with it a fragrant aroma. The scent was warm and comforting, with notes of earthy richness and subtle hints of bitterness. After taking a refreshing sip, Gram looked deep into the eyes of each of her young charges. Perrin saw in her eyes that she longed for more time with each.

'Boys, this squad of soldiers is more than we anticipated. They have with them an apprentice to one of the Circle of Seven mages who ultimately rule the empire through their puppet, the Emperor. The hooded one we saw this sun intends to delve into the minds of all eligible males for any indication of rebellion and any knowledge of the heir to the Southlands,' she said. 'The soldiers caught Ernst and his son and beat them fiercely. Although the boy was spared broken limbs, his father had both legs broken, and I fear his wife and daughters are being mistreated by the soldiers. I see you have not been idle and have prepared to go. Good, good,' she said.

'But Gram, we can't leave you,' Perrin said.

He turned to see Bren nodding vigorously in agreement.

'Now, boys. You can and will. The soldiers won't do anything to an old woman like me. They need my skills. Now I have much to tell you, so listen carefully and do not interrupt,' she said.

Perrin wondered if his grandmother could withstand the attentions of an apprentice of the seven. He was about to protest when she raised a finger at the boys to forestall any interruption.

'You both know all the game paths and trails within two suns travel, so you have an advantage over the soldiers. Use your skills and talents, and you should avoid the patrols. Get yourselves to the high valley. I took the opportunity to send for assistance when we first suspected the muster was near at hand, and someone should be there to meet you and guide you south and west. Perrin, you must accept responsibility for your cousin's safety and protect him at all costs. He must reach the rebel pathfinders. Be sure to take the package with you,' she grasped Perrin's hands in her own, 'These two charges I entrust to you.'

The old woman looked into the eyes of each of her wards to ensure they had a complete understanding of the severity of their plight.

'Our preparations were none too soon, it seems. I have taught you both the care of the land and the importance of living in harmony with all manner of man and beast who share it with us. The northerners who rape the land and destroy all must be beaten back and overthrown. We were unprepared for their invasion. We must not repeat that mistake,' she said.

'But, Gram, what's all this about? Rebels, secrets, and strangers. We can't leave you. You will be in danger,' Perrin said, bewildered.

'Perrin, you must go now, and for all our safety, get Bren far away from the Brocken. I have something more for you to carry and protect,' Gram said.

Gram rose and pulled her chair over to her curtained alcove. She climbed on the chair, reached into the thatch and pulled out a long, wrapped bundle, which she brought out and placed on the table. Gram unwrapped the bundle and held out an old sword in a plain but serviceable scabbard and belt, offering it to Perrin. The hilt was well-worn leather wound with a dull metal wire, and when Perrin drew the sword, he saw it was oiled and retained a fine edge. The blade was balanced, and the sword looked well crafted.

'Perrin, you hold the sword your grandfather and those before him have always used to defend this land. Carry it well. When the time comes, the sword will reveal its secrets,' his grandmother said.

The boys were shocked. Never had they seen their Gram do anything but obey empire directives. Certainly, she had never said a single word about the resistance or hiding weapons. The boys donned their packs, and Perrin strapped on the sword, but neither cousin could avoid glancing at each other and their Gram, puzzled expressions on their faces.

'Head away from the village before you turn for the high meadows, it will confuse the Brocken, and they cannot track you in the dark. Go now and be watchful,' Gram ordered.

Perrin and Bren hugged their grandmother fiercely before slipping out the door. They flitted around the corner of the cabin, using the shadows as concealment until they reached the underbrush at the forest fringe. As they crouched and listened, Perrin wondered how much of the night's events Bren had understood. They studied the forest and decided the best course of action.

Just as Perrin was about to rise and head onward, Bren grabbed his sleeve and pulled him back to a crouch. Bren pointed. In the faint glow from cottage lights, Perrin could just make out a patrol leaving the village and heading in their direction. The boys held their breath as the patrol neared. When the soldiers rounded a copse of young alder next to the path for a short time, hiding them from sight, the boys crawled deeper into the forest. They moved quietly away from the only home they knew and the woman who had taught them that they were just another part of the land and that there was no greater sin than to abuse its bounty.

The boys crept along a disused game trail that headed well away from their intended direction of travel. Just when they intersected a path they knew well and could follow to make better time, Perrin tripped over the unfamiliar sword and fell to the ground with a clatter. As Bren helped Perrin to his feet, a shout came from the direction of the village, and a squad of soldiers rushed towards the sound. A whistling and occasional thud filled the air as the squad began shooting flatbow bolts through the darkness. When a bolt sprouted in Bren's tightly loaded pack right in front of Perrin's face, he urged his cousin to greater effort and hoped his ankle would hold up. The boys dashed along the path, only their knowledge of the area keeping them ahead of the pursuit.

Perrin reached forwards and snapped the bolts shaft as he hurried Bren away from the village and the chasing patrol of Brocken warriors. He knew of a switchback path that was easily missed in full sunlight and would be almost impossible for the pursuing soldiers to see in the gloom and pitch-black shadows of the forest. As it was, the cousins bolted past the hidden track and had to quickly double back when Perrin realised his error. The boys made it to the switch back just as the patrol could be heard reaching the last bend in the trail they had been racing along. To avoid making noise or showing movement that the soldiers might detect, the boys quickly hid in the undergrowth, thanking the gods for the training and patience they had mastered while hunting. They waited with bated breath as the patrol thundered past their hide at double time. Having seen some of the training these soldiers were given, Perrin was not surprised at the professional way this patrol was conducting the chase, often swapping leaders to have fresh eyes and legs in the lead. Perrin knew the patrol would soon come to a fork in the track, and they would either have to split up or discontinue the chase and return to discover the identities of the villagers they had been chasing.

With renewed fear for their grandmother, Perrin signalled for Bren to take the lead and head up the path, while he fell back to keep one ear out for the discovery of their ploy or the resumption of any pursuit.

Knowing the terrain, the cousins kept up a steady pace as they headed towards the high meadows. After a short while of keeping watch on their back trail, Perrin knew they had made good their escape from the Brocken patrol, so he caught up with Bren and took the lead to hasten their journey. He knew these paths well and was not about to let Bren wander off or take a wrong turn, as he was sure their identity would be forced from someone in the village. The soldiers would be on their way to the upper grazing grounds as soon as the sun rose and gave them enough light to follow the well-worn path from the village.

Perrin and Bren made good time, and Perrin was once again thankful for his grandmother's forethought in packing his large hunting pack the sun before. It meant that he and his cousin were only hampered by their small travel packs, and, although tightly filled, they predominately held spare clothes and only a few personal items. The packs were relatively light and easy to handle.

The forest seemed to help them along, as each boy travelled well and did not have any further falls or injuries, and apart from a dull throb, Perrin's ankle caused him no ill effect. A barely discernible lightening on the horizon indicated that they were approaching the small pass that gave access to the high meadows. The cousins had been climbing the foothills at double pace, and Perrin decided that a short rest would be welcome. A quick reconnoitre of their trail followed to satisfy Perrin's niggling feeling to expect the unexpected and ensure the patrol had not somehow tracked them. Perrin shucked off his pack and had Bren sit with his back to a tree, watching down the trail as he retraced their path, stopping and listening for any disturbance to the natural sounds and flow of energies in the night-time forest. Satisfied that there was no one in a position to endanger them, Perrin made his way back to his cousin and a short respite from their escape.

Bren was happily working by moonlight, stripping twigs from a branch and smoothing its surface with his belt knife. Perrin realised his cousin was fashioning a crutch. He was amazed at the level of understanding Bren showed about the possible damage their flight may have done to his already injured foot. As he bent down to examine the work, he braced a hand on the tree at Bren's back and was astounded when, with a whistle and a thud, an arrow appeared and embedded itself not a finger width from his hand, the shaft and fletching vibrating right before his eyes.

'Hold and identify,' a voice called from the dark. With barely a rustle, Bren and Perrin were surrounded by four men with arrows nocked.

Perrin was well aware that the lands had changed and that there was trouble brewing for the south. The four men were clad in forest garb to blend in and camouflage them, and each was hooded in a green mask with only holes for the eyes to break the concealing effect of their clothing.

'We are only the village herders, returning from Sixth Sun,' Perrin said.

He knew that in times to come, their identity and trust would be commodities to be guarded well. These men clearly worked well together, and it was unlikely that they were a band of brigands or stock thieves. It was also clear these were not soldiers of the invaders.

'We take them to the commander,' a man said.

Perrin identified him as the squad leader. He was also the one to retrieve the arrow from the tree and replace it in his quiver. Perrin realized how serious these men were when he saw the sharp hunting broadhead arrow tip the man had used rather than a simple target point. Perrin and Bren were briefly searched, and save for Perrin's sword, their belt knives were identified as their only other weapons. They were each handed their packs and were marched towards the pass under heavy guard. Eventually, they reached the high meadows.

Perrin was surprised to see a campfire burning on the far side of the meadows somewhere near their lean-to. He also noted several silhouettes moving between his line of sight and the fire. As they were marched across the meadow, Perrin decided sticking to his story was the safest thing to do. After all, it was virtually the truth, and he knew he could trust Bren not to talk and give away any of their secrets. This commander fellow may have made himself at home in their camp, but there was no need to panic. Hunters had often stopped overnight if they came across the boys on their travels, and, in keeping with the tradition of hospitality in the mountains, the boys had never had any problem with it.

The group were nearing the opposite slope when the leader jogged forwards to approach a figure crouched before the fire. As Perrin and Bren were ushered up the slope, the crouching figure rose and turned towards the cousins. He was a large man, well-proportioned, with long flowing hair currently loose across his shoulders. No more could be ascertained as the fire behind him held his face in shadow, although the hilt of a large sword could be seen jutting above his right shoulder, and the light of the fire flickered in the depths of the large polished stone set into the butt end of the sword's two-hand hilt.

'Hello, Perrin,' a voice said.

Perrin could not make out the features of that face, but a strange feeling of recognition overcame him. Perrin was sure he had met this man before. Perhaps he was a hunter who had spent time with the boys or a regular traveller to the village? Then, without warning, Perrin was enfolded in the man's strong arms and swung off his feet. This was something that Perrin had not experienced since he was a boy, as he had outgrown most men in Hightop, especially not since his return from his forced service to the empire.

'It is good to see you, brother,' the commander said.

Perrin was released, and tears filled his eyes as he made out his brother's features hidden under a light beard.

'Garat, but you...?' Perrin managed, before his throat tightened and tears began streaming down his face.

'No, I did not die, but I did have to disappear, and no one could tell you for your and my own safety,' Garat said.

'What? where?' Perrin stammered.

'We are the Pathfinders of the resistance. When we received word of your need, we came to guide you to safety and protect the secrets of the Southlands. Come, we have much to catch up on and little time before we must leave,' Perrin's brother said. 'You have grown so much. I can not believe our little bull has become the man you are.'

'Just a moment, Garat, have you met our cousin Bren? He's a little different but is handy with both blade and axe and has been like a brother to me since I lost you,' he said.

Perrin grabbed Bren's arm and brought him into the firelight. Once again, Perrin was dumbstruck and confused when his newly returned brother bowed his head.

CHAPTER THREE
Pursuit

Each abysmal night, a battle rages
In pitch-black, the balance dips.

PERRIN WAS ABSOLUTELY confused by the recent direction his life had taken. The sudden appearance of a brother he thought dead these last turns. Then, the strange behaviour Garat had shown toward their cousin, whom the entire village of Hightop had always treated as a beloved but simple herder. His thoughts were interrupted when his brother grasped his shoulder and turned him towards the lean-to.

'We will talk, Perrin, but first, we must get you away from these meadows. If I know the Brocken, they will be on their way here already with some knowledge of who they let slip through their net. Get your pack ready. We will be travelling fast. I suggest you sling this over your back.'

Garat passed over the sword that had recently been taken from Perrin. Perrin grabbed Bren by the wrist and dragged him into their crude shelter to pack all the herbs and remedies their grandmother had sent with them. He was sure many of them would be needed in the suns to come. He also wanted plenty of cover as he retrieved the package he had promised to keep secret and safe at all costs.

By uniting the packs, Perrin and Bren could equally distribute their belongings so that each was not hampered by an overly cumbersome load. The large hunting pack was scooped up by a member of Garat's band. It would not slow the men down if the lugging of it was shared among them. Finally, Perrin reached down their axe and gravely handed it to Bren, hoping that his cousin would not need to use it anytime soon.

They emerged from the lean-to into a scene of frantic activity. Garat had ordered his men to erase any sign of their presence, and several green-clad men were fanning out with burning torches to check and re-check the immediate area and pathways to and from the campsite.

'Ready, I see,' Garat said. 'Perrin, I want you and one of my pathfinders to head down and through the valley. Don't bother to hide your tracks and use that crutch. We want the empire's men to think you are alone and heading south towards the next village. The rest of us will head to the snow line where rocks and scree will hide our tracks. We will shadow your direction and meet later to make our way to safety.'

Garat signalled over a warrior who, as with the others, was garbed in shades of green and wearing that strange mask with just the eyes visible. Standing next to Bren, Perrin could see why this rebel was chosen. He had a lithe body and height to match his cousin, so he would leave almost identical tracks. As most mountain men wore soft leather thigh boots, even the impression left in softer soil would be hard to differentiate.

Without preamble, the warrior turned Perrin downhill and began to jog towards the valley floor. Perrin had no time to ask questions or even farewell his brother and cousin. With just a wave, he set off to catch up to the figure that was fading fast into the background and the deepening shadows of the meadows. The warrior led Perrin through the longest grasses and softest ground on their run, leaving an obvious track that any southern hunter could follow. Perrin knew that the warrior was showing skills he would usually hide his tracks rather than leave a trail to follow. He hoped they would not become bait in a deadly game of hide and seek. Perrin and his silent companion steadied into an easy jog that each could keep up for some time. As they ran side by side, Perrin's breathing aligned with the warrior's as they made good pace across the valley. The new moon, now rising to its zenith, provided ample light, and the meadows were easily traversed with streams and ponds showing slivery reflections so the pair could avoid them.

'The Brocken patrol had horses,' Perrin said.

The only answer he received was a grunt and a quickening of the pace being set by Garat's man. Perrin concentrated on running and using the crutch to create the illusion of an injury and two youths fleeing the muster. Perrin knew it would be a close race to reach the valley rim before dawn reached the valley floor. His main concern was that they would have to climb the far escarpment of the valley.

While it was steep, the climb would not be impossible. However, it was also the first part of the valley to come into full sunlight. In the dark before dawn, the terrain climbed beneath their feet, and Perrin began to tire from their pace. Although he prided himself on his ability to stay with the best in the village, he had, after all, been on the go through the night. With everything that had happened, his adrenaline could only lend so much to his stamina.

'I think we should take a break while we still have the cover of darkness,' Perrin said.

He reached over and grabbed his companion's shoulder. A snort of derision was the only answer Perrin received as they slowed to a walk, allowing their legs to recover to avoid the risk of cramping when they stopped. When they finally rested on a boulder about a third of the way up the base of the valley's rock face, they made out the faint glow of flaming torches wending back and forth over the valley floor in the direction they had come. The hunt was on.

Perrin watched as the torches became a straight line pointing in their direction and began to creep across the meadows, following the path laid down for them. As he looked up at the climb facing them, Perrin noticed the morning sunlight touching the heights and the small pass they would have to take to break out of the valley into the surrounding forest. Taking the lead, Perrin guided his companion to the valley wall. From experience, he knew that the climb was precarious but not difficult for experienced mountain men. His only concerns were for the climbing skills of his silent companion and his own level of concentration in his current fatigued state. As they began to climb, the glow of the morning sun crept down to meet them, which would only serve to highlight their movements against the pale stone long before they could reach the pass.

Concentrating on picking his way through the rubble littering the base of the incline, Perrin knew that the sound of any dislodged rock bounding down the slope would echo across the valley and alert their pursuers long before they could be seen. Even as the Brocken steadily marched in their direction, the trackers could never be sure that their quarry had not headed in a contrary direction. Not until sunlight on the valley floor made tracking them much easier. He was careful to pick the easiest route up the cliff face. The cousins had often raced each other up to the pass. Perrin once again called a rest on a small ledge to gather strength before the final ascent. The sunlight had just lit the ledge, and they sat and watched the shadows lift from the valley below them.

The squad of Brocken appeared from the gloom, and the dozen afoot were followed by four mounted soldiers, travelling behind so as not to confuse the trail of the pursued. The dawn's light gave confidence to the trackers as they picked up their pace, and the mounted soldiers spread out across the trail when they realised it led directly to the valley rim. As the companions resumed their climb, Perrin noticed that the mounted warrior's actions were practised moves. Foot soldiers grabbed stirrup leathers, and the horses outstripped the remainder of the squad. Each horse effectively carried three, with two foot soldiers running and leaping with the assistance of the horse and rider.

Climbing steadily, Perrin's confidence in his companion grew as they continued without hesitation or complaint. The wall's incline steepened when they had approximately seventy paces to go. This exposed the climbers to their chasers while slowing their ascent to a crawl. Using hands and feet, they continued climbing by crab-walking their way across and up the wall, ignoring the happenings below them. Any distraction would only serve to slow them down. Two bolts suddenly pinged off the rocks on either side of the climbers, only serving to add determination to their effort. They kept moving, knowing the flatbow was the preferred weapon of the Brocken. While lethal at close quarters, the flatbow was most inaccurate over distance. Given the archers were shooting almost straight upwards, any bolt would be most unlikely to hit. Perrin and his brother's man doggedly continued towards the pass just above. Perrin scrambled over the lip of the pass and immediately reached down to aid his companion. As the warrior rolled through the gap, Perrin noticed blood soaking the back of his tunic.

'You've been hit,' Perrin said.

'It's nothing. Let's go,' was the response.

'No, hang on a moment. We need rest, and I should look at that shoulder of yours. If we throw down a few rocks, I'm sure we can keep them from climbing until we are ready to go.'

He cast around collecting fist-sized rocks, then shucked off his pack and sword. He casually lobbed rocks over his shoulder, knowing the threat would be as much of a deterrent as any direct hit. Keeping away from the edge to avoid stray flatbow bolts seemed more important than aiming his projectiles. As his rebel companion collected more missiles, Perrin was finally able to study the man. Dressed in some sort of uniform with the green hooded tunic and strange mask, he carried only a rather large hunting knife and the standard longbow and arrows of an experienced woodsman.

'OK, let me have a look at that shoulder. We don't want the blood to give away our trail, and I think we have plenty of time to rest at the moment,' Perrin said, flicking a few more rocks over the edge.

The warrior shucked off the tunic, turned away from Perrin, and began to slip the wooden toggles of the shirt free. When the shirt followed the tunic, Perrin immediately noticed tight bandages binding his chest.

'You're already wounded. Cracked ribs?' Perrin asked.

Perrin reached to examine the rib injury only to have his hands slapped away. When he looked up, he saw danger in the eyes of Garat's warrior. Perrin was confused by the reaction but the shoulder injury was the priority. He reached into his pack to retrieve a packet of echinacea and some soft lint that he moistened with his water flask. While Perrin was distracted with his preparations, the warrior removed the rebel mask, releasing a cascade of long blonde hair.

'You're a g... girl,' Perrin stammered. 'Does Garat know you're a girl?'

'He should by now. I am his wife, and my ribs are just fine,' she said. 'We can get to full introductions later. Right now, I think we have greater problems than our relationship. I am Heleana, but you can call me Leana.'

Perrin had so many questions, but the immediate need to care for the damaged shoulder and give themselves a head start on their pursuers was paramount. Leana was of similar build to Bren, with long legs and fine bones, but the resemblance stopped there. Her hair, when released from the confining mask, tumbled down her back and was a shimmering corn-stalk gold. Her mischievous eyes were of a tawny brown with hints of green and gold, and when she smiled, it was as though the sun had just risen. He saw how captivating she was and understood why his brother would have been smitten. He himself was immediately a little jealous.

'I have to stitch that wound before we go anywhere,' Perrin said. 'Just keep lobbing rocks over the edge while I do this.'

As Perrin prepared and cleaned her shoulder, Heleana sat safely back from the cliff edge and casually began throwing rocks. She carefully timed her throws so she didn't hamper Perrin's treatment of her wound. Perrin completed his ministrations, repacked and then, while Heleana was dressing, he checked on the Brocken.

'They've split up,' Perrin said. 'Three horsemen are heading back up the valley, and two units are heading along the cliff, looking for another way up. I think we only have until mid-morning before they are back on our trail.'

'Those horsemen will be going for reinforcements and will come back through the foothills to join the hunt with more men,' Heleana said. 'We will get a good start, but they will soon have these hills flush with soldiers hunting us. Even if they have not guessed who has escaped them, they will still want your brother.'

As they prepared to leave, they threw more rocks to give themselves as much time as possible before the soldiers began the climb they had just completed.

'Heleana, what is going on? Right now, my head is spinning. I have not had a moment to think since leaving our grandmother back in Hightop.'

'I will try and give you some answers as we travel. You know these hills better than me where should we go, and would your cousin lead Garat to the same area?' Heleana asked.

'Even though travel has been forbidden Bren and I often come up here and explore. We always planned an escape route if we ever needed one. I am sure he will lead Garat in the same direction.'

He indicated uphill and headed away from the pass into the thickly forested foothills. Perrin kept to game trails to make their way easier and reduce the chance of creating a simple-to-read trail as they would if they traversed virgin bush. He knew where Bren may lead Garat and his men. Speed was essential at this stage, as the Brocken had cut roads and had squads stationed throughout the hills that could respond as soon as the message to join the hunt came through.

Perrin set a steady pace, and Heleana stayed well behind to cover the back trail and hide any obvious tracks. After a time they judged that the Brocken would have achieved the climb the pair came together.

'I see you have learned well from your brother. You match the skills taught by the pathfinders and easily traverse the forest. You leave little or no sign of passing. I think now stealth may be to our advantage. Let's slow down and consider the best way forward and I will try to answer some of your questions,' she said.

Perrin slowed to a steady walk that most mountain bred could maintain over various terrains.

'First, what happened? Why did Garat disappear? What is going on? How long have you been married? Who is my brother that the Brocken want him, and why was he so strange towards Bren?'

'It was necessary to keep many things from you, and I will try and explain some of it,' Heleana said. 'If you keep us heading in the right direction, I will tell you the story of your parents and your brother and their fight against the oppressor.'

She paused for a moment, then began.

'The invasion began in your twelfth turn. For almost two seasons, we restricted the advance of the Brocken to the city of

Sudhemere and its immediate surroundings. It was thought that the original invasion was little more than a treasure-seeking expedition. Eventually, with greater numbers and superior armour and tactics, the Brocken gained supremacy. Even now they do not enter the forests or foothills unless travel is easy and there is a village to occupy.

That was when you were sent to live in Hightop with your younger cousin, Bren. Many of the reasons were not explained to you then, as you could not divulge information you did not have. I will leave the telling of that part of the story to your brother.'

'As to your family, they were advisors to the Duke and leaders in the community. During the incursion, your brother became a Squad Leader in the resistance and then the Commander of the Pathfinders. They are the major force of the resistance against the Northern Empire. He has a price on his head, and they do not know his identity, that is why he had to disappear. The masks we wear hide our features in battle and are a symbol to the people. Anyone caught with a mask is summarily executed by the Brocken. We have been keeping up a campaign of hit-and-run with the northerners until our leaders can come up with a way to force the empire to retreat or surrender. They think we will only have enough forces to counterattack and achieve those ends by combining with the other races the Dini and the Elves.'

Perrin watched Heleana as she took a moment to reflect on the simpler times and the hope of returning to the joy of the past. Heleana's breathing was becoming shallow due to their exertions and the storytelling. He could tell there was a deeper hurt in her past.

'When the Duke was murdered, and Sudhemere was threatened by siege, your parents took charge of the city's defence. They evacuated as many of the residents as they could before the siege began. I am sorry for your loss, but your father and mother were great heroes and gave themselves up for their people and the land they loved.'

Perrin had stopped and turned back towards her as she finished the tale. He was gasping down huge breaths, trying to keep composed. He stared into his sister in-laws eyes.

'Why wasn't I told?' he demanded.

'You have been through the Brocken's conscription and induction. Because of your importance, it was decided that ignorance would keep you safe,' Heleana said. 'You have experienced the mind probe and hateful training regime. The whole exercise is designed to identify children of the resistance leaders and ferret out the hidden prince,' she added.

'What importance do I have? And we all know the prince disappeared turns ago and no one knows where,' Perrin said.

'Perrin, we cannot stop. We must keep going. I promise, as soon as we rejoin Garat we will have time to answer all your questions. But rest assured, you have played one of the most important roles of all in the defence of our land,' Heleana said.

She turned Perrin around and gave him a gentle shove. He led them slightly uphill as the forest of beech and oak began to give way to the spruce and firs of the upper reaches at the feet of the mountains. They reached one of the new roads cut through the trees to give the Brocken a faster means of communicating via a system of dispatch riders. Perrin halted when he heard a clattering of hooves heading in their direction.

Heleana grabbed Perrin's arm and whispered, 'A rider comes. They may be carrying word about us. We must stop him.'

Perrin motioned for Heleana to hide behind a bush beside the road and then crossed over to hide behind a tree trunk opposite her. Heleana armed herself with a fallen branch while Perrin slowly drew the sword over his shoulder. The rider galloped around the corner of the road, clearly in great haste. Perrin and Heleana jumped from concealment, scaring the mount, which reared up at the apparitions and dumped its rider in the middle of the road. The horse whinnied, bucked, and took off up the road as the saddle slipped, further antagonising the beast.

'What have you done?' demanded the indignant rider. 'I only just stole that horse from the Brocken.'

Perrin and Heleana looked down at their captive and realised this could not be a northern soldier. He was garbed in grey, but his choice of clothes featured sandals, leggings and a robe, with a bag strung across his chest. A grey beard and heavy black eyebrows were features dominated by a shiny bald pate. The rider closed his eyes for a moment then suddenly looked up at his captors.

'That's all right. I asked him to stop just up the road. Help me up, please,' he said.

He held out his hand to Heleana, apparently not liking the look of the sword in Perrin's fist. Perrin suddenly recognised their captive.

'You're Martyn the tinker,' he said.

'Young Perrin Omholt. Fancy seeing you way out here and keeping such salubrious company. The Lady Hell, as I live and breathe,' the tinker said. He bowed to Heleana. 'So, you are the two the Brocken hunt. The message just came through to Norgay's Trading Post, and the squad there is right on my heels. This horse was the only one they had, so I stole it to make sure any pursuit was on foot alone. Ahh, here he is,' Martyn said.

When they rounded the bend in the trail, the bay gelding was grazing on new grasses growing in the sunlight, shining through a break in the canopy. Perrin realised it was past mid-sun, but there was still some time before darkness descended.

'The poor beast has bruised a hoof in his flight. We will have to move on as best we can,' Martyn said.

He grabbed the horse's reins, adjusted the saddle and handed Perrin a flatbow and quiver that had been sheathed on the saddle. Martyn then continued up the track.

'We best hurry on. The Brocken squad was well rested, and you two look as though you have had quite the adventure.

'Young Omholt, do you know whom you have taken up with here?' Martyn paused for maximum dramatic effect. 'None other than Lady Hell, the most feared sub-commander in the Southland's resistance. She has led many of the most dangerous and bloody missions and attacks on the Brocken. She is also the daughter of and heir to the Duke of Sudhem, thus deserves both her honorific and the sobriquet,' Martyn said.

Martyn looked at Perrin for his reaction and saw he had no idea of the Lady's reputation.

'No, Martyn, I didn't know that,' Perrin said.

Perrin looked towards Heleana, who only shrugged and nodded.

'Martyn, why are you here?' Perrin asked.

'Perrin, my boy, do you know what the Brocken do to horse thieves? I can normally get away with cheating them at pokr, but stealing a horse from the captain, even with the horse's permission, is perhaps a bit more than I could talk my way out of,' Martyn said.

'Mitchum always said it was best to keep an eye on you. He thought you were a bit of a charlatan,' Perrin said.

'The tavern keeper just can't play pokr. I never cheat to win more than my opponents can afford. Is it my fault he keeps challenging me?' Martyn asked.

Perrin was watching their back trail and, with his sense of the forest, noticed the disturbances increasing behind them.

'The Brocken are coming on quickly. We had best find a defensive site or set up an ambush. I am almost done in and would prefer to keep some energy if it comes to a fight,' Perrin said.

Heleana nodded wearily in agreeance. 'I am also stretched and my shoulder pains me.' They studied the trail. Just behind them, it cut around a small landslide that would at least protect one flank, and a drop-off on the other side gave them a high-ground advantage.

'This looks about the best place we could hope for,' Heleana said.

She strung her bow. Perrin was unsure how many shots she could manage with her damaged shoulder.

'Martyn, how many are in that squad? Is it the standard six men?' Perrin asked.

'There were eight, including the captain and his manservant, when I left,' Martyn confirmed.

'You don't mind if I just continue on, do you?' Martyn asked. 'I'm sure you two are better suited for a visit from the Brocken.'

Heleana and Perrin prepared themselves as the strange man casually wandered up the road, leading the stolen horse. At least he had taken Perrin's pack with him, allowing Perrin more freedom of movement. Perrin considered the situation. Between them, they had a flatbow, a longbow, a long knife, and Perrin's sword. The Brocken would have flatbows, short swords, and the advantage of numbers. Perrin hoped to down three or four with the element of surprise but knew that, ultimately, two could not hope to stand against eight trained soldiers.

'Leana, take my sword and go after Martyn. I will hold them here as long as I can. I cannot let my brother's wife die at my side,' Perrin said.

'You are just like him,' Heleana said.

She was drawing on the mask of the resistance. 'To stand together is strength, and we will not retreat any further.'

Perrin began to understand the reputation Martyn had described.

'Yes, my Lady,' he said, then turned to her with a slight bow. He was rewarded with a smile and a kiss on the cheek, followed by a swift kick to the butt.

'Now find some cover and make sure of your targets,' Lady Hell commanded.

RESISTANCE

The point guards of the Brocken squad rounded the bend, not expecting to find two rebels opposing them. In a strategic error, the captain had force-marched the soldiers, so the squad was bunched up and coming on at pace. Three of the Brocken fell with arrows, piercing their gambesons before the remainder could regroup and coordinate their attack from cover. Flatbow bolts flew but were fired as deterrents to give the captain time to order his men rather than to cause injury. The wounded and dying screamed in pain and pleaded with their comrades to no avail. With only one flank to utilise, the captain sent a man down the slope and gave him covering fire with their flatbows.

When the Brocken soldier had reached his position, he began to shoot at Perrin and Heleana, forcing them to take cover. Perrin knew any advantage they had was now slowly turning in the other direction. They could not return fire without exposing themselves, and the superiority of numbers and firepower would eventually win. Perrin grasped his grandfather's sword and indicated to Heleana his intention to charge the squad and allow her to escape.

Heleana viciously shook her head and indicated with hand signals for Perrin to stay down. Perrin knew it was only a matter of time before one of the soldiers could find a clear shot. A flatbow bolt is devastating from only twenty paces. Perrin jumped up and screamed a war cry as he charged the squad's position. A grey garbed soldier rose up before him with his short sword held high. Perrin's downward stroke met no defensive parry. Moments before Perrin's sword shattered bones and cut through flesh and muscle, a cloth-yard arrow pierced the man back to front. As the soldier fell under the sword's stroke, Perrin continued on hurdling a fallen trunk only to find a number of green-clad, masked figures standing over the bodies of the Brocken squad and their captain.

Adrenaline pumped through his veins as he stood prepared for another attack, but no foe was there to face him. Perrin surveyed the tableau before him. Reality was no reflection on the imaginings of two young boys' pretence while herding their flock. Striking down the Brocken soldier did not compare to slaughtering and dressing a lamb or goat for sustenance. The horror of so much death conflicted with everything he had been taught by his grandmother. There was no balance here. His stomach roiled and he rushed to the side of the path bringing up what little the organ held until the acidic taste of bile coated the back of his throat.

He slowly came down from the height of tension and realised he and Heleana were safe. Perrin thought it ironic that the Brocken assimilation officers provided him with the scars and memories that allowed him to focus and not completely break and give in to the tears that threatened to burst forth. As he cleaned and sheathed his sword he was greeted by the squad leader, who also signed a silent greeting to Heleana as she rose from her place of concealment. Heleana strode over to Perrin and handed him her water flask. Perrin could see in her eyes the compassion of one who had had the same experience. A flurry of hand signals indicated orders being passed along. One of the rebels led Perrin and Heleana up the road in the direction that Martyn had gone. The rest of the squad were to clean up the scene, leaving little evidence and creating a mystery about the now missing Brocken squad.

Around the next bend in the road, they found Martyn, his horse, and another Pathfinder. The Pathfinder motioned Martyn to follow them and turned up-slope away from the road, towards the scree-covered slopes of the mountains. As the group laboured uphill, Perrin looked back and saw the other man carefully sweeping their tracks and hiding all signs of their passing. After a period of silence, Perrin could no longer stand the uncertainty the last two suns had cast upon him.

'Where are we going? I must find Bren. He will be confused,' Perrin demanded.

'Perrin, in just a short while, we will join your brother and can rest. Then, you will get all the answers you need. Up ahead, there is a well-guarded and concealed valley we sometimes use as a raiding base. We will be safe there,' Heleana said.

'Will there be any food?' Martyn asked. 'Running from certain death tends to make one hungry.'

'It has not been as if we had time to hunt,' Heleana shot back at the tinker. 'Travel rations will be about all.'

Perrin watched as Martyn closed his eyes and moved his lips. The strange man suddenly looked up and said, 'Thank you.'

'My Lady, if you could send this fine young man up around that spur in the rocks, we may be able to do better than travel rations,' Martyn said.

Perrin could see Heleana was fatigued, and the pain in her shoulder had been aggravated by drawing her bow. He was concerned how she would react to the Tinker's suggestion. Heleana's body had stiffened and her fists had clenched then with an exhalation of breath she relaxed and looked towards the leading Pathfinder.

'Do as he says. We are not far away now. I know the required pass signals,' she said.

Heleana led Perrin, Martyn, and the horse onwards as the scout peeled off and started stalking towards the indicated spur. Not long after, Heleana was confronted by the first sentry, and they passed on towards the safety of the resistance base. Heleana indicated a small rock fall that looked impenetrable until a cleverly painted canvas screen was moved aside, showing a small tunnel just tall enough to allow the horse's passage. With a clear field of fire and steep walls, the valley, little more than a glade, could be defended by a small number of archers against a much larger force.

Exiting the tunnel, Perrin saw a well-ordered camp, although it was strangely quiet as most communication was done via a series of hand signals. Perrin was glad to see his brother and cousin striding towards them across the floor of the valley and was soon enveloped in a family bear hug. Garat stepped back and greeted his wife, who winced at his embrace. Garat noticed the blood on her tunic and, with great care, peeled the cloth away from the dried blood to expose the wound.

'Come, my love, we can get that cleaned and dressed. It looks as though someone has done a good job of those stitches,' Garat said.

He looked at his younger brother and mouthed the words *thank you*. Perrin turned to his cousin, and taking him by the arms, looked him up and down. Bren was clearly overwhelmed and hugged his cousin once again.

'Bren has not been hurt. He kept up with my squad members and even displayed tracking skills to outshine my own,' Garat said before leading his wife towards a cave mouth set into the valley's wall.

Although Perrin had to bend through the mouth of the cave, it soon gave out to a larger chamber about the size of his Gram's cottage in Hightop. As Heleana was being attended to, Garat looked at his younger brother, and Perrin realised that his older brother now had to slightly raise his eyes to look into Perrin's own.

'Well, brother, you have certainly grown. I am very happy to see you,' Garat said.

Garat motioned to Perrin and Bren to take stools around a small fire and indicated with his hands that refreshments should be brought. Martyn sat and, with obvious relish, greedily took the tankard offered and downed it in one swallow, resulting in a coughing fit.

'Water? Water! You can drown in water, you know,' he stammered.

Garat looked at the strange addition to his wife's party and asked, 'And just who are you?'

'Garat, this is Martyn. He comes through Hightop every now and again. He is a tinker but also a mountebank and gambler, according to Mitchum the tavern keeper,' Perrin said.

'Don't forget horse thief and cook if you could direct me to the hearth,' Martyn said, indicating a rebel entering the cavern bearing a dressed buck over his shoulder.

'I got this just round the spur this man sent me to,' the scout reported.

Heleana and Perrin looked at Martyn, who just smiled and asked Perrin, 'What herbs have you in this pack that I've been lugging around for you?'

Perrin checked his pack and handed Martyn a series of sachets. Perrin also took a packet and said, 'I'll just check on your horse.'

Martyn's eyes glazed, then he looked at Perrin and said, 'Do not bother. He is being very well cared for.'

Martyn turned towards the hearth, taking a well-honed skinning knife from somewhere in his robes. Enticing odours soon wafted around the small cavern.

The Omholt family took advantage of the time to bathe and refresh, then returned to relax around the fire.

'Perrin, I suppose you have a great many questions?' Garat said. 'If you can wait until your tinker can serve that venison stew he is preparing, I will tell the tale that has brought us to this point. But while we wait, may I formally introduce Lady Heleana Edwina Loretta L'Atchett, my wife and second in command of the Pathfinders. My Lady, may I present Perrin, your brother-in-law?'

Garat had risen and brought Perrin to stand before Heleana. Perrin bowed, unsure of the forms, considering the events of the recent past. Heleana, looked every inch the refined woman of stature. She had changed from her forest garb into an open-necked embroidered shirt with split riding skirts and polished knee boots.

She rose from her stool and, to Perrin's delight, kissed him on each cheek.

'Welcome, brother, and thank you for your service to the Southlands,' she said.

Perrin was about to ask yet another question when Martyn bashed a tin pot with a ladle.

'Come and get it,' he announced. 'I cook. I don't wait tables.'

Martyn was serving a generous amount of stew onto his own plate when Garat indicated that Perrin and Bren should remain seated and moved to the hearth to prepare two plates. After a moment, Garat handed the boys plates of stew with thick slices of camp bread.

Perrin looked to his cousin and said, 'I'm sorry, Garat, but Bren does not eat meat.'

'Whatever gave you that idea?' Garat and Bren said in unison.

Perrin looked between the two of them, bewildered by their comment.

'Well, it would seem that your grandmother kept you very ignorant of who each of you really is, as well as the fact that she is not related to you at all,' Garat said. 'I know you will be concerned for the old woman, but be at ease. She can handle her own affairs, and I am sure we have not seen the last of old Gram. I may as well get to the point, Perrin. The boy you have been protecting is not your cousin Bren but is really the crown prince of the Southlands, his majesty Brycen Ronan E'Nakor.'

Garat then bowed and indicated young Bren. Both Perrin and Bren stared at him, puzzled and dumbfounded.

'What?' they both began.

'Wait on here, first, you say Gram is not our grandmother, and now Bren is not Bren? What is going on?' Perrin asked.

'Just relax, boys,' the older Omholt said.

He placed a hand on each of their shoulders and gently forced them to resume their seats.

'I see the telling of this tale will stretch your belief, little bull,' Garat said.

By using the old nickname, he indicated his brother should be calmer and understand the facts before rushing to conclusions.

'Bren, do you know any of this?' Perrin asked.

'Cousin, it has been as though I have been living in a fog, but it is clearing. I am remembering more and more, but not from too long ago,' the younger boy replied.

'You were sent to live in Hightop to avoid detection. The plan was to keep you from understanding your origins so that any integration would be seamless. The villagers would accept you as refugees and orphans of the conflict, like so many others. We knew the northerners could discover your identities using their mind probing in their inductions and interrogations, so the fewer who knew, the better.

'As you would be living under the Northern Empire's influence, you could hide in plain sight. It was only after the North began their conscription and basic training that we knew the truth would eventually be found. Perrin, you were able to survive the conscription only because you were completely unaware of the role with which you had been entrusted. Mother and Father would have been so proud of you, and even I was a bit jealous that our 'little bull' was being given such an important task in the future of the Southlands,' Garat said.

Perrin still did not believe what he was hearing and looked to Heleana for verification, only to have her smile and nod at him. She flashed a series of hand movements that Perrin, to his surprise, understood as *listen and learn*.

'Over the last five turns, you boys have been one of the resistance's most important and best-kept secrets. Perrin, you have become the man our parents meant you to be, even more so than I,' Garat stated. 'If we of the South are ever to be free, we need to bring new hope to the people and align ourselves with the elves and other races that call the Southlands home. That hope is the unveiling of our lost prince alongside the Elven heir.'

'But Bren, he um... He sometimes forgets things,' Perrin said. Perrin was trying to be as diplomatic and caring as possible. 'If he is the prince, how does he not know?'

'Mushrooms,' Martyn mumbled. Martyn was unaware that the talking had subsided, and those sharing the fire with him could clearly hear his musings.

'What do you mean mushrooms?' Perrin asked.

'Well, you did live in Hightop with a well-known witch, and there are a number of mushrooms that can confuse the mind,' he said.

Perrin and Bren stared at the tinker.

'Witch? Our Gram is not a witch,' Perrin said. He was on the verge of doing something physical as the last few suns had stretched him almost to breaking.

'Calm yourself, Perrin Omholt. I meant no insult. As a matter of fact, I consulted with the good lady any number of times,' Martyn said. 'Yes, I can see how that would work. A regular dose of golden top would keep young Bren in a sunny and ebullient mood. Why, that cunning old battle-axe even fooled me. She managed to cheat a cheater.'

'Many plans have been laid in the hope that we can finally push back the Brocken and force a truce. We were on our way to get you and Prince Brycen as we have been ordered to travel to the south to meet and plan,' Garat said. 'We will set out tomorrow and head south. We must meet on the rising of the next full moon. A guide is being sent to join us.'

'Oh, yes,' Martyn said. He then began to tick off on his fingers. 'Tinker, charlatan, gambler, horse thief, cook, guide. Did I forget to mention guide?'

CHAPTER FOUR
Nordinium

Evil triumph a first for ages
Fear and doom take hold and grip.

THE KING EMPEROR RAILED at his chamberlain in a never-ending cycle of complaints and incriminations. His temper was always at its worst when the blizzards blew.

'Was it not my family that were the ones to unite the North under one rule? Had not my ancestors planned, schemed, fought, and died to create this empire? Well, Harta?'

'Yes, Majesty, it was you and yours,' Harta intoned.

'Am I not the sole superior commander of the forces of the north? Why did I ever agree to the ministrations and conjurations of those damned mages? Is it not my wealth and my gifts that they now enjoyed as they lord about the estates and palaces I provide? Yet still, they have the temerity to ask for more. Do they think wealth grows in the snow?'

Lothar the Great, King-Emperor of the Nordinium Empire, paced the length of his council chambers and continued to rant his displeasure at the latest expenses and demands made on his treasury to support the invasion of the Southlands. Yes, the pillage of the southern lands provided a steady stream of taxes, slaves, and food.

The bounty eased the burden of feeding his subjects during the harsh season of the long moon and strengthened his grip on the College of Barons. Still, the contentious matter of the mages and their continued demands for slaves and gold was undermining his rule. Could he afford to risk the completion of their great task and allow them to finally bring the Southlands to heel? What exactly were they doing with the many slaves that entered their monastery and never came out? Was mastery of this vast world of Tol achievable or even desirable?

'What now, Harta?' demanded the King.

'Majesty, the Fourth of the Seven requests audience,' said the chamberlain.

Harta was well aware that Lothar understood he had tempered the mage's demand and had used the word requests to ease the mood. Harta was the third appointed chamberlain for this turn. The previous two holders of the position now resided on spikes at the gates of Lothar's capital. It does not do to displease the King - Emporer. Lothar nodded understanding of Harta's diplomacy. In the depths of the season of snows, the transport of fresh supplies from the south was hampered by the weather that limited the passage of their fleet. This always caused tempers to flare, and the consequences were dire.

A huge fire roared in the central pit, fed by logs the size of a fully grown boar. The council chamber wreathed in smoke that escaped the flue and drifted above them, slowly dissipating into the cracks in the stone work of Lothar's keep. Two drudges entered, wheeling a new log on a barrow. The King-Emperor judged them as below his notice and ignored them as they rolled the heavy log into place. An ember from the resulting shower of sparks landed on the back of the King-Emperor's hand. The burn snapped his attention from his diatribe against the mages, and he lashed out at the nearest drudge, who tripped on the hearth and fell into the fire. Screams of anguish echoed off the chamber walls. Harta grabbed the other drudge and ordered him to drag his companion out of the pit and take him to the kitchen for aid.

'Use the barrow, fool,' ordered the King-Emperor. 'Harta, send in the fourth.'

The King-Emperor returned to his throne and watched for the entrance of the mage.

Why do all those mages look almost identical? Each had a bald, almost skeletal head, piercing close-set eyes, dark brows, and a pointed beard. Their bowed backs and long arms were clothed in hooded robes, with variously coloured bands around the hem indicating their rank in the seven. The colour of the band referred to a gem with which they controlled their power.

'Lord Lothar,' began the mage, 'great advance has been made. We will soon have the means to subjugate the power in the Southlands and bring all its wealth to your service.'

'You forget yourself, mage. You dare enter my presence without obeisance and supplication?' Lothar raged.

Lothar rose and stormed towards the mage. The Fourth stood his ground in defiance and only dropped into genuflection when he was sure the king-emperor was conscious of the slight, but before outright disobedience was undeniable.

'What do you want now?' Lothar demanded.

'Majesty, we have nearly discovered the way to control the gems. We will soon have the means to control the south. We need more slaves and gold,' the fourth said.

Lothar looked down upon the mage.

'Tell me again, mage, why I need you and yours when I can crush the south at my leisure.'

'Majesty, as we have explained in the past. There is great power in the Southlands that is symbiotically linked to all life forces in a harmonious accord that has lasted for millennia. If it is aroused, it will overpower your barons and their men, and threaten all you have built in the north. Without a means to gain full control of the life forces in the south, your barons and their men could meet with forces beyond the mundane. Once conquered, the Southlands will open the rest of Tol to your empire.'

Only the crackle and pop of the resins and saps in the pine logs burning in the pit punctuated the silence that followed the fourth of the mage's petition.

Lothar and his chamberlain's eyes met. Harta watched his lord's face and noted that Lothar understood the stare from the mage was defiant and dangerous. Lothar rued the sun he had ever agreed to listen to the first of the mages. While it had seemed harmless that their conjuring would help his conquests, the growing power and wealth of the mages was beginning to rival the ever-hungry College of Barons. Not only was Lothar battling resistance in the south, but his own capital had become a hotbed of control-hungry nobles demanding more and more wealth and power.

'Well, mage, in the middle of this freezing season, there are no more slaves, and you can just summon up your own gold. I will not continue to finance your experiments when the outcome is hidden from me. Get you gone, and when one of you can prove to me how these gems will benefit my empire, I may consider your further use. This great power of the Southlands seems no more than your own conjuring,' Lothar said.

Harta winced as the king-emperor spat angrily and turned to his throne. Only Harta witnessed the murderous expression that crossed the face of the persistent mage. The Fourth was the third mage to appear before the King-Emperor Lothar this week.

The wind howled and moaned through the corridors and a blast of chilly air rushed into the chamber when the mage threw the doors apart to leave. Two guards surprised by the action rushed to secure them.

Harta considered the growing chasm between the crown, the barons, and the mages. The season of snows in the north was harsh enough without the added concern of barons with nothing better to do than cement discord and gossip behind his back. Lothar preferred a simpler time when the strength of arms was the determining factor to his rule. The time of snows then was a season for planning raids, discussing opponents' strengths and weaknesses, making and developing weapons, and training for conquest.

When a land was under a mass of snow, it was time to hunker down and await the first melt. When those first long boatmen came to them with stories of lands free of snow and filled with endless fields of grain and stock begging for the taking, Lothar could no sooner hold back the barons and their sons than hold back the wind.

Lothar had ascended the throne after the untimely death of his brother and father in strikingly similar hunting accidents. The power of his rule was derived from strict obedience to his decrees. He had forged an entire empire, but this had now brought the need to rule and manage over the need to battle and conquer. He was the prisoner of his own successes, and, until he could ensure the succession with an heir, he would be ever pursued by the barons to name one of them to follow, with the conundrum that as soon as he did, he would be open to his own accident.

Lothar had heard stories of the beauty of the daughter of the Duke of Sudhem, the now-deceased ruler of the Duchy of Sudhemere. Lothar considered a union between north and south a way to amalgamate his holdings and cement the Southlands as the latest adjunct to the empire of Lothar the Great.

Harta studied his king and emperor. He had flaming red hair and a beard, along with piercing green eyes that warned of his intelligence and temper, while his freckled countenance belied the raw power of his mighty frame. Given all his success at forging the Northern Empire, this man was a warrior, not an administrator. This was clear by his insistence on the use of all his titles. As far as Harta's lord was concerned, all should remember his rise to Emperor using the positions he attained during his conquests. Yet the opportunities and wealth he had created for his Barons and their vassals had only increased those hard-to-control human failings of envy and greed.

With the passing of every season from one snow solstice to the next, his empire grew, yet the mentality and bickering of the barons did not abate. Life had grown easier for the empire's subjects as Lothar's rule of law and swift, decisive justice decreased the loss of life through petty squabbles and border clashes. The hidden consequence of advancement was that the barons had more sons to be gifted land and larger households to feed. While the King-Emperor understood the need to supervise one's own estates and ensure that enough food was produced during the seasons of the sun to sustain life during the seasons of snow, the short-term answer had always been to take what you wanted. After all, it had always been he who has the strongest arm survives.

Lothar's chamberlain had always been a practical man and had previously been the supply officer in Lothar's war band. His jet-black hair, long nose, and hooded eyes gave him the appearance of the black bird of death, adding his broad shoulders and massive chest, meant no one attempted to play the fool or cheat the right hand of the King-Emperor. Lothar relied on Harta to guide his lands towards a self-sustaining empire. He was also acutely aware that the occupation of the Southlands currently provided the best chance to weed out the weakest of the Barons and their progeny.

Understanding the duplicity and greed of the Barons was easy. All one had to do was believe that if their mouth was moving, they were lying. His greatest fear was the machinations of the mages and the increase in numbers of the seven with their new apprentices. The mage's secrets were hidden behind the forbidding walls of their monastery.

Having just celebrated the solstice, everyone was aware that this season of snows would be longer and harsher than most. Many of the barons had ignored the warnings and spent their season of the sun campaigning in the south instead of administering their own holdings. With the thaw, would come the clamouring of demands to increase the production of larger ships to return with more booty from the Southlands. The practice of raiding south during the snows and managing your holdings during the growing seasons was becoming blurred by the ease of pillaging the Southlands and the ever-growing greed of the barons. Harta had reported that a faction in the College of Barons was secretly planning to grasp control of the Southlands and withdraw from Lothar's empire.

The worst of these was Baron Lord Tod Du Tek and his two sons, his heir and his spare. Each of the clan members was worse than the previous. It was hard to imagine when each was devious, immoral, pernicious, and just downright dangerous. The baron had bullied his way to leading the invasion of the Southlands and was currently enjoying the warmth in sunny Sudhemere while his holdings in the empire were covered in snow. He had taken his second son with him, leaving his heir to oversee his estates. Lothar could not think of a more dishonourable man than the second son of Baron Lord Du Tek.

Du Tek now enjoyed leadership in the Southlands as he had manipulated and murdered his way into control, ever reliant on the rule of strength. His assassins had murdered the sovereign of the Southlands in his own capital and arranged timely accidents for any number of his fellow barons and their sons. Du Tek would always refer to Lothar's own rise to power as his own inspiration.

In his various roles as an officer in Lothar's warband and now as chamberlain Harta had often warned his King-Emperor of the dangers of letting Du Tek and the barons hold sway in the Southlands. They should not have control over the flow of riches and the honours and powers granted to the most successful. When Lothar had united the Northern Empire and stabilised the chain of command, he had managed to combine the war bands into a cohesive force while also eliminating any immediate opponents. Lothar maintained the perspective that without an enemy to fight, the barons and this new army would look for enemies domestically. As Lothar himself was then the greatest enemy of all, it was smarter to have his barons looking outwards and southwards than at him.

The King-Emperor was in a quandary. He knew the beast he had created as the army was now abundantly supplied, armed, trained, and commanded. Wealth and reward could be won through spirited adventure and strength of arms, but only if it had a focus and a land to conquer. Yes, the barons often had their own agenda, with their ships and raiders filling their own coffers, but if they did not interfere with the King-Emperor's overall push into the Southlands, Lothar was prepared to let them have their fun. At least until he decided he needed to bring them into line with his own plans.

'Majesty, would you take wine and refreshments before open council?'

'Harta, why must these sycophants parade every daughter they have at every opportunity?' Lothar said. Despite this, he nodded approval of Harta's suggestion.

'Lord, an alignment with your august person would elevate the father of your bride to the head of the College of Barons. You understand the value and prestige of such a position. You also understand the danger of such a position,' Harta said. Once again, repeating the warning he oft gave to the oft-asked rhetorical question.

'Harta, perhaps my barons could do with a reminder? I have not exercised my arm for some time. Clear the courtyard. On the sun after the next full moon, we tourney,' Lothar declared.

Harta saw that the King-Emperor was smiling for the first time that sun.

'Lord, there is an oxen's depth of snow out there.'

'Have the drudges clear the courtyard. I will melee!' Lothar roared. He punctuated that decree by banging his fist on the shield that always leaned against his throne.

'Advise the barons that any who bring me to submission can name their female kin as my betrothed. Harta, this is exhilarating. We tourney in the depths of the snows. Let us see how many of those sons of barons can hold a shield against Lothar the great.'

Harta was unnerved but not surprised by his lord's decision. It had always been his first response to adversity—the strongest survive. Harta wished he would live to bring Lothar's empire into harmony and peace but knew that strength alone could not stand against deceit and greed.

'Harta, the council is postponed. I must see to my armoury and replace the bindings on my mace and shield. Have any scrolls sent to my rooms, we will deal with them there,' Lothar said.

Harta could see that Lothar the Great was in an ebullient mood as he scoffed down the wine, grabbed the fowl he had been served, and stormed from the council chamber.

CHAPTER FIVE
The Seven

As hope diminishes the light is lost
In deep despair, a pact made.

DOLMUN, THE FOURTH of Seven, raised the hem of his robes above the slosh and mire that ringed the pathways between the citadel and monastery. He did not care to have the pale white hems of his robes muddied. He did not relish returning to the First of the Mages with the news that the King-Emperor would not fund any more experimentation or even supply slaves for those experiments. His only redemption for his frustrating defeat was that he had not been the first of his brethren to fail in the task.

He knew he had time to formulate the best way to pass on the news because Reaver the Black, First of the Mages, would be engaged in his favourite pastime until the bell called the monastery together for vespers. Dolmun could not believe that they still maintained the sham religion but saw the benefit of having some autonomous control over the population. It gave the mages access to information not necessarily known to that red-headed barbarian who currently occupied the throne.

The First Mage, Reaver, had been the Monastic Abba and had cared for his congregation as well as any Abba who had come before.

When Lothar had created his empire, the wealth and power of the Abba were impacted, and Reaver looked for ways to reassert his dominance. At the urgings of some of the disgruntled barons, the Abba was asked to research ways to circumvent the King-Emperor's power.

If Lothar could not be defeated by force of arms, perhaps there was a mystical path to his downfall. In his studies, Reaver the Black discovered a path to total dominance, not only over Nordinium but the empire and all the lands beyond. Even the Abba did not know exactly what was beyond other than untold riches and ultimate power. The keys to his mastery over all would be the wealth from Baron Du Tek and his cadre of disgruntled barons while keeping them ignorant of the true level of power that the life essences—which the mages study and collect—can unleash.

Dolmun was an administrator and did not much care for the ceremonies and practices that went on in the monastery's catacombs, but he was an integral cog in ensuring the First had the vital components to continue his studies. One did not anger Reaver if one did not want to experience his experiments as a subject. Shortly after the abundant wealth of the Southlands was discovered, Reaver had withdrawn from the daily management of the monastery, locked himself away in the library, and later barred any entry to the catacombs and deep cellars. Coincidentally, that was when the urchins and low-lives of the streets began to disappear, and the previously affable Reaver became dark and secretive. Just after the sun solstice of that turn, Reaver called each of his monks to attend him, one at a time. Each monk returned changed and wearing a ring with a coloured stone.

The first monk to be closeted in Reaver's workrooms was a young novice who returned two moons later with a ring featuring an emerald green stone and the title of the Seventh. The burly monk, whose passion was his gardens, became the Sixth and bore the blue topaz. The waspish studious brothers, Ulian and Worian, were converted together as Reaver became stronger and more aligned with his dark arts. Ulian the Fifth proudly displayed the silver star sapphire, while his brother boasted of being the Third, showing off his yellow sapphire. These two had never shown any desire for a life outside of dedication to the monastery but now were Reaver's strongest supporters.

Agross the Red, now Second of the Mages, had been the military arm of the monastery. The man was as big as the King-Emperor and had the strength to match. In the past he had always trained for the defence of the monastery while observing all the teachings. These sun's his ruby ring was often seen flashing as he assisted Reaver at their mysterious and dark practices.

When Dolmun was summoned to attend Reaver, he agreed to participate, becoming the Fourth with the diamond ring to seal the dark pact. During the ceremony, Dolmun hid the extent of his own powers from Reaver and now waited for his chance to usurp the First at the culmination of his plan.

Dolmun was not completely at ease with the Circle of Seven. Nor the increased need for bodies to feed the practices necessary to create the power the First needed. Each time Dolmun was forced to enter the catacombs, he believed the chill and odour were not totally attributable to the weather or the gore that splattered the walls and blood that ran in the gutters. Dolmun kept his participation to the bare minimum needed to maintain the facade of obedience. He would quickly dispatch his allotted slaves and capture their essences without adding torture and pain to heighten the yield. Dolmun kept the slow but steady stream of life force he garnered to himself without resorting to the murderous practices of the others.

To gain power, each mage had to harvest the life forces of his victims and build up and store the power in a gem. With these, he would eventually be able to draw the life essence from the

Southlands. Each mage was linked to the others through their ring. In an effort to gain complete control over the Southlands, Reaver had the mages build and strengthen their power, practising for the final ceremony during the season of the sun solstice, when seven virgins would complete the rite. This rite would be held in the citadel at Sudhemere, where seven large gems linked to the mage's rings were protected by Baron Du Tek. Du Tek's fear of the mages was the only thing keeping the gems from disappearing into his own vaults. The previous baron to hold his position had not been so circumspect and had suffered for his avarice.

The first toll of the bell brought Dolmun out of his reverie, and he prepared himself for the coming confrontation. It irritated the Fourth to bend to Reaver's rants, but it was easier to acquiesce than to directly defy the First. Reaver burst into Dolmun's chambers without any announcement.

'Well?' Reaver said.

The perfumes the First had sprayed over his robes did not completely mask the cloying odour of the cellars where he spent his suns. He did not even bother to change his robes anymore, and the dark stains on the soot black robes could not be mistaken. The First's pallid complexion and his squinting eyes displayed the fact he had rarely seen the sunlight even as it was the depth of the season of snows.

'Lothar laughed at your request, my Lord Abba,' Dolmun said. 'He insisted that no more slaves could be obtained for you until the 'between seas' could be navigated and that you should have enough gold already. He did ask for you to update him about your experiments and how they benefit him directly.'

Dolmun had deftly redirected Reaver's anger at his failure to obtain support from the King-Emperor and turned it to undeviating resentment at Lothar.

'Vesper's now,' Reaver said. The anger and loathing in his voice were undeniable.

Dolmun would repeat the chants and devotions and go through the motions only to be seen to support the First and to ensure the spiritual needs of the population of the capital were being cared for. The changes in the mages had not gone unnoticed, but the comforting customs and practices kept the people mesmerized and content, which was important to Dolmun. With the scarcity of slaves to progress his experiments, Reaver had brought a number of new acolytes and apprentice in to the monastery. These men were less followers of the monastery than ruffians and kidnappers. Reaver had finally revealed to the circle of mages as a method of storing life forces and building up power only to have the raw material unavailable. There are only so many souls that could be bought off the streets or stolen.

After the minimum requirements were met to give some semblance of mystic rites being performed, the Circle of Seven Mages was ordered to the catacombs to plan the coming season of the snows' solstice. This would be the shortest and darkest sun, and some of the most caliginous rites were to be conducted on that night.

Dolmun ensured he was early and made his way around the chamber, checking the hidden slivers of diamond he used to siphon off small quantities of the essences released to Reaver's main repository. He kept hidden his own knowledge and secret passage access to the First's office with its treasure of ancient scrolls and tablets. Dolmun had discovered the means to collect and store life force the moment Reaver had rushed from his office to experiment with his own new discovery. There was always an advantage to studying one's surroundings.

The chamber held seven throne-like chairs in a semi-circle facing a long table that separated the chairs from the far wall. The tools Reaver and the other Mages used to collect their power were arrayed upon the table. The light glinted off wicked-looking blades with a variety of functions, straight and razor-sharp for slicing and bleeding, curved for flensing, and hooked for evisceration. These lay alongside irons for heating and branding and braces and vices for crushing. The instruments gleamed with light reflecting off the well sharpened blades, the blood-soaked table top providing the perfect dark backdrop.

Along the far wall were three racks currently hosting two old hags dragged from the drug dens of the waterfront and a young boy bought with gold from a mother. The mother would soon become much like the hags and may well feature in this rite in her turn. The Circle of Seven Mages was waiting for the mind-numbing drugs to wear off before the torture and pain could begin. It was only at the height of the ceremony that the strongest essences were captured. Dolmun was just completing his preparations when the other mages started to arrive.

'Welcome brothers,' Dolmun showed each to their place. 'We are blessed this night to have three subjects who are to provide tonights offerings.'

He knew he was stating the obvious but he was ensuring the distracted mages did not notice his collector placed strategically where each mages head would rest. Dolmun would not be an active participant in the activities tonight, although he appreciated the fervour with which his fellow mages attacked their roles. The more fear and pain inflicted, the less chance anyone would discover his redirection of a portion of the results.

After the First arrived he delivered a blessing over the three subjects and anointed each with scented oil. He traced crux anasta on each forehead to awaken them out of their inertia. The First then invited the brothers to join him. Reaver, Ulian, and Worian placed their rings in the required housing above the victims and proceeded with the dark ceremony. The captured trio was subjected to a display of the weapons and in-depth explanations of how they would be utilised. This instigated a steady increase in fear, but the mages required more.

The brothers used large hunting knives to cut away the filthy rags that clung to the women's bodies, protecting what little modesty they had left. The wilted mams, slackened stomachs, and unkempt quims on display had the women squirming to try and hide from the men before them. The flash of the knives and the activity brought them fully out of their stupor, and the screaming started. Reaver had placed a ward about the cellars that deadened the noises that emanated, thus avoiding any prying ears and uncomfortable questions. The forces of fear and pain heightened when the mages took up wickedly sharp hooked blades and began slowly drawing a long cut from sternum to pubis. The hags did not last long under the brothers' knives and clamps, but the young boy put up an amazing resistance for his size and age.

Just as Reaver and the brothers were completing the rite and collecting their rings, an amazing burst of life energy was funnelled through the connection between the rings from their sister stones in the citadel of Sudhemere in the Southlands.

'What was that,' the twins said in unison.

'That was resistance,' Reaver said.

Each mage felt a warmth through their rings and a feeling of almost rightness in opposition to the results of tonight's practices. The silence in the chamber lasted for many heartbeats before the feeling dissipated. The Circle of Seven Mages sat stunned. None knew what this new reaction meant, but all knew it was not the outcome they had come to expect and that it could only be a harbinger of opposition.

'Perhaps our inquisitors have finally captured the hidden prince. That was definitely a surge in the power from the south,' Agross said.

Stuck without news from the Southlands during the storms of the season of snows, the mages could only speculate on the meaning behind the event. The only interpretation ultimately agreed upon by the Seven was that there may be a new player in the game. Reaver was determined to get a message to Baron Du Tek in the captured city of Sudhemere as soon as the weather allowed a ship to sail. The gems held in the city and linked to the mage's rings must be protected at all costs.

'I fear we have just witnessed a new player being placed on the board,' Reaver said. 'I must meditate and seek guidance over this occurance.'

Prime morning prayers were observed the next sun while the mages still argued over the events of the night before. Reaver was not prepared to leave the monastery until the level of power required to capture the Southlands was stored. The Seven would travel south on the last ship that left before the next season of snows, almost a full turn away. The ceremony to infuse the gems would be carried out during the Southland's sun solstice when the life forces would be at their strongest.

'One of us must travel south on the first available ship,' Agross argued. 'We must investigate what had transpired last night.'

He insisted that waiting would only allow the opposition to gather strength and become organised. Reaver would not hear of it. His sole focus was to become master and claim ultimate power over all. Dolmun enjoyed supporting both sides of the fierce argument as he wandered the monastery's halls, checking his collectors. So much emotion was being expended in the discussions that Dolmun could almost feel his power growing.

'The longer we wait the greater resistance we will face,' Agross continued his argument. 'We should not rely on Baron Du Tek to keep the gems safe as they had with the previous governor. We need a representative in the Southlands.'

When the First threatened dire consequences for any disobedience among the Seven Mages, Dolmun realised there must be a reason Reaver would not leave his cellars. This intrigued the Fourth, who decided this would require careful and secretive investigation. Why would the First insist on staying until the last minute unless he had a specific reason or conduit he could not part with?

'Master Dolmun,' an acolyte said. 'King-Emperor Lothar has called for a tourney on the next full moon. He sends riders to inform the Barons.'

The young acolyte raced off to spread his news to each of the Seven. Dolmun welcomed the news. Having just had the mid-season moon, there would be sufficient time to plan. A gathering of the population featuring excitement, fear, pain, and a myriad of other emotions would drastically boost the power he could store. As long as Reaver guarded and kept his own council regarding the storage of the life forces harvested, Dolmun was confident that no one else would consider or have the skills for harvesting the crowd.

Dolmun was beginning to see the value of a holistic approach. Why only limit oneself to the dark practices when just as much passion, zeal, and emotion could be garnered from the lightness in everybody's life. It may take longer to collect and be less intense but careful storage and condensation could produce as powerful a result. He would need to prepare more of his collectors to spread about the crowd. A sudden inspiration came to him. He would manufacture some small gifts for some of the ladies in the crowd. Just a sliver of diamond would make them attractive.

REAVER ENSURED HE WOULD not be observed before sneaking into the deep cellars. He had agreed that no other should discover their meetings. Reaver prepared to contact his muse as he did after vespers on every sixth sun. At this time of the turn, it was also the sixth full moon. The numbers were auspicious for intense contact. In a small room no bigger than a closet, Reaver channelled a small amount of the precious life essence he had gathered to open a compact window between existences. The apparition that appeared before him was exactly as he had dreamed. The voluptuous, naked woman beckoned to the First, enticing him closer. The night before each summoning, the First would dream, and the woman who appeared in his dream grew more and more appealing and attractive each time. The woman begged the First to hurry, capture more essence and feed her more power so she could cross over and be his forever.

Reaver reached beneath his robes and, taking up a sharp blade, sliced his inner thigh. The pain was excruciating yet rapturous and euphoric. He sliced again, and the vision arched her back, opened her legs and ran her hands down her body to touch that which Reaver longed to do, she then moaned in unison with the First. A third slice brought the pair to ecstasy, and the First felt himself giving in to oblivion. Just before he completely lost himself, he imagined he saw the wicked claw and curved beak of a monstrous entity superimpose itself over his greatest love.

DOLMUN WATCHED THE exchange between the First and the creature through the keyhole. He now understood the changes in the First, even while not understanding the connection. This would take a great deal of secret study. The hideous monster he saw had the strangest effect on the First, but Dolmun was in no position to ask why.

Without the steady flow of slaves from the south, the mages' opportunities to gather power were limited. Dolmun also noticed that over the last turn, the quality and number of that commodity had suffered greatly. As the administrator, Dolmun was aware more than the rest that someone was depriving them of their due. It could only be Baron Du Tek.

The baron's arrangement with the First put him in the best place to control the flow of riches from the Southlands back to the Northern Empire. With Reaver's attention otherwise directed, the Baron was getting away with this fraudulent behaviour. Dolmun would make sure that upon his return to the south, the baron would be brought to a reckoning. Even so, Dolmun was secretly appreciative of the Baron's greed. It limited the First's power until they reached the Southlands, which would put distance between the First and his strange lover.

He knew that the conscription of the youth of the south had begun, so there would be a good selection of fit young men available in the season of the thaw. The Fourth would ensure this turn's inventory would be held in the Southlands, and kept healthy and well to allow the greatest harvest when the time came. If the mages arrived in the Southlands and little was available, the total subjugation of the region could be jeopardised. Dolmun hoped that the First would agree with the plan but determined he would send a missive to Du Tek ordering the same, even without the First's approval. By the time the mages headed south, Dolmun would be the most powerful by a large measure. Dolmun agreed with one aspect of the First's plans. The life forces of the south were the key to total domination.

He would also order that this crop of the south's youth not undergo the mistreatment and physical and mental tortures usually inflicted upon them by the sadistic guards and instructors. They could be mind-probed by the apprentice mages attached to the garrisons in the south, but only to determine alliances and relationships with known resistance leaders and the whereabouts of the prince. The slaves must be maintained in peak condition to maximise the return on the ceremonies and rites at the sun's solstice.

CHAPTER SIX
Melee

Great sacrifice for each the cost
If evil to transcend is willing paid.

DOLMUN STALKED THE battlements choosing the best places to surreptitiously place his collectors. He watched when three suns before the tourney, teams of drudges began the mighty task of shovelling the mountains of snow that choked the forecourt. This was an often-repeated process in the early onset of the snows and again when the thaw was imminent, but never before had this been attempted in the depths of the season of snows. All feared that if they failed to appease Lothar, some would join the ranks of those who had displeased him in their current abode.

Dolmun was impressed when a young kitchen drudge of about ten turns came up with the ultimately successful plan of maintaining massive bonfires in the courtyard that melted the falling snow and provided a layer of ash to aid footing on the slick, wet cobbles. The store of wood and black rock used to heat the citadel would be sorely depleted, but that was a problem to be solved another sun. The young drudge earned himself the reward of ensuring the fires were kept fed throughout the night. He and a small army of his fellows ran an endless relay of sacks of black rock and logs from the stores to the fires.

Many of Lothar's barons maintained apartments in the capital, but they were mostly occupied by the baron's female kin, while heirs and male relatives saw to the estates and manors. If any noble house hoped to gain an alliance through marriage, they would need the strength of their sons. Many messages were sent demanding the presence of their menfolk in the capital, and while most would make the perilous journey, others would freeze in the saddle.

The Circle of Seven welcomed the distraction the King-Emperor's little fight provided. It would be no use to 'Lothar the Great' if he aligned himself with one of the noble houses. Once the mages had control of the power of the gems, no force could stand against them, and the seven would create an empire covering the known world and spread out to all corners of all the lands.

The sun dawned, and Lothar heartily thanked the sun god for the clear skies and weak sunlight that bathed the courtyard as did Dolmun even as it would have been considered blasphemy within the monastery. The fires had been allowed to burn out, and the ash spread across the courtyard with an added layer of rushes and chaff to give the combatants the best footing possible. While not ideal, any northern soldier had spent time fighting during the first thaws or on the slippery deck of a longboat.

To all the sudden festivity of the sun was a welcomed benefit, along with the possibility that one of the noble houses would be betrothed to the King-Emperor. Dolmun had heard that many first, second and third sons had braved the snow—a number had only completed their journey that very morning. Even as the barons begged for time to recover, Lothar ordered the grand melee for mid-sun. He was not about to delay his chance to prove himself and tweak the noses of his barons. If they did not honour his words, they would fear his arm.

RESISTANCE

Dolmun was pleased. Lothar had done well in choosing the sun to host his tourney. The sun was chilly but clear, and the expectant crowd was already buzzing with anticipation and approval. These positive life essences were weaker than those gained by Reaver's black arts, but there was much more to be had. Dolmun felt warmth growing and flowing through him during the early contests at arms. The excited crowd created a steady stream of life essence through his small, strategically placed collectors. As the expectation of the main event grew, Dolmun had to excuse himself from the viewing stands as the feelings began to overpower him. He had two fears, one was obvious—discovery. It would not do to have the rest of the mages uncover his secret. His second fear, was giving into the flush of power and becoming no better than the First—a slave to its enticements.

LOTHAR KNEW HE HAD the support of his war band and would usually count on his chamberlain to cover his back, but in this instance, Harta was to act as overseer. His responsibility was to ensure that not too many fatal injuries occurred and that no one used the event to settle outstanding debts of honour. In all, a full four score and more had marked the list, with barons and their heirs combining with their most trusted men at arms, hoping that weeding out the field would lead to the most fruitful and sought after harvest in the empire.

The displays of the morning and the stalls exhibiting the latest in weapons development and production were cleared to make way for the King-Emperor's grand melee. By ballot, each house entered was chosen to be on the inside or outside team. Without some rules, the sun's entertainment could decimate the noble houses of heirs for turns to come, although these rules were few and often very fluid in their interpretation. Each team was identified by a white or a green armband with the intention that each team should clear the field of the opposition before reverting to a free-for-all.

As a weak, watery sun reached its full height in the pale blue skies, a horn blast from the citadel's walls announced the beginning of the grand melee. The inside team was led by Lothar, the King-Emperor, and it was a great honour for a house to be chosen to flank his own guards. With a glorious roar, Lothar leapt out of the ranks and charged towards the battle, a wedge of men in his wake. The outside team, those with green armbands, opposed his advance as one by overlapping their shields. The melee did not allow spears or pikes. Weapons were limited to blunted swords and axes, maces or flails and shields with a warrior's choice of armour.

Lothar's distinctive red hair flowed from below his simple iron helm, topped only with a thin circlet of gold. While his gambeson was a rich, deep green quilted with gold studs, he wore his old serviceable mail shirt to battle. Many of his opponents had steel breast plates and helmets that shone with silver or gold adornments. Lothar carried his iron-bound wooden shield and heavy mace. The King emperor had won his empire with these weapons and saw no reason to change to the new weapons and shields on display before him as he launched himself into the fray.

When did warfare become so uniform? Lothar wondered as he broke the arm holding the shield before him. He burst through when the line buckled against the power of his relentless assault. The melee dissolved into a free-for-all when the press of bodies limited the full swing of weapons, and participants were simultaneously prodded, pushed and punched from all sides. Shouts of victory and screams of pain rang out in equal measure, echoed off the walls, and then mixed with the excited cheers and leers of the assembled and invited audience. Drudges risked severe injury by rushing into the bedlam to drag out the unconscious bodies of participants before they could be trampled into the mud.

Lothar had decided this was just the thing to work out the pains and strains that grew when snow forced inaction. He roared his battle cry and flayed about him with his mace, not caring whose helm he dented. The melee was at its peak, where the champion would be decided by the last man standing, and Lothar the Great would be that man.

Two men working in tandem stood before their King-Emperor and bravely tried to defend against the onslaught but went down when Lothar bashed one shield to shield while lashing out low with a backhanded blow of his mace, popping out the knee of the other. When he turned to acknowledge their attempt, he felt a knife thrust to his lower back that was only turned away by the combination of his mail shirt and his twist to salute his foes. Lothar continued the turn and was cunning and fast enough to grab the knife-wielder and disarm him.

'Enough!' bellowed Lothar.

Harta called for horns to be sounded and the remaining warriors to cease and desist their entertainment. Shoving his captive into the arms of one of his remaining war band members, Lothar called on his chamberlain to assemble the council and take the family of his unlucky assassin into custody.

Lothar lounged on his throne, enjoying the aches and pains in his arms and the general warmth that lingered throughout his body after exertion and hard work. Before him stood Baron Du Ague, his wife and daughter, and the Du Ague heir, currently bound in chains. The boy was of an age to rule a barony and had been audacious enough to try for a greater seat. Lothar could appreciate the aspiration—and even the bravery of the attempt—but could never condone the treachery and, more than that, the interruption to the most fun he had this season of snows with his clothes on.

'Harta, these two can adorn my gates,' Lothar said. Without a preamble, he indicated the baron and his son.

'Send the women to the mages with my compliments,' he judged.

When the Baroness began to wail in fear, Lothar rose and added to his instructions for his chamberlain.

'Send my bath slaves to attend me.'

Lothar, the Great King-Emperor of the North, stormed from his chambers with only the thoughts of the delights and pleasures ahead and no regard for the summary punishments he left behind.

WHEN THE MELEE HAD suddenly halted as the King-Emperor bellowed and grabbed the son of Baron Du Ague, the flash of fear and panic added to Dolmun's power and sent his temperature plummeting. Dolmun had staved off possible embarrassment but only by Lothar's good timing in capturing his assailant. When Dolmun and the rest of the court had gathered in the King-Emperor's council chambers, the First charged towards the chamberlain to request the punishment be left to the mages. Reaver was becoming most insistent when Lothar summarily declared his verdict. The First railed at the lost opportunity to bleed the baron and his son, taking solace only in plans for the futures' of the baroness and her daughter.

CHAPTER SEVEN
Respite

Seven warriors battle the horrors
Seven warriors bring back the light

'YOU ARE GETTING DANGEROUSLY close to suffering a severe injury, tinker,' Heleana warned. 'Unless you explain your part in this, I will personally hand you over to the Brocken.' The clenched fists and white knuckles at her side were a clear indication that her threat was very real.

'Calm yourself, my Lady. I am merely the messenger sent by others to gather those needed to fulfill destinies and lead the defence of all the lands. As a matter of fact, on the morrow, we will be joined by one of the small folk and his life partner, after which we must collect the twins, whom I believe you have met, from the village of the Salient Buck.'

Perrin began to collect the platters and pulled Bren up by his collar.

'Come, your highness, we have dishes to do.'

The pair gathered the pot and wooden spoons from the hearth and ducked out of the cave to wash the pot and platters in the small stream that ran through the vale.

'I don't know about you, Bren, but this is all a bit too much for me to understand.'

'Perrin, much is hidden from me, but as I hear more, it is as though a fog is slowly rolling back to reveal the truth.'

'Well, my prince, we had best listen and learn, as Gram used to say, and leave things up to those whose plans we seem to have a part in.'

Bren stood slowly and, with quick hands, dumped a pot full of water over his cousin's head.

'Do not call me that. You, most of all, must be my cousin. My family.'

Perrin immediately rose to retaliate, but paused in his plan to dump Bren in the stream. Perhaps it was now time to grow up. Perrin smiled as Bren backed away from him holding a pile of freshly washed dishes.

'You may be a prince but you know I will get you for that,' Perrin warned.

Perrin grabbed up the remaining dishes and followed his fleeing cousin who was just disappearing into the cavern. Perrin could feel the tension upon his return.

Heleana was leaning forward, staring intently at the tinker. Perrin glanced at Garat, who appeared relaxed with a strange smile of satisfaction playing across his features.

'What have we missed?' he asked.

'Nothing of importance. Just my wife ensuring she has all the information she needs, and for once, her ire is not directed at me,' Garat's smile widened.

Heleana turned to her husband with eyes blazing.

'If you knew any of this without telling me, Garat Omholt...' she warned, leaving an open threat of reprisal hanging in the air.

'Be at peace, my Lady. All will be explained when we gather. There will be many who do not understand the part they must play in the future of our lands. Might I suggest that we start by educating our young Prince?' Martyn gestured for Bren and Perrin to take their seats.

'Will you not tell him your story so he can discover the trust he must have in his closest advisors?' Martyn said. 'After all, you, Lady Hell, are the focus of the resistance and the leader most highly wanted by the Brocken. As heir to the duchy of Sudhem and your role with the pathfinders, you provide a double focus for those fighting for freedom.'

Heleana sat back with a sigh even as she pointed at the two men in front of her, promising that the answers to her questions had not been satisfactory.

'Garat, please prepare some mulled wine. This telling may take some time, and I think this misbegotten tinker may like something more than clear mountain water.'

'Civilisation, at last. My Lady, you are most gracious,' Martyn said and bowed where he sat.

Heleana waited until Garat had served each of her audience with a warming draft, all the while ruminating on her tale and how best to impart it. She had sat at her father's knee during council and often had her tutor urge her to tell the stories or sing the teaching songs. Heleana sipped her wine as she pondered the best way to begin the story that had brought her to her current station in life. Remembering her losses would be painful, but vital for the education of the young prince.

'My horse had become fractious and pawed the ground as it picked up on my inattention and nervousness. I should have known better, so I firmed up the reins and leant forwards to pat the mare's neck, acknowledging my failing. At fifteen turns, I had fallen into reflection about how I came to be astride the piebald mare looking down upon my father, uncle, and two of their counsellors backed by forty of the household guard on the plain below.'

C.S.R. KEELEY

'Father's party was arrayed just above a landing site on an inside loop of the river Rayum, where a spit of sand provided easy access to land the boats and barges that plied the river in trade. I had been included in my father's council at fifteen turns after completing one turn of the season's exchange in the court of the elven peoples of the Sunset Islands. Father was progressive, and along with having closer ties to the elves, he often relied on the council of his vassals and even commoners in ruling his Duchy. It was not uncommon to have a provincial Earl or Goodman be given a full hearing in the council chambers.

'That sun's excursion came about after a strange man I had never seen or heard of before burst into the council chamber demanding a private meeting with Father. To my surprise, my father immediately acquiesced to the demand.

'The stranger was taller than average, with a balding head, and the most luxurious eyebrows complemented his neatly trimmed, small beard. He was dressed in well-worn but cared-for calf-high boots and leather leggings with a black velvet doublet over a crisp white shirt. The fashion was three turns out of date, but the man was imposing nonetheless.'

Heleana paused her tale to look closely at the tinker, then shook her head and continued.

After instructing the prelate to excuse the court, Heleana's father and uncle rose and indicated that the man should follow.

'Heleana, join us,' her father said.

Once ensconced in the duke's private study, the man gave his report, 'The Southlands have been invaded.'

Heleana was astounded, but, to her surprise, her father did not question the man's announcement, instead demanding an account.

'Father, what does this mean?'

'Heleana, my love, this is the Earl of Lotan's Rest, and he brings grave news. This man has always been a friend of the South and is to be

86

listened to and respected for his devotion. His council was invaluable to your Grandsire, and now he comes to me.'

The duke returned his attention to the stranger.

'Sir, this is most unexpected. I know better than to question your motives, but is there any chance you may be wrong?' Heleana's uncle asked.

'Unfortunately not my Lord.'

'Perhaps it would best if we save our thoughts until we hear your tale?' Father said.

'Gladly, my Lord, but first, I ask you to call in the captain of your guard and order the stand-to of your entire garrison.'

'Your infrequent council has always been for the best for my Duchy. It will be as you ask. Heleana, please see to the orders and return as soon as possible. Kindly ask Lady Cornwell to see to refreshments.'

'My Lord, a glass of wine would be well welcomed. May I have a pipe while we wait as my journey to Sudhemere has been arduous?' Heleana heard the earl's request as she hurried from the room.

When Heleana returned she knew the three men had waited in silence while the Earl prepared a pipe and lit it from a taper taken from the mantle over the fireplace that continually burnt in the duke's study. The duke's brother also had lit a cigarillo from the taper, a fashion that had only become the norm in the last turn or two.

Heleana had returned to her father's study, alongside two serving girls, carrying trays of cold meats, cheeses, and fruits, with wine, ale, and chilled water. The earl helped himself to a cup of red wine with a dash of water and a small selection of cheese and fruit. Heleana was shocked at the man's temerity to serve himself without an invitation from his Duke, but when she turned to her father, he gave a small shake of his head.

The Earl of Lotan's Rest helped himself to a second cup of wine and rose to clean his pipe and tap out the detritus into the fire.

'My Lord Duke, I carry grave news and must hurry to our capital and advise our sovereign, but I will give an account of what I have seen and heard. Some of it will seem strange, but I ask that you hear me out before questioning my tale.'

'As you wish. My father always said there is more to you than others may know. Please tell us all you can,' the duke said.

'Invasion is the only word I can use to describe the multiple incursions along the coast. After dragging a young seafarer from the ocean, I gleaned from my contacts that many 'large, well manned boats have landed along the coastline as far as a skiff can be rowed in two suns. The Southlands have never experienced such a widespread attack. This is clearly a well-prepared and supplied invasion.

'From the description I received from the fisherman, these raiders had only one intention; to shock an unprepared opponent. Casting about, I soon realised that I would not get any coherent information from the behaviour of the beasts of the forest, as fear of a large predator was the overriding sensation. The birds were heading deep into the woods, and even the sea birds were flying inland to the marshes and lakes of the plains,' the strange earl continued. 'If I was to provide any worthwhile warning and intelligence, I would have to see for myself who these invaders were.

'Keeping low, I crested the headland above the fishing village of Wurt with a horrible suspicion of what I would see. I was sure of my own safety, as I would be well warned before any enemy could come close. Not so the residents of the village.'

Heleana studied the man when as he described his first sight of the invaders. His demeaner was of one frustrated by inaction due to an overriding duty. When the Earl paused in his narrative his far away look and the clenched fist pounding on his thigh indicated he was remembering the attack he witnessed. And was feeling once again the pain and frustration of knowing his duty was to carry warnings to his Duke over assisting those who suffered below.

RESISTANCE

'The smoke from many fires filled the small cove, and screams of terror reverberated and echoed off the cliffs. The raiders continued to torment their prisoners, seemingly in search of riches and booty. What had me mostly perplexed was the well-ordered camp set up along the beach. Clearly, this was a highly drilled and organised enemy with little fear of immediate reprisal.'

The earl paused to look each of his listeners in the eye.

'Just as I was about to withdraw, I noticed movement through the smoke near the edge of the village. Squads of six men were being drawn up to stand before someone who appeared to be their leader. Each man was similarly attired in grey garb and armed with a flatbow and short sword. Heavy backpacks indicated that these men could survive an extended march without needing to hunt or pillage for supplies. As the squads marched from the village, I noticed two vital pieces of intelligence. There seemed to be two distinct cadres making up the invaders. The sailors seemed nothing more than raiders, looting, raping, and killing, in contrast to the well-controlled and uniformed soldiers. The second and most important intelligence was that they had no horses yet.

'With that information gleaned, I reversed my course, keeping low against the skyline to find sanctuary deep in the forest. I knew I could outstrip the invaders and reach Sudhemere with my warnings well in advance. I am possibly the only person with an overview of the danger facing the Southlands. After warning you, my lord, I must ride to the capital and warn the House of Peers and the Sovereign of the Southlands.'

He paused to place his hands in his pockets, retrieving his supplies to prepare his pipe. He continued his narrative as he rose and approached the fireplace to light it.

'I followed an old game trail, often having to push my way through new growth and bramble. My Lord, I was tired and depleted after helping the fisherman and my labours after. I had not taken any food *nor gained sustenance from my surroundings. The idea of organised squads of men fanning out into the countryside was not to my liking, as they may have stumbled upon the same trail I was on. Travelling well into the dark of each sun, often with guidance from inhabitants of the forest, I kept well ahead of the invaders' scouts and foraging parties. Breaking free of the forest, I walked for another sun over undulating river plains until I saw smoke rising into the clear blue skies. Taking a great deal of caution, I crawled up the final slope before the River Rayum and looked down upon a trading place abuzz with activity.*

The earl rose and replenished his plate and cup, allowing his audience to absorb his tale before he continued.

'Kimee's trading place is a stopping point along the river between the coast and Sudhemere. The wily Kimee and her partner established the trading post and barge service, cutting the need for farmers and traders to travel to your city to sell their wares and goods, my Lord. I observed many people rushing hither and thither on unknown errands while the trading place's namesake stood atop a wagon directing what appeared at first to be a panic.

'Fortunately, I could relax as I watched the goings-on, which, upon reflection, I realised was early season goods and crops being loaded onto two large barges in preparation for the journey upriver to Sudhemere. I took a moment to study Kimee. She is a woman beyond middle age but still statuesque and desirable. She wore dark green skirts falling to mid-calf with a matching corset top over a white lace-up shirt which gave a tantalising glimpse of ample breasts. Tooled calf-high boots of a deep brown hide almost matched the waves of hair that flowed down her back even as strands of grey were becoming more noticeable. I had to smile as I am somewhat intimately aware of what lies under the skirts and petticoats.'

At that point, the Earl's recount drifted off as he looked out the window to the river flowing past the city.

'My good Earl, your report,' The Duke demanded.

'Ah, my apologies, your grace. It has been a tiring journey.'

The boots Kimee sports are a relic of a past career as a Pathfinder. We first met more than twenty turns ago when she was a troop leader in the service of the sovereign of the Southlands. It is wise to keep on her good side. If she reaches under her skirts, she is on the verge of pulling out one of the wickedly honed hunting knives sheathed in each boot, and her waistband holds a brace of throwing knives just as sharp. I have, on more than one occasion, looked down at the glistening edges of one or the other. Fortunately, more often than not, I can talk my way around the blades to enjoy the pleasures of her company and curvaceous body.

Heleana was not unaware of the flirtations of the members of her father's court. Her snort of derision broke through the Earl's musings. He bowed his head in her direction and continued.

'I rose and headed towards what was going to be an awkward reunion. When last in her bed, I had left in the predawn with nary a word. Although known to Kimee as a traveller and part-time trader of horses and small, easily carried, and costly trinkets, I have not told her of my other services to the Southlands. I made no effort to conceal myself as I walked down the slope directly towards the ire I knew would meet me.

The trader noticed my approach, jumped lithely down from the wagon, and strode purposefully towards me with hands firmly planted on her hips. I was brought up short, although not surprised, when two knives thudded into the ground a finger width in front of my feet.'

'You old reprobate. Do you think you can just wander in here anytime you like? Give me one good reason not to gut you where you stand.'

'Kimee, my love, would it be wise to eviscerate your business partner?'

'Do not tempt me. You had better have something to ease my wrath, or you can just turn around and keep walking.'

'Kimee, raiders have landed in Wurt and along the coast. I can only assume we are being invaded by an organised army. Gather all your goods and people and get upriver to Sudhemere. I need two horses. I must take warning to the duke.'

Kimee stood transfixed, disbelief slowly draining from her features. She knew I was a lothario, a cheat at pokr, and a questionable business partner, but I always had the best for her and the Southlands at heart. She grabbed the shoulder of the first man she could reach and gave orders for two horses to be saddled and readied with provisions for four suns travel.

'You,' she pointed at me. 'Come and have some ale and a bite. You never cease to amaze me. This was the last thing I would have expected. You had best ride at pace to Sudhemere.'

'Well, we could take some time for ourselves.'

'When you have finished your meal, I will be most happy to walk out with you, personally put you on your horse, and set you on your way. Your news, as always, has only added to my responsibilities and workload. Now, sit down and eat while I gather my folk and give them their orders.'

'From there, my Lord, I rode directly to your city to bring the news, as I must for our sovereign. I believe the invader's boats will come upriver and arrive at Sudhemere's river gate within seven suns.'

The Duke turned to Heleana.

'Heleana, see to the earl's comfort and needs. Ensure his horses are well cared for and have the head groomsman select two fast horses as replacements. Your uncle and I have much to prepare.'

Heleana paused in the recital of her story and she took some time to compose the next painful stanza. Garat was well aware of the next excerpt of his wife's tale and had moved close beside her to provide the strength and love she would need to forge ahead with her reminisence.

'My recollection of that meeting ended when my hand fell and stroked the silken shaft of my family's heredity weapon that sat sheathed across my knees.' Heleana looked at her hands in memory. 'Since that time and having many suns to reflect the weight of the axe's wooden haft brought me fully out of my reminiscence and back to the task at hand. We were waiting for the invaders boats to come upriver.

Father's men stopped fidgeting and stood tall and proud in their ranks when my guard captain touched my knee and pointed towards the bend in the river. Two strangely designed boats were being rowed upriver by a single bank of oars. We counted 15 oars per side. Each boat had a mast, but the winds would have made sailing difficult. The lead boats raised a pennant as a signal to its follower, and the boats angled towards the beach.

The boats ran up upon the sand, and men jumped ashore, securing the boats with lines and anchors. Planks fell to the beach, and we counted thirty men disembarking from each boat. Strangely, several rowers remained on board, and I noted that those men were chained to their oars. I could only assume that these were criminals or our own people, newly enslaved.

The soldiers from the boats were uniformed in ankle boots, grey leggings, and dark grey jerkins. As they climbed up from the beach, they formed two ranks facing father's troops. Each was armed with a strange-looking bow and had a short sword at their hip.

My guards and I watched the Duke of Sudhem raise his arm in a signal of parley. His honour guards knelt and placed their longbows and swords before them on the ground as a show of peace.

As a mirror image, the leader of the grey soldiers repeated the duke's actions, and the front rank knelt, then, without warning, fired their bows. A volley of thirty arrows decimated the duke's ranks, taking down my father, uncle, and most of their guard. The remaining guards took up their swords and charged the invaders, only to be taken down by a volley of arrows from the second rank.

We were were horrified by the brutality of the action, and my guards looked to their new Duchess for guidance. I sat transfixed until my captain grasped the reins of my horse.'

'You three, take the horses and get our Lady back to the city.' He indicated three of her guards. 'Leave your bows and quivers. We two will hold as a rearguard. Now go!'

'Perrin, Bren, I know you have not visited Sudhemere, but the city's walls were built over many turns to hold back flood waters, not defend against a siege. Perrin, your parents were in the city. They were vital in saving the many residents who could leave and stayed behind to coordinate its defences. They, and the remaining councillors, sent me away, insisting that as heir, I must remain at large to give the defenders hope and a focus for the future. I carried a missive from your mother to Garat. Since then, we have led the resistance together and find ourselves here united. The betrayal and murder done that sun have steeled my resolve to never trust the Brocken and fight until the last has been driven back into the sea!'

Bren had sat and listened, transfixed by Heleana's telling.

'My Lady of Sudhem, the story of your loss and the resistance you have put before the invaders, along with your bravery in battle, has been whispered and rumoured about, even reaching us in Hightop. Would you accept the thanks and high regard of all you protect?'

'Well put, young prince. Now, it is well into the evening, and Perrin looks about to drop,' Martyn said. 'Might I suggest we retire? Tomorrow, we begin a new phase of resistance.'

CHAPTER EIGHT
Allies

Seven warriors are faith restorers,
Seven warriors force chaos back.

PERRIN WOKE IN THE pre-dawn as was his habit to ensure the safety and wellbeing of his stock. As the only one stirring in the cavern, he took the opportunity to head out to the stream to complete his ablutions and find the privy. While the darkness made traversing the sleeping bodies difficult, the lightening of the sun outlined the cavern's opening with a silvery shadow. He used his hunting skills to avoid waking any others and slowly crept outside. He started to edge around a boulder that he did not recall seeing just beyond the mouth of the cavern when it growled and rose up before him.

The wolf's head came to his chest, and the ivory of its teeth glinted in the dull light as the lips drew back in a snarl. Perrin was transfixed. He could not run in either direction as he had just ducked out of the cavern and had no space to outpace a full-grown wolf. Perrin was flabbergasted at being face-to-face with a snarling wolf in the middle of a Pathfinder stronghold. His senses were reeling. He completely forgot about his need for the privy. His only thought was to warn the others, even though it may force the beast to action. Raising his arms for protection, Perrin drew in a deep breath.

'No yell.'

Perrin's disbelief grew. Did the snarling apparition before him just speak?

'Varellon, guest here.'

Perrin's shock and fear were mitigated when a boy standing no taller than the wolf stood from where he had been resting against the far wall of the cavern's entry.

'Youngling wake her. She angry no sleep,' the boy continued.

The lad stepped up, put his arm around the wolf's neck, and drew its head into his chest, affectionately tousling the fur between the beast's ears. The wolf huffed at the lad, then pulled away from him, turned, and stalked away into the early morning shadows of the vale.

The noise of the interaction must have awakened the others as a torch was lit within the cave, and voices began to ask questions and demand answers. The torchlight drew closer as Garat called out for his brother. Perrin was already left incredulous at the start of his sun when the light fell about the speaker and showed him as being somewhat older than either brother. The brothers could not move as they stood, astonished by the sight of something from legend—a wolf rider from the distant mountains.

Before them was a man of middle turns, although he only stood as tall as the brother's chest. His hair was a mixture of browns, and his skin had a slight greenish tinge. He regarded them with clear, green, almond-shaped eyes. The small man's mid-length hair was held back by a rawhide band, displaying pointed ears tufted with dark brown hair. He wore forest garb, much like Perrin, and showed no sign of carrying any weapon.

'Devron, have you and Varellon finally decided to join us?' Martyn said as he squeezed past Garat.

'Tinker, is you. Varellon learn dangers on plains.'

'Well, before any discussions or travelling are done, I think breakfast is in order. We have a fresh kill that we can share with your partner and some venison steaks that would go well with mushrooms and eggs,' Martyn said as he retreated into the cavern. 'Come along, you lot.'

The three men looked at each other but could do no more than follow the tinker. Heleana and Bren had armed themselves with their axes but relaxed their stance when the trio followed Martyn into the cavern.

'Ah ha, the famous bardiche that spreads fear in the hearts of the enemy,' Martyn said. 'Gentlemen, the lady's weapon is a symbol of the resistance. She has led many sorties against the Brocken, brandishing this fearsome axe and earning her the well-deserved title of Lady Hell. Will you let the boys examine it?'

Heleana offered the axe to Bren, who, after replacing his own axe, grasped the weapon's haft. It could not have been more different. This was clearly not designed with versatility in mind. While Bren's axe could be used as a domestic tool, as well as a weapon, this was designed for a far different purpose.

The blade was as long as Bren's arm, and while it had a sharpened cutting edge, it also came to a point that could only have one use—stabbing. The axe head was intricately carved with scrollwork and inlaid with gold. The vicious but somehow beautiful blade was affixed to the shaft at two points, and when the shaft's butt was placed on the floor, the axe came to Bren's shoulder. This weapon would be equally useful from horseback as it would be afoot. Bren tested the weight and balance, then took a stance.

'Not in here!' exclaimed Heleana.

Bren remembered his surroundings and sheepishly offered the axe for Perrin to study.

'If you lot have finished playing with your toys, I believe introductions are in order.'

Martyn brought the wolf rider forwards, who had hung back in the crowd of so many Plainsmen.

'My Lady Heleana, may I introduce Devron of the Dini, wolf rider of the far ranges pack and life partner of its matriarch, Varellon.'

A huff and a clatter had all in the cavern turn towards the entrance. There, seated just inside, was the large wolf that had greeted Perrin earlier. At her feet was a long bone from the deer slaughtered the previous evening. Martyn stepped over to the beast and bowed with his hands outstretched. The wolf sneezed and shook her head to clear it. She seemed confused.

'This is Varellon, the leader and strongest of her pack. Under her guidance, her pack has become predominant.'

The wolf rose and padded towards Perrin, who followed the tinker's example, as did each of the others in turn. Varellon returned to the entrance, stopped to regard the tinker, then took up the bone and exited the cavern.

'You respect. She hard to please,' Devron said.

'Will she be all right out there? The Pathfinders are renowned for their hunting skills,' Bren asked.

'Rest assured, young prince, Varellon will only be seen if she wishes it so,' Martyn said. 'Well, as we will be travelling together for some time, I suggest a hearty breakfast. Cooked meals may be hard to come by for a while. Varellon has found our midden, but I am sure she would appreciate some fresh red meat.'

Martyn ducked under the sackcloth that separated the hearth from the cavern and returned, handing Devron a platter with a selection of offcuts and bones.

'Please deliver these with our compliments,' Martyn said.

'While we await Devron's return, you boys can cook breakfast. Hopefully, Prince Brycen, you know a good way to prepare mushrooms.'

Bren glared at the tinker for a short while then turned to Heleana.

'My Lady, I am beginning to understand your view of this tinker, exasperating may just not cover it.'

'My Prince, your grasp of the situation does you proud,' Heleana bowed.

'Can we all get back to the matter at hand? I have just been formally introduced to a wolf,' Garat said. 'We have all heard stories of the small folk and their partners, but few of us have ever seen one, let alone been sniffed by one. Martyn, how has this come about?'

'Well, a good yarn always helps with digestion. Perhaps we could ask Devron if I can impart his tale as we eat. Our language is very difficult for the Dini. Devron's home range encapsulates the Grove of the Ancients and he seems to have been gifted with a greater understanding of our tongue. It seems it is time we all learnt a bit more about with whom we share our lands.'

Devron returned as the boys placed platters of grilled venison, stewed mushrooms, and fried eggs before those gathered. Each took the wooden plates offered and began to serve themselves. When each was seated with their meal, Garat spoke.

'Devron, we are all wondering how you met this tinker and what has brought you here?'

'Blackness, death. Give message Earl. Ikat attack. Warf hunt. Tinker save.'

Devron and Heleana looked hard at the tinker, sure there was something they were missing, but they turned away, shaking their heads.

'Devron, if it is your wish, I can convey the story as I know it,' Martyn said.

'Yes. Be better.'

'Well, Tinker, you do seem to get yourself in the middle of everything,' Heleana said.

'Just one of my many talents, my Lady, along with story-telling. It is often the difference between a good meal and jack of ale, or an old crust and beaker of water. I learnt of Devron's tale through my experience with him and himself filling in the gaps.'

Martyn soaked the gravy and egg yolk off his plate with some trail bread and wiped his fingers and mouth with a kerchief he pulled from one of the many pockets of his robe. Taking a last sip of watered wine, he prepared to tell his tale.

'I first came across Devron and Varellon in the Red Ranges somewhat north of here. They were having a bit of difficulty with a troop of warf. Devron explained his predicament to me.'

Devron replayed the encounter with the Ikat, determined to discover how they had missed its presence. They had been skirting a small gully where a pungent odour hanging in the still mountain air masked the usual fresh, clean scent of pine and sap. The odour, carried by a slight breeze, revealed the evening resting place of a large troop of warf. Devron and Varellon crept through the underbrush, ensuring they stayed downwind of the small, canine carrion eaters. Devron knew that warf, with their elongated front legs and protruding lower jaw, are a constant nuisance to lone travellers and any animal separated from its herd.

During the attack Devron found it hard not to strike out and kill. His survival and protective instincts battled against his training and the vows he had embraced. Adrenaline coursed through his veins, and fear for Varellon heightened the anxiety. Varellon, the matriarch of the Far Ranges pack, stands at the shoulder half as tall as any man of the southern plains. Her usually impeccable russet coat was matted and snarled with blood and detritus from the vicious mountain Ikat's attack.

RESISTANCE

The most unfortunate outcome of the surprise ambush was that it had attracted the attention of a scavenging troop of warf.

The carrion eaters became Devron's immediate concern.

Warf appear to be distant relatives of wolves, but they share no common line. Although they band together in loose troops like wolf packs, the similarity ends there. Their slight build, single-mindedness, and willingness to eat almost everything—including their young in times of want—make them formidable when they combine to run down prey, particularly when the scent of fresh blood is in the air.

Devron and Varellon had to find a place to defend against the troop.

Devron realised that the usual strength of their combined resources was now reliant on only his own skills and resilience. Actions that had until now been easy and natural had suddenly become life-or-death decisions.

The first Devron knew of the mountain feline's presence was the spine-chilling, menacing growl and breaking of branches as the Ikat launched itself. The solitary Ikati of these mountains are a third the size of Varellon, with spotted fur for camouflage, a vicious temper and claws to match. Slashing talons and a piercing snarl caught the Dini and wolf by surprise as they had been concentrating on the warf.

The Ikat landed on them, ripping, slicing and biting with abandon. The pain as claws raked through flesh shocked both, as each felt the other's reaction through their bond. The Ikat disappeared as suddenly as it had attacked, but the real damage had been done. The blitz attack had left them both with deep lacerations. While the injuries were not immediately life-threatening, the noise of the ambush and metallic tang of blood in the air had attracted the attention of the warf troop.

Devron could only assist Varellon down the game trail while looking for any defensive position where they could stop to try to stem the flow of blood and dress the wounds properly. There was no chance to hide their bloody trail, so there were limited options. Starting a fire would be paramount for keeping the warf at bay. Varellon was the strongest and bravest of the Far Ranges wolf pack and would normally have no fear of any number of warf, but she was in no shape to fight or run and would be at their mercy if they had no other aid.

Varellon valiantly maintained a limping pace, but with each lurch of her hindquarters, a small pain-filled yip escaped her. Devron found it hard to differentiate between Varellon's pain and his own, as their close link blurred the individual's resistance. Varellon turned her head to lick her wounds, but Devron insisted she concentrate on staying ahead of the warf. Her black-tipped ears flicked in annoyance and a quick message of I hate you, *flashed into his brain. Their love for each other was reflected in those words and her quickened pace.*

During the ancient ceremony for bonding with wolf partners, the Dini accept an unconditional vow. No bonding is achieved unless each of the pair is found honest in their promise never to take the life of any creature, except for sustenance or protection of the wolf pack. This millennia-old agreement balanced the strength created by the mating bond between wolf and rider. For every action the ancients have taken to protect Tol, there is a reaction that offsets the benefit created. This ensures that an arrangement such as the wolf riders enjoy does not overpower nature and upset the natural order.

Varellon's hindquarters had been slashed by a full set of the Ikat's claws, and Devron had suffered a gash to his thigh. A glint of bone was visible through her wounds, and he saw her pain in her sharp green eyes. When she turned to regard her rider, a slow blink of the eyelids confirmed it. The high-pitched barks and lingering odour of death brought them back to their predicament. It indicated that the warf troop was spreading out to surround their prey, as was their usual hunting tactic.

Devron feared that without proper care, the damage to Varellon's leg would be permanent. He quickly tied a moss and bark dressing over Varellon's wound using the rawhide band from his hair. The blood oozing from the crude dressing would still leave a trail that was almost an open invitation, welcoming any predator to their next meal. As the pre-eminent wolf and rider pairing on Tol, their skills needed to be unsurpassed in adherence with the bonding pact and its rules. Wolves do not take kindly to permanent injury, so Devron considered the death that was stalking them may be the better outcome. Still, in true wolf style, they would not make the kill easy. At least the news they had been entrusted with had been delivered.

Devron watched the flitting shadows and heard the yipping barks coordinating the troop. Varellon's bleeding had eased, and although there would no longer be a visible trail of blood to lead directly to them, the scent in the air was all the warf needed to continue their pursuit. Devron ushered Varellon into a small void in the hillside. While not ideal, the depression left by an uprooted tree protected them from behind and above, and the tangle of dead branches provided tinder and fuel for a fire. The scent of smoke and crackle of flames might keep the warf at bay, but only until hunger overrode the species' natural hesitation. They were still in danger, but at least they had a small window of time to see to their wounds.

Laying hands gently on Varellon's oozing wounds, Devron channelled a small amount of his weakening life energies. A rider donating their life force is rare, as the wolf-mate is stronger by far and recovers much quicker from sharing or expending energies. At last, he was able to repair some of the damage and close off the last of the seeping blood vessels. He then washed the injury with clean water from a waterskin before packing the area with a proper poultice and binding it well. Devron was still bleeding, but did not have time to treat his wound. He had to get a fire going to fend off the circling warf and give himself time to think. He struck a flint with his belt knife, and as smoke curled from the tinder, he blew on it and watched, dismayed, as the spark petered out and the smoke dispersed. Striking the flint again, he carefully breathed the spark in the tinder to life, his hands shaking from the shock of their situation. He slowly fed the flames with kindling until he had a good-sized fire crackling. As the smoke permeated the woods, the warf troop became agitated, and their annoying high-pitched yapping closed in on the hasty camp. The scent of blood would eventually overpower the warf's natural cowardice.

Although Devron stands as tall as Varellon, he was under no illusion that he could carry her, as her weight is more than double his. The Dini had been a very short race of people who lived in the forests of Tol, making their homes in the treetop canopy. They inherited their skin's slightly greenish tinge and the ability to mottle against any backdrop, which allows them to seem to disappear at a whim. Riders are masters of hiding, and their furred, pointed ears give excellent hearing. Unfortunately, none of that could help them this time. All Devron could do was attend to his own wounds and prepare to wait out the coming night in the hope that the fire and smoke would deter the warf troop and they would leave to find easier prey.

Devron had enough jerked meat and water to see him through until morning and hoped Varellon would be recovered enough to help bluff these beasts into leaving them alone. Even then, he was not certain he would have the strength to last through the night. His light-headedness was either due to the smoke or blood loss. He could not tell which.

As the season of the long moon had passed, many mountain animals were stirring and hunting, getting ready for the season of birth. The Ikat would normally have remained hidden rather than attack. Devron could only assume it had recently birthed young and was protecting them. This would explain why it was a hit-and-run attack. The warf being in the vicinity would have agitated the Ikat and added to its fear for its kits.

Devron reached for Varellon's mind and was pleased to find she had fallen asleep. The shock of the attack and her injuries had affected the normally stoic wolf more than usual. Devron was grateful he could provide her with the security to sleep and recover even a little. Thus, he was determined to watch through the night to give Varellon the best chance to regain some strength.

He collected as much wood as possible without exposing his back to an attack and settled in for a long, tiring vigil. He sat and watched the surrounding woods with his back to the fire to save his vision as the snap and crackle of the burning dead wood affected his hearing, and the smoke affected his sense of smell. He needed his sight more than ever to watch for any sign of the advancing menace. The sunlight filtering through the maple, oak, alder and ash trees weakened as dusk approached and the yammering of the warf increased. The troop had scared off the usual local inhabitants, and instead of the bustle and noise of birds and small animals, the woods were devoid of any sound other than the crackle of flames and cackle of the warf.

Weakened from blood loss and the effort of finding their small refuge, the sudden rushing attack of three of the beasts surprised Devron. He grabbed a brand from the fire and jumped to his feet to defend his mate. He swung the flaming brand at one of the warf while another came in low and latched onto his ankle. The feel of the jagged teeth ripping flesh and the pain as a fang struck bone caused him to scream out aloud. He drove the brand into the eyes of the warf, and with the sickening stench of burning fur and flesh, the warf released its grip to run howling into the deepening dusk. The heat and fire were deterrent enough to send the remaining warf scampering out of reach. As night fell, the flaming brand reflected in the eyes of the troop as more of the beasts took up a position just beyond the reach of the feeble light given off by the fire. Devron sensed the warf were overcoming their fear and readying to attack as one. He refreshed his brand and took up another. His only chance was to keep the fire going and defend Varellon with these burning branches.

One after another, the warf rushed forward, yapping and gnashing their teeth, each trying to entice the rest to rush forwards in a combined attack. Any single warf, or even a mating pair, was easy to handle as they were easily intimidated by larger beasts. The carrion eater is no larger than the small mountain goats and baby deer they often corner and kill and were only feared when running in a pack. The strength in numbers gave the warf a level of bravery not displayed by any individual. Devron understood the need to have a creature like the warf in the grand scheme of things, but this did not mitigate any frustration and fear.

The tang of blood was driving them to a frenzy. Each feint brought the pack closer, and at least a dozen creatures were now clearly bunched just beyond the firelight. Devron added wood to the fire and refreshed his burning brands, despite knowing his efforts were almost useless.

The small-minded creatures were now united in but one thought—kill.

Suddenly, the warf began scratching their noses and behaving in the most curious of manners. As one, the troop rolled on the ground, rubbing their snouts and faces in the grass. Then they jumped up and bounded, howling, into the darkness as a figure emerged from along the game trail.

A big foot of the plains strode forth. Attired in a plain black robe and rope sandals. He had an ample belly, and the firelight reflected off an almost hairless dome, although strikingly large black eyebrows rose in question of the predicament.

'Yes, it was me,' Martyn interrupted his tale to confirm his part in the tale.

Perrin noted that Heleana and Devron looked curiously at Martyn once again. The tinker had a strange grin on his face as they both shook their heads and turned away.

'Hello, the camp. May I come forth?'

'Welcome, I thank. Use spell?'

'Spell? Pah. No spell, just my whole sack of ground pepper and the wind in the right quarter.'

'Thinking saved by warlock or mountain god.'

'Warlock? No, just a humble tinker who now has even fewer goods to trade.'

'No coin. Offer services of Devron, Varellon, Far Ranges pack. Far from any village.'

'I am on my way to pay my respects to the Earl of Lotan's Rest. I never visit these woods without stopping to say hello. He often has news from far afield, gathered through his travels. Some of his stories are worth the extra walk.'

'We see Earl. Forest herds dying no cause. Blackness. Curse. An evil in forests.'

The tinker's brow wrinkled in consternation at the news. He sat, lost in thought for a moment, then looked over at the recumbent form of Varellon.

'May I suggest we attend your wounds? Then we can discuss your sojourn over a cup of tea. You do have tea, don't you?'

'Yes. Travel lightly for tinker.'

Devron rummaged through his pack, brought out a drawstring bag, placed a small pot in the embers at the fire's edge, and filled it with water.

'Tinker by trade. I can always find just what is needed.'

With the tinker standing guard, Devron could finally complete his ministrations of all their injuries. With a new poultice of herbs and the correct bandaging, Varellon had a good chance of recovery. Devron was finally satisfied with the aid given to his wolf mate and gratefully sipped the flask of tea the tinker offered. He sipped the tea but shortly succumbed to sleep from the emotions and expended energies.

The clear warbling of a nearby magpie and an annoying beam of sunlight woke Devron. Shocked into full consciousness, he looked around. The teapot was empty, but the fire was still burning well. When he stood and stretched his injured leg, he found no sign of the visitor. He backtracked along the game trail but found no clear indication of the black-robed man's passage. When he turned to retrace his steps, he *noticed his leg gave him no more pain than a pulled muscle would. He rushed to Varellon's side and inspected her hindquarter. An injury that could have been permanently debilitating and certainly disfiguring was now almost completely healed. Devron stood over his mate and watched her chest rise and fall in a deep, steady rhythm.*

'You tell good,' Devron said.

'Now Devron, it was only as it must be. In the mountains, we must all show hospitality and give succour when needed,' Martyn said,' Talking of succour, Devron, did you happen across any leaf in your travels?' Devron proceeded to take out a pouch and offered it up to the Tinker. The pair then went through the process of preparing pipes which they lit with switches from the fire. After ensuring a good draw the tinker continued.

'Right now, I act as a guide to those selected to attend the moot. We must prepare ourselves for travel. We have others to collect.'

CHAPTER NINE
Sudhemere

Lotan's ruby red as fire, bravery in battle, warrior's desire.

S'JANE SHUDDERED, TOOK a deep breath and shouldered the baskets before tentatively approaching the barracks. Ever since the beginning of the season of the sun, the soldiers had begun to look at and treat her differently, and collecting their washing for her mother had become uncomfortable.

Life had become very hard for them since the occupation of Sudhemere. S'jane's mother had gone from being a valued member of the Duke of Sudhem's court to a washerwoman of the Northern Governor's detachment of soldiers. S'jane was to mark her twelfth turn at the coming solstice. She knew this was a significant age, but her mother was reluctant to tell her what the whispers from the soldiers meant and the actual meanings of the terms they spoke behind her back when she handled their small clothes and grey uniforms. She wasn't a complete innocent but was still young enough that she dreamed of being whisked away and saved by a handsome pathfinder.

Life for all in Sudhemere was a sun-by-sun proposition since Baron Du Tek had taken governorship of the Southlands.

Unbelievably, that was an improvement over the previous governor's reign of terror. Du Tek at least saw the value in having his slaves in a workable condition rather than dying in the streets.

S'jane's mother suffered scrubbing and washing uniforms by sun and the indignity of the soldiers' forced attentions at night. S'jane spent many evenings pretending to sleep in the corner of the hovel they had been forced into while her mother had no choice but to entertain one soldier after another. These night-time visits often ended with her mother bruised and beaten when her feigned participation was not convincing enough.

When Baron Du Tek had noticed a decrease in productivity, he wisely legislated against violence in his soldier's nightly entertainments. The men of his garrison were no longer allowed to permanently damage the baron's chattels on pain of a lashing. This did not completely stop the bashings and violence, but curbed the severity of the injuries received, ensuring the continued performance of the enslaved population. S'jane's mother never fought back or complained, as only those who proved their worth were allowed the rations and housing distributed by the Baron's commissar and warders.

Fortunately, most of the garrison were out on patrol, and S'jane had chosen mealtime to collect yestersun's dirty uniforms. This meant S'jane would only have to put up with minimal pinching, prodding and lecherous remarks while she worked. The only men left in the barracks were from the commissary platoon overseeing the slaves who were cleaning the soldier's housing and bedding.

S'jane stood out with her flaming red hair, often worn in a loose braid reaching well down her back. Her height was not remarkable, but the growing strength in her body was becoming obvious. Unfortunately, these features attracted attention, which was the last thing a slave girl needed at this time. S'jane had learnt from her mother to remain in the background and try and avoid being noticed, but as the season of the sun solstice approached, she received more attention from the soldiers and, surprisingly, the gangs of ruffians that inhabited the streets of Sudhemere.

These gangs of kids, most no older than S'jane, survived on petty crimes against the invaders and populace alike. Many had been orphaned and had no other means to feed themselves. The Baron often ignored these transgressions, understanding that as long as they did not get out of control, he did not have to find a way to house and feed them. Also, as soon as they reached twelve turns, they would swell his ranks of slaves. Another of the Baron's initiatives was the law that children under the age of twelve be protected from the attention of his soldiers so the next generation of slaves could develop. Baron Tod Du Tek was becoming well-known for understanding the commercial side of invasion and occupation. This had earned him grudging respect from the other Northern barons and bought him the governorship of the Southlands.

S'jane tucked her hair beneath her shift before she entered the barracks and made her way to the storeroom towards the rear of the building. She kept her head bowed and walked down the centre of the aisle between the bunks. She hoped that by avoiding eye contact with slaves and soldiers alike, she could load her baskets, sling them about her shoulders, and leave without any interaction. She had noticed that once loaded and intent on her job, there was less chance of a soldier stopping her and asking her age. Her mother had told her to say that she was only eleven turns old but her growing body was proof of the lie. S'jane knew her mother was trying to protect her, but knowing how her mother suffered from the soldier's attentions S'jane believed forewarned is forearmed.

S'jane was near the door to the barrack's storeroom when her peripheral vision noted the presence of a pair of scuffed boots. She raised her head and came face to face with the worst of the lot, Corporal Otero.

Otero was the most slovenly soldier S'jane had ever seen. His mouth of rotting teeth lent him a permanent odour of decay, while his lank hair and broken nose clearly showed he had no care for cleanliness or appearance. Otero took S'jane's chin in a hand covered in food scraps and fats from his lunch and brought his face down to hers. He kissed her firmly on the lips and forced his tongue into her mouth. His breath and his taste nearly made her gag. While this was going on, his hands groped her young body and stroked her thighs, drawing a moan from deep in his chest.

'Only a few more moons and you will be mine,' Otero said. 'I just bought you in the barrack's sweep, so I rushed over to give you the good news. You can now savour our future together. You cost me a great deal of credit, so I will get my value before leasing you out. Many have noted your growing assets, and the bidding was fierce. I even had to promise double midnight duties for the next six moons, so I will be looking forward to as many nights spent enjoying my property as possible. Now go about your business, and do not let any other touch my goods.'

Even though S'jane knew that taking a ladle of water from the barrel in the storeroom would result in a whipping, or worse, she had no option. If she did not rid her mouth of the taste of Otero, she would surely vomit. A small mercy had no one watching, so she rinsed her mouth out and, in a small act of rebellion, spat the water back into the soldier's barrel. With her skin still crawling from the meeting with the corporal, S'jane loaded the clothes and strung the baskets from the yoke she used to spread the weight across her shoulders.

S'jane could not wait to go on her way. She did not want to meet Otero again and needed to report this to her mother. S'jane did not fully understand the implications, but did know she did not want to become Otero's property if she could avoid it.

RESISTANCE

She retraced her steps towards the wash house where her mother sweated away her youth, sun after sun. She could not ignore the depredations of the occupying soldiers as it could be seen in every corner of Sudhemere. The previous governor, who had, according to gossip, upset the first of the Northern Mages and his plans, hung from the walls. The gutters and alleys were filled with the crippled and emaciated citizens who had run afoul of the Northern Empire and its occupying forces. S'jane's own hunger reminded her that all in Sudhemere had run afoul of the Northern Empire occupiers.

Even though she made this trip every other sun, she always flinched before dashing through the city's main square. There, Baron Du Tek meted out his summary justice. There were only two levels of infraction to the Baron's laws. The first was crimes against the North, treated as treason, and crimes against Sudhemere, treated as misdemeanours. If a starving child stole a loaf of bread from a baker designated as a supplier to the garrison, the crime committed was treason. If the baker was supplying Southlanders, the punishment was less severe.

The punishment for treason was being nailed to the walls of the square using iron spikes through each hand. Their cries for mercy or release were a constant reminder that the Baron held Sudhemere firmly by the shortest leash. Crimes against the populace earned the perpetrator punishment by being chained in the square for seven suns, the chain not long enough to reach the centrepiece of the square, an elaborate fountain. The combination of relief from thirst being just out of reach and the screams of the condemned traitors could easily send one mad. Upon being released from the chains, perpetrators were branded on the forehead with the mark of the thief. If a criminal received two such brands, they were marked as incorrigible upon the third offence and treated as committing treason. There was only one release from the punishment of treason. Death.

S'jane steeled herself and tried to close her eyes and ears to the despair evident in the square, rushed forward, dodging and jumping the clawed hands of those chained. The guards would often wake up or throw things at the somnolent criminals to make a game out of those preparing to cross the square. Any attempt at helping the condemned or providing any succour to these poor souls was immediately regarded as treason. As she skipped around the grabbing hands trying to close about her ankle, she heard the failing voice of her aunt calling her name. Her mother's sister had been spiked to the wall suns earlier after dropping a cabbage as she passed through the square while delivering her vegetables to the commissary.

Her crime was considered treason when the vegetable was pounced upon by those in chains, and she was punished accordingly.

Although the plight of the population of Sudhemere had improved slightly under Baron Du Tek, it was certainly not out of any intrinsic compassion for the Southerners but merely out of commercial considerations.

With the laughter and catcalls of the guards ringing in her ears and tears for her aunt streaming down her face, S'jane ran from the square and ducked into the nearest alley to rest and compose herself. No sooner had she eased the yoke from her shoulders than she was surrounded by one of the local street gangs. Seven kids, ranging from nine turns to her own age, could behave unpredictably.

Depending on the sun, they looked for care and guidance, or were prepared to kill for what they needed.

S'jane's only comfort was that she was close enough to the guards at the square that they would hear a scream. As she was well-known among them, they would investigate. S'jane looked at the two boys who obviously led this gang, each proudly bearing the brand of the thief on their forehead. The brand had become a badge of resistance to the children of Sudhemere and many went out of their way to earn the title of thief, despite the punishment resulting in some dying in the chains.

'Did youse see Gilly? She still alive in there?' the tallest said. 'She's da one in da blue vest.'

'I think so. She must be the one closest to my aunt. I am sure she reached for me when my aunt called my name,' S'jane said. 'Aren't you Avan, the son of the old Duke's Master of the Stables?'

'Dey be all gone. I'm da master here,' Avan said. 'I know youse Red. Youse are da washer woman's daughter.'

S'jane looked closely at the boy. Underneath his coating of dirt and grime, she saw a lad just younger than herself with a tangled mess of brown hair and green eyes that stared defiantly. She cast her eyes over the rest of his gang and saw hunger, the desire for hope and release from the depredations of their current ordeal. Even though many of them could not remember any other way of life. S'jane had had the beginning of an education in the duke's household and vaguely remembered a younger girl just joining in the classes.

'I remember Gilly now. She's your twin sister, isn't she?' S'jane asked.

'What of it, she tough, she'll make it,' Avan said.

S'jane heard the words, but the look on Avan's face told the real truth. These kids were fast running out of any real hope and reason to live. S'jane had always pondered a way to help the prisoners in the square, but each plan to give them succour or hope would lead to her own incarceration and punishment as a traitor.

'Can youse get er a message when youse goes through?' one of the youngsters asked.

'No, I can't. It would mean my death,' S'jane said. 'But I think you could.'

This announcement surprised the gang. The older two pulled wicked-looking rusty knives, and the next two eldest pulled sticks sharpened to a fine point. The remainder armed themselves with rocks and stones taken from their pockets.

'Whatcha mean? Youse trying to get us kilt? Youse goin to turn us in to the Brocken?' Avan said.

'No, wait. I think I have a way to get a message of hope to your sister and for her to hang on as long as she can until she is released,' S'jane said.

'Talk fast, Red. Don ave all sun,' Avan said.

'Not here. Help me get these baskets back to the river gate, and I can explain the plan,' S'jane said.

S'jane knew she had the most knowledge of the layout of the square, as very few were allowed passage. The only ones with a more intimate knowledge were the likes of Avan, who had survived their incarceration within, and only if their young minds had not blocked out the despair and pain of their time at the pleasure of the Baron. S'jane and the gang were not hindered in their trip to the washrooms, as no patrol or citizen were prepared to interfere with the young street gang without backup and support.

When S'jane was safely returned to the workrooms with her washing baskets, she explained her plan to Avan and his gang. She set each a task and outlined what she regarded as the safest way to get a message of hope to all those chained in the square. The most important task was for Avan to find a safe refuge where the gang could hole up for a time and to stock it with as much food and water as possible. Gilly would need time to recover from her ordeal, and the gang would need to hide out if any of them were recognised.

S'jane explained to the gang that the safest way to send a message was to send it to all those currently chained so that Gilly could not be singled out and punished or convicted of treason. The gang dispersed to complete their tasks. They were to meet S'jane in the alley near the square just before the moon's apex. That night, the moon would be a dull crescent and would cast a clear glow, but it would be the best chance they had.

Once the gang were away about their tasks, S'jane shook out the uniforms in the baskets and piled them ready for washing. Unrolling a grey cape, she felt something solid caught in its folds. She turned so that no other could see her find and slowly peeled back the cloth to reveal the sheathed dagger of a Brocken soldier. S'jane immediately suspected a trap and knew she should report the find to a squad leader. She feared that her delay in returning to the washrooms would be held against her, and without a valid reason, she could be seen as committing a crime against the North.

S'jane secreted the weapon in her clothes and finished her work, all the while waiting for the heavy hand of a supervisor or Brocken officer to land on her shoulder. Later, during a short break between the uniforms being washed and hanging them to dry, she hid the dagger in her mother's room. As the work sun came to a close, S'jane's continued fear of discovery abated slightly. She wondered if the word had gone out that she was to be the property of Corporal Otero, and this was why she had not been harassed or questioned.

S'jane shared a meagre meal with her mother in the early evening. The stale half loaf of grainy bread was spread with a rind of cheese, showing mould that was only lightly scraped off. The slices of browning apple that topped their dinner were a rare delight that had come from the gardens her mother's sister had worked in. Each looked at the withering fruit and was painfully aware it would be the last of such gifts.

S'jane considered her parent. She was aware of the pain within her mother and that she had no way of helping her own family without suffering a similar fate. S'jane knew her mother would not hesitate in the sacrifice if it were not for her. She had been an honoured lady in the Duke of Sudhem's court. Not yet forty turns, the rosy cheeks and lustrous auburn hair of her youth were now sallow and faded. S'jane had always tried to feed her mother the lion's share of any meal they managed, but the meagre diet did not replace the body's needs used during the gruelling suns of work and nights of suffering the attentions of the soldiers.

S'jane waited until the mid-evening bell that sounded the curfew for all citizens and was grateful that none of the baron's men had arrived to partake of what they saw as their right as the conquering force. S'jane's mother had fallen asleep shortly after their meal, and S'jane welcomed the chance to sneak out and put her plan into action. Her wish was that their actions tonight would give all incarcerated in the square some hope that others were thinking of them.

S'jane snuck quietly into the alley. She kept to the shadows and travelled well out of her way so any casual observer would have no reference of direction for her point of origin or destination. She had hidden herself and her hair under one of the grey cloaks of the Brocken, which nearly proved fatal when she came face-to-blade with Avan's knife. Only a last-second flash of her hair in the moonlight saved her from injury. Avan's grunt of exertion and S'jane's squeal of surprise were dampened by the fold of cloth each wore over their mouths and noses. S'jane was grateful that a plan to hide their identities had saved their mission before it could start.

S'jane sent the two oldest boys to the rooftops, where stale bread and rotting fruit had been secreted earlier. It was all that could be safely stolen, but to those in despair, anything would be welcome. The smallest and quickest boy was sent as a diversion. The guards would not expect anything but the usual tedious duty after curfew. The rest of the escape had been prepared.

The youngster raced towards the square and, at the last second, threw a stale loaf of bread towards the chained prisoners. The surprised guards hesitated, conflicted between giving chase and retrieving the loaf from the chained prisoners. The clamour of the now awakened prisoners for the bread set their course.

They began running after the fleeing figure that appeared nothing more than a will-of-the-wisp and was clearly too elusive for a flatbow bolt. The guards entered the now-deserted alley to see the lad disappear around the corner. They called out and increased their pace as they raced after their target. Each was intent on catching their prey, and as they raced down the alley, none of the four guards saw the pieces of cord that had been knotted together. The line had been stretched across the darkest section of the alley, and the pursuit ended in a heap of flailing arms, legs, and injuries caused by their short swords and daggers that had been unsheathed at the outset of the chase.

When the hue and cry had gone up, and the guards were intent on their pursuit, the two senior members of the gang began lobbing their offerings down into the square. What little they had managed to steal or spare would at least send the message to those with fading spirits or no hope that others were prepared to risk all just for them. The remaining part of the plan was for the gang to lay low in their hideout until Gilly was branded and released, and be there to care for her and bring her back from her ordeal.

S'jane was further pleased that no mention of the mission was made in the following suns. She assumed the guards were too afraid to admit their lax efforts for fear of reprisal from their sergeant.

When she next ventured to the barracks to collect the washing the familiar chills had her skin crawling and made S'jane shudder. She stopped and took a number of deep breaths before shouldering the baskets and tentatively approaching the barracks. When she entered and moved down the centre aisle towards the storeroom, she felt the eyes of soldiers following her every movement, but they were strangely silent. None spoke the usual ribald comments and suggestions. She completed her collection of the washing with the least amount of interference. S'jane could only put this down to the coming night of the sun solstice and Corporal Otero's claim upon her.

When S'jane neared the square, she prepared to rush past the fountain at its centre, ensuring she stayed as far from the grabbing hands as she could. When she completed the crossing with her load of washing she stopped to catch her breath. She sobbed as she drew in gasping breaths, realising that her aunt no longer called her name. Then, resolutely shouldering her burden, she looked towards the alley where she had met Avan. Someone had decorated the wall with a large swish of red paint, clearly visible to all in the square.

CHAPTER TEN
Red

Mwindo's silver star does cure, intensity and honour ensure.

THE SUN THAT GILLY received her brand was looked upon by S'jane as a small win against the Northern Empire's ongoing occupation. Her help in this small measure of resistance gave her a great deal of satisfaction, even though she could tell no one, not even her mother.

S'jane continued to deliver the washing between the barracks and the river gate washrooms. Each trip she made and each comment or pinch she received made it that much easier to deal with the secret knowledge that she had done something to make others' lives more bearable against the oppressive occupation.

Many turns ago, when Sudhemere had expanded due to the wealth and productivity of the Duchy, the businesses that fed overflows of water back into the river or tainted the water by industry were moved downstream and centred around the outflow from the city at the river gate. The change kept the river clean for drinking and casual uses like swimming in the season of the sun. The sewers had also been diverted to the same area, so care had to be taken that products produced or washed here did not end up with an unpleasant odour. Often, as during the current hot weather, the smell from the sewers became most irksome, and S'jane's mother would have to add crushed flowers to her work to hide the smell that permeated the garrison's washing.

S'jane was helping her mother chop and crush the old flowers delivered from the citadel, including those too wilted or faded for use by the flower gatherers, when Avan appeared before her. The young ruffian looked distressed and had clearly sought out S'jane as a last resort.

'It be Gilly. She sick,' he said. 'She don't move an won't open er eyes.'

'Mum, I have to go with him,' she said. 'Come on, Avan, show me.'

S'jane knew she had left her mother with no explanation, but the thought of losing Gilly after the risks they had all taken was devastating. Avan led her through the alleys and back-ways of the city, pausing often to check their way forwards and as often to check they had not been observed or followed. S'jane welcomed his precautions and was careful to blend into the shadows and crowds they passed through so that no one would remark on or remember her distinctive hair. She often had to restrain Avan in his haste to get back to Gilly as she knew none of the population of Sudhemere moved quickly unless under the lash of one of the Baron's overseers.

He eventually took S'jane down a stinking alley that previously led to the dumping and cleaning area for the night pots of the citadel and grand houses of the city. The alley was so narrow that S'jane and Avan had to turn sideways to traverse it. Even though it had not been used for many turns, the walls were still caked with dried crap, and the ammonia smell of piss even now pervaded the air.

Avan stopped in the darkest recesses of the alley and held up his hand to demand silence. He waited for a long while to be sure no one was close or could hear, then he tapped four times on the grate of an opening into the sewers. The grate moved from below, and Avan was able to grip it and set it aside. One of the smallest kids in the gang popped out of the hole and gestured for Avan and S'jane to climb down. After S'jane had begun her descent, Avan replaced the sewer grate with the help of the kid above. They climbed down a short ladder made from materials scrounged from the city. The ladder shook and creaked under their combined weight but held together.

Avan took S'jane's hand in the dark and led her, bent over almost double, along a now-defunct sewer pipe. The pipe brought them to a convergence of several disused sewer outlets. The floor space here was as large as a small warehouse, although the ceiling was easily within S'jane's reach. The closeness of the ceiling, held up by a series of arches, evoked a feeling of being closed in, and their shadows gave the area an almost haunted aura. S'jane could see the wisdom in the choice of hideaway. Any full-grown man would find it difficult to manoeuvre to any degree in the confines of the space.

The gang had made an impressive lair, with bedding and some storage areas for their food and loot from foraging in the city. They had even managed to acquire two of the smokeless lamps and oil used in the grand houses rather than the tallow and wick lamps used by most of Sudhemere's populace.

'Over ere, Red,' Avan said.

He took one of the lamps and guided S'jane to Gilly. Avan's sister was groaning and tossing in her sleep, and S'jane saw from the state of her bedding that she was burning up with a fever and sweating profusely. The odour also indicated she had soiled herself.

'Avan, get me some clean, cool water and some clean cloths. I will also need clean bedding and a girl to help me,' she said. 'Gilly is sick with a fever, and we need to cool her down.'

Avan rushed to do her bidding and sent over a small girl who was clearly a new member of the gang. At about ten turns, she was slight in stature, and her wild, knotted head of dark brown hair looked like mice had nested there. S'jane and the girl, Eist, moved Gilly off the pallet that was soaked in sweat and urine and placed her on the cool stones of the cavern's floor with just a thin cloth beneath her. S'jane had Eist undress Gilly while she made sure none of the rest of the gang could see. Eist then bathed Gilly with the fresh water, and S'jane instructed Eist to keep Gilly cool by placing cloths on the forehead and dripping water onto a cloth covering Gilly from knees to shoulders.

While Eist cared for Gilly, S'jane found Avan ordering the rest of the gang to find the cleanest bedding and clothes that might fit Gilly. The way he got these kids to follow his instructions was impressive. He was firm and clear with his orders, giving the other kids a purpose and direction.

'Avan, she is really skinny. Has she eaten since she was released?'

'Na. She weren't hungry and giv er bit t'others.'

'Okay. We need to get her to eat something. She needs food to fight the fever. Show me what you have.'

S'jane was impressed with the quality of food the gang had stored. When she mentioned this to Avan, he said that when she ordered him to find a hideout and supply it with food, he had decided to steal the best they could. He even proudly showed her two chickens kept in a small alcove off one of the sewer inlets.

'Avan, is this area safe? Won't water come through here?'

She was worried about what effect moving Gilly would have on the girl.

'Dry, less we get a storm. There be only a coupla street grates that lead here. This time of turn should be okay.'

S'jane set a pot of water to boil and told Avan to kill and clean one of the chickens. With a broth simmering, S'jane instructed Avan on how to complete the soup with some root vegetables and carefully feed Gilly. She was thankful for the time she had spent in the duke's household. She had often acted as a runner for her mother and the duke's apothecary.

'It will take several suns of keeping her cool but not too cold, and feeding her broth and clean water before the fever will break,' S'jane said.

Avan assured her they could get the job done and instructed the other senior boy to lead S'jane home and ensure she was safe. When they approached the washrooms, S'jane noticed that the wall next to the entry was marked with a large swish painted in red. She was surprised, as she had not noticed it before. She wondered at its appearance and the likeness to the one painted on the wall near the square and others that had appeared around the city.

When S'jane re-entered to the washrooms, the sun's work was nearing an end, and everyone was working slowly. With only two more suns to the solstice celebration, the workload would double on the morrow because the squad leaders and the Northern officers would try to outdo each other with clean uniforms and equipment when presenting their men to the governor and his court. The season of the sun solstice was celebrated throughout Tol and was the only sun of the turn when the populace would join together and share whatever they could with friends and neighbours.

In the coming suns, the number of soldiers in and around Sudhemere would increase as Northern Empire Barons from outside the city arrived with various honour guards and troops. Baron Du Tek would use this celebration to solidify his leadership in the Northern occupation and ensure the visiting barons knew exactly whom they looked to for the ongoing flow of wealth into their coffers.

That night, S'jane and her mother shared a simple meal of stale bread soaked in a weak broth made with an old lamb bone and carrot tops scrounged from the commissary's midden. While they shared the meal, S'jane became aware that her mother had something to tell her. She could tell her mother was finding it hard to find a way to start what was clearly an important conversation.

'S'jane, when you were born, I was the happiest woman on Tol. Your father was in the Duke's guard, and I was a lady-in-waiting to the Duke's wife. You gave us so much delight and pleasure. You were always the cheekiest child, and even the Duke often asked after you. I did not know any other life. I had never lived anywhere else. When the Northerners came and your father was killed, I had nowhere to run, and you were but six turns,' her mother began. 'Even as your true birth sun was earlier in this turn, this sun solstice will see you officially twelve in the census records. I have tried to protect you as much as I could, but now you will be regarded as being of age, and the soldiers will be allowed to use you.'

'Mother, what do you mean? Do you think they will give me another job?'

'S'jane, Baron Du Tek ordered that no child younger than twelve turns could be used by the soldiers as slaves. My darling girl, you will no longer have that protection. That is what Corporal Otero meant when he saw you. That is why the other soldiers have stopped accosting you.' S'jane's mother took her hands across the wooden crate they used as a table. 'When the soldiers come to me in the night, I have had to let them use me. I have had no choice. I have seen them break and kill others who resisted. I had to protect you.'

'Mother, do you mean Corporal Otero means to use me as those others treat you?'

'Yes, S'jane. I had hoped we would be free of the occupation before you were made to suffer. Every young girl's first time should be with the one she loves. Your father made it very special for me, and I cling to that memory every time one of those beasts forces himself on me. Otero will come for you on the night of the solstice. I will try and give him what he wants, but you must be prepared. You must find a happy place to go to when he uses you. Do not fight him, or he will hurt you.'

S'jane's mother dropped her hands and sobbed. S'jane had always wondered at her mother's acceptance of the attentions of the garrison soldiers. She now saw the strength that had carried her mother through turns of torment to give S'jane a small glimmer of a chance of a normal life. That night, as she curled into a ball trying to sleep, she grasped the handle of the illicit dagger she had hidden in her bedroll. She had no idea what was to happen to her, but the comfort of the weapon eased her fears, and she eventually found sleep.

THE MUSIC AND NOISE of the garrison celebrating the solstice echoed along the city's walls. The bands of soldiers wandering the streets had been swelled by the visiting Barons, and most of the original inhabitants of Sudhemere stayed in their hovels and nooks, trying to avoid attracting attention. In tomorrow's light of the sun, it would be safer to move around the fringes of their area and quietly observe the solstice with friends.

S'jane's mother had tried to prepare her daughter for what was to come and had even cleaned herself and wore a garland of wilted flowers in an attempt to be more appealing. They sat together, waiting for the inevitable. If it were not Corporal Otero, it would just be another. As the night bell rang out the midnight peal, the flimsy door to their room burst open, and Otero crowded in, swigging on a jug of the cheap local spirit.

'I am come for my due. I own you bitch, now come to me. I will see if you are as good as your mother.' Otero drunkenly grasped for S'jane, but S'jane's mother stepped in before his hand could close on her.

'Would you not like me first? We can show her how best to please you, Corporal.'

Otero stood back and laughed. His rotted teeth and sun's drinking led to this filling the small room with a nauseating smell. He stared at S'jane's mother.

'You think you can distract me, you whore. I have paid for the bitch, and I will have her.'

Otero lashed out with the jug and smashed it across the older woman's head. The garland flew off and S'jane's mother fell, hitting her head on the corner of their makeshift table. S'jane ran to her mother and cradled her head in her lap. It had finally happened. One of the bastards had gone too far. S'jane closed her mother's clouded eyes with the thought that her mother was now free and vowed that she would also find that freedom.

'Now, my red-haired bitch, let's see all of you. I have spent moons dreaming of your unsoiled pleasure pot.'

Otero threw down the broken jug and reached for S'jane. She dodged but tripped over her mother's legs and fell heavily onto her bedding. It would be useless to scream.

No one would come.

Otero stood over her, laughing and undoing the buttons on breeches that her mother had probably washed just yestersun. S'jane backed into the corner of the room as Otero displayed himself to her and made crude hand gestures indicating his intent. As he moved towards her, S'jane closed her eyes, not knowing what to do. She lashed out at the corporal to keep him away.

His surprised gasp and immediate bellow scared her even more, and she opened her eyes, only then realising she was holding the dagger that had given her so much comfort over the previous nights. Otero held his hands across his bulging belly, and S'jane fervently hoped he could not feel or see what she had done to his manhood. Otero fell to his knees as his eyes glazed, knocking over the crude oil lamp. The corporal made small mewling noises as the pool of blood spread. He was staring at S'jane as the light faded from his eyes. She huddled on her pallet, covered in Otero's blood, rocking backwards and forwards as shock slowly took hold and the flames from the lamp spread and caught. She would not be given the punishment of a traitor. For killing one of their own, the soldiers would tear her apart.

Just before passing out from shock, S'jane felt hands grab her and pull her away from the bodies of her mother and attacker. The movement sparked something in S'jane, and she stumbled through the streets of Sudhemere, led by two small boys. S'jane had no idea where she was being led as the scene of her mother's death played over and over in her mind.

S'jane woke coughing with water dribbling down her throat. She felt someone holding her head, and when the coughing fit passed, saw the arches and ceiling of the gang's hideaway. When she turned her head, a grinning Gilly held a cup to her lips and nodded encouragement. After taking another swallow of water, S'jane sat up and looked around. Dried blood cracked and crinkled as she moved, reminding her of her mother's murder and her own near attack at the hands of Corporal Otero.

S'jane sat up and saw the gang all standing back, watching Gilly attend to her. Oddly, every wall of the hideaway was decorated with one of the red swishes that had been appearing on various walls across the city.

'Hey Red, bout time ya waked,' Avan said.

He pushed through the others and brought over a platter holding bread, fruit, and cheese. The bread was suns old, but some of the fruit was not too badly decayed. S'jane realised the gang had saved her and given her sanctuary.

'Ya save Gilly. We save ya,' Avan said.

It was a matter-of-fact statement. Avan was announcing a debt settled.

'What happened?' S'jane asked.

'Dunno, weren't der. We was keepn an eye on ya, and ya needs us, so we come,' Avan said.

He turned and walked away into the darkness of the shadow cast by one of the arches. Gilly smiled at Avan's display of manly disdain.

'Avan says we had to look out fur youse. Member da red mark on da wall near your room? Dat's our mark. Avan as called us da Reds. We put dat mark as they dun for me at the square to let people know dat we can have hope and we need to hold on, just like Avan dun in the square and like youse showed me,' Gilly said.

S'jane looked around the hideout and saw two distinct changes. There were more kids and a lot more loot piled around. Gilly noticed the direction of her gaze.

'When them gets stuff for the solstice in the citadel, it much easier to filch it, now we gots more an twenty mouths ta feed,' Gilly said.

Gilly helped S'jane to her feet and proudly took her for a tour, introducing her to the group and explaining some of their special talents. Some were pickpockets, while some were grab-and-run experts. Others helped plan the getaways based on S'jane's plan from the alley. One or two older ones, including Gilly, were rooftop break-and-enter specialists.

Later that sun, the gang had gathered for their own solstice celebration. Food had been prepared, and some watered wine had been added to the festive occasion. S'jane looked around at the gang. Some had donned bits and pieces of finery stolen from the better parts of the city, while others had bathed and tried to brush their hair. S'jane herself had been given a near-new dress of a deep green that really set off her eyes and hair. S'jane was so happy to see the joy and hope in the kids that she vowed that she and the gang would take to the streets and spread that very same feeling and message of hope. The red swish would become the symbol of freedom to come.

Just then, a disturbance on the far side of the cavern alerted the girls. When whispers and laughter followed Avan as he led Eist over to them, the fear of discovery that had been their immediate reaction waned to relief.

'Hey Red, youse got a price on ya head.'

S'jane instantly thought of the deaths of her mother and the vile corporal Otero. There had not been enough time for an investigation. The fire would have made identities and the manner of death almost impossible to determine. There must be some mistake.

'Eist here heared it her very self. Ten gold royales for ya,' Avan announced. 'Eist got a boot shinin op next ta da barracks. She get good info. Tell her what you heared, Eist.'

'Yea, two soldiers was gabbin about da money da Baron has on capturin the rebel leader. Ten gold royales. Da local guy was tellin da other one about da Red. He says he stands over two span, wit long red hair and beard, and carries sword across hes back.'

Each of the group looked to S'jane for her reaction, and after a short pause, they all burst into fits of laughter. S'jane watched, bewildered at the group who were all laughing and some were pointing at her as they whispered to their fellows, eventually realisation came to S'jane.

'Wait, wait,' she said. 'Who is the Red?'

Avan stopped laughing and became serious.

'Why, youse da Red. Youse our leader.'

CHAPTER ELEVEN
The Ancients

Zahhak's yellow lights all shadow battle glow does inspire.

'PERRIN, IF YOU AND Bren prepare your small packs with only what you need for the next few suns, I will send your large packs on to our destination with my men,' Garat said.

Perrin was pleased by his brother's suggestion as he remembered his promise to Grams. So much had happened. The change of direction his life had taken in such a short time could easily have him forgetting about the package the old woman had counselled him to keep a secret from all. The boys were finishing sorting through their gear when Perrin was brought short by a question from Bren.

'Lady Heleana, if you and your husband are leading the resistance and Devron's wolf partner is preeminent in the wolf packs, who is calling this gathering? Who is in a position to bring together all the peoples of the South?'

'A most astute question, my young prince. I had thought one of the others would have asked it much earlier,' Martyn said.

He and Devron were sitting around the fire sipping from flasks of tea while Garat and Heleana prepared their own travel packs.

Heleana turned towards the tinker but took only one step before being restrained by her husband's hand on her shoulder.

'A question I want the answer to as well, my love. I suggest we have him explain before you take your axe to him,' Garat said.

'But Garat, it would be so, so satisfying.'

'Martyn, your answer to Bren's question had better be good. I have seen her in this mood before, and I cannot guarantee a pleasant outcome for you,' Garat said.

Garat led his wife to a seat and directed the two younger ones to join them. To his dismay, Heleana had scooped up her bardiche and seated herself next to the tinker. She took up a soft rag and began oiling the haft with long, slow movements.

'Yes, perhaps it is time for an explanation,' the tinker said.

The two boys moved to place their packs in the pile of baggage set for transport but were brought up short when Devron's wolf rose from the shadows. None in the cavern had noticed her enter. She padded over and sat at Devron's shoulder, towering over the diminutive rider.

'Varellon has no equal amongst all the packs, but even she will bare her throat to the Wolven. The Wolven are of the ancient races and are the ones that guide the meat eaters. They are the sires of the wolves and revered as the largest, strongest and wisest. The ruminants and grass eaters bow to the great Bucks while all adhere to the wisdom of she who is at the centre of the grove. The Grove of the Ancients holds the sum of all knowledge in the history of our world of Tol, particularly regarding the elevation of the three races. The Dini, some of whom share our world with their wolf partners, the Elves of the Sunset Islands who have an affinity for the seas, and you, the Peoples, tillers of the plains,' Martyn said.

Heleana stormed to her feet and slammed the butt of her sheathed axe upon the floor.

'Are you suggesting our destiny is in the hands of some animals?'

Varellon sprang to her feet with hackles raised, and a deep growl echoed around the cavern. Before anyone else registered the danger, Devron moved to stand before his partner. There was a nervous relaxing of tight muscles when Varellon sank to her haunches, and Devron regained his own seat.

'Well, that certainly got the juices flowing,' Martyn quipped.

'Elaborate, tinker!' Heleana said through gritted teeth. Her composure was on the brink and her stance and preparedness was that of a warrior.

'Be at ease, Lady of Sudhem. Just as we all have structure within our societies, the ancients also adhere to the counsel of the Druids. The Druids are the guides to the peoples and go-betweens for the ancients whose council has set the direction of the three races of Tol.'

Heleana sank down onto her seat, confused.

'Ancient animals and Druids. I thought that was all just tales and myths made up as bedtime stories to amuse young ones,' Heleana said.

'The ancient ones are bringing together those needed to lead us against the coming threat. We are being gathered at the behest of the Druids,' Martyn said.

An audible huff came from the wolf as she eased herself into a prone position. It was clear to those sitting around the fire that this was not the first time the partners had felt the same lack of control over their choices. Devron cocked his head as though trying to hear a distant whisper.

'Varellon say start. Wilder Wolven join at moonrise,' Devron said.

Garat stood quickly and held up his hand to forestall his wife's objection.

'My love, we have to get moving either way and I, for one, want to meet this wolven. If there is help to be had from the Wolf Riders and the Elves, I will welcome the support.'

Heleana nodded her agreement and—as if none of the recent revelations had been voiced— took command of the group.

'Right. You boys, get this area cleaned up. Garat, take the tinker with you and bring in enough firewood to replenish what we used. Oh, and arrange the transport of this baggage,' Heleana ordered.

Garat had sent out scouts, even though they were at the very limit of Brocken influence. There was always a chance that a rogue bunch of Northerners or deserters had ventured further into the mountains and forests in search of plunder or a base to raid from.

At times during their march, Garat would study a pile of sticks beside a path or a strange arrangement of branches in saplings that grew where direct sunlight could reach. Each time he paused, he checked each side of their path and rearranged the sign before moving on.

'Your precautions do you proud, Pathfinder,' Martyn said. 'Devron advises that there is no sign of invaders within two sun's march. We can rest easy in the knowledge and increase our pace. Wilder awaits.'

Garat and Heleana called for a brief stop at the news as it was mid-morning and the group would benefit. Garat could also call in the Pathfinders following their line of march, erasing any sign of their passing, and dismiss them from their task.

'How do you know of the movements of the enemy?' Garat asked.

'There is much life in these forests, and word is passed so all may avoid the Brocken. They do not adhere to the same rules of hunting as do your people.

'This is where I leave you,' Martyn said. 'I will see you all at the Village of the Salient Buck. I have had the twins and their blacksmith working on a project, and I must prepare a suitable introduction.'

'You said you were our guide, among other things. Now, you desert us when I have more questions than answers. You have mentioned the twins. How are a pair of rustic siblings involved in all this?'

'You, Heleana L'atchett of Sudhem, have much to learn. It will be difficult for you to develop the trust that will be needed in those who will band together under your banner. As myth and bedtime stories become real, it will be up to your husband and yourself to bind together the Elves and the Peoples to bring the Brocken to submission. Follow Devron and learn from the Wolven. He will have answers to some of your questions.'

'Join me in the village six suns hence, where we just may take a huge step in rectifying our deficit in power compared to the Brocken's manpower, training, weapons, and strategies. Oh, and I used the term guide only in the broadest sense,' Martyn said.

Heleana bristled as the group repositioned their packs to continue on their way. She drew in some deep breaths as her husband turned her in their direction of travel. Martyn settled at the base of the healthy oak tree whose canopy shaded the clearing. When Devron led the group away, Perrin was confused to see him recline and close his eyes.

'Not exactly in a hurry, is he?' he said to Bren.

'Per, I do not understand anything that man does.'

The pair followed their companions on what Perrin considered a very pleasant trek through a forest thick with the vivid greens of healthy plants, and a rustle and twitter that suggested the animals and birds had little to fear. The only indication that this was anything more than a hike was that each party member bristled with easily reached weapons. Devron only carried a belt knife but had little need of a weapon, considering he was riding a wolf. Each of the brothers had a long sword strapped to their back in addition to their knives and longbows, with quivers hung belted at their waist. Heleana and Bren carried their axes, short swords and knives.

Half a sun after leaving their guide the travellers came together as a gut-wrenching feeling of wrongness overcame each of them. The usual twitter and hum of movement in the forest was silent and when they attempted to forge ahead the feeling of evil grew. Varellon was growling continuously and Bren was especially affected. Garat turned them from their line of march and found as they retreated the effect of the feelings dissipated and eventually cleared.

'I don't know what happened back there but everything felt just wrong,' Garat said. 'It was the strangest thing I have never felt anything like that before.'

'Unfortunately Bren and I have,' Perrin said. 'Up in the valley we came across a similar feeling when we discovered two warf completely dried out. Every living thing grasses and even mosses were blackened and withered and the feeling of evil was strong enough to make you want to throw up your lunch. I told Gram so she could let your pathfinders know. We should add this experience to her knowledge.'

The travellers all took drafts of fresh mountain water to cleanse their mouths and throats of the lingering taste of the evil they had felt. Garat had them circle around and brought them back to the direction of travel indicated by Devron and his wolf.

When the shadows of the forest began to deepen, Devron halted the group.

'Wilder. Varellon greet. Wait.'

It was not long before curiosity won out, and the four humans crept forwards to get a glimpse of the wolven. Heleana was surprised at the tableau playing out before them. Varellon had shown no fear or submission back in the cavern, even to the point of bristling up to defend her rider. Yet here she was, laying on her back while a beast twice her size had its jaws on her throat. To add to the scene, Devron knelt before the two beasts with his head on his hands in supplication. The wolven then sat back on its haunches, and Varellon rose to sit on the animal's right, although slightly behind. Devron remained bowed until a deep-throated rumble echoed across the clearing. The noise caused a rustle and flutter to rise in the branches above the trio. Perrin then noticed a myriad of birds perched overhead. Ensconced in the lowest branches, he was surprised to see, were exclusively hunters—owls, kites and hawks. Devron stood and took his place beside his partner.

'Come,' Devron called.

The four warily entered the clearing, wisely keeping their hands well away from their weapons. Each was stunned by the size of the beast before them. Perrin judged that the size and power of the wolven, with its teeth and claws, would probably match the four weapon-for-weapon. Remembering the way Martyn greeted Varellon Perrin strode forth, bowed his head and extended his arms with his wrists exposed. Perrin waited, unsure of his next move, but relying on the teachings of his Grams. *Manners always matter*, was one of her oft-repeated maxims.

Following his lead, Bren and Garat quickly followed suit. After a short pause, Heleana came forwards and presented her wrists beside her husband.

The wolven stood and stepped forward, bringing his snout frighteningly close to Perrin. After a brief sniff, it moved on. Perrin noted that the beast smelled of pine with a hint of crushed new grass. Far from fear, Perrin's immediate sense was of life and growth, a sensation so different to that expected that, although welcome, it was disconcerting in its own way. His musing was interrupted by a squeal from Heleana. The beast had licked her cheek as he turned away from her.

'Wha... wha..?' she gasped.

'Wilder has scent. Make camp. He hunt. Food for all.' Devron said.

Before anyone could ask one of the many questions evident on their faces, the wolven had disappeared. It was amazing that so large a beast could move between heartbeats with nary a leaf or blade of grass disturbed. Twittering and fluttering drew their attention to the branches overhead, where the roosting birds all took flight. Within a snap of the fingers, the party was once again alone in the forest. All three men turned and regarded Heleana.

'Ok, stop gawking and get to it,' Heleana ordered. 'Devron, will we be able to have a fire?'

'Yes, fire gift of the ancients.'

Within short order, the camp had been set to Heleana's liking, and a supply of dead wood had been collected to feed the small cooking fire that had been started. The wolven returned and stalked around the camp, clearly inspecting each member's preparations.

'Perrin, go Wilder.' Devron said. 'Take knife.'

'Ok, Garat, while Perrin is off with our host, take our young Prince and dig a latrine. Make it deep. It would not do to upset any sensibilities at this juncture,' Heleana ordered.

Garat retrieved a sharpened stake from his pack along with a carved scoop, ideal for the job at hand and evidently well-used.

'Come along, Bren. When her ladyship commands, we obey.'

Garat ducked and laughed as a stick swished past his ear.

'That was a little close, my love.'

'You are damned lucky I was feeding the fire and not cutting up these roots.'

When Bren and Garat returned, Heleana, Perrin, and Devron sat around the fire, discussing the best herbs to enhance the vegetable stew starting to bubble away on the campfire. Beside a selection of root vegetables were some leaves, fresh mushrooms, cress, packets of herbs from Perrin, and a pouch of salt. As the discussion grew louder, Garat smiled as the trio all had a view on the correct amount of seasoning to add.

'Where are our companions?' Bren asked.

'Wilder thought it best if he and Varellon enjoyed their dinner out of sight,' Perrin said.

'Darling, I think a little more salt?' Garat suggested.

'This time, I do have a knife to hand. Aren't you living a little dangerously, my love?'

'Ever since I met you, light of my life.'

As he moved to sit on a log that had been pulled close to provide seating, a knife thudded into the wood a hand span from his thigh. He pulled the knife from the wood and offered it hilt first back to his wife. The wry smile on his face and the raised eyebrow on hers clearly indicated that this was an ongoing battle of wits.

'Keep it and trim this meat for cooking,' Heleana said. 'Wilder was kind enough to offer us the choicest cuts of venison for our dinner.'

The group enjoyed a fine camp meal and were just finishing cleaning the campsite when the two canines returned. The pair settled into a relaxed position with the wolven clearly to the fore. Even with his head resting on his paws, Wilder looked impressive and ready to pounce at a moment's notice. He huffed as smoke from the fire drifted his way but did not look unsettled. The flicker of flames was mirrored in his large, clear golden eyes. When Perrin noticed this, he looked deeper and wondered at the depth of understanding and history those eyes had seen.

'I have gained permission from Varellon to speak through her partner.'

The four companions looked at the Dini and realised he was in some kind of trance and linked to the wolven.

'I do not have the throat and mouth to speak your words. The Dini does but does not fully comprehend your language. I can speak directly to you through him. Ask your questions. We break camp before the sun.'

'Garat and I lead the Pathfinders, and Bren is our prince. Who else is being brought into this gathering to help us against the Brocken?' Heleana asked.

'The coming threat to all will need to be turned back by the work of many. It has been discussed and identified that you must work to equalise the strength and power the enemy has and you currently lack. Their weapon is very powerful even if the bows of your hunters have a greater range. Their leaders understand that limitation and devise training and strategies to be most effective against any who come before them in battle. The tinker, Martyn, will introduce you to another option that may go some way towards tipping the balance in your favour.'

Devron held up a hand to forestall any questions and cocked his head in a listening pose.

'It has been noted that the Brocken's occupation and strategies are based on holding an area that is easily defended, and where communication and ease of moving men about aids their influence. This is why we have seen limited incursions beyond the plains. Although they have begun cutting roads through the forests and setting up fortifications in the foothills, these are only within a sun's march of occupied villages and well-used trading routes. It is assumed that as more men and resources are assigned to the occupation, they will increase their sphere of influence and bring more and more of our peoples under their rule. You were fortunate that the warning brought to you by the Earl of Lotan's Rest gave you time to divest your lands of horses and other beasts of burden, limiting the enemy's shock and awe incursion.'

Wilder rose to his impressive height and stalked around the clearing, as if pondering his next instructions.

'We have identified four areas that, as leaders of the resistance, you will be assisted in by all who have a stake in preserving our way of life.

'First, weapons and tactics. It is not the intent of the ancients to destroy the invaders, but to bring them to submission. This can only be done by showing that we outmatch them at every juncture. At this point in time, the Tinker, the twins, R'chal and A'lek, and their blacksmith are refining a weapon that will give you far greater accuracy and range.'

'Second is a chain of command. You will need captains who stand out and will be eagerly followed by your men. Thus, persons such as Prince Bren, Devron, R'chal, and the elves will play major roles.'

'Third, communication. The wolf riders will be able to relay messages across greater distances and much faster than the Brocken could hope to manage.'

'Fourth and finally. Strategies. The Brocken rely on brute force to overcome their opponents and only ever face one battle at a time. We believe that coordinated incursions into their territories, carefully planned and executed through rapid deployment and communication, will stretch their resources to breaking point, allowing the general population to come together in revolt. To that end, the Earl of Lotan's Rest is attempting to reach the leader of the resistance in Sudhemere, someone known only as *The Red*.'

'We regard the efforts that your Pathfinders and others have made to date as vital in halting the invaders' advance, but as you can now see, a much greater opposition will be launched with you, Lady of Sudhem, at the fore.'

The wolven returned to his place alongside Varellon and once again sank to his haunches with his head on his paws.

'Your Ancient Ones seem to be placing great faith in an itinerant tinker and a provincial earl from a distant holding, not to mention backwater twins and a young Prince who, until recently, had no idea of his heritage.' Heleana said.

Perrin watched as Garat, who had been deep in thought was stirred by his wife's statement. He stood and emulated Wilder as he strode about the circle, clearly rehearsing his next words.

'Wilder of the Wolven, you have given us much to consider. Not long ago, Heleana and I could only manage to contain the invaders to the plains. I see now that our success was more based on their limitations and desire to fortify their holdings before continuing their encroachment into our lands. We would welcome the assistance you have laid before us, but we need to know and understand the people you have told us of before we can lead them and trust in their abilities.'

'Garat Omholt, you have always displayed leadership in its most desired form through knowledge, respect for your men, and balanced planning to ensure the greater outcome over risk rather than strength of arm or ruthlessness. As we travel to the village, I will tell of the twins, or at least that which I know, and your good wife can tell that which she knows of them. Rest now. We will leave with the coming of the sun.'

Garat stood before his wife and offered his hand to help her rise. It seemed she was not in the mood to retire and Garat had to lean back heavily to haul his wife to her feet. Perrin nudged his cousin and nodded towards their bed rolls, suggesting retreat as the better part of valour. Devron spoke before Heleana could voice her objection to being sent to bed by a wolf.

'Wilder gone. Sleep. He guard.'

Perrin stirred early, as was his habit. Taking care not to awaken the others, he groped in through the pre-dawn light to the latrine. Upon returning to the camp, he could make out the bulk of the wolven as a black shape against the background of the forest. Even with the sun not yet risen, the forest had its own outlines, shapes and shades.

Perrin stoked the ashes of the campfire, hoping to find a coal he could coax into life. With shaved kindling and bark, he soon had a steady fire going that he fed with the gathered deadwood. He placed a pot to boil, knowing a cup of hot tea would be just the thing to start the sun.

Wilder huffed to gain Perrin's attention, then stood and disappeared into the forest again. Perrin saw what the wolven was indicating. In a pile next to where he had been seated were a variety of mushrooms, some tubers, wild onions, and a selection of eggs. With the liver saved from the previous evening, the group would enjoy a full breakfast before they began their trek for the sun.

Wilder returned just as Perrin and Heleana were inspecting the campsite to ensure that there was as little evidence of their passing as possible. The practice of leaving everything as it was found was not from fear of discovery by the Brocken, but was usual for Pathfinders and those of the forests to leave any campsite in the same condition as it was discovered. It showed respect to and an understanding of the forest and those they shared it with.

'Wilder say start. Rain coming,' Devron said.

As they donned their packs, Perrin noticed the dullness of the sun and the clouds gathering overhead.

Wilder led off with the others in single file behind him. Heleana, Bren and Perrin followed the wolven with Devron atop his wolf, followed by Garat at the rear Perrin understood his brother's choice, from that position he could keep all in his charge in sight. Even assured there were no enemies near, it was his practice to put caution before chance. Communication was difficult while wending their way around the trunks of trees and through brush thickets, but that did not stop Heleana from demanding answers to her many questions. Each time she asked for information, Devron would reply that all would be answered when the time was right.

The pace quickened as they worked their way down from the mountains. The wolven moved fluidly, as large a beast as he was Perrin noted he took some effort to protect the forest from his bulk. They were moving almost at a trot when the rain came shortly after mid-sun. They had not stopped at all since setting out, but the going had been relatively good downhill, and as long as they remembered the rules of hunting, they avoided the roots and snags that could cause a fall.

Wilder kept up the pace, and no one complained about the drenching they were getting as the wolven's luxurious coat became waterlogged and bedraggled. None in the party would be the first to complain, but it was becoming almost unbearable when the beast led them into a clearing at the base of a tor rising up through the forest. Heleana was about to front the wolven about their predicament when her husband pointed out the mouth of a cave at the base of the tor.

'No fear. Safe enter,' Devron said.

Gratefully, the party gathered just within the mouth of the cave and waited until Garat could light a small oil lantern he carried in his pack. Garat led them inside as the lantern folded back the darkness before them. Perrin noted that the cave would easily accommodate them all although his brother and himself would have to take care when standing as the ceiling was to low to stand fully upright. Devron walked over to the others and suggested they face the cave wall. Heleana took her time in complying and was showered in water droplets as the two canines shook out their coats.

'Varellon sorry. Instinct,' Devron said.

Garat moved around the cave and found a circle of stones on the sandy floor blackened by fire. Someone had used the cave previously and, fortunately for their group, followed the code of the mountains and brought in a good supply of firewood for the next occupants. With a fire started and the warmth and light filling the cave, Heleana set about organising the camp. The packs were piled near the fire, not too close but close enough to dry out, and the adventurers took turns to change from their wet forest garb into their spare clothing.

'As that storm is settling in, I assume we are here for the night?' Garat asked.

When the question was answered in the affirmative, Heleana handed Garat a comb and sat before him so he could attack the knots within her hair.

'Now would be a good time to tell us of these people who are gathering. There is no need to hunt. We will survive on travel rations tonight.'

'My Lady of Sudhem, I will be most pleased to tell you what I know of the twins, and you will be able to fill in the story with what you know of them,' Devron said. The Dini again had the look in his eyes that indicated the trance-like bond with the wolven.

CHAPTER TWELVE
Hunter

Druk diamond, white and pure, no dedication more secure.

THE MIASMA IN THE CAVE was redolent with the odours of wet wool, wood smoke, unwashed bodies, and damp canine. The smell was made bearable by the underlying sweet whiff of a wild, flower-rich meadow, the same essence each of them had noted when introduced to the wolven. Perrin and Bren made a drying rack from sticks and branches while Garat attended to the important job of combing out his wife's hair. The smoke rising above the fire disappeared through a fissure in the cave's roof, and the storm continued to rage outside.

With the camp in order, they made themselves comfortable and began to care for their weapons. Garat and Perrin's yew bow staves needed to be dried and then waxed to avoid being affected by the proximity to the fire. Bren and Heleana inspected their axe heads for any sign of rust. They cleaned and oiled the heads but refrained from sharpening the cutting edge in deference to their companions. Once all metal surfaces were cared for and handles oiled, waxed, or resined, the weapons were stacked in the furthest corner of the cave, and the party settled down to a meal of dried venison, dried fruit, hard biscuits, and cups of tea.

Heleana and the men sat across the fire from the two beasts. Both rested their heads on their front paws, looking almost somnolent, although an ear would flicker or a tail waver every now and again. Devron leaned against his mate, clearly entranced.

'We of the ancients have been observing many who may be instrumental in leading against the invaders. She who is the sum of all knowledge, tasked me and others to monitor individuals who could act against the coming threat. Some of those I have mentioned.

'The twins, R'chal and A'lek were raised in the forests. Their line has always been closely linked to those of us who marshal the growth and strength of the links between all in the wild. They adhere most closely to the covenants guiding those who share our world's bounty. I will now tell of what I know of these siblings.

'I have many sources that I use to observe and gather information without being noticed. The raptors and owls are keen-eyed and attentive when watching from afar, while rodents and weasels can live close by to gain an understanding of any subject. Individually, each is limited in focus and capacity. To appreciate an overall picture, many views are combined, and a concise opinion is revealed.'

Heleana found it difficult to reconcile that the words were coming from Devron, yet the timbre of his voice and use of current language and words were those of the largest wolf she had ever seen.

'How do you combine all those individual views. It must take great patience and time to gather together your spies?' Heleana asked.

'That, my Lady of Sudhem, is a component of our existence that you may find hard to understand. The greater trees provide the receptacle in which the knowledge is placed and compiled. It does take some time for the oaks, ash, and elms to impart a cohesive story, but the strong links that run through our world are much like the roots of those trees. Every being in our lands has their place, and the largest and strongest of us protect the natural order. It is the knowledge and wisdom of the long-lived that allows me to think in the languages of the peoples. It is also the shared instincts of those who eat meat that links us.'

'Would you be able to talk through any of us?' Perrin asked.

'Only at great need. It gets more difficult to communicate with one who is removed from existence within the natural order. Even though you share a close bond with the forest, Perrin Omholt, you rely heavily on life within a village, and the stronger those links are, the weaker your connection with the natural order becomes. This is in no way disapproval but rather the plan of the ancients when raising up the three races.'

'Your theories on our link to the natural order are most thought provoking,' Garat said. 'It may take me some time to accept and understand those. I am still in awe that I am communicating with a beast out of myth. Perhaps we can put aside our evolution for a time and hear what you have gleaned about these siblings you are taking us to meet.'

'To tell of R'chal and A'lek, I view them from the many angles as seen by the creatures of the forests. Please forgive me if the story seems disjointed in any way. I was tasked with observing the twins from the time they reached maturity. She, who is all knowing, has tasked each of the ancients to attend and watch those deemed invaluable in the times to come. R'chal and her father were often together in the forests and are closest to the old ways.'

Wilder seemed to relax and closed his eyes with a sigh. Heleana found it reminiscent of her tutor when Aunt Winifred was imparting the histories.

R'chal huddled in the hunting blind, predawn chill seeping through her leathers. She was unwilling to move because any sound she made would echo through the dark, silent forest. She shed a tear, missing the bulk and warmth that would normally signal the presence of her father. This sun's hunt was more to keep to his routine than the need to replenish stores or for meat and hides to trade in the village. Perched in the branches of an old oak that overlooked a well-used game trail, the blind was one of many she and her father had built over the turns.

When all one can do is wait, the mind tends to wander, and the sun's intruding thoughts were no different to the many previous suns.

What had happened to mother and father on their trading trip to the plains? How long could she keep A'lek from charging off to find the answer?

This was a real quandary as it would usually be her that would never consider the consequences and just charge ahead. She just hoped that A'lek was currently foraging for the fungi, herbs, and medicinal plants their mother was famous for throughout the countryside.

How could twins be so different?

R'chal had always shadowed her father and, after nineteen full turns, had come to best him with bow and arrow. He deferred to her for the first shot, claiming her gentle hands caressed the bowstring on release, giving her greater accuracy. He was always ready for the kill shot if she was off target, but rarely was it needed. A'lek was studious, learning everything from their mother about the balance needed to maintain the forest. They even made a point of planting trees and spreading seeds for every animal R'chal and her father brought home from the hunt.

A rustling in the branches and the first bird calls signalled the awakening of the woods, and R'chal prepared her gear as the light strengthened. She selected two of her meticulously made arrows—straight, true, with wickedly sharp heads, and fletched with the tail feathers of a red hawk. These arrows could be used for a perfect kill shot over 200 paces.

She silently brought out a flask containing the musk scent of the last buck she had taken from her pack. Although the process of squeezing this essence from the buck's glands was one of her least preferred jobs, her father had proven time and time again how effective it was in the hunt. She sprinkled the musk over a swatch of dried grass and lowered it from her perch with a leather thong. The gentle morning breeze would disperse the scent, overlaying the smells of the mulch and new growth that indicated a healthy forest. Finally, she took a pair of antlers down from a peg in the trunk of the oak tree and set to sawing them together, making the noise of a buck rubbing their rack against a tree marking territory.

The noise of the antlers and scent of the musk would not fail to bring any male in the area to investigate whether he needed to maintain his dominance over the surrounding forest or if another Buck was challenging for the right to his domain.

Now all there is to do is concentrate and wait.

The sun rose fully, and R'chal repeated the sound with the antlers a number of times before detecting noise and movement downwind. She recognised the dominant buck when he finally revealed himself, and was pleased to see a trio of does timidly following his lead, one obviously heavy with young. Although she had promised herself, she would one sun take this magnificent animal, it would not be until he was older and deposed as herd-boss by a younger, stronger buck. The fact that he was investigating R'chal's lures meant that there were other solitary bucks around that may make a play for his harem. This was a good sign for this sun's hunt.

The buck grunted a warning and made short dashes towards R'chal's blind but appeared confused when no challenge was forthcoming. Finally, he squirted his own scent around the base of the oak and trotted off along the trail, dutifully followed by his does. R'chal smelled the acrid ammonia and was pleased that the fresh scent would strengthen the attraction for any bachelor buck prepared to fight for the right to his herd.

Hunting was a game of patience and R'chal had learnt early how to sit quietly and motionlessly for long periods. She slowly went through the exercises her father had taught her to keep her muscles from seizing at the worst time. R'chal flexed her legs, arms, and back with small movements, avoiding noise. She was ready when a low grunt heralded the arrival of a solitary buck. Through the dappled light, she watched the newcomer hesitate to completely reveal himself. This animal was large with an impressive rack of ten points, but R'chal noticed he did not quite flow through the forest. Instead, he moved with a stuttering step. He had been injured at some stage, but the need to breed in this season overpowered any handicap he suffered. The buck grunted again at the fresh scent he caught in his soft, moist muzzle, and R'chal let him come closer to investigate her lure.

She decided to take the great buck, as his injury would probably see him severely wounded if he fought.

Drawing her bow, she looked over the animal as it moved broadside to her position. The shot could not be easier. Upon sighting her arrow, R'chal noticed a strange dark patch of hide on the buck's rump buck. This was the injury that left him hobbling, but what would have caused it?

The bow twanged, and the arrow flew true, hitting just behind the shoulder blade. The buck staggered and then bounded towards the densest part of the woods, hoping to escape. R'chal knew the shot was a kill as the arrowhead would cut through more blood vessels, muscle and sinew with every move the buck made. She collected her pack and climbed down from her perch to follow and ensure the beast suffered as little as possible.

Bright blood dotted the foliage as she forced her way through the increasingly thick undergrowth. The buck would not be able to go much further. She wriggled her way through holly and blackberry, leaving her own splashes of blood on the wicked thorns until she broke out into a relative clearing under the spread of another of the huge oaks that dominated the forest. The buck lay panting at the base of the tree, and

R'chal stood at a distance as it drew its last breath. Bubbles of blood appeared, mixing with the saliva from the animal's lips and snout. The deer went limp with a clearly audible sigh as bright arterial blood flowed free.

R'chal doffed her pack and was preparing to dress her kill when a deep rumbling growl emanated from across the small clearing. In the stippled shade, R'chal could just make out the form of a wolf, but to her astonishment, it was bigger than any other wolf she had seen. She could not be sure due to the shadows masking its form, but she could see its head was at least at eye level with her own. The grey of its fur was offset with a red ruff running down its spine, and R'chal guessed the bush of its tail would have the same tinge. With her pack and bow at her feet, she determined that retreat would be the best choice in the encounter. As she bent to retrieve her things, a deeper growl echoed, and she would later swear to A'lek that she clearly heard the word 'Go!'

'This was the first time I had allowed R'chal to see me,' Wilder explained.

Dragging her pack and bow, R'chal wormed her way back into the thicket, once again suffering the pain of the grabbing, stinging thorns. R'chal forced herself to away, constantly alert for any sound indicating the beast was about to rush to the attack. The further she made her way through the thicket, the surer she felt the huge wolf would satisfy itself with her fresh kill. Hunters usually gave a wide berth to the packs of wolves that shared the forests, but R'chal had an inkling that this was a lone beast, and it was bigger than any she had ever heard about.

With the sun indicating late morning, R'chal realised she had little choice in the matter and decided to head home and check in on her fractious sibling.

As she started the familiar trek home, her thoughts wandered again to her missing parents. At first, their delayed arrival home was easily explained, as they had no need to rush. R'chal and A'lek could care for the chores and animals on the small farm they had cut out of the deep forest. Reports of the invasion took the siblings by surprise because they did not learn about it until they needed to travel the two suns to the village to trade. The most horrifying tales told of the capture of Sudhemere and the atrocities inflicted on its citizens. Even if only half the stories the twins heard were true, the invading soldiers sounded merciless and cruel.

As she reached the stream that flowed towards the small vale her family had tamed and turned into a completely self-sufficient holding, R'chal suddenly wondered about the wolf she had encountered. Why did she not fear it? Why did she feel no maliciousness from its presence in the forest? The largest wolf she had ever seen gave her a feeling of serenity and completeness. Having spent her life farming and hunting deep in the forests, this was another anomaly to ponder. Perhaps A'lek would have an insight.'

R'chal stood on the brink of a small babbling waterfall and looked down on the vale that held their home. In the distance, she saw her sibling working among the drying racks, fussing about with the drying meat and herbs and preparing them for trade in the village. Now that the season of birth was upon them, they could again travel the two suns to the village of the Salient Buck. There, they would replenish the stores they had used during the long moon and, more importantly, get the latest news on the occupation and, if possible, their parents.

R'chal cupped her hands around her mouth and called a high, 'Kooeeeee.'

A'lek turned and waved both hands overhead in their signal of safety. If A'lek had only raised one arm, R'chal would have melted back into the forest. They had taken the precaution of creating the signal when they had heard of the atrocities enacted on farmsteads and isolated holdings by the invading soldiers. R'chal bounded down the slope alongside the stream and began to lope along the well-used path towards home.

A'lek had clearly been busy. A pile of bales and crates waited to be loaded on their two-wheeled cart. Alongside bundles of herbs and medicinals were sacks of dried venison, and chickens and ducks were housed in latticed crates. The well-hung and aged haunch of a recent kill would top the load as the innkeeper of the Salient Buck would trade a few suns of room and board for the prized meat.

'I thought we would have a fresh beast to round out the load,' A'lek remarked.

'I was beaten to my kill by a wolf.'

'I haven't heard any wolves of late. You sure it wasn't a fox?'

R'chal grinned at the usual byplay that underlined their relationship. Each took great delight in bringing the other down a peg or two at every opportunity.

'No, A'lek. This was no ordinary wolf. It was solitary and the largest I have ever seen or heard about, and before you belittle my decision to retreat, there was something even stranger about it.'

'What? Did it have two heads?'

'No smart-alek, this is something I have been wrestling with all the way home. It growled at me, but I swear it spoke to me. I clearly heard it tell me to Go.*'*

'Ok, now I know we have to go to the village. You are clearly suffering from cabin fever. You do realise wolves don't talk?'

'Well, one word may not be a conversation, but it made more sense than some of the heart-to-hearts we have had lately. Fortunately, I agree with you. The sooner we leave, the better. Let's hitch the cart and get going.'

A'lek looked askance at R'chal with concern for her and her adventure. Her words etched across her features showed an anxiousness with what had happened out in the forest. With a small shiver, A'lek turned and gathered the harness.

'Why don't you get Bluebell from the yard. We can take her with us and turn her out with Bartimaeus's bull. If we are lucky, we can

get another calf out of the old girl,' A'lek said. 'I have already penned the goats in the barn with plenty of feed and water, and the remaining chickens and ducks will be fine for a seven sun or so. Also, if I'm not mistaken, it will be your turn to clean out the barn this time.'

'If I didn't know your mother and father were married, you would certainly fit the bill.'

With each twin chuckling at the comeback and without needing further discussion, they confidently went about tasks they had repeated many times over the turns. In short order, the pair were ready to depart. With only the need to prepare their own packs and collect travel rations, they would manage near half a sun's travel before nightfall.

R'CHAL AND A'LEK SPENT the second night of their trip in a well-used and supplied way station. Their family had initially set up a lean-to and small corral with a supply of firewood next to a small stream. Over the turns, other travellers had added various features, such as a water barrel and crude furniture, making the stop almost civilised. Arriving in the mid-afternoon, the twins decided to stop the night rather than travel to the village and get in after dark. If they left with the first glow of dawn, they would arrive just in time for breakfast at the tavern.

'I know that look, R'chal. What's going on in that head of yours? You haven't even bothered to set out any snares or tripwires around the camp. Not even last night.'

'You're right, I have been mulling over something. Ever since coming face-to-face with that wolf, I have felt a strange serenity within the forest. Right now, I have a queer feeling that we are being protected. More worrying though is the strong belief we are being watched.'

'We're half a morning's travel from any settlement, and the only thing to watch us would be the trees.'

'Or, one mother of a big wolf,' said R'chal.

A'lek remained silent after that and fussed around the camp preparing the evening meal. R'chal wandered the edges of the clearing, looking deeply into the surrounding forest. As the afternoon deepened to twilight, the twins settled around the campfire with a pot of tea after seeing to the animals in their care. Like most farmers, they lived by the rising and falling of the sun. On full dark, they retired to their swags.

The travellers prepared to resume their trek before even the ducks and chickens had stirred. The annoyed squawks and angry clucking of the birds amused the siblings. It was clear to R'chal that her twin was impatient to get underway and reach the village as soon as possible.

'I am sure Quinn will be too busy to notice your arrival,' R'chal said.

'Teasing does not become you, wolf girl.'

'Good comeback. Just check that rear lashing while I clean up the camp. Dad would have our hides if it was not ready for the next traveller.'

The sombre thought had the duo completing their tasks and heading down the track in short order. The creaking of the cartwheels and slap of the harness were the first sounds in the slowly awakening forest until a ripple of disturbance became apparent ahead. Rustling leaves and birds taking sudden flight indicated something approaching along the path.

'A'lek, secure the cart and stay behind me.'

R'chal strung her bow and drew an arrow from her quiver, holding it loosely but ready to nock and draw. The pair waited, ready for anything in these uncertain times. Pounding footfalls soon indicated someone was running at pace towards them. Not until they spied a shock of almost white hair on a fast-moving youngster did they relax.

Kjieran, Quinn's younger brother, was so intent on his errand that he nearly ran into R'chal as he rounded a bend in the path. Sliding to a halt, it took a moment for the lad to realise who had blocked his way. Then, his searching gaze locked on the cart.

'A'lek, Quinn says come quick. Your mother. In the tavern. The Brocken hurt her bad,' Kjieran squeaked out the words between rasping breaths and tears of relief at finding the twins so soon.

R'chal helped the boy to sit and passed over her waterskin. She noted he had run to fetch them without any of the usual requirements for such an effort. As he took a great gulp of water, R'chal eased the skin from his grasp.

'Slowly, Kjieran, steady now. Catch your breath and tell us what happened.'

'I don't know. The Lady Hell came to the village last night. She had your mam in a cart. She is hurt real bad. Quinn sent me. I know the way, so I left before the sun to come get you.'

A'lek knelt before the boy.

'Kjieran, you have done well. We have to go. You rest here and catch your breath. Can you bring in the cart for us?'

Kjieran looked up at A'lek and nodded between deep breaths and slowly diminishing sobs. R'chal returned the waterskin to the boy. She stood and looked at her twin, and without the need for words, the duo took off at a steady, loping run.

CHAPTER THIRTEEN
Wilder

Bazu topaz blue for the freed, diligence others cede.

'YOU PAINT A VIVID PICTURE. Your intelligence gathering is remarkable,' Heleana said.

'Each animal and bird shares its own observations, even the beasts of burden and the domestic breeds. Over many suns, the singular thoughts of each were shared, and a full portrayal of the twins was compiled by the keepers of knowledge. There was a time when the great trees would convene and share their news. Now it is up to those like myself to gather all the threads together,' Wilder explained.

'Perhaps we could pause at this juncture. I, for one, need a moment, and the rain has abated somewhat. I will be back shortly,' Garat said.

'Hold up, Garat. I could do with some relief, too,' Bren said.

Perrin had been engrossed in Devron's recital of Wilder's story. When Garat stood, he looked over at Heleana and saw that her husband had styled her hair in a series of fine braids that enhanced her look as a fierce warrior. He wondered at the resilience of one who had gone through so much and still maintained the aura of a well-bred lady.

Garat returned to his seat, and his wife settled herself comfortably resting, her arm across his lap and her head against his chest.

'I suggest that you, my lady, take up the story of the twins now,' Devron said.

The Dini shook himself and looked around the cavern as though he did not know how he came to be there. Varellon nudged him with her muzzle, and her rider calmed down and rested his head against her flank. Heleana moved away from her husband so that she could sit upright to tell what she knew of the twins.

My squad and I were patrolling the edges of the plains to discover any incursions or advancement of the Brocken when one of my scouts reported that a farmstead had been razed by a group of Brocken deserters and raiders. Many of the worst atrocities committed by the Brocken are by small groups of these deserters or lesser barons seeking to enhance their wealth by sending out marauders to pillage farms and small communities. One such band had fallen on a well-established farm, four suns travel from the village of the Salient Buck and at least a six sun march from Sudhemere. One of the farthest attacks we had seen so far from the safety of their occupation of Sudhemere.'

Heleana repositioned herself and sat up with her back against the cave wall. The memories obviously having a sobering effect and deserving a more reverential attitude.

'When we arrived at the farm, we were greeted by the smouldering ruins of the house and the grisly sight of the farmer and his son, possibly only ten turns of age. Their bodies were spreadeagled along a fence rail and had clearly been used as target practice for a variety of weapons. Their deaths, although barbaric, would be more merciful than the treatment his wife and daughter were to suffer. We knew of the women because of the garments strewn about the stoop.

'Dresses of similar fabric but differing sizes were discarded as the women were stolen.

RESISTANCE

'It did not take us long to track the raiders, and we found the mother and daughter in a copse where they had spent the night being badly abused by their captors. The girl, only slightly older than her brother, did not have the strength to fight her abusers and had succumbed following the repeated misuse. Her mother, on the other hand, showed wounds indicating that she fought against every attack and eventually suffered the same fate as her husband and son.

'I left three of my men to ensure the family was reunited and interred together.'

Heleana's head drooped and her eyes brimmed with tears at the memory. Garat slipped down beside her and held her against his chest until she could continue. The Lady Hell was fearsome in the face of the enemy yet in her husband's arms she could let her real emotions to the fore.

'At that point, my men vowed to eradicate this group from our homeland and leave no evidence pertaining to their disappearance. We marched at the double through the night to make up the time they had ahead of us. At the sun's rising, we stopped for a cold camp and sent our scouts out to ensure we had not lost contact with their trail. My men were impatient to catch these thugs, so we resumed our march at a steady pace.

'The scout came in about mid-morning. He reported the raiders, approximately fifteen strong, had waylaid a trader's wagon and were torturing the trader and his woman. There was no complaint when I ordered a forced march at double time. From concealment, I saw the wagon had lost a wheel, which had allowed the raiders to surround it and attack. I counted three with serious wounds, indicating the traders had tried to fight them off. The man was now clearly riddled with flatbow bolts, and the woman was being made to suffer the same fate as the farmer's wife.

'I had six Pathfinders, each a bowman, and surprise to utilise in my attack. After setting the targets for my men, I stood to the fore and raised *my axe. It had the desired effect. The raiders each rushed for weapons except two, who were too engrossed with their turn at the woman. My archers took out their initial targets and two more as we charged the remainder. The flatbows that had been used to kill the trader had been left uncocked, and we only faced badly aimed sporadic bolts as we swept through with sword and axe.*

'My bardiche served its purposes, first instilling fear in the enemy and then tasting their blood. Killing is never easy, but in this instance, my men and I had no qualms. The only raiders left alive were the three injured by the trader.

'The woman was alive but barely able to speak through swollen lips and cracked teeth. She had not allowed herself to be used without a fight and paid the price. Her only words were 'The Buck'.

'We made a pyre of the wagon and the draught horse that had been killed in the raider's attack and threw the bodies of the raiders upon it, dead or alive. The wagon had held two barrels of lamp oil, which created a hot flame to purge our land of these vile brigands. I ordered two litters made, and we took the trader and his woman and started for the village. We buried the trader under an oak when we entered the foothills and rushed to do what we could for the woman, but she died before we reached the village.'

THE SUN GLINTING THROUGH the leaves reflected off a slight mist, and the distinctive smell of smoke permeated the air. R'chal noticed A'lek's back straighten, and the already punishing pace quickened. Rarely did her sibling outpace her, but A'lek steadily drew ahead as they raced towards their destination.

The village of the Salient Buck was built on the high side of a bridge that spanned a fast-flowing mountain stream. A large, cleared meadow on the low side served as common grazing land and was surrounded by a mixture of woven twig, and post and rail fencing. The two-storied tavern dominated the square from where various houses and outbuildings had started to spread. R'chal noticed that A'lek's eyes were firmly fixed on the smithy, set slightly apart, hoping for a glimpse of the smith's daughter.

Her own attention was fixed firmly upon the group of people milling about the stoop of the tavern. As the pair emerged from the shade of the forest fringe, one of the villagers in the group noticed them and turned to point in their direction. As the twins approached, the small crowd parted to allow a woman to come to the fore. She was clearly a woman of authority with a physique and demeanour to match. She held out her hand in the universal signal to halt. With the backing of two masked green-clad attendants and the press of villagers behind them, the siblings had little choice but to stop and catch their breath.

'A'LEK, R'CHAL, I AM Heleana of Sudhem. I am very sorry, but we were too late.'

The realisation of my words took a little time to filter through their burning lungs and the pounding blood in their temples. The siblings dropped their packs and, with groans of pain, seemed to meld together as they embraced the loss of hope and impact of grief.

'Come, sit.'

I took each by the hand and led them to the steps of the tavern. From someone in the growing throng, mugs of watered wine were offered and accepted. The twins were no strangers to the harshness of life lived in isolation, although they had hoped their parents would return. The sudden understanding that only the death of their father would result in their mother suffering harm from the invaders deflated the pair, and sobs of grief wracked their bodies.

As the Lady of Sudhem, I had witnessed similar sights all too often since the Brocken's invasion. I quietly instructed my attendants to disperse the villagers and give the pair a chance to recover somewhat from their shock. Understanding the stoicism of our people, I waited patiently until the pair took long draughts from their mugs and turned tear-stained faces towards me.

'Your mother is being well cared for. The tavern keeper's wife and the smith's daughter are cleaning and wrapping her. She was obviously well respected, as many have come forward to offer their assistance. The smith's daughter was most insistent that she direct the preparations.'

'We must go to her,' A'lek said.

They stood and turned towards the tavern door just as it opened and Quinn's leather-clad figure emerged from the darkened interior. With head downcast, it took her a moment to realise who stood before her. With an uncharacteristic squeal that was equal parts delight, anguish and concern, she rushed into A'lek's embrace.

'Oh A'lek I am so sorry. Your mam, she was so dignified and wise. She fought them. She fought hard but A'lek, what they did to her. A'lek the bastards hurt her, hurt her bad.'

With Quinn's words, the last vestige of hope that this was all some horrible mistake fled the twins' thoughts. Quinn reached for R'chal's hand and drew her into the embrace. The three of them shed tears, as only the closest of friends can over the loss of one truly loved. Quinn's leather skull cap only just reached the twins' shoulders, and the pair looked at each other, seemingly afraid to ask the next question. R'chal finally drew in a deep breath and turned Quinn towards her.

'Quinn, did the Brocken...did they violate her?'

'Oh R'chal, you know she would have fought them alongside your father.'

At that point, I stepped forwards and gently separated the trio.

'Perhaps it is time to see your mother.'

I followed as Quinn took A'lek's hand and led them into the tavern and down into the cellars. She paused outside a small cool room a common feature in provincial inns often used to store vegetables over the long moon. Quinn drew aside the curtain and gestured for the pair to enter. The bare plank walls and two barrels of apples were the only features apart from the body laid out on a trestle.

I did not wish to intrude on the families grief but understanding the power of the emotion I stood ready to assist. Their mother was bound from feet to shoulders in white linen with an ornately embroidered shroud covering her head. R'chal looked at the shroud and realised someone's wedding shawl had been donated for its current purpose. The twins slowly moved down each side of the trestle and stood looking down at the woman who had been such a solid foundation in their lives. With no words spoken, the twins each moved to lift the shroud and take a last look at the face of their mother. Quinn's sudden whimper gave them pause.

'Oh, A'lek, don't. Don't look, please just remember her as she was.'

R'chal drew back the shroud and gasped. Her mother was no longer recognisable. Her beautiful auburn hair had been so severely hacked off with a knife that, in places, they had taken the scalp with it, leaving angry red gashes. Her eyes were blackened and nose broken. Split lips, slightly parted, did not hide her lost and broken teeth.

Just as it was for me I was sure R'chal would never remember gently replacing the shroud but she would forever remember the promise she made right then. The Brocken would pay dearly for their sadism and depravity.

Quinn's sobs eventually broke the trance the twins had fallen into. Each had been remembering their mother as she was and vowing vengeance on those who had taken her away. They backed out of the room and, with reverence, drew the curtain closed. Quinn once again took A'lek's hand and led us back up the stairs and into the common room, where I had ordered a table set and spread with bread, cheeses and fruits.

'Come and sit with me.'

The twins had little understanding of the forms required in the presence of noble folk, so just nodded and sat in the seats indicated. I sat with my back against the wall, facing the main entrance. R'chal's eyes wandered about the room eventually noticing the covered, oddly shaped object leaning against the wall.

'You as well blacksmith. You obviously were very close to the poor woman. Eat, and I will tell you how we came upon your parents.

The Pathfinders have been keeping an eye on the increasing incursions of the Brocken. My band and I were sweeping the lowlands, knowing that small bands of soldiers have been looting farms and settlements. We were tracking a patrol that had razed a small farm and butchered the family that lived there.'

I paused and indicated that the trio should eat something.

'My scout went forward to investigate and returned to report that the soldiers had waylaid some travellers and were toying with a woman while tormenting her companion, who was clearly injured. There were fifteen of them, but three appeared to be badly wounded. I instructed my band to spread out and leave no witnesses. We took them by surprise, there was to be no-one to tell of their fate.'

Heleana paused to let the implication pierce their grief.

'Your mother was still alive when we got to her, but I am sorry to say your father had already succumbed to his injuries. We carried them both for two suns until we reached the foothills and buried your father at the base of an oak that looks towards the rising sun. Your mother was fading and only said, "The Buck." We came here as fast as we could, giving her as much care as we were able. I am sorry, we were too late.'

Of the three, Quinn was the most used to dealing with the wealthy and worthy, so she was the first to speak.

'Lady Heleana, we thank you for returning our loved one to us. Please accept our gratitude. If ever we can repay your kindness, please do not hesitate to ask.'

With that, I retrieved my weapons and pack, bowed to the still-seated trio and strode to the tavern door. As I placed my hand on the doorknob I turned, they remained in their seats, slowly chewing on *the food before them with little or no desire to eat but using the time to gather their thoughts and strength.*

The Dini resumed his faraway look.

'Thank you, Lady Heleana, I will again take on the telling from here,' Devron said.

'I must commend this rider. It is an intimate bond he shares with his partner, and allowing me to intrude would have been a difficult decision.'

It was strange for the group to hear Devron talking about himself in that manner. Each looked to the others and silently agreed that strange was becoming mundane. Devron continued the wolven's story.

'We will take her home. She would want to be there,' A'lek said.

R'chal and Quinn only nodded understanding A'lek's close bond with the natural order of things taught at the knee of the twin's beloved mother. They rose to begin the sorrowful task of returning their mother to the home she had created deep in the forest. As they left the tavern, they saw Kjieran holding the harness of their cart. The cart had been unpacked, and their cow replaced with Quinn's mule. The villagers had dispersed their goods to where they were usually sent and had filled the wagon bed with layers of fern and early season wildflowers. Many of the villagers stood some distance away, giving the twins space but also strength from knowing how much their mother was loved. Four of the women of the village, dressed in their best, filed into the tavern and returned bearing the body of the highly respected practitioner, healer and midwife.

Upon beginning the homeward journey, the twins were glad to fall into the ingrained practices they each had been schooled in by their father. It served to distract their thoughts, and it seemed only right to honour his memory. The quiet clop of the mule and creak of the lightly loaded cart were small sounds in the forest, but it seemed to R'chal that there were many more bird calls and animal signs than she would normally notice.

They cold camped that night, having discovered well-stocked hampers of food supplied by their friends. In the morning, the smell of the fresh ferns and flowers permeated the camp, which was markedly different from the usually pungent odour of a cold campfire. An early start without needing to hunt or cook would have them reaching home by mid-morning the following sun. As the sun passed overhead, the smells and colours of the forest gave them comfort, even as R'chal pondered the increase in animal and bird life.

As the pair neared the last bend in the trail before their vale home would come into sight, R'chal suddenly chilled as a feeling of foreboding overcame her. Putting out her arm, she halted A'lek, who was leading the mule, and unlimbered and strung her bow. She retreated into the underbrush alongside the trail and silently moved at an oblique angle to open up her view of the barnyard while staying completely hidden. What she saw shocked and surprised her.

Smoke rose from their chimney. Small, pale puffs gathered and floated on the almost still air until an errant gust dissipated them. Almost matching the chimney puff for puff was the stranger lounging on their stoop with his sandalled feet propped up on an upturned wooden bucket, enjoying his pipe. Even more surprising than the stranger were the birds that flittered about the large oak that dominated the yard and shadowed the cabin during the season of the sun. Garlands of flowers twisted about with vines hung from the lowest branches of the great tree.

'Come forth, hunter. You have no need to fear me.'

R'chal nocked an arrow before she stepped from her hide. It was never wise to believe the first words out of a stranger's mouth.

'I am simply an acquaintance of your mother and have come to pay respects, as have all our friends here,' he gestured towards the tree.

At those words, R'chal noticed the mounds of freshly dug earth at the base of the tree on the side that greeted the sun for most of a full turn. Gentle huffing and the creak of the cart indicated A'lek's approach.

'Well, if you haven't shot anyone by now, I assume we have a visitor rather than raiders.'

'Well met, apprentice. My name is Martyn. I am a traveller and friend to all who practice the healing arts.'

The stranger was dressed in tight rawhide leggings and a dark over-garment that seemed to share the requirement of a robe by sun and a blanket at night. He just topped the twins' height, and his bald pate was surrounded by a thatch of unruly greying hair.

'No time like the present, I think you will find everything to your liking,' Martyn said.

A'lek and R'chal stood looking down into the grave that had been dug deep and well. It was just as they would have prepared. R'chal turned towards Martyn.

'Don't look at me. It was all his doing.'

Martyn pointed at the small waterfall that marked the boundary of their vale. Sitting upright but barely visible against the backdrop of foliage and shadows was the large wolf R'chal had stumbled across on her last hunt. R'chal grasped A'lek's shoulder and turned A'lek towards the beast. Not knowing its intention until it bowed its head to the duo and appeared to melt into the forest.

'Your mother and father were well loved throughout the woods. They only acted according to the needs of the forest, and their reputation was carried far and wide. The beast who just blessed you is of the Wolven, one of the ancient races and very rarely seen. Now let us see to the needs of your mother and lay her to rest.'

After the interment, Martyn withdrew into the cabin with the remaining hampers. He had fetched them from the cart after unhitching the mule and turning it loose into the corral. He left the siblings to stand together over their mother's burial site. Upon dusk, the cabin door opened, and the twins entered to the enticing odour of a stew gently bubbling away on the hearth and freshly baked bread.

'By the looks on your faces, you would appreciate a hearty meal. Luckily, I have a variety of skills that come in handy at times.'

Martyn was ensconced on their father's chair with his feet stretched towards the warmth of the fire. Even as he drew upon a mug of ale from their mother's latest brewing, they could feel no malice either towards him or from him.

'Eat, eat. And while you do, I will tell you a tale.'

They were amused by the outlandish mannerisms of this strange fellow who had done much to alleviate their grief. Hunger suddenly had both their stomachs rumbling.

'Good, now load up those plates.'

He sat back and tamped a full bowl into his pipe while waiting for them to sate their hunger. He was pleased when A'lek rose and topped up both plates for seconds. When the twins sat back, obviously replete, Martyn spoke.

'The beast you observed earlier is of the Wolven, one of the ancient races. His name is too hard to pronounce, so I call him Wilder. He has been watching you for some time as your destinies are intricately woven into the future of Tol. A'lek, if you would be so kind as to get the door, he would like to come in and be formally introduced.'

The twins looked up from their now empty plates and, in unison, turned to the door. A'lek slowly stood, approached the portal, raised the locking bar from its bracket, and cautiously eased the door open. Few in the forests were taller than the twins. The surprise A'lek got when he found himself looking directly into the honey-brown eyes of a seated wolf overrode some of the immediate flash of terror that had both twins reaching out for any weapon near at hand. Almost instantaneously, feelings of calm and goodness overrode their natural instinct.

'Be at ease. You have nothing to fear. Consider your surroundings. Your beasts and birds are quiet and calm. Wilder assured them that *they are under his protection and no harm will befall them. It took some time and effort to calm the chickens and ducks as they tend to be flighty and have very limited attention,' Martyn said.*

'Hunter, I ask permission to enter.'

R'chal stared at the apparition filling the doorway, and her mouth dropped when she realised the wolf had spoken to her. It was the twig that broke the donkey's back.

'That's enough,' R'chal stood and slammed her hands on the table. She turned her ire towards the stranger sitting in her father's chair. 'What is going on here? Where have you come from? What are you doing here?'

'Hunter, be at ease. We come to honour your mata.'

R'chal strode to the door. A'lek looked dumbfounded when R'chal fronted the still-seated wolf.

'I thank you for your preparations. We have lost much and have not yet had the opportunity to grieve. Being confronted with a talking wolf or Wolven *is just a bit beyond reason.'*

'R'chal, what are you on about? No one has spoken,' A'lek said.

He pulled her back from the beast as she was nearly nose to nose with it.

'Only you, hunter.'

The wolven stood, revealing just how much bigger it was than any other wolf, and stalked off into the night. R'chal, still vexed and now just a little embarrassed, turned and stormed at their guest.

'Did that animal just talk to me? What has just happened? What is going on here? Where have you come from? What are you doing here? I want answers, and I want them now!'

Her voice grew more menacing with each question. A'lek had rarely seen R'chal this worked up. She was always methodical, taking one step at a time through problems to achieve the best result. Patience was a major facet that made her a great hunter.

'R'chal, stop. Help me clean up. After that, we can get all the answers we need. I will even dry.'

This last statement brought R'chal's attention back to her sibling more than anything else. Drying and putting away was always a bone of contention between the pair. This necessary daily task had bred any number of contests and arguments over whose turn it was. R'chal realised A'lek was trying to fill her hands with mindless work that would give each of them some time to process the evening's strange happenings. Just the tactic their mother would use.

'Okay, A'lek. But afterwards, I will get those answers and more.'

R'chal stalked over to the alcove that served as their food preparation and cooking area and began the familiar task of heating water and scraping the platters.

'She is going to need more from you. I know my sister. You had better have some good explanations for all this.'

A'lek turned from the seated man and cleared the table on the way to join R'chal in completing their after-dinner chores. In short shift, the pair had the cabin clean and presented the way their mother liked it. The mundane task had had the desired effect, and a somewhat calmer R'chal sat before their guest while A'lek fussed at the hearth preparing mulled wine.

'Wolven? Explain!' R'chal insisted.

'In the beginning, before the three races of men were raised up, our lands were completely different. Many of the creatures we share our world with were sentient, as were some of the trees. Young oak, elm, poplar, and pine would traverse the lands, communing with other ancients until they found their place in the scheme of things. After all, they had all the time in the world before rooting themselves in the place meant for them. Sharing the land were the animals. Each species had a hierarchy to ensure the symbiotic balance was kept. The hunters, wolf, ikat, even the warf, were overseen by the Wolven. The ruminants and herds were headed by the great bucks, and the burrow dwellers and rodents answered to the badgers. Even the seas, which I know do not mean much to you as you live so far away, have their leaders. The relationships between all were harmonious where the rules, taught to you by your father, prevailed. Only the old or infirm were offered and taken, keeping each race strong.'

Martyn accepted a mug of spicy mulled wine.

'That was before chaos came to Tol. Plague, evil, blackness, and death came from nowhere. The corruption expanded to threaten any who came into contact with it. On the heels of the chaos were the warriors who came to fight the expansion of the evil. Fighting valiantly for many hundreds of turns but ultimately taking too many losses to do more than hold the blackness at bay in a stalemate that could never be maintained. That was when the ancients were forced to intervene. Debate was long, but the end result inevitable. The power of Tol had to be utilized in the defence of all.

'The captain of the defenders was called to the grove of the most ancient. It was explained that all the beings of Tol were prepared to give up most of their sentience to imbue the remaining warriors with the inner light and power of Tol. Each of the seven remaining warriors of her cohort were fortified with the power of Tol and given the colour of one of the seven sacred gems linked to the inner power of our world. The gems imbued the warriors with light to fight the darkness. The warriors gained ascendancy and banished the evil from our lands.

Our ancient ones agreed that no more than two elders from each phylum or group of species could be fully sentient, thus Wilder of the Wolven and the ancient elder of the grove. But even the wisest can make mistakes. Now, come and join me in a draught of this exceptional wine. We must discuss what fate has in store for you.

'Tol needs the hunter, and I need the apprentice.'

CHAPTER FOURTEEN
Challenge

Dreq emerald to revive ensures a world will survive.

HELEANA'S PARTY MADE good time coming down from the mountains. The terrain had started to flatten out, and the going became easier as the trail wended through the oaks, elms and alders of a healthy forest. Travelling with two very large wolves did not seem to affect the natural inhabitants of the area.

'Devron, I would have thought the wolves would scare away the locals,' Heleana said.

'Ancient one respected. Rare he seen. Animals curious,' said Devron.

Setting up camp each evening had become easy as each of them fell to the chores needed to ensure Heleana had no reason to critize. By using game trails and with advise from the inhabitants of the forest the group had travelled a direct route and reduced the usual travel time substantially. On the morning of the he seventh sun of travel Devron announced they would reach the village just after the sun's zenith. Heleana's immediate thought was of a soak in a hot tub, and she shivered at the memory of washing in the mountain streams and pools. Her recollection was abruptly interrupted. She had to do a quick side step to avoid the wolf when Varellon suddenly stopped just in front of her. They had halted in a small, clear area of the trail. The wolven, who had been walking with Garat at the back of the group, came to the fore and sat in front of Devron's partner. Wolf rider and the four plainsmen took up positions behind the two beasts.

From the bend in the trail ahead approached three wolves and their riders, who were on foot, following their partners at a respectful distance. These beasts were uniformly grey with various patches of black fur at their ears, on their chests or on their paws. All three came before Wilder and repeated the actions Varellon had taken upon meeting the ancient one. Their companions followed suit, genuflecting in unison.

'Black Peaks pack. Varellon larger, pelt closer to ancient one,' Devron said.

Heleana smiled to herself. It seemed even the diminutive wolf riders had a hierarchy and were not immune to boasting about whose partner was better. Devron went forwards to talk to the three in a language that seemed more like birdsong, whistles and clicks were interspersed with some recognisable words. Devron returned, leading one of the riders. The pair looked alike with their bow-legged walk, hide clothing, fur-tufted pointed ears, and—the feature Heleana could not completely reconcile—the two thumbs on each of their five-digited hands. They differed in their colouring, as Devron's colouring matched his wolf's brown with russet highlights, while the newcomers was grey with black tips to his ears.

'Heit, leader go gathering. Scout, warn Brocken move. Show respect, ancient one. Look afar at village. Many plainsmen.'

With some yips, huffs and sharp barks, the three new wolf riders sent their partners off into the woods, and took to the trees, running along the low branches and lithely jumping from tree to tree. While there was some disturbance of birds squawking and taking flight, the party disappeared in short order. Heleana resettled her pack and hefted her bardiche, eager to reach the village. Devron halted her first step by abruptly grasping the handle of her axe. A dangerous act, as at any other time, the perpetrator would feel the extent of the lady's wrath.

'Hold, Lady, Pathfinder. Guests,' Devron said.

Somewhat bewildered, Garat moved forwards and joined Devron a short way down the trail. As soon as the pair stopped, two figures stepped from the shadows of the woods. They glided from their concealment with no discernible movement or rustle of the thick foliage bordering the path. Garat and Devron did not reach for weapons but instead crossed their arms in front of their chests and balled their fists.

'*Ek sien jou, krygsman,*' Garat said.

'I see you, warrior,' the strangers said, repeating the actions of Garat and Devron.

After the ritual greeting, Garat stepped forwards and shared a handshake with the tallest stranger.

'Well met, Chelke,' Garat said.

'Pathfinder, we come at the request of Orkoiyot S'anie to observe and report.

The pair moved forwards but remained at a respectful distance when they went down on one knee before the wolven. They rested their elbows on their knees and placed their foreheads on their closed fists.

'*Ons sien jou, wyse een, en is joune om te bevee,*' they said in unison.

'Live in peace and be welcome,' Garat spoke the words for the others in the party.

Heleana smiled when she sensed the excitement of the lads clustered behind her. She heard the whispers—elves, warriors, weapons, tall, powerful, flawless were only some of the hastily mumbled superlatives bouncing between Perrin and Bren. Heleana took the opportunity while the elven pair greeted the ancient one to move forwards and stand beside her husband. Chelke and her companion rose to their feet, bowed to the wolven, and took one step back before turning to Garat.

'Chelke, may I introduce my life's partner, Lady Heleana Edwina Loretta L'Atchett of Sudhemere.'

Garat's formal tone set the mood. There were formalities to be observed before any news could be shared. The elven warriors bowed their heads in respect, not taking their eyes from Heleana's. As it was far from the greeting offered to the ancient one, Garat felt the bristling emotions emanating from his wife.

'Be still, sweetheart,' he whispered. 'They are showing you great respect by not taking their eyes off one considered a dangerous warrior.'

'Lady Hell is well-known amongst those who wander the lands. I see your formidable weapon is at hand. If your braids are to be believed, you are certainly one to fear,' Chelke said. The elf flicked some of her own braids back over her shoulder.

Heleana turned to her husband, who stood by with a wry smile. He shrugged.

'If I can't boast about you and your achievements, my love, what sort of husband would I be?'

'Well, Pathfinder, I see you have met your match. I did not think you would find a mate who could tame you.'

Garat was unsure about the comment until he observed the amusement in the elf's eyes.

'Chelke, will you take salt?'

Garat had decided to get the greeting back on track. Garat took his wife's hand and pulled her down with him as he sat cross-legged. The elves almost flowed into the same sitting position. Chelke withdrew some dried meat from a pocket while Garat unknotted a small pouch from his belt. When the elf offered up the meat, Garat pinched some salt from his pouch and sprinkled it over the jerky. The four shared the seasoned meat in the formal giving and receiving of life's sustenance. With formalities observed, they rose to complete the introductions. Garat motioned to the still-overawed boys to come forward.

'Balju Chelke, may I introduce the heir to the sovereignty of the Southlands Prince Brycen Ronan E'Nakor,' Garat said.

'*Goed ontmoet, leier van mans.*'

'And my brother, Perrin Omholt. Our prince's boyhood friend.'

'*Goed ontmoet, beskermer.*'

'Garat, Devron, my companion is Boid. He was with our young Koiy when she went missing. He has been charged by Orkoiyot S'anie to tell of her plight at the coming gathering and not to return to the Sunset Islands without news of the heir.'

While Garat was being introduced to the second elf, Heleana could hear muttering behind her Perrin and Bren had taken the opportunity to whisper to Devron.

'What did she say to us?' Perrin asked.

'She respect. Give titles on Pathfinder's word. Bren leader of men. Perrin she name protector. Elves skills, abilities see knots and braids in hair,' Devron said.

The expanded group continued their trek to the village with the elf and Garat leading the way. Heleana recalled the elves she had met when she had travelled to the capital with her father. It was the practice of the leaders of each race to send their heir and a companion to live in the court of the other for a time to learn and understand the laws, languages and customs of their neighbours. Heleana had been told that trade with the elves was expensive and time-consuming, but since the invasion, all commerce with the peoples of the Sunset Islands had halted.

Heleana remembered the furore caused when the elven heir went missing. Unfortunately, the elven heir, Koiy Aayla, had been in residence in the court of the Southlands sovereign when the Brocken swept through the plains and captured Sudhemere. She and her retinue had left to return to her mother's lands, but all knowledge of Koiy Aayla had been lost shortly after leaving the capital, except the story Boid could tell.

Bren had been too young to have begun his time at the court of Orkoiyot S'anie when he went into hiding.

Heleana studied the elf Chelke as she walked beside her husband at the head of the group. She was taller than all, even Perrin, but only by a finger width or two. While Perrin had broad shoulders and exhibited strength and power, the elf was long of limb and slender, but by no means was any less impressive. Heleana could easily believe the stories told of the endurance and speed of the elven people. Chelke was garbed in rawhide trousers with a hardened leather vest decorated with beads and shells in small intricate patterns. The vest looked to be a type of hardened armour that was shaped and fitted tightly over her ample breasts yet left her midriff bare. One of her most striking features was the dark hair that fell in rows and rows of braids, many knotted with coloured string, ribbon, beads, or gems. She was clearly a hunter as she matched Garat weapon for weapon, longbow and arrows, knives and sword. Only the sword worn across her back that differed.

While Garat preferred a broad sword, hers was finer in the blade and clearly designed for one-handed use. When the light through the leaves began to brighten, it was clear that they were getting close to the village. Devron stopped the group.

'Wilder, Varellon leave. Village busy,' he said.

Heleana nodded and turned to the canines. She bowed low in a show of thanks and watched as they disappeared into the shadows of the forest. Garat led them to the village of The Salient Buck. While traders and travellers were commonplace, a group comprising elves, a wolf rider afoot and the Lady Hell emerging from the forest would have raised some notice. Instead the inhabitants largely ignored

Heleana's group as they rushed about, intent upon their own doings. Heleana understood the canine's reluctance to stay with them.

The party entered the picturesque mountain village where thatched roofed houses were brightly painted and clustered around a square dominated by a two-storey building with an attached yard and stables. Heleana led them towards the village inn, heralded by a swinging sign painted with a rearing deer under a crest of five stars and the wording *The Salient Buck*. Beyond the village was a bridge over a mountain brook and, further away, an open meadow with grasses rippling in the breeze. With a welcome sigh, Heleana sat down on the steps of the inn. Each of her companions doffed their packs and stretched out well used muscles.

'Innkeeper, do you keep guests waiting?' she called.

At her call, a rather rotund gent bustled out from the door, wringing his hands and wiping flour onto his apron.

'My lady, my apologies. Never enough time,' he said. 'How may I help?'

'Two rooms and send for the smith. Kindly heat water and tell your good wife that many more are expected,' Heleana ordered. 'You boys can share I intend to get to know R'chal better.'

The landlord indicated the group should follow.

'Heleana, my love. I will find your tinker and see what mischief he is concocting.' Garat kissed his wife and turned to leave, followed by Devron and the elves.

'Well, boys, let us enjoy a lunch of more than just trail rations,' Heleana said.

Heleana herded the two before her through the door of the inn. She was shown to a room overlooking the bridge and meadows. While looking out at the vista Heleana pondered the meaning of the tinker's plans. *'I hope you know what you are doing. Much hope and planning is being attached to a none too trustworthy itinerant.'* Her musings were interrupted by a knock.

'Come,' she called.

The innkeeper peered around the door. 'I have prepared a luncheon in the common room and sent my boy for the smith if it pleases m'Lady?' he said, tugging a lock of his hair.

'That would be most welcome, my good man,' Heleana replied. 'Please lead the way.'

Heleana was joined by Perrin and Bren at the board. The spread consisted of loaves of freshly baked bread, cold meats, cheeses, fresh and preserved fruits, and an array of mushrooms served in a spiced broth.

'Are you not having the mushrooms?' Perrin asked Bren.

'I hope never to see another mushroom in my life. I also hope that one sun you will stop teasing me?'

To drive home the request, he flicked a blackberry at his cousin. Perrin stared at the purple mark left on his vest and reached for a bowl of nuts.

'Do not even think about it, Perrin Omholt,' came the ominous command.

'Yes, Lady Heleana,' Perrin conceded.

A glare at his cousin promised future retribution. Perrin held up two fingers to remind his cousin of the debt he was accruing.

'I think you two can take your meal outside and enjoy the village before the others come,' Heleana said.

The two youths began piling flatbreads with meats and cheeses until each hand was filled. Just as they bustled towards the door, it opened. They nearly collided with a young woman of an age with Perrin and a younger boy. The girl was clad in a leather apron, with a leather cap over her hair and ash-stained face and hands that she wiped with a grimy cloth.

'Who demands the smith?' she announced.

The two youths stepped back. They looked toward Lady Heleana and, as they slipped past the woman, whispered in a tone that carried across the room, 'The Lady Hell.'

The girl came forward, wiping her hands on the cloth. She stopped before Heleana and nodded in recognition.

'My Lady,' she said. 'How may I serve?'

'Where is Bartimaeus the smith?' Heleana asked.

'My father is collecting more black stone and ore from the quarries. He should return in the next two or three suns. I am Quinn, and this is my brother Kjieran. He has just started his apprenticeship,' she said.

Quinn was clearly proud and protective and, although respectful to Heleana, had defiance in her tone. Heleana could see her brother looked up to his sister. He was as tall as his sister but was gangly in stature, promising to fill out as he reached maturity. He had a very memorable shock of pure white hair. Heleana wondered about the title of apprentice smith, as he would be seriously hampered by the metal brace strapped to his left arm. The brace supported a withered and scarred forearm and hand, the aftermath of a serious burn. The brace somewhat explained his sister's attitude.

'I believe you and the children of that unfortunate couple we encountered when last here are working on some project or other for that man, Martyn.'

'More R'chal than her twin,' Quinn said.

'Might I know the outcome of your endeavours?'

'Come and meet R'chal, and we can show you what the tinker has us doing.'

Quinn and Kjieran led Heleana to the smithy. She spied the twins with their heads together, charcoal stick in hand, bent over a scrapped hide in deep discussion.

'R'chal, A'lek, Lady Heleana is here and wants to understand our work.'

R'chal and A'lek looked startled and attempted, without success, a bow as a proper greeting for one of Heleana's station.

'None of that now. We are all equals when it comes to defending our lands. Just what has that horrible man got you so intent on?'

'My Lady, it would be far better for us to show you rather than try to explain. Do you have someone adept with a bow?' R'chal asked.

'Yes, as a matter of fact. Quinn, they nearly trampled you when you entered the inn.'

'Kjieran, run and find those boys and tell them to bring their weapons,' Quinn ordered.

'Young man, please find Martyn the tinker and ask the Inn Keeper to prepare a basket of food. It does not look like any of you have taken the time to eat lately,' Heleana added.

'What is so interesting about a bow that needs displaying?' Heleana asked.

Quinn went deeper into the building and returned with a strange mechanical device resembling a strung bow but with extra strings and small wheels at either end. When Heleana handled the device, she saw that the multiple strings were actually one.

'The comparison between a normal bow and this one is what we want you to see and understand,' R'chal said.

'I made that for Kjieran when he was smaller. He was able to hunt birds using blunts and became very accurate with it. He put it away once he could draw a traditional bow so he would not be ridiculed by his peers. Martyn believes this toy is the key to turning back the Brocken.' Quinn said.

Heleana now appreciated the connection between the boy's handicap and the current project. It seems an accident that befell a small boy would impact the efforts of the resistance.

'I am but the messenger. The ancients and druids are guiding this gathering.'

The twins, along with Quinn and Heleana, were startled by the voice that emanated from the smithy's loft. With a rustle and a small fall of straw, the bald head of the tinker appeared as he drew on his brown robe. He shuffled along to the ladder and climbed down. He came before Heleana, brushing the clinging dried grass from his attire, and nodded in recognition.

'Well met, my Lady, now we can have some fun. Here comes our young prince. Shall we proceed?'

As the group turned to join the three young men, a further noise came from the direction of the loft.

'Was someone up there with you?' Heleana demanded.

Heleana looked deep into the gloom of the loft and thought she saw the flash of white petticoats being gathered.

'A gentleman never tattles. Show and tell time. R'chal, lead on,' said Martyn.

'I don't think you need us. Kjieran and I will clean up around here a bit,' A'lek said.

R'chal and Quinn took their guests to a clearing in the forest, beside a small pool that had formed above an overflow that splashed and bubbled down a series of heavy boulders. Perrin and Bren laid out a blanket and unpacked a basket of bread, soft cheeses and preserves. Heleana insisted that R'chal and Quinn eat before their demonstration. Martyn needed no encouragement and tucked in with fervour, washing down each bite with a swig from his waterskin. Heleana was sure the skin was not filled with the crystal clear water of the mountain brook they sat beside. Perrin and Bren wandered the clearing, leaving the women to enjoy the repast. Various strategically placed stumps and a defined fire pit indicated this was a well-used picnic and swimming spot.

R'chal rose and asked Perrin if he would permit her to inspect his bow. She recognised the wood as yew and noted it was of good quality because the natural lamination between the heartwood and outer layer was evident, giving the longbow more consistency and power. Upon drawing the string, she turned to Heleana.

'This longbow has a draw of more than ninety pounds of force. I could never hope to maintain accuracy and distance for very long, maybe four arrows over one hundred paces, and I would be done,' R'chal said. 'Perrin, would you please demonstrate?'

R'chal handed Perrin his bow. Perrin retrieved his quiver and arrows.

'It would be a pleasure, my Lady,' he said. 'That scar on the trunk of that oak, I judge at about fifty paces. Would that do?'

'Very nicely,' R'chal said.

Everyone came to stand behind the two. Perrin took his stance and placed two arrows within the target before turning to offer the weapon to R'chal. She had noticed that Perrin used a different method of drawing than she was used to. He held the arrow and longbow to his chest, then pushed out the bow with his left arm, using the power of his body to extend the string. R'chal had never used this method before but understood its effectiveness.

R'chal took up an arrow and, with calming breaths, drew and released, and then repeated the action. Both of her arrows landed inside those of Perrin, and she was rewarded with a satisfying gasp from the observers. However, she determined that the number of times she could repeat the feat would be limited.

'Perrin, how many times could you hit that mark from here?' she asked.

'R'chal, I am a hunter rather than an archer, but I would guess no more than four in any one stance,' he replied.

He left to retrieve the arrows. Heleana came to R'chal's side as they watched him walk to the target.

'While powerful and accurate over distances beyond one hundred paces, any archer quickly loses that accuracy with repeated draws of the bow. To continue to hit a target effectively, they would have to move closer and closer as their muscles tired,' R'chal explained.

'A full-sized version of the contraption I made for Kjieran would vastly improve the number of times an archer could maintain accuracy while keeping a safe distance from the range of the Brocken flatbow,' Quinn explained.

'How is that possible? What makes it work?'Heleana asked.

'That, my Lady, must remain a secret until we can gauge the effectiveness and viability of our new weapon. To that end, in two suns, we contest. I put a call out to the best archers and hunters, near or far, to come and test their skills against Quinn and R'chal. Even Balju Chelke, the elf champion, will shoot,' Martyn said. 'I must hurry off now and see to preparations. Your Pathfinder will be overseeing the challenge.'

BY LATE AFTERNOON, the village had filled with curious spectators and challengers. A tent village of near-equal size to the permanent settlement had sprung up on the meadow to house the Pathfinders, the Elves and some of the Wolf Riders who had come down out of their range.

Wilder and Varellon had come forth and now sat on the far side of the bridge, each like a sentinel, knowing that coming any closer to the village would cause unnecessary concern for the inhabitants and their beasts. As Heleana crossed the bridge to find her husband, each canine nodded their recognition. She returned the acknowledgement and continued on, finding Garat directing the construction of archery butts made of straw and tightly bound green saplings.

'Finally found a skill worthy of your talents,' she said.

Garat embraced her and kissed her formally on each cheek while his eyes promised a more intimate welcome once they found a less public setting.

'How goes your young charge R'chal?' he asked.

'I am not sure of her plan. She is currently ensconced with the smith, working hard on their project. What is the general feeling of the people?' she asked.

'Heleana, my love, much will ride on this challenge. Many will not follow the lead of a young woman without a great deal of convincing. You have the status to demand obedience, but R'chal will have to prove herself over and over again to command followers, and at her first mistake, all could fail,' he said.

'Is that not always the plight of the venturous?' Heleana stated.

Heleana moved through the village and was greeted by many who knew her in person or by reputation. She watched as the people of the village made the most of the unexpected gathering and opened their doors to feed and entertain their guests. Music and singing continued into the night. While all felt a sense of joyous reprieve, the tension from the occupation of their land and the importance of the coming suns simmered just below the surface of the impromptu celebration.

The elves, while subdued in their participation, occasionally joined in and added their voices to some of the more well-known folk songs. At those moments, the mountain valley echoed with their high, clear voices, countered by the rougher tenor of the villagers. Heleana was never out of sight of the smithy. She kept one eye on the continuous glow of the forge and the shadows of Quinn and R'chal, working steadily.

HELEANA WOKE THE NEXT morning to the sounds of the village coming to life and invading her slumber. She had always woken at the first sounds of the morning. She believed that to lead is to participate. As she dressed, she noted that R'chal's bed had not been slept in she had not returned to the inn to take rest overnight. Heleana ventured out to discover the reason and headed to the smithy after instructing the innkeeper to prepare the bathing room and breakfast.

Heleana found R'chal and the smith testing various versions of a strange device that was little more than a wheel attached to a small cup-like object. Both girls were wearing leather aprons and covered head to foot in soot.

'If you two have time, I think a meal would be in order. R'chal, you have had little time to rest. We will need you at your best tomorrow. Come now, I have had the bathing room prepared,' Heleana said.

As R'chal doffed the apron and turned to follow, Heleana pointed to Quinn.

'You too, smith.'

Quinn nudged the recumbent form of her brother, who had not managed to stay awake the night through, and directed him in the clean-up and banking of the forge before following R'chal.

Heleana led them to the bathhouse at the rear of the inn, where they were welcomed with steam roiling out the door as they entered. R'chal grasped the chance to get clean and undressed quickly. She entered the large tub set into the floor that was easily large enough for six persons. Heleana followed and sighed as the hot water enveloped her. Quinn was reluctant to bathe with the Duke of Sudhem's daughter. Let alone Lady Hell, whose reputation as a vicious fighter and leader of men was well-known throughout the Southlands.

Heleana noticed the concern on the face of Quinn as she studied the woman. Heleana was used to the surprise of those that saw her scars glowing white against the tanned skin of her arms and legs.

More shocking was the puckered cavity, an angry red in colour a wound, that stood out against the pale skin of her upper chest. None of her injuries detracted from her well-muscled, powerful warrior's physique. Instead, they only proved that the feats of courage attributed to Lady Hell were not exaggerated.

'Now, Quinn. Before we enjoy all the heat,' Heleana said.

Quinn quickly undressed and, using a bucket, attempted to wash off the worst of the soot before entering the pool. Quinn's most striking feature was revealed when she removed her leather cap. Her hair was cut in a bob and was an intriguing deep emerald green.

When Heleana expressed her approval, Quinn explained that she had to keep her hair short over the forge, but coloured it to make sure she could keep her independence and make the statement that she could still be a smith and a woman.

Heleana had provided clean clothing for R'chal, including linen britches and chest bindings as undergarments, along with the shirt, jerkin and trousers of the Pathfinders and the ankle boots common to the mountain folk. R'chal's pleasure in donning the uniform was evident to Heleana. To be seen to be a pathfinder was a great honour.

After sharing an enjoyable breakfast and discussing the next step of the project, Heleana sent for Perrin and Bren. When they appeared, she instructed them to find a selection of the best longbows available to purchase.

BOTH BOYS KNEW THE value of the better bows and that a true hunter would not part with his best. With this in mind, they purchase a selection of six very serviceable bows with a variety of draw power. Upon the success of their mission, the boys were instructed to deliver them to the smithy, where R'chal and Quinn had once again retired to develop their strange device.

When the boys approached them with the bow staves, Perrin noticed R'chal was plaiting gut and silk thread into a long, continuous string. She stopped and used an iron ingot to hold the threads securely in place while she tested the variety of bows for pliability and rebound.

Having selected two bows of a similar style, she took them to show Quinn and asked for a saw. Perrin and Bren followed her actions, and with increasing trepidation, realised her intent. After carefully measuring, then re-measuring, R'chal began to saw the staves about one hand span from each end. At first, Perrin began to protest, but Bren led him away, muttering about doings beyond their ken.

LATER THAT EVENING, as Heleana prepared for bed, R'chal softly knocked on the door.

'Come in,' Heleana called. 'R'chal, why are you knocking? This is your room.'

'Heleana, you have a husband,' R'chal replied. She cast her eyes around the room.

'He sleeps with his men. While I admit he comes in useful at times, we really need him to keep the rumours in check. There have been men coming in who are questioning the contest, and that terrible man, Martyn is taking bets on the outcome,' she said.

At that, R'chal held up two wrapped packages and, with a smile, advised Lady Heleana to back her at whatever odds she could get. Heleana was intrigued but was more concerned with R'chal's physical abilities and insisted that she prepare for bed. Heleana went downstairs to bring back a plate of the stew that was always simmering in the cauldron over the coals in the kitchen. After R'chal had eaten, the anticipation of the tournament tomorrow kept her turning in her sleep deep into the night.

RESISTANCE

The morning dawned and promised a glorious early season's sun in the foothills, meaning a soft breeze and the heat being tempered by the valley's elevation and shade offered by both forest and mountain. After having a breakfast tray prepared, Heleana returned to the room she shared with R'chal.

'R'chal, the challenge has stirred a hornet's nest. We have many wanting to test themselves against the hunter. Garat is holding eliminations to determine eight to face your challenge. We have given two spots to the elves and will find six from the Pathfinders and hunters. We will not begin the final challenge until after mid-sun,' Heleana said. 'How did you sleep?'

R'chal stretched and smelled the enticing odour of grilled meat, toast, and eggs, along with what she hoped was coffee.

'Well, thank you, my Lady. I did take a while to drop off, but the singing helped me relax.'

'We cannot hope to keep this contest secret for long. We have to assume the Brocken will hear of this gathering, so we will be leaving to convene the council at a more secure site as soon as we can,' Heleana said.

As they enjoyed their meal, R'chal remained deep in thought and worried that even if she was successful, could she really right the balance and give the Southlands a chance to turn back the Brocken advancement?

When R'chal looked towards the meadow from the window of their room, the transformation was staggering. The vacant meadow now boasted a small village of tents, and enterprising locals had set up stalls selling any variety of foods and drinks. Further out, she saw the range, flanked by small pennants fluttering atop thin posts. The archery butts were set at the various distances. R'chal was unwilling to leave anything to chance. She spent the morning selecting and weighing arrows and preparing gloves and arm guards to give her a consistent feel. A knock on the door brought her back to reality. She had lost herself in the preparations.

'Come,' she answered. A'lek slipped into the room.

'Where's Martyn? Is he not your mentor?' R'chal asked.

'He's off somewhere trying to cheat the whole village. He sees it as a challenge and a bit of a lark to maintain his villainous reputation. But I have come about you. We have not had time to compare our experiences here, but that can wait. How about some meditation to relax and centre yourself?'

'A'lek, that is just what I need.'

She sat before the fireplace and gestured for A'lek to sit, too. The twins joined hands and relaxed, then slowed their breathing and remained that way until a knocking on the door disturbed their reflection. R'chal collected her things and had A'lek carry her selection of arrows as she took the two covered bows she and Quinn had produced. Perrin and Bren were waiting outside, bouncing with excitement about the afternoon's entertainment.

'Hunter, the competition has been fierce for the right to challenge you,' Perrin said.

Perrin and Bren led her downstairs and towards the bridge. R'chal was grateful for A'lek's thoughtfulness as the anticipation began to grow and adrenaline started to build. Fortunately, R'chal had faith in her skills, even if the outcome was far more than a clean kill and food on the table. As they crossed the bridge, the festive vibe of the gathering became more subdued as word passed of the arrival of the competition's main event. The friendly competition had now become somewhat more serious.

R'chal approached a slightly raised dais. In front stood nine archers, each holding their preferred bow. Garat Omholt stood and announced the rules of the challenge. Six arrows each, at ranges of twenty-five, fifty, and one hundred paces, with the bottom three archers dropping out after each round. The order was to be decided by ballot, with the challenger shooting last. These rules were greeted with a general hubbub of agreement and a rush to get to the best spectator points. R'chal went down the line of her opponents to shake hands and wish them luck. She noted that other than the elves, she was as tall or taller than most. There were four dressed in the garb of the Pathfinders, three hunters dressed in leggings and furs, and two elves, one of which, to R'chal's delight, was a woman. R'chal felt a tug of recognition as she took her hand.

For the first round, R'chal requested to borrow Perrin's longbow and placed second in points behind the female elf. One of her arrows had clipped another and fallen outside the inner ring. The round saw three Pathfinders eliminated, although all scores were extremely close. The second round commenced at the fifty pace butt, and the fatigue of the continuous pull, aim, and release started to become apparent as scores became more varied. R'chal noticed that the elves had maintained the best scores, but the female had once again outscored the others. R'chal took up one of her bows and slipped it out from its cover. As she approached the firing line, a ripple of whispers and mutterings passed through the crowd.

R'chal drew her arrow, then stood relaxed as she looked at the wind, distance and crowd. As she stood with her bow drawn, the crowd became agitated as more and more realised the impossibility of maintaining that draw. When the crowd hushed, she took careful aim and released. The judge at the target held up a yellow flag for an inner, and when R'chal repeated the performance another five times for a perfect score, the buzz throughout the crowd rose in anticipation for the final round.

After some refreshment and removal of the shorter targets, R'chal's final opponents were the two elves and one remaining hunter. When R'chal stepped up, it was the female elf she had to beat. She once again displayed her relaxed approach and ability, and easily matched the hunter and the male elf in score after only four arrows.

Before she could draw her next arrow, the female elf approached and conceded R'chal's claim as champion by laying her bow at R'chal's feet.

R'chal nodded her thanks and asked the attendants to move the target out another twenty paces. R'chal turned to A'lek and indicated to bring over the other wrapped bow. She took the bow from the cover and handed it to the elf woman. At one hundred and twenty paces, the two archers could not be separated, as arrow after arrow flew accurately and easily. The villages and their guests cheered each and every arrow as the two proved the claim that the resistance now had the means to match the power of the Brocken. Even more so perhaps they had found a Hunter to lead them.

CHAPTER FIFTEEN
Possibilities

Seven warriors bring light to black

HELEANA HAD REWARDED herself with the luxury of staying in bed after allowing R'chal to use the amenities first. She lay there considering the possibilities the new weapon could provide. She remembered the feast and rounds of congratulations and questions about the strange new bow. Too many people had too many questions, so Heleana and R'chal escaped the festivities and taken refuge in their room at The Salient Buck.

Stretching and longing to wash the sleep from her eyes, Heleana got up and headed for the wash basin and jug of water. As she passed the window, she glanced towards the scene of the contest only to be caught short.

'There were no longer any tents, stalls, nor pennants flying. The meadow looked just as it had when they arrived. Heleana smiled inwardly and once again thanked the ancients for her husband. She and Garat had snuck away in the early evening to attend to her husband's earlier promise. Heleana had remembered the tinker's previous dalliance and had led Garat to the loft at the smithy. With the celebration providing a backdrop of song and laughter Heleana demonstrated to her husband how much she had missed him and how grateful she was to be his wife. Garat had planned to lead his Pathfinders away from the village at first light to create a confusion of trails. She could only wonder at the work that had returned the area to this pristine mountain vista under his direction. She smiled to herself still in awe at the man's stamina. Her hand slid low on her abdomen, remembering the night and enjoying the pleasurable ache of being well satisfied.

A knock on the door pulled her from her musings, and she turned and opened the door to the young stable boy.

'My Lady, I was sent to get you for your morning meal. It has been served in the great room,' he said.

Heleana smiled and watched as he backed away, tugging a lock of hair. 'Thank you.'

He turned and scampered down the stairs. She returned to the washstand and rejoiced in the icy freshness of the water, which served to clear her head and bring the events of the past few suns into focus. She dressed in her Pathfinder travelling clothes and turned to face what was sure to be another round of questions and explanations.

Heleana found R'chal enjoying a plate of stuffed mushrooms and fried eggs. She looked up and gestured for Heleana to join her. Heleana was pleased to see that the only other diners present were Martyn, A'lek, Perrin and Bren, who were enjoying their own repast at another table, away from R'chal. Two elven warriors stood by the door, looking not unlike sentries. Heleana nodded recognition to the Chelke, who dipped her head in response. Heleana was pleased and surprised that the inn's common room was not overflowing with eager Pathfinders and hunters wanting to know the secrets of the new bow. Secrecy at this moment would be vital.

The Brocken would come to know about the contest and, through bribes or torture, would attempt to gain all knowledge of the weapon. The invaders communications were being improved with a system of dispatch riders. Horses had become a focus of their recent raids into areas of the plains long thought to be beyond their interest.

'Heleana, I am surprised. Where is your husband and the throng that wanted all the answers last night?' R'chal asked.

'R'chal, the Brocken will soon hear about this gathering and investigate. We are fortunate that this village is so far from the centre of their occupation, but we are certain a squad will shortly appear. We have adjourned the council to reconvene at a safer base further south. We dare not risk these good folk, so we have dispersed the crowd and will leave this village as though we had never been. Word has come from the leader of the council that we must make haste,' Heleana said.

Just as the women sat back feeling pleasantly full, there was a ruckus at the door as the elven sentries held back someone who attempted entry. Heleana noticed the leather cap of the smith as voices became raised.

'Please let her in,' Heleana called.

Through the opened door Heleana could see that Quinn was not the only one vying for a glimpse of their champion. It looked like most of the village had assembled in the stable yard. The smith was allowed entry by the stoic warriors and entered, carrying a long cloth-covered package. Quinn crossed to the table and, placing the package on the table, bowed to Lady Heleana.

'R'chal, you have given the Southlands hope. We can begin to believe that we can overcome the Brocken and the Empire of the North.

'My father has a secret process for making steel and is the best swordsmith in the Southlands. I have brought you a gift that he made for me. Because women cannot hope to wield a long sword effectively in battle, he made me this,' she said.

Quinn indicated the gift and pulled aside the cloth covering.

'He calls it a rapier. Strong enough to parry a long sword with a tip sharp enough to penetrate any Brocken uniform. You must have a weapon that will protect you and as a symbol when you lead us against the Brocken.'

Quinn finished on an exhalation, indicating that public speaking was not common for her, but her speech was heartfelt and well meant. Heleana watched R'chal handle the sword.

Even from her position, Heleana could see that it was beautiful. It had a bright scroll-work blade paired with a basket hilt inset with gold dragons. Heleana recognised the quality and workmanship of the weapon and matching scabbard. She could also see the importance of this gift in Quinn's eyes. The young woman was giving this gift to her friend in the hope that it would save R'chal and help to return the Southlands to its people.

'Quinn, it is a magnificent gift. All I can do is try my best to help, and your own skills went a long way towards providing the weapon and the hope that you speak of. I have never held a sword before I will have to find someone to teach me or I might cut myself instead of an enemy,' R'chal said.

R'chal reverently sheathed the sword just as Devron ducked under the arms of the grasping elves and bustled into the inn.

'Lady, Brocken come. Leave. Wolves go range,' he said. 'Two suns.'

Heleana stood and looked towards Martyn, A'lek and the two cousins.

'Get going, you louts. We don't have all sun,' she ordered.

Heleana's pose stiffened when all but Martyn jumped to her command.

'You too, Tinker,' Heleana said. Her tone was ominous.

Martyn was busy hiding bread and cheeses in the various pockets within his robe. Heleana glared at him.

'We have word from the leader of the Druids and meet in three suns,' she warned.

'Yes, yes my lady, but don't worry overly much about him I am sure he knows exactly what is going on here,' Martyn said.

'Heleana, we must have Quinn with us. We cannot leave her. Her skills and knowledge will be essential to the Southlands. Others have seen what our new bow can do, but only Quinn can make the cam wheels that give the bow its mechanical advantage,' R'chal said.

As the shock of understanding spread over Quinn's features, Heleana turned to her.

'How soon can you pack?' Heleana asked.

'But I... I just... leave the village? I just can't,' Quinn stammered.

'R'chal is correct the Brocken would pay handsomely anyone that divulges knowledge of the new bow. If they were to take you they would extract the information under torture. You would suffer greatly,' Heleana said. She had placed a hand on the smith's shoulder in an effort to calm the conflict within.

Heleana glanced over the smith's head at R'chal. She could see R'chal felt for the smith as she herself was trying to adjust to the upheaval of a complete change in their circumstance. She saw the understanding that only two people knew the workings of the bow and the value that information would be to the Brocken slowly dawn on Quinn.

'Where would I go?' Quinn asked.

'R'chal, you have seen the value of your gift to the Southlands. The smith will come with us and train others in the making of this new weapon. Quinn, gather what you need. I will send Perrin and Bren to assist you. Go now, we leave shortly,' Heleana ordered.

Heleana and R'chal rushed to their room and quickly packed their belongings and retrieved their weapons. R'chal carried her two wrapped bows and the two quivers of arrows she had meticulously chosen. Fortunately, Quinn had provided a belt with the gift of her sword, so with no other encumbrance, she and Heleana with her sheathed bardiche stepped out of the inn and into the tumult of packing and preparing for a trek. Martyn had regained his horse and was at the centre of the bustling mayhem. Backpacks were being repacked and balanced while A'lek and Devron concentrated on supplies of food and water. Martyn saw R'chal and waved her over.

'Hunter, the ancient one awaits you beyond the village. Go to him,' Martyn said.

'Why me? I have done everything you wanted. Everything is changing.'

R'chal's distress was noted by Heleana.

'Tinker, what is the meaning of this?' Heleana demanded.

'Wilder awaits the hunter. R'chal, take the Lady of Sudhem with you. She has travelled with the ancient one.'

Heleana understood R'chal's reluctance. She had been forced to re-evaluate her whole future when Sudhemere had fallen to the Brocken, and she had become a wanted fugitive. She took R'chal's hand.

'Come with me. It seems our futures are indelibly linked to these lands and all their inhabitants.'

Heleana led a reluctant R'chal along the trade road away from the village. When they rounded the first bend, R'chal suddenly stiffened, and her features paled. From the shadows lining the route, the immense form of Wilder came forth. The wolven sat before R'chal for some time and then, with a nod in Heleana's direction, disappeared back into the undergrowth.

'What just happened?' Helana asked.

'He talks in my head. I'm scared, Heleana. He called me Hunter, and said I have been chosen. He said he will be my guide in the battles we are all to face.'

'The ancient one spoke to you? That is unprecedented. I, too, was confused when Devron first conveyed the wolven's thoughts to us.

Since then, I have discovered that the ancient one is knowledgeable and wise. By communicating directly with you, he shows you respect and honour.'

'Heleana, I am completely flummoxed and scared to my bones. It was bad enough when the tinker came to us and started Quinn and me on this path. He has also labelled A'lek as the Apprentice. Apprentice to what?' R'chal turned and looked back along the path, then did an about face back in the direction they were to travel. Heleana understood it to mean she was thinking about the past and now what lay before her. 'He said the Hunter and the Apprentice are essential to the future of Tol. Wilder said our line has always remained closest to the ways of the ancients. I don't know what is happening to me.'

'R'chal, we travel to meet the druids in three suns. Be steady. I am sure we will gain the answers we all need then. Come. We had best check on the preparations before that itinerant, our supposed guide, swindles half the village.'

On their return all was calming down, and it seemed the group was finally ready to depart. Yet another commotion came from the direction of the smithy, and a braying mule harnessed to a two-wheeled cart was led out. The cart had wooden slats on the floor and sides with man-high wheels and no seat for a driver. It was sturdy and meant for collecting and delivering farming equipment, firewood, or black stone. Quinn led the mule while Perrin and Bren followed, brushing off the soot and dust of the smithy. Quinn was busy giving her brother instructions about caring for the forge until their father returned and messages for the master blacksmith.

Heleana was about to protest that the cart would slow them and make it harder to cover their tracks when she realised a smith without tools and forge could not teach others. Quinn drew the cart up before R'chal and Heleana and indicated she was ready to go.

'Did you pack the whole workshop?' Heleana inspected the interior of the cart. She spied metal ingots, bags of black stone and various sands, tools, anvils of different sizes and uses, a small forge, and Quinn's personal needs.

'This is just a travelling forge we use when repairing farming equipment on site. I would never be able to forge a sword with it, but it will do to make more of R'chal's devices,' Quinn answered.

Quinn's innocent answer indicated she did not understand the dilemma Lady Heleana now faced. Heleana had planned to travel swiftly and change direction often to confuse any followers. Now, with the addition of the cart, she would be limited in the paths she could take, and the Brocken would find it easier to pick up their trail.

'Perrin, you and Bren can take the lead. We travel the main road so we can move as fast as the cart will allow. Watch for riders and look to the crests of the hills for any observers. Go now,' she ordered.

All in the party could see that Heleana was well suited to command and watched as the two boys took up an easy jog along the road leading south from the village with no questions asked.

'Will you two take rearguard and confuse our tracks if you can?' Heleana asked the elf warriors.

Without a word, they turned, walked to the road, and waited. Heleana, R'chal, and Quinn, followed by A'lek, Martyn, and his horse, passed them, and then the elves slowly turned to follow. Devron and Varellon took to the woods, where they would shadow the expedition and be on hand if needed.

'We need to make good time. The council has been summoned. In three suns, we will begin to plan our defiance against the Brocken and turn the tide of deprivations against our people. We will meet with the leaders of the Druids, the Wolf Riders and representatives of the Elves to combine our efforts to push back the Brocken and free our lands,' Heleana said.

RESISTANCE

R'chal and Quinn were suddenly aware of the importance of this mission and their place in it. The expedition made good time while on the main trading route but would soon have to turn to confuse followers and head in the general direction of the hidden base used by the Pathfinders and others of the rebellion as a planning and training centre.

The travellers made cold camp that first night to ensure a fast departure the next morning. Heleana intended to confuse any trackers by creating multiple false trails and eventually breaking up the group. At first light, they packed and left following the same order of march. After the sun had fully risen into a clear blue sky, Heleana signalled for A'lek to come forward.

'A'lek, would you run on ahead and get Perrin and Bren's attention? We need to turn from this path soon,' Heleana said.

She was sure the Brocken would not stop long in the village. She had instructed the innkeeper to point out the various paths leading away from the village, hoping that the village's population would not suffer and the gathering could be passed off as some sort of travelling troupe.

'I will look after that, Heleana. I may as well get used to this,' R'chal said.

R'chal's brow creased and her eyes closed. She took on a pose of deep concentration then relaxed and opened her eyes.

'It worked Heleana I felt Wilder on the periphery of my mind and took the chance to test out our connection, it that is what this thing is. I thought *Wilder, would you round up those two lads ahead*, and then I felt *Hunter* in my mind. The whole thing is so very different. Felt may not be the right word for it but I just don't know.'

'I travelled with Wilder and he talked to us through Devron but I believe that was a link through his wolf partner. With you it is as though he has partnered directly. It may be the same style of partnership only stronger.'

Not long after, and before the cart rounded a bend in the path the women were met with the sight of the two boys being held at bay by a very large wolf. Although Wilder had been seen with the Wolf Riders, no one had connected the wolven with R'chal. Perrin had his sword drawn and was between the canine and his young cousin. Wilder was sitting in the middle of the road with a bass rumble emanating from deep within his chest. Both boys looked around with wild eyes and welcomed the appearance of Heleana and R'chal. When they turned towards the approaching group, they indicated the blocked track, but when they turned back to the defensive position again, they found the track completely clear.

'Wilder said he would scare the Mule,' R'chal whispered to Helana.

'Where did he come from? He nearly had me soiling my pants,' Perrin said.

'Cousin, my thanks for jumping to the fore. I have to agree with you. No matter how far we travelled with a wolven when a wolf of that size growls at you it is enough to freeze the blood and weaken the knees of the most fearsome warriors,' Bren concurred.

Perrin sheathed his sword across his back while studying both sides of the well-travelled path between villages. The path passed between forests of oak and elm and was bordered with younger bushes and trees where the sun could reach through the canopy of old growth.

'I saw a fox run across the path,' R'chal said. 'What about you Heleana?'

'Definitely a fox,' Heleana said.

The timber of her voice may have given away the joke, but Heleana realised that R'chal wanted to divert Perrin's attention from studying the verges too closely for signs of Wilder. Heleana knew R'chal was still coming to understand her link with the wolven and probably considered it best to keep that between herself and Heleana for the time being.

'A fox? Hardly,' Perrin said.

Perrin's argument was cut off when Heleana called all the party members to gather.

'Speed and confusion are our best weapons at this stage. I am sure the Brocken will be following, and we must move as quickly as possible. Just ahead is a small track leading into the mountains. There, we will split up. Perrin. You, Bren, and Martyn can lead the horse. Follow the track, and do not hide your passing. Just before dusk, while it is still light, make your tracks disappear. This will sow confusion with any following Brocken squad. R'chal and the elves will go with you to assist,' she said. 'Quinn, A'lek, and I will travel as fast as we can until we can also leave this track. This will split any force following and give us time to come under the protection that distance in the Southlands offers.'

'No, I will stay. Quinn and her knowledge must be protected,' R'chal said.

'I also. Boid will aid the prince,' said Chelke.

Before Heleana could protest this small mutiny, R'chal had drawn the cover from her bow and slung a quiver of arrows over her shoulder. R'chal indicated the elf should take up the other new bow that she had used during the challenge. Heleana realised that giving R'chal the lead would strengthen the reputation of the Hunter and the resolve of the Pathfinders and civilians who would need to follow this young woman.

'So be it. Go,' Heleana said.

A'lek and Quinn took up the mule's lead ropes. Perrin's party went on ahead and soon broke off from the path and headed up slope, leaving a well-defined trail Heleana could follow. As they disappeared in the undergrowth, Chelke the female elf jogged forwards to lead Heleana's group while R'chal dropped back to take the rearguard position. As the cart was lost to sight around a curve in the path, Wilder moved out of the shadows and came to walk beside R'chal, who placed a hand on the huge head and expressed her thanks.

Although they had separated the expedition, the cart still dictated their pace, as pushing the mule too hard would only chance injury to the beast or damage to the cart. Because of this, Heleana planned to travel into the night by the light of the waning full moon.

R'CHAL WAS WALKING with Wilder, thinking of the events of the last week, when the wolven suddenly disappeared into the growing afternoon shadows. Shocked out of her reverie, R'chal heard the clattering of hooves coming up behind her. She turned, selected an arrow from her quiver, then nocked and drew her bow.

Two horsemen came upon her at a gallop, but jerked to a stop twenty paces away when they saw the lone archer.

'Hold there,' ordered one rider. 'We have a squad not far behind.'

He motioned to his companion to take up his flatbow. As the weapon was raised, Wilder slipped out behind the horses and growled loudly. R'chal had never heard the wolven growl, but it was deep and full of menace. The horses immediately reared and bolted, causing both riders to be thrown and the flatbow to be fired prematurely. R'chal walked forwards with her bow trained on the leader. As she approached, she asked Wilder to watch the men as she disarmed them. The mental link between the two was proving very useful indeed.

With Wilder standing over the two Brocken soldiers, R'chal calmed one of the horses and retrieved a coil of hemp rope from the pommel. And with Wilder threatening to rip out the throat of the first to soldier move, R'chal could securely tie the two men together with their arms behind their backs and also bound their ankles. They would be found by the squad eventually, and R'chal had managed to delay a decision she had been grappling with. She was warring internally. She had a lingering doubt - *would she be able to fight and take a human life?*

The soldier who had spoken glared at R'chal with the clear intent that he would do some serious harm to her if he did not have an extremely large wolf breathing down his neck.

'Do you know who I am? I am Captain Rankin Du Tek, son of Baron Lord Tod Du Tek. You would do well to release me.'

R'chal smiled at the red-faced captain. With curses and threats ringing in her ears, R'chal watched Wilder blend back into the undergrowth.

R'chal approached the horse she had secured and took up the reins. She led the horse onwards and soon came upon the cart, where Heleana had gained control of the second runaway beast. R'chal approached the scene as Heleana turned towards her with the obvious need for an explanation.

'There were only two riders. One was a messenger,' R'chal said. She pointed out the message satchel on her horse's saddle. 'The other was some sort of squad leader, a Captain Du Tek, I think he said. At least he gave the orders. He did say a squad was not far behind,' she completed her report.

'These two horses have been ridden hard and look to be spooked or ill-used. We will lead them until we can care for them, and perhaps we can use them in the traces to speed our trip,' Heleana said. 'What did you do with the riders?'

'I tied them up and left them on the side of the road. I don't expect they will be too happy when they are found by their comrades,' R'chal said. 'As the Brocken soldiers have travelled farther and harder than we have, I think securing their only horses may give us enough advantage to keep ahead of them. Keep going. I will keep our back trail safe.'

R'chal turned to retake the rearguard position. This time, she was determined to keep her mind on the job and not allow the repetitive pace to lull her into inattention.

Shortly after dusk, R'chal asked Wilder to drop back and check on the Brocken squad and their whereabouts. He soon reported that soldiers followed. They had released the riders and come on quickly, but the extra pace had caused the men to tire, and the squad leader had called for a halt. Wilder told R'chal he would watch the squad while she went forwards to advise Heleana and Quinn they could safely stop for a while.

R'chal jogged forwards and was careful to ensure that Heleana and Quinn knew it was she who was approaching in the gloom just after the sun had gone down and before the moon's light was strong enough to illuminate the forest.

The cart slowed as she approached, and Heleana walked to the rear of the cart to receive R'chal's report. Upon hearing they could stop and rest, Heleana instructed Quinn to unharness the mule and care for the beast while she cared for the horse, ensuring they were adequately fed and watered. She asked R'chal to mount the remaining horse and go forward to bring in the elven warrior who had tirelessly scouted the path ahead all afternoon.

R'chal was sure not to rush and maintained a steady, unthreatening trot to allow the elf to discern her direction of travel and the lack of haste as the echoes of a horse's hooves striking the ground may be misread. Her own recent experience dictated a certain level of caution. She rode forwards until the green-clad elf stepped from concealment and touched her knee. Although she had been watching for and expecting contact with the elf, it came as shock and she tried but failed to stifle a yelp of surprise. R'chal used the sign language the Pathfinders had learnt from the elves to ask her to return to the cart for a meal and rest. At least that was what R'chal hoped the signing had meant.

As the group sat around a small brazier Quinn produced from the cart, it occurred to R'chal that she did not know the elf's name and only knew she was highly skilled with bow and arrow. R'chal was not aware of any break in good manners that would transpire if she conversed with the elf, so she assumed a leader would gather all knowledge of their companions and just ask.

'Hi, my name is R'chal,' she said. She held out her hand.

'Chelke,' the elf replied.

She grasped the out stretched arm wrist to wrist.

'You may call me Che, as my hunters do. You have proven yourself worthy.'

'And this is A'lek and Quinn,' R'chal indicated each as she continued the introductions.

'When we competed, Heleana called you Balju. Is that your title?' R'chal asked as Quinn handed around slices of travel bread spread with honey.

'Yes. It means keeper of our leader's laws. I fill the same role in our society as Lady Heleana's husband.'

Not wanting to give any advantage to the following Brocken squad the stop was very short. The bread was washed down with ladles of water. Each taking it in turns to dip from the barrel lashed to the side of the cart.

'Let's get on,' Heleana said. 'We are in luck. The horse you liberated from the messenger is a farm hack the Brocken stole. By the marks and calluses on its coat, it is broken to the harness, so we can use it to spell the mule and travel a little faster. This other horse, though gelded, is well-bred and well-trained. It is an officer's horse. I am sure he will not be pleased to lose such a valuable creature.'

Heleana grinned at R'chal's expression and the accompanying groan.

'I'm just making friends wherever I go,' R'chal said. 'Let's stick together in the dark. I will be told if the Brocken start to gain on us, and I do not want that cart to become stuck or damaged.'

R'chal busied herself with helping Quinn cool the brazier and pack the cart. Her suggestion was based more on wanting to walk with A'lek and discuss their current predicament and the possibilities they may face than any real fear of being caught. At the same time, she mentally advised Wilder of the plan.

Soldiers sleep, came back.

I am leaving food at our campsite, R'chal thought. R'chal left a dried haunch of goat where they had stopped hoping that Wilder would not mind the less succulent cut of meat.

Wise. Less noise than the hunt, Wilder sent, closing off the silent conversation.

When the bay mare was harnessed to the cart, the group could travel at an increased pace, but R'chal thought the mule was a little put out as it refused to move and tossed its head in the halter until Quinn pulled its ear, stared in its eyes and told it to behave.

PERRIN'S GROUP WERE not as lucky as R'chal's. The plan of leaving an easily read trail worked. It had divided the Brocken force that was trying to catch the fleeing cart. Unfortunately, that force was larger than a single squad. A full squad of six soldiers were now in pursuit.

When they left the path to head towards the mountains, the elevation allowed them to occasionally see the Brocken squad that had broken off the main force to track them. Whenever the soldiers traversed the clearings and openings in the forest canopy, it was apparent they were making ground on Perrin's party.

Following Heleana's instructions, they left a clear path, but this allowed the Brocken soldiers to close the gap in the chase. Perrin did not know their ultimate destination, but Martyn assured Perrin that he had been there before and could guide their group to the mountain refuge.

Perrin decided that, to honour his oath to protect Bren at whatever cost, he had to send Martyn and Bren on while he delayed the Brocken with ambush and misleading tracks.

When he outlined his intentions to Bren, the younger man vehemently decried the plan. Until Martyn stood before him, staring into his eyes, with hands firmly planted on each shoulder and explained that it was the best way to delay the soldiers. Thus ensuring Bren would arrive at the council three suns hence. The elf warrior added his agreement and indicated that he would stay with Perrin to even the odds. Two experienced woodsmen against six Brocken seemed to be about even.

Martyn and Bren redistributed the packs to allow Perrin and his companion less encumbrance to ease their concealment and movement through the forest. Once their task was complete, Perrin and the elf were armed with only longbows and blades and were free to flit from cover to cover.

Martyn and Bren led the horse in a more westerly direction while Perrin and the elf ensured their tracks were concealed from all but the best mountain trackers. After some time spent in this endeavour, Perrin signalled to the elf that it was time to turn their attention to the closing squad of Brocken soldiers. The obvious first step was to take down as many as possible with an ambush and a volley of arrows. Perrin and his companion returned to the trail they had blazed and set their trap.

The leader of the Brocken squad must have been well trained as they came on spaced apart from each other, with one tracking the fleeing horse and men while the next in line relayed back the findings. After these two, the following four were on guard and free to travel quickly in a defensive formation with flatbows cocked and loaded.

Perrin realised he could not change the plan, and taking out the two leading men would even the odds but would make it harder to silence the rest. With the sun setting behind them and a gloom enveloping the forest, Perrin could not risk a protracted battle. Therefore, he signalled to the elf that he would take the nearer soldier as he assumed the elf was the more experienced archer.

Their arrows flew true, and each soldier was pierced through the chest. Perrin was a farmer and hunter and had never wanted to kill a man. The revulsion he felt in his gut at his action was tempered by his love for his cousin and the oath he had taken to protect Bren, even at the cost of his own life and convictions.

The sudden loss of two of his men startled the Brocken leader, but he soon recovered and had his men under control.

The element of surprise had not been as successful as Perrin had hoped. Now it seemed they would have to fight until full dark could cover any retreat. With the Brocken under cover, the use of their longbows became less effective than the Brocken flatbows. The flatbow could be cocked and held until a target presented itself, while a longbow had to be aimed, drawn, and released in one fluid motion. To achieve the most accurate shot the archer had to step from concealment, providing a larger target for their enemy. Perrin now understood the great value of the new bow R'chal had introduced at the contest.

With Perrin providing cover, the elf made his way to Perrin's side to plan the next phase of this engagement. They decided the elf should flank the Brockens' position and try for a clear shot. This cat-and-mouse game could be played by both hunter and hunted. Perrin had lost sight of all members of the Brocken squad but had to maintain cover for his elf partner. He could only assume the squad leader was trying the same manoeuvre and had sent a squad member to silently and skillfully flank their own position.

Perrin was well protected by a fallen tree and the thick trunk of a mountain ash. He understood that trained soldiers may gain the upper hand over two young woodsmen. In preparation of possible hand to hand fighting Perrin drew his sword from its sheath and plunged the point into the loam of the forest floor. Leaning the hand and a half grip against the tree providing his refuge.

The Brocken kept up a steady rate of fire in Perrin's general direction, limiting the covering fire he could provide to the elf, but the growing shadows in the forest provided cover and concealed some movement. Added to the elf's ability to move silently, this eventually gave the elf a headshot that took down the leader, followed quickly by an arrow to the chest of a flatbowman. The remaining soldier turned to flee, only to be brought down by Perrin's arrow at almost exactly the same time Perrin was pierced by a flatbow bolt through his left breast that threw him backwards.

As Perrin struggled to regain his feet he heard the distinctive sound of a sword being drawn from a scabbard. The snapping of branches and a war cry only just registered in his brain through the haze of pain and shock. The soldier was intent on a kill. He had drawn his short sword and was running straight at Perrin.

When he vaulted the log Perrin had used as his hide, he came face to face with Perrin holding his own long sword while blood seeped through his jerkin and down his arm. With little time available, the soldier immediately attacked Perrin's wounded side, only to come up against a strong parry and solid defence while his quarry gasped in pain.

In his desperation to succeed, the soldier went for a high slice, figuring his opponent could not lift his sword quickly. Desparation gave Perrin one chance. Griting teeth against the pain he grasped the blade of his sword at the ricasso two span ahead of the crossguard with his left hand. He knew that hand was almost useless as strength bled from his side. By steadying the blade at the blunted section he could use all the strength in his right side. With his last effort he thrust with all he had left toward his attacker. Perrin felt his blade meet the resistance of the soldier's padded gambeson. Then slide through as his falling body weight forced the point of the blade through muscle and organ. It was arrested against bone deep in the soldier's torso. Perrin detected all strength deserting his assailant's body only a brief moment before the pain and shock overcame him and his own energy faded.

It was a death blow, and the combatants fell with their life's blood leaking from their wounds.

CHAPTER SIXTEEN
Hunted

One above all, to battle and lead.

PERRIN OMHOLT SWAM against the tide in a sea of hurt.

He fought to master the flood even as the pain blossomed and became hypnotic in its intensity. Perrin was hanging on to a promise. There was something he had to do. He had not completed his task. He could not remember what it was, but he had to stay and finish it. All he could picture was an innocent young boy reaching out to him as he was enveloped by a malevolent cloud. Perrin escalated his determination to fight against the soothing flow of pain attempting to drag him to oblivion. Perrin groaned as the searing pain intensified once again, and then he heard voices that seemed familiar.

'Bolt bites bone. No cut here. Not move.'

Perrin vaguely recognised the stilted speech accompanied by a deep throbbing rumble.

'The blood loss is not slowing, but if we cut, we may make matters worse. I am no healer.'

Perrin this this other voice as Boid, the elf warrior. Perrin once again surrendered pain's grip on his conscious thoughts.

DEVRON AND BOID WERE greatly concerned for the young woodsman. They had been told he was important to the resistance, and neither welcomed the thought of losing a comrade in arms. Devron was not aware of the hierarchy of the plainsmen but decided he was invested in the current happenings. He would not give up easily after all Varellon had been through.

'Search Brocken. Bandage, healing herbs. Fire, heat water. Poultice. Slow bleeding, find help,' Devron said.

When Devron gave the instruction to the elf, he expected derision at his orders. Instead, the elf nodded and sprang into action. Devron asked Varellon to lie down next to Perrin to warm him in a vain attempt to hold shock at bay while he used his small axe to shred kindling and wood for a fire.

It was now full dark, although the rising moon reflected a good deal of light. That and the elf's exceptional night vision allowed for a quick search of the dead soldiers. He did need to use his knife when one of the Brocken groaned as he was turned. The arrow had pierced him through the gut, and the knife was used more with mercy than anger.

'I have blankets, a cooking pot, bandages, a small sack of yarrow powder and a wild honeycomb wrapped in leaves,' the elf said.

' Make fire. Make warm. Varellon find herb for poultice.'

While they prepared, Perrin continued to groan as he neared the surface of consciousness and tried to remember why he must fight the darkness growing at the corners of his mind. Perrin occasionally heard voices, and the soothing lack of panic gave him the extra hope from someone was fighting for him. He again surrendered to the vortex of pain that dragged him deeper and deeper only to bring him back to the surface in a tortuous, never-ending cycle. And with each cycle, the periods of darkness grew.

Perrin was shocked into full consciousness when the pain sharpened to searing intensity. His eyes flew open, and he saw the large wolf laying across his lap.

'Hold Varellon,' Perrin heard from behind his shoulder.

'Perrin, hold fast,' the elf ordered as he pushed hard against the shaft of the flatbow bolt still protruding from Perrin's breast. Perrin swooned when the pain became unbearable.

DEVRON WAS GRATEFUL for Perrin's state of unconsciousness as he continued to draw the bolt through his shoulder and out below his shoulder blade. Devron quickly applied the poultice of honey, garlic and yarrow, used the moss to hold the mixture in place and then bound Perrin's wounds front and back, and securely bandaged it all in place.

'I find Wilder. Help.'

Leaving the elf as a guard and Perrin wrapped in blankets with a fire going, Devron and Varellon backtracked to find the Brocken squad. The fire would be a beacon to any pursuing Brocken, so before Devron could go for help, he had to ensure no one could come across the fire and the patient who lay at the mercy of time.

Devron knew that the ministrations given Perrin were, at best, rudimentary, and he would need a real healer as soon as possible. Night was no obstacle to a Wolf Rider and his partner, so Devron headed for the trading route to locate Wilder and find the Hunter and Apprentice.

Varellon loped along the path at a pace that ate the distance and could be sustained for an extended time. In the early morning, Varellon gave warning of enemies ahead. Devron asked his partner for speed, as stealth would take too much time, and they blasted through the camp of the eight remaining men of the Brocken force. The sudden rush of a flitting shadow and the surprise of a tired and nodding guard allowed Varellon to thunder past the soldiers, leaving shouted orders and stumbling men in their wake. They were well past when a lone flatbow was released in their direction, and the bolt skittered harmlessly behind them.

'Wilder.'

Varellon slowed to a walk as a shadow detached itself from the surrounding darkness. Devron had Varellon pass on the report of Perrin's injury as the two large canines stood nose to nose under the setting moon. Varellon shifted and told Devron that Wilder was communicating with the Hunter, and her pack was being woken. Wilder and the wolf took off up the path, but Wilder's paced outstripped Varellon's as the more rested wolven's longer gait held advantage. His partner reported to Devron that the Hunter was at least a half sun's travel at this pace, which was a full sun's travel for the Brocken squad.

Wilder would run down the Hunters' pack in half that time.

R'CHAL WAS RUDELY AWAKENED just before dawn after only a brief, broken sleep following her midnight guard duty.

Hunter, Perrin injured in the mountains. I come, blasted into her sleep-deprived brain.

R'chal's shock at perceiving Wilder's voice brought her back to her current reality. She approached the recumbent form of the Lady of Sudhemere.

'Heleana, Perrin has been injured. Wilder is coming.'

Heleana woke with a start at R'chal's whispered news. The words took some time to register. 'R'chal, you have a rare gift. It is as magic to me, but I trust your insights.'

'R'chal, what has happened?' asked a groggy A'lek.

'Wilder reports that Perrin's party were attacked. Perrin has been wounded,' R'chal replied. 'Wilder is coming to take you to him. We can take the mule. Gather whatever you need, and we will head back and meet Wilder on the trail.'

Heleana looked at the practiced movement of the twins. It was obvious that they had training in the care of the injured. In the gloom A'lek was checking and packing medicinal supplies while R'chal tacked the mule ready to take the supplies A'lek was wrapping in blankets.

'Heleana, I must go with A'lek. We will see what can be done for your husband's brother,' R'chal said.

'R'chal, it is against my better judgement. It seems that the two of you are enmeshed in the future of our resistance,' Heleana said.

'Heleana, A'lek assisted our mother in her healings. I don't think we have a choice. Wilder is coming and will lead us.'

'Alright. We are far from the Brocken influence. No squad has come this far into the ranges. Go, I have grown rather fond of my brother-in-law. I wish to unite the Omholt family and retrieve a small portion of that which was stolen in the invasion by the Northern Empire. We will stay awhile and travel slowly so we can aid you if needed.'

'Come on A'lek, Wilder is coming on fast,' R'chal said.

'A'lek hold the mule tight. Wilder is near. He has told me he will ease the beast,' R'chal said.

R'chal turned to A'lek to help hold the mule as the whites of its eyes showed and it danced at the end of the lead rope. With its snapping teeth and stamping hooves, A'lek wanted no part in securing the beast but was not about to ignore R'chal's need.

Help me calm the beast, Apprentice. I will not eat it. A'lek understood the words that came into the minds conciousness. It was as though the mule was relaying Wilder's instructions.

A'lek concentrated on radiating calmness and companionship. It was understood that the herd mentality relied on the support of all in the herd. A'lek also projected calmness towards R'chal and

Wilder as herd mates, indicating that the mule was now of this herd and would always be protected by A'lek's herd. When the mule had calmed and become less recalcitrant, Wilder could approach without the beast bolting.

When R'chal hugged the huge canine, A'lek felt a push in the shoulder and understood the mule wanted an arm around its neck as an assurance of the promise of protection.

'Wilder says wisely done,' R'chal said.

'I could hear him. Why can't I hear him now?'

R'chal stood for a time staring at the Wolven.

'Wilder says you are the apprentice and you will understand in time. The connection only works when you can share a mind,' R'chal responded. 'Wilder is apparently bonded to me in a similar way that Devron is to Varellon only while he wants to be. Wolven are of a high order and can choose to participate or withdraw at will. I am not completely sure, but that is the feelings he projects to me,' R'chal said. 'He also said it was wise to bring the mule as they are smarter than horses. Horses can run faster, so they do not need to be so intelligent. Wilder doubts we would be able to control a horse in his presence. He has directed Varellon to head into the mountains. We can cut off the track here, and Wilder will lead us to Perrin.'

R'chal turned to the mule and retrieved a small pack along with her bow and quiver. As she prepared herself, A'lek was left holding the mule, which was standing quite strangely with its head firmly planted against A'lek's chest.

'You lead the mule and follow Wilder. I am going to sweep our trail and make certain that we can't be followed. Get going, Wilder is worried by Devron's description of the wound. You will be needed,' R'chal said.

'Ok, but I only helped mother treat the worst cuts and breaks. I am not sure I can save a life.'

'Let's just get to Perrin. I am sure we can help.'

Wilder was waiting at the top of a rise ahead when A'lek turned uphill. The mule immediately followed A'lek and did not show any form of the wilfulness normally associated with the breed. A'lek maintained a steady pace as the mule often pushed forwards and assisted when the slope became steeper. The wolven flitted ahead and stopped often to await the Apprentice and the mule. A'lek had lost sight of R'chal but was sure that Wilder maintained contact.

A'lek now had the chance to explore a growing number of sentient consciousnesses that touched an awareness within him as they travelled. What startled A'lek most was the variety and differing strengths of these consciousnesses. Ever since joining Wilder in the mule's mind, it was like a switch had been thrown, and a link was growing with the forest and all its inhabitants.

In the late afternoon, A'lek was snapped out of his musings when R'chal stepped from behind a large tree.

'Just who is leading who?'

A'lek was holding the lead rope while the mule pulled him towards a copse of mountain fir. Wilder was nowhere to be seen, and Devron stood atop a downed trunk peppered with flatbow bolts. A'lek smelled smoke and realised they had arrived at Perrin's camp.

'R'chal looked fondly on her twin as A'lek fell straight into healing methods. She gave the mule water and asked Boid to feed the beast oats when it was ready. They would need the mule to help transport Perrin.

A'lek had immediately moved to the patient. Glancing with concern at R'chal, A'lek's countenance expressed worry. R'chal nodded reassurance as she shared those fears for the patient. A'lek examined the aid that the elf and Devron had provided and was greatly relieved that the poultice included infection-fighting ingredients.

A'lek peeled back the blood-soaked bandages to get a look at the damage. As the bandage came away, the tree moss that made up the bulk of the poultice fell away, allowing a flow of fresh blood to trickle down Perrin's chest. A'lek quickly replaced the moss and applied pressure to the gaping hole of the entry wound.

'R'chal, come here and press down on this bandage firmly. We will have to clean these wounds with hot water and repack the sites with a fresh poultice. He has lost a lot of blood, but the blood flow does not indicate the severing of a major vessel. I am more concerned that the bolt may have pierced a lung, but his breathing would be more erratic if that was the case. Shock and the blood loss may still take Perrin from us.'

R'chal's pride in her sibling grew as she watched A'lek's training and practice from their mother come to the fore. A'lek quickly finished the ministrations needed to give Perrin the best chance of reaching more experienced healers. The tightness and neatness of the bandaging would maintain pressure on the wounds and keep the poultice well positioned during the trip down through the forest.

'This will need stitching. You did well to stem the blood flow. The yarrow and garlic are doing their job,' A'lek explained. 'If he starts to bleed again, we may have to cauterise the wound, but that would cause permanent damage to his shoulder. It looks as though the bolt has not caused major damage to any internal organ, but it has caused damage to the muscles and ligaments. The more intense pain relates to the bone being chipped. While I clean up, R'chal, can you rig up a travois?'

While A'lek, with Boid's aid, finished attending to Perrin, R'chal and Devron took to the forest in search of some stout poles. R'chal explained the theory to Devron, who immediately understood the principle because his people used a similar device when moving families about their range. He soon found what they needed and felled three green saplings with his axe. It was not long before a very sturdy travois was hitched to the mule, using blankets taken from the packs of the Brocken soldiers. Once the patient was secured to the travois, they were ready.

'Devron, can you be our scout and watch for any nearby Brocken?' R'chal asked.

Hunter, I am nearby, came from Wilder.

Perrin moaned as the jostling spiked his pain level. R'chal and A'lek noticed that Perrin was vaguely aware of being moved onto the travois. This may be a sign that he was starting to come around.

The strange procession started their journey out of the mountains. An anxious A'lek kept watch on the patient while R'chal led the mule, always looking for the easiest route down so as not to jar Perrin too much.

R'chal was trying to balance speed and the comfort of the patient. The main concern was finding the trading route and ensuring they were well enough ahead of the Brocken to give Perrin a chance to get the healing he desperately needed. At times, the going became so rough that A'lek and the elf had to take hold of the travois poles and carry the patient over the broken ground to ease the bumping and swaying of the contraption.

R'chal continued to lead her group downslope as the forest opened up, with the trees becoming larger and more spread out. She held up her hand in the signal to stop and remain still. R'chal studied the trading route from the safety of the undergrowth that grew thicker closer to the path. Before she would commit to the faster travel, the trading route offered, she wanted to confirm the position of the Brocken squad. When she tried to contact Wilder, she received no response. R'chal suddenly became fearful that her reliance on their link had overshadowed her own decision-making skills. It was a valuable lesson, but a most inopportune time to learn it.

R'chal waved Boid forward.

'Can you range ahead and study the signs? We will wait awhile, before following.'

No sooner had they stepped onto the path than both the elf and Devron appeared from ahead. So much for that plan, R'chal thought to herself. Both scouts reported that the Brocken squad had passed this site recently, and the signs showed they were under forced march. A'lek took the opportunity to check his patient as R'chal received the reports of the wolf rider and elf.

'R'chal, he can't take much more of this rough travel. We need to get him onto the cart and find a real healer as soon as we can,' A'lek said.

R'chal's only choice was to continue on the path and send Devron and Varellon ahead as scouts while she and the elf provided protection for A'lek and Perrin. Fortunately, the need to travel slowly would keep them well behind a squad of soldiers being forced to march. It would be up to Devron to give them ample warning if they were getting too close to the soldiers. The smoother travelling conditions made the going easier on the patient. However, A'lek was scared that the decreased moaning and periods of semi-consciousness may not be attributed to that greater comfort.

When Devron reappeared from a trip of scouting ahead, Wilder communicated with R'chal.

Cart, attacked, Lady of Sudhem and Elf defending blacksmith, R'chal heard from Wilder.

Varellon rushed forwards with Devron waving his arms in warning.

'Cart attack. Broke wheel. Brocken,' Devron reported.

'How far ahead?' asked R'chal.

'Not far. Orders, Hunter.'

Devron was relying on the knowledge of an experienced leader. R'chal knew each of the others also looked to her to make the tough choices while keeping them safe. R'chal felt Wilder's presence on the right flank and knew the Brocken would soon try to outflank the defenders. R'chal wondered at the understanding of tactics that had suddenly come to her but did not have the time to delve into the phenomenon.

'Devron and Boid, take the left flank and ensure no Brocken get close. Go quickly,' she said.

Wilder, please defend your flank, R'chal projected and welcomed the warmth she got when the feeling of affirmation filled her senses.

'A'lek, get off the path and protect Perrin,' she said.

R'chal was surprised when the mule began edging off the path even before A'lek had acknowledged her order. R'chal steeled herself and checked her weapons. She could outshoot flatbows in distance, accuracy, and rate of fire by at least three to one. She also knew she could rely on Che and Heleana to hold firm under pressure, so an attack on the squad's rear would be relatively safe and sow discord amongst the ranks of tired, hard-pressed men.

R'chal had left the rapier Quinn had gifted her in the cart as she had rushed into the forest on Perrin's rescue mission. She vowed she would learn swordcraft and always have the backup available from now on.

As R'chal stalked forward, her conscience battled the same question that befell her when she met the soldiers on the road. Hunting and killing game for survival while always following the ways taught her by her father was one thing but?

Could she kill a man?

R'chal took in the scene. The squad was being held back by very accurate bow fire and had not managed to organise beyond finding shelter. Che and Heleana had made the most of their first volley as two Brocken lay bleeding on the path. From the rear, R'chal saw the officer goading his men to follow his directions, shouting threats of retribution and promises of punishment. His ranting indicated his lack of actual control over his men. He clearly only led through his rank and the position his father held in the occupation. His tactics were that of a bully.

R'chal gleefully took the opportunity to shut him up by placing an arrow in his right buttock and pinning his hand to the tree he fell against with her next shot. When the squad realised they were surrounded, some broke off into the protection of the forest on either side of the path. The two that broke cover on the left were immediately felled by arrows from Che and Boid.

The two Brocken soldiers who had slipped into the forest on the right immediately ran screaming from cover to throw themselves down, begging for mercy. R'chal approached from the rear, keeping the remaining Brocken cowered by the threat of her bow while Heleana and Che moved forwards to assist in keeping the soldiers subdued.

When Devron, his wolf and the second elf warrior appeared, the squad saw the value of surrender and became compliant as Quinn moved amongst them, collecting weapons and belt knives.

Thank you, Wilder, R'chal projected.

Hunter, was all she perceived in return.

R'chal welcomed leaving the disposition of the prisoners to Lady Heleana as she returned to A'lek to bring up the injured Perrin. By the time they returned, Quinn was supervising two of the prisoners as they fixed the cart under the watchful arrows of the two elf warriors.

Lady Heleana questioned the officer as his wounds were being attended to by the third uninjured squad member. Perrin became the focus of the group when it was discovered the Brocken squad carried basic medical supplies. With the prisoners under the watch of the wolf and rider, and the elves, Lady Heleana and A'lek prepared to clean out Perrin's wounds again and sew them closed using the Brocken's medical kit.

'How is the patient?' R'chal asked.

'Still delirious and in and out of consciousness. Fortunately, the soldiers have a decent medical kit and we can now close his wounds. Sewing will allow an almost complete recovery bar some impressive scarring.' A'lek replied. 'Can you and Quinn use the travois to rig a stretcher in the cart? If we string it from the sides, we can limit the jarring of the cart.'

'Heleana, what shall we do with these men?' R'chal asked.

'Four unarmed Brocken with their Captain injured should be no danger. I would usually march them with us, but Perrin is our priority, so we must send them on their way.'

'We watch,' Devron said.

'Devron and Varellon can escort them until they are safely distant,' R'chal said.

She also knew Wilder would soon appear to the squad to lend support to the wolf and her rider. After the three soldiers were sent off, carrying their leader and well-guarded, the group prepared to leave.

Although Perrin had received further treatment, A'lek and Heleana had concurred that he was far from out of danger. The group would not stop until Perrin was safely under the care of more experienced healers.

With the horse in the traces, Quinn led off in the cart. Heleana had identified the tiredness in R'chal and insisted she ride the other horse while Heleana led it.

'You shot to wound rather than kill,' Heleana said.

'I wanted to give you the opportunity to question the leader.'

'As it happens, I did want to know why he had goaded his men to come this far into the foothills. It was all about the horse you confiscated from him. He took it as a personal insult and wanted the beast back. It seems the horse was more important than his men.'

R'chal could only wonder at the folly of men and the effect one event had over the lives of others. Once again, she felt a tugging towards understanding that decisions made in battle generally meant someone would die. R'chal was grateful for the steady swaying of the horse and soon became very drowsy. She was not sure she wasn't dreaming when she looked over and saw A'lek draped over the back of the mule, fast asleep, while the animal took great pains to keep his somnolent load safe and steady.

R'chal was only partially aware of the continued clop of the horse's hooves during the night when she was righted in the saddle after slipping to one side in her sleep. She woke when the horse stopped, and she heard voices surrounding her.

Their party had met with another group heading to the council meeting. Heleana decided it would be faster if Perrin was carried on his stretcher by a relay of Pathfinders. They had experience in transferring the wounded to safety, and running men could outstrip a horse and cart when the duty was shared.

Dawn was just breaking. Heleana assured R'chal and A'lek they would reach their destination by mid-sun, but Perrin would be in the hands of the healers well before then. The second group of Pathfinders loaded much of their gear onto the cart to transport the wounded Perrin more swiftly. After a quick farewell to Lady Heleana, they vanished down the road, leaving R'chal unsure of the events that had just transpired.

'Time for a good hot breakfast. We are safely beyond the occupation and within easy distance of our objective,' Heleana said.

With the relief of no pursuit and confirmation from Heleana that their trek would soon be at an end, R'chal and A'lek could sit quietly over their cooked ham, bread and cheese and discuss their companions. Lady Heleana had proven welcoming and supportive. Quinn was well known to the siblings, even more so to A'lek. Che and Boid had not questioned her orders. She had not spent enough time with the others who had set out with them to determine their alliance but none had given any negative indications.

RESISTANCE

Was this her leadership or the presence of Lady Heleana?

CHAPTER SEVENTEEN
Pathfinders

Zammok's black, by example, extort the cohort to thrive.

'LET'S GET GOING.'

With breakfast over, Heleana ordered a start to the sun's travel. It was a much-relieved group that packed the cart and hitched the horse. The morning was bright, with sunbeams slanting through the leaves and the birds and insects of the forest singing and buzzing as they began their sun's work. R'chal could almost forget the questions that had so recently plagued her. There was no need to scout or backtrack, so Che and Boid could walk with the group. Only Devron and Varellon stayed well clear, moving deep in the forest to give space to the horses and mule.

R'chal had been lagging behind, deep in her own thoughts, when she shivered from top to toe and shook herself out from her doldrums. She strode up to walk beside Heleana.

'Finished second guessing yourself?' Heleana asked.

'How did you know?' R'chal said.

'You would not be a leader if you did not dissect every aspect of an engagement and see if you could have done better. It was as I would do and as I had hoped you would do,' Heleana said.

'Heleana, so much has happened. I hardly know which way to turn. I have to know more about this conflict if I am to help you the best way I can. I am but a country hunter, I have no knowledge of the machinations of those in power. What exactly am I walking into?' R'chal asked.

'Until now, we of the Southlands had little understanding of the best way to defend ourselves other than by passive resistance. We acceded to the demands of the invaders to try to ease the pain and suffering of the population. The Pathfinders have only tried to limit the spread of the Brocken influence and curb their most vile acts. This stalemate has lasted turns, and now we must unite and fight back.

'We travel to a meeting of the three races of the Southlands to plan our push against the tyranny and occupation of the Northern Empire,' Heleana said. 'The Elves, Wolf Riders and people of the Southern plains will unite and develop a plan to push the Brocken from our borders.'

'A'lek and I will help in the best way we can,' R'chal said.

She watched her sibling ahead on the path and smiled as the mule nudged A'lek for attention.

The two women fell into a companionable silence as they marched along, ruminating over their parts in what was to come. Could the Southlands push back an occupier that was better armed, trained and equipped? R'chal only hoped these leaders had a good understanding of the Northern Empire.

She knew that one must know and understand one's enemy in the same way she had to know and understand what she hunted. At least she was sure the new bow to the south would greatly improve their defence and give their attacks a clear advantage over flatbows. She had only to ensure that the design and knowledge of the new weapon did not find its way into northern hands.

R'chal was shocked out of her musings when a green-clad and masked Pathfinder jumped down from a branch and landed directly in front of A'lek, startling the mule, which brayed in fright and skittered behind the Apprentice.

'Lady Heleana, well met,' the Pathfinder said. Then he followed up with a series of hand signals, only some of which R'chal understood.

'Lead on, Aitien,' Heleana said.

She turned to her fellows and indicated they should all follow. Quinn brought up the cart, and they were led to a cleft in the wall of what otherwise seemed an impenetrable cliff face. The group was led through a passage that opened onto a vast valley, the remnant of a substantial volcano crater. In its centre was an almost perfectly round lake, the still surface mirroring the far wall of the crater and the white clouds scudding in a clear blue sky.

R'chal surveyed the sight. The crater's walls were pockmarked with various cave mouths, and the valley floor was set up as an organised camp. Tents were neatly erected in rows with more permanent structures that could be mess halls or cooking facilities, as they were the only places smoke wafted from. While it looked well planned, the encampment also looked like it could be easily dismantled. R'chal determined that part of the safety of the resistance lay in its mobility.

R'chal and Heleana waited at the mouth of the pass as their group halted to take in the vista. Beside R'chal, Heleana relaxed and sighed as they saw her husband striding towards them. Perhaps he had news of his brother. Perrin had never been far from her thoughts. As he advanced, Heleana ran to him and threw herself into his arms.

R'chal wondered if they were conflicted by feeling their love and joy from being together again while also worrying about his brother. And if she would ever find a love like that.

'How is Perrin?' Heleana asked.

This was an answer the whole party were eager to hear.

'He is resting comfortably,' he said. 'A'lek, R'chal, thank you for seeing to Perrin. Our medics say your actions have given him the best chance to fully recover. He sleeps now, and his colour improves.'

'I must give credit to Devron. His initial care went a long way to stopping infection. Where is Devron?' A'lek asked.

'The Wolf Rider will join the pack high on the rim. They will only come down to the valley floor once the horses and mules are cared for and stabled,' Garat said. 'They are most aware of the effect their partners have on our livestock. Heleana, have you had word of Prince Brycen?'

Garat glanced around the group. The Pathfinders who had brought in Perrin had also delivered the news of the group's separation to avoid pursuit.

'He was with Martyn. They had a horse. Have they not arrived?' Heleana asked. She was suddenly worried that her plan may have put the prince in harm's way.

'Do not be overly concerned, my love. I have sent out squads to bring them in,' Garat said.

He took Heleana's hand and signalled to the group to follow him. Garat led them around the lake, towards a group of tents set apart from the rest. As they walked, the shimmering reflection from the lake mirrored the changing views of the crater around them.

Indicating the largest of the tents, Garat said rather pointedly, 'That, my darling, is our tent.'

R'chal saw the wicked grin that crossed his face. She hoped it would put Heleana at ease over the still-missing prince.

The rest of the party members were shown to a tent and took their belongings from the cart. Once they were settled, Garat called a squad of Pathfinders over to take Quinn and the cart to the armoury and the horse and mule to the stables.

As a warrior tried to lead the mule, it kicked out and broke away to run and into the tent that A'lek had just entered, threatening to collapse the tent around them. A bewildered A'lek coaxed the beast out of the immediate danger.

'A'lek, I think you had better go with them and take your friend. He seems to like you,' R'chal said. A smile crossed her features at the absurdity of A'lek now having a mule attached at the hip.

'Well, I don't have much to unpack, so I may as well look around,' A'lek said.

A'lek stared at the beast before taking up its lead rein. R'chal watched Quinn, leading the cart, and A'lek, leading the mule, follow a Pathfinder to a cave mouth where a post and rail fence had been erected. The corral also looked like it could be dismantled and moved with very little warning.

R'chal was standing near the lake, staring at the reflections in its waters, losing herself in the safety and beauty of her surroundings, when she noticed Quinn walking towards her. The other young woman carried a pack in one hand and a long-handled, heavy-looking hammer in the other. Quinn dropped the pack at R'chal's feet.

'We are bunk mates apparently,' she said.

'Surely you don't use that thing at the forge?' R'chal asked. She pointed at the hammer.

'This is for northern heads, not plough shears,' Quinn said. 'It was my father's and his father's before. I could not leave it and will carry it proudly into battle.'

'Quinn, you have far more value in your craft than as just another arm in battle,' R'chal said.

R'chal pointed to the tent they were to share and invited Quinn to settle herself in. R'chal was sitting on her pallet watching Quinn unpack her few possessions when the pair were hailed from outside.

'R'chal, Quinn, come. I have a surprise for you,' Heleana said.

R'chal looked at Quinn, who nodded and followed R'chal as she left the tent. Standing outside were Heleana and Che, looking rather pleased with themselves and much more relaxed than they had at any other time over the last six suns. R'chal welcomed the mood as their travels had tired her, and she had used muscles she had not worked for some time. Heleana led them towards a screen of woven saplings hiding the opening of a cave.

As they approached, R'chal could see pale puffs escaping from the mouth of the cave and moisture settling on the stone.

'Is that steam?' asked R'chal.

'Come on and see,' Heleana said.

R'chal entered the cave and was delighted to see a grotto lit with candles and a pool of steaming water fed by a trickle of boiling water bubbling from a fissure in the rock. Although the thought of a bath was delightful, R'chal was still not totally accustomed to communal bathing with relative strangers. Sharing a mountain stream or bucket of lukewarm water with A'lek was more usual. Her previous experience at the village was the first time she had bathed with anyone else.

As Quinn and Heleana disrobed, R'chal considered that the benefit would be greater than any embarrassment. R'chal was confident in her body and knew her two-span tall frame was well proportioned. She had always considered her breasts a bit too large for archery, but her long legs and wide shoulders were always commented upon as perfect for farming and hunting. R'chal sighed as she sank into the inviting waters.

Che also hesitated to join the three women in the pool, and at first, R'chal thought it may be for cultural reasons until she observed the elf considering the various shelves in the rock walls. When satisfied, Che divested herself of boot knives, belt knives, hunting knives from her hip sheaths, a large knife strapped to her back under her shirt, and even a selection of throwing stars hidden among the intricate braids of her long hair. R'chal was fascinated and wanted to ask Che the story her braids told, but deemed it was too soon to ask such a personal question.

R'chal watched Che shuck her jerkin and unlace the thong of her shirt. The first thing R'chal noticed as she drew her shirt over her head was the pattern of dark tattoos enveloping each arm. The intricate designs were nearly lost on the elf's glowing, dark-ebony skin. R'chal was captivated and watched Che unwind her chest bindings, releasing plump breasts, slightly upturned at the dark brown nipple. The tattoos crossed her chest and met at her cleavage. Four jagged scars bisected the design just above Che's left breast. An even more horrifying set of scars ran from her hip down to her knee. R'chal felt a strange attraction as she studied the now fully naked Che.

In an attempt to disguise her growing blush, R'chal fully immersed herself and scrubbed her hair. R'chal burst from underwater, spluttering, and turned from Che when the elf entered the pool. R'chal had not had such a reaction to Heleana or Quinn, who both now shared the bathing pool. What was going on?

R'chal knew she should hide her shock until she understood her feelings and was grateful that the water was hot enough to put a rosy glow on her pale skin and hid her flushed features. As the four women relaxed in the pool, R'chal glanced once more at the scars showing vividly on Che's left breast, floating just above the waterline.

'That is an impressive set of scars you have,' Heleana said.

'Felion, the cats of the savannah on our side of the great desolation, are larger and far more fierce than your little ikats. On occasion, one will attack a lone traveller or a child. This one proved more cagey than most. His pelt adorns the floor of my lapa. I lay next to his cooling body for half a sun before I was strong enough to see to my wounds. This is one of his teeth.'

Che flicked one of her braids over her shoulder, showing a large yellowing incisor bound between knots and coloured beads.

'That is not an insignificant scar you carry yourself, Heleana,' Che said.

'Flatbow bolt. I was fortunate it was at extreme range and a lucky shot. It lodged in as far as the barb and did no permanent internal damage. They had to cut it out on the run, so the scar is worse than it could have been. I was delirious for a time but had a wonderful night's sleep under an old elm tree and woke up sore but stronger. None of my squad could understand the turnaround. At least it matches the scratch Perrin stitched on my shoulder.' Heleana turned to display the reddened scar of a recently healed wound.

The blasé way the women spoke about their near-death experiences spoke volumes about the tenacity and strength in their well muscled and toned bodies.

The mineral content of the waters did wonders for their tired limbs. Later, a relieved, clean and refreshed R'chal sat outside her tent dressed in the embroidered shirt and riding outfit Heleana had given her while Quinn lightly oiled and plaited her hair.

As evening neared, the valley became animated as hunting parties returned with game to be cooked over open fires. R'chal noted an array of offerings, ranging from large fish from the mountain streams to ducks and geese. One group even brought in two large deer. The bustle of cooks and their assistants was busiest around the wooden huts as the lazy wisps of smoke became a haze that floated on the still air within the valley of their safe haven. A'lek approached R'chal and Quinn while towelling wet hair.

'Well, that was a refreshing swim, wasn't it? I stunk of the mule and the stables so took the opportunity to bathe.'

A'lek was shivering from the icy coldness of the lake and looked perplexed when Quinn and R'chal burst into laughter.

'Why not use the hot spring?' Quinn asked when she could finally take a breath between fits of laughter. 'It is very warm and relaxing.'

'There is a hot bath? No one told me there was a hot bath,' A'lek said.

'Come with me, I will show you,' Quinn said.

Quinn took A'lek's hand and headed towards the screened cave. R'chal watched them leave and noted that Quinn did not relinquish her twin's hand.

'I think our young smith has taken a liking to the Apprentice,' Heleana said.

'They have been dancing around the issue for several turns. The amusing part is they think no one else can see the attraction.'

'We have time before this evening's meal. Perhaps I can begin to answer some of those questions you had for me earlier,' Heleana said.

Heleana approached and came to sit beside R'chal on a stool looking out over the darkening waters of the valley's lake. As each star appeared in the night sky, a twin appeared in the still waters.

'Heleana, thank you. The tinker came to us and helped us bury our mother. That was when he introduced us to Wilder and told us we had a part to play in the future of the resistance. I did not believe him until Wilder talked to me. Then the tinker set in motion the plan to rebuild Kjieran's bow in a size that a full grown man could use. That was as far as he would explain other than insisting that A'lek was to become his apprentice. What do you know of our future?'

'None of us knows what tomorrow brings. We are here to meet with those who represent the ancient ones and pool our knowledge. Bren, if that horrible man has not lost him, will be the leader that those under the thumb of the invader can focus their hope on. You, Garat and I will unite the Pathfinders, Elves and Wolf Riders into a force to match the Brocken soldiers. A'lek, on the other hand, has been singled out to follow in the footsteps of the healers.'

'Everything that has happened is overwhelming. You are lucky you have someone to share it all with.'

'Yes, I am.' Heleana looked about the camp as a sinister smile spread across her features. 'Come, let's find my errant husband. I want to make sure he knows he has been ignoring his duties.' Heleana jumped up from her seat and pulled R'chal up after her.

R'chal and Heleana enjoyed an evening stroll around the lake, which seemed a popular pastime as they encountered other groups walking or jogging past. At one point, they stopped to watch a knife throwing contest a number of Pathfinders had challenged Che and her companion to. The target was a split log with a rough figure of a Brocken soldier outlined in charcoal. Che stepped to the line, then looked around at the growing audience of Pathfinders. She turned and took five paces back, then, in the next heartbeat, she let her belt knives fly, striking the centre of the head and body mass.

Her achievement was met with resounding applause, then cheers when she added her throwing stars in a single line across the chest. The growing appreciation of Che's feat was suddenly replaced by a collective groan as the large hunting knife from her back sheath thumped impressively into the groin area of the figure.

Heleana and R'chal's clapping from the rear of the group was the only sound associated with admiration as many of the audience's hands went instinctively to protect their personal property. Che acknowledged the applause as she strode forwards to retrieve her various weapons. The wry smile on the elf's face only added to her mystique.

As R'chal and Heleana neared the completion of their trip about the lake, a flustered A'lek approached them, followed by Quinn, looking somewhat perplexed. A'lek kept looking back at Quinn, even after grabbing R'chal's hand and leading her away with a wave of apology to Lady Heleana.

'R'chal, the bath... they share... share,' A'lek stammered.

'A'lek,' R'chal said. 'Just enjoy the adventure and make sure you do not embarrass Quinn. She is important, and I think she rather likes you.'

'Do you really think so?' A'lek asked.

'Yes, everybody does. Now, say something nice to her. I think she does not quite understand your reaction,' R'chal said.

R'chal ushered A'lek back towards Heleana and Quinn, who had been watching the animated discussion. As they approached, R'chal was amused in the knowledge her welcoming smile contrasted the look of sheer terror on A'lek's face. A groan emanated from R'chal and a guffaw from Heleana when A'lek announced to Quinn, 'I like your hair.'

Quinn turned and ran to her tent.

A'lek looked from R'chal to Heleana and back again completely flummoxed. To save A'lek from complete apoplexy, Heleana asked, 'Why don't we go and check on Perrin and see if he will be well enough for the summit on the morrow?'

Heleana led the still shell-shocked A'lek and R'chal to another series of tents set apart in an alcove off the main valley. It was set closest to the entry pass, so it could be the first area evacuated if such a situation arose. The tents surrounded a more substantial hut, built of logs with a chimney and a porch, yet it still had a canvas roof, belying the impermanence of the camp.

Heleana stepped up and knocked on the only wooden door in the entire valley. The door was opened by a small woman in the process of gathering her long hair into a bun. The one or two strands of grey did not help R'chal determine the woman's age, but Heleana's reaction pushed that consideration aside.

'Aunt Winnie!' Heleana said, gathering the woman in a warm embrace and lifting her off her feet.

'Leana, put me down. I taught you better manners. Now introduce me to your companions,' the woman said.

'But Aunt Winnie, where have you been?' Heleana asked.

'Later, my girl, right now I have patients to care for, and you have still to introduce me to the Hunter and the Apprentice,' she said. 'I have known of you both for many turns.'

Heleana gathered her wits and introduced R'chal and A'lek to Lady Winifred, former nanny and tutor to the king.

'My Lady,' A'lek said. R'chal nodded and noted that A'lek was becoming quite adept at this strange level of courtesy.

'Aunt Winnie, we have come to see about Perrin and his recovery. A'lek and R'chal were instrumental in bringing him down out of the mountains,' Heleana said.

'Yes, that was a job well done. The speed of his travel saved blood loss and possibly even his life. A'lek, I believe we have you to thank for saving his shoulder. This boy has a part to play in what is to come,' Aunt Winnie said. 'After some hard work, young Per is sleeping and resting. He will completely recover and be well enough to attend tomorrow.' Lady Winifred said before suddenly changing tack. 'Where is that twice damned Tinker? He should have seen to this.'

'Aunt Winnie, he was sent off with the prince. They should have arrived by now. I did not have another option,' Heleana said.

'Leana, my girl, do not fret. I will deal with that charlatan upon their arrival. Right now, I think you have other important matters to attend to,' she said.

Lady Winifred indicated the approaching figure of Garat Omholt.

CHAPTER EIGHTEEN
Moot

A world gives up freedoms and sentience
Endowing inner light to each defender.

A MUTED BELL'S TOLL echoed throughout the valley. The morning call to breakfast was hardly needed as the smells of baking bread and frying meats hung in the clear mountain air, making mouths water.

The meeting to be held this sun promised direction and clarity. Everyone present was aware of the pivotal nature of the discussions, even if they were not to attend. The scouts and other members of the Pathfinders understood that their jobs in the valley were valued and important. As much as the jobs of the leaders of the three races in preparing the plan that would guide the Southlands back from the oppression of the occupying Brocken forces.

The stories told around the campfires about the Hunter's performance at the challenge boded well for the dire decisions that may well be made. Each person in the valley had a job that would culminate in an outcome they had fought towards. Some directly in the face of the enemy and some secret, hidden within the occupied territories. The only two points of concern raised in the whisperings were the missing Prince and the age of the person said to be the Hunter.

The summit was set to convene in the mid-morning in one of the largest caverns of the valley floor. R'chal sat outside her tent as Quinn once again attended to her hair. Quinn had begged for a chance to present the Hunter with hair braided in the style of the Elven warriors. While R'chal didn't mind, she knew Quinn was more interested in talking about A'lek than practicing a change in profession.

As Quinn finished R'chal's braids, she pointed out Lady Heleana and her husband approaching. Quinn was still so overawed by the importance of the company she now kept that she bowed on their approach and slipped into the tent behind her.

'You know you don't need to do that, Quinn. You are just as important as anyone here,' R'chal said.

'R'chal, it is near time,' Garat said.

He held out his hand to assist R'chal to stand. 'Where is the apprentice?'

'A'lek has become fascinated by the healing qualities of the mineral hot spring, and I believe is making a hands-on study of the benefits,' R'chal said. 'I will ask Quinn to go and collect my sibling.'

Before R'chal could turn to the tent, Quinn emerged and sprinted towards the screened cave mouth.

'I don't think she needs a reason to be with A'lek,' Heleana quipped.

'I see that we will be joined by the other races. Che is over there with other elves I have not seen before, and Devron's Wolf Riders have also come in.' R'chal said.

'They are all waiting for the signal from Garat to convene the meeting,' said Heleana.

Suddenly, and with a little guilt, R'chal thought of Wilder. Before she could cast out a thought, she heard, *Hunter, I am near.*

Garat and Heleana looked a little concerned as R'chal sighed in relief but were distracted when Quinn and a still dishevelled A'lek joined them. Quinn quickly picked up the brush she had used on R'chal's hair. Not having the time to match the twins' hair, Quinn ran the brush through A'lek's locks. She quickly bound the hair into a loose braid using several leather ties. This ensured the Apprentice would be presented looking somewhat tidy even if completely bewildered.

Garat raised his outstretched arm to shoulder height and brought his closed fist to his chest in the universal signal of "come and unite". The waiting groups began to move towards the meeting place and entered the cavern one at a time. Garat led his group around the lake, ensuring they would be the last to enter, not so much as a gesture but to give him the greatest chance of saving face by producing the still-missing Prince.

'My search for Prince Brycen has been for nought. Every squad has reported back that there is no sign. It is as if all trace of them has been erased,' Garat said. 'Hunter, we may need your tracking skills sooner rather than later.'

The cavern was set with stools, stumps and logs arranged before a rock ledge that held only three high-backed chairs, one occupied by Lady Winifred. She stood and indicated they take the five stools set for them, closest to the right hand of the dais. As Garat helped his wife to her seat, R'chal and A'lek sat, but Quinn looked around and, bowing, began to back away only to have the twins grab one of her hands each and plant her firmly on the stool between them.

The murmur and whispers between each group subsided as Lady Winifred rose and drew their attention. Just as she was to begin, there was a commotion outside the cavern.

As the tumult grew, all eyes were drawn to the cave mouth, where a bald-headed, bearded man leading a horse walked in, followed by Bren Omholt and his cousin Perrin, whose arm was in a sling. Perrin's wide smile and good colour indicated the arm may be his only lasting injury. A number of the attendees jumped from their seats.

The berobed man spoke clearly enough to be heard by all, 'Sorry we're late. I had to convince my horse that he would not be eaten.'

Martyn followed his strange announcement with a bow towards the Wolf Riders and their partners. Garat, who had yet to take his seat, strode towards the pair of boys, ready to welcome and introduce the prince. The two boys pushed past him in unison and cried out as they rushed to the dais, jumped up and embraced Lady Winifred.

'Gram,' Perrin and Bren's voices rang out.

The family reunion went on for some time in front of a stunned yet mildly amused gathering.

'Boys, boys. We have guests,' she said.

Lady Winifred, whom the prince had called Gram, signalled Garat over to assist her in settling down the emotional cousins.

'Take your seat, your highness,' Lady Winifred said.

She pointed to the left-hand chair on the dais beside which leaned an old but serviceable sword and shield.

'Garat, be a good boy and get a stool for your brother, please,' Lady Winifred instructed.

'Yes, Aunt Winnie.'

The response from the Pathfinder's highest officer was automatic. When he returned with a three-legged stool, Winifred indicated for him to place it at the right hand of the prince, then led her young charge over and bade him sit.

R'chal was bewildered by these events and noticed that Perrin seemed to share her feelings. His expression made it obvious that he had known this meeting was happening but had no idea he would be sitting in, let alone be on the dais. He looked unsure about his cousin's identity and further confused by his Gram's apparent importance. Lady Winifred retook her place, a frown creased her brow. R'chal followed her gaze to see that the tinker was still holding the horse and was talking into its ear.

'You there, Tinker. Get that horse out of here. Have you forgotten where you are, you horrible, horrible man?' Lady Winifred said.

Martyn handed the horse's reins to a waiting Pathfinder, turned, and strode purposefully to the dais. The bemused attendees became restless as he approached and stood before the dais.

'Why Winifred. What would mother say? That is no way to talk to your big brother.' Martyn stepped onto the dais and sat in the remaining chair. Turning to Perrin, he held up his fingers and counted down. 'Druid, did I forget to mention Druid?'

R'chal found herself as confused as the rest of the assembled guests, and a cacophony of questions and noise began to rise until Martyn once again made himself heard.

'My friends, we are here to answer your questions,' he said. 'I think we may benefit from some introductions. Many of you know each other, so we will stick to the representatives.'

Martyn then walked over and stood behind Bren's chair. 'Might I introduce His Highness, Crown Prince Brycen Ronan E'Nakor, heir to the Southern plains.'

This announcement, although expected, was met with immediate applause, cheers, and small yips of delight from the crowd. It was further backed by horn blasts as the news filtered out from the cavern to all those who had worked to bring this sun about.

Martyn turned to his sister and said softly, 'This may take awhile.'

Martyn held up his hands and once again called for calm. He knew the power of his vocal cords and chose to keep his tone well modulated until a stronger voice may be needed.

'Her Grace, Lady Winifred, Marchioness of Druk's Tor, Aunt Winnie to some, Gram to others–' he nodded to Perrin and Bren, '–and that old witch, to one,' he said, skipping well out of his sisters reach. 'Tutor to the king, teacher to the prince, and Druid of the Ancients.'

Polite laughter was mixed with gestures of deference while the lady looked daggers at her brother. Martyn continued over to Perrin, who looked up from his stool confused, clearly not believing he would be presented to such an august gathering. Martyn placed his hands on Perrin's shoulder and announced, 'Perrin Omholt, companion, protector, and adviser to our Prince.'

R'chal was amused by the look of shock that replaced the bewilderment on Perrin's features. He was startled at both the titles and the clapping and cheering that were the acknowledgement of the attendees. Martyn then returned to his seat and waited until these announcements had sunk in.

'Many of you know me or have heard of my various reputations. I am Martyn Ricar D'Kley, leader of the Druids and foremost councillor to, and representative of, the Ancient Ones,' he said. 'Now that we have established who is who, I will ask the representatives of the races to come forward and be welcomed.'

Six people approached the dais, two with their wolf partners in attendance. Martyn once again stood and moved equidistant between the prince and the gathered representatives.

'Your Highness, may I formally present Garat Omholt, Leader of your Pathfinders and his most capable sub-commander, Lady Hell,' he said.

R'chal saw Martyn pinned with another set of daggers from Heleana, who then looked to her Aunt Winnie, who nodded in silent agreement that this would not go unpunished.

'Chelke and Boid of the Elves. Che, I believe you are to speak for Orkoiyot S'anie.'

Martyn turned his attention to the wolf riders and their wolves. 'K'dnce and Selkin of the packs with Devron and Varellon. K'dnce and Selkin speak for the Deep Forests Pack while Devron and Varellon represent the Far Ranges Pack.'

'I do believe we can now get down to business,' Martyn said.

Martyn retook his seat, an action everyone else followed, barring Che, who remained standing in the centre awaiting acknowledgement from Martyn. Martyn waited until all were settled, then nodded to the Elf.

Che stood before the group dressed in the traditional garb of her people: boots, trousers, and a vest. This left her well-toned arms bare and displayed for all to see the tattoos that contrasted with her dark skin and indicated her status and importance in the elven hierarchy. In contrast, Boid's tattoos, also showing around his uniform, were not as complete as those of Che.

'Friends, I bear apologies from Orkoiyot S'anie. After the loss of her first daughter some turns ago, she has recently been blessed with another, and I can announce the arrival of Princess Elsi.

'The Queen is healthy but loath to put her heir within any sphere influenced by the Brocken. She begs forgiveness and does in no way intend slight,' Che said. She bowed to Prince Brycen. 'The Orkoiyot has decreed that I attend and speak for the Elves of the Sunset Islands.'

Martyn stood and moved to the centre of the dais. As he surveyed the attendees, he noted there were some among the three races who were clearly unsure in the presence of others. While each of the races traded with and knew of the others in general, they each remained in their own range and did not interact on a daily basis. This was due to the factors of distance, differing customs and needs. While dalliances occasionally occurred, breeding between the races was impossible.

'Perhaps it would be best if I give a briefing on how we have come to be here and why it is becoming imperative that action must be taken,' Martyn said. 'All present must be commended for the actions you have taken against the occupation. Although the Elves and the Wolf Riders have yet to be directly affected by the Brocken, they are acutely aware that only time and the resistance of the South have allowed this state to exist. We are here to formally unite and decide the best way forward for all.'

He paused to allow a general murmur of approval to ripple around the room.

'But you have been fighting the wrong enemy!' Martyn said.

His statement caused an upheaval, with shouts of derision and some very personal insults.

'I am not adding any of those to my accomplishments,' he said.

R'chal heard the comment spoken under his breath but as he turned to the prince and Perrin she assumed it was for their benefit. An inside joke perhaps. The druid stood centre stage waiting for the commotion to subside.

'My friends,' Martyn said. 'My friends!'

His words echoed throughout the chamber as Martyn stood upon the dais and projected his voice without shouting. This brought the meeting to order, although a few remained standing.

'My friends, we have been working towards this union for many turns. We bring before you those who have recently been revealed to us. The Hunter and Apprentice have been foreseen by the Ancient Ones as being critical to our success against the real enemy – The Circle of Seven.'

Martyn sat back down and surrendered the floor to his sister, who stood.

'The Circle of Seven Mages hold the strings that control the north. The Brocken occupation is but a symptom of their nefarious disease. If we cannot defeat the mages, it will not be just the Southlands under their dominance, but all who call Tol home will be held under the sway of but a few,' Lady Winifred said. She sat again before continuing. 'We druids need the strength of the Apprentice, as do the Ancient Ones if they are to help. Meanwhile, the Hunter and the Pathfinders must plan the push against the Brocken that will relieve the citadel of Sudhemere. We must now ask what each group can offer that will best serve this alliance.'

While the words of the Lady Winifred were sinking in, Devron and K'dnce approached the dais, flanked on their right-hand sides by their wolves. When they approached the dais, Martyn signalled that they should step up and address the meeting. Selkin and Varellon took station in front of the dais and sat at the feet of the riders.

'Friends,' K'dnce said. 'Packs support. Riders Red Ranges, Deep Forest, Far Ranges keep ancient law of Wolf Rider, "Not kill that which cannot be eaten." '

At this K'dnce and Devron stepped towards the prince and laid their small axes at his feet, thus pledging the loyalty of the packs while ensuring the alliance would not violate their laws.

This startling admission was met with some consternation and discussion amongst the Pathfinders. After all, they had faced the brunt of the resistance against the Brocken and had come to the meeting hoping for some relief through the aid of allies and reinforcements. Voices were once again raised as various squad leaders, many of whom were village elders, decried the value of having the Wolf Riders present.

R'chal saw disappointment in Devron's face and Varellon's bared teeth and raised hackles, and decided she would not let her friend's sacrifice and efforts go unmentioned or unrewarded. R'chal stood and took the hands Garat Omholt and Lady Heleana, leading them onto the dais. They walked to the centre and looked out at the continued turmoil. After standing for a short while, R'chal turned to Martyn and gestured towards the assembly.

'Quiet!' Martyn said.

He had not raised his voice or left his seat. R'chal was grateful for his assistance as the astonished participants quieted and retook their seats, after all confirming, R'chal's claim to be the Hunter was one of the main focuses of the meeting. Was it possible that this girl was indeed the leader they hoped for?

R'chal looked around the cavern and noted that there were many more people crowded around the walls. R'chal knew she could not prove she was the Hunter. She had yet to fully come to terms with the possibility herself, and although she had proven her abilities with a bow, she could not hope to compete in any other competition of arms.

'My name is R'chal,' she said. 'A'lek and I were brought here by Devron and Varellon, who made considerable sacrifices and faced great danger. They were instrumental in saving the life of our prince's cousin, Perrin.

'I do not claim leadership, but I have come to help. Some of you were at the challenge and saw me introduce a new weapon. It will give you an advantage over the flatbows of the Brocken. But we need a lot more than weapons to defeat an army. It will take the unity of all inhabitants of the Southlands. It will take communication, supply chains, intelligence, speed, knowledge, training, and strategy. The Wolf Riders will fill vital and life-saving roles in the conflict to come.'

This announcement was met with yips of agreement and clapping from the Wolf Rider contingent, and a murmur of understanding and agreement from the rest of those in attendance. R'chal's voice had grown stronger as she had spoken, and her confidence had grown in the knowledge that she could help these people. Even as she stood with Garat and Heleana, she stepped closer to the edge of the dais, aware that the Pathfinders, in particular, needed to see her confidence.

'You are not the Hunter,' someone yelled from the rear of the cavern.

A very large Pathfinder strode forward. 'Omholt, do you really expect us to follow this girl into battle?' He pointed at Garat. 'We need more than some fancy shooting.'

'Kurbah, you forget yourself,' Garat said.

'Omholt, we have waited turns under the yoke of the Brocken, and most here have lost more than they can count. You promised us a leader, the Hunter, not some slip of a girl. I have willingly followed you for turns, but this is just not right or reasonable. I demand proof, or I will challenge your leadership by dint of arms.'

Kurbah's tirade was reinforced by an undercurrent of agreement and followed with a cheer at the possibility of a trial by combat. Before the growing commotion could fully take hold, a deep rumble, growing into a growl, echoed throughout the cavern with no discernable source. As more and more in the crowd grew concerned with the growl sending inherent shivers up and down spines, they turned to the Wolf Riders, only to see the wolves and their partners bowing in a display of obedience.

From a dark recess in the rear of the cavern, a shadow formed and stalked towards the gathering. Wilder stalked past the now silent Kurbah, stepped upon the dais, and sat at R'chal's right hand. R'chal noted that Wilder was tall enough to reach her shoulder when he sat. It was the first time many of those present had seen a wolven.

Martyn had jumped from his seat and was clapping the theatrics of Wilder's appearance. R'chal was surprised at his reaction evidently not even he had known of the presence of one of the ancient ones in the cavern. Those of the high order could keep themselves shielded from all but another Ancient One. When R'chal looked into Wilders eyes *Only you Hunter*,' was the reply.

'Friends, before you resume your seats, may I introduce Wilder of the Wolven, one of the Ancients of the High Order. I am sure he would welcome any challenge you care to offer. He has deemed R'chal the Hunter, so I daresay you have your proof.'

Martyn came to stand with R'chal and Wilder. Garat and Heleana stepped up to the group to add their acceptance, and when Bren and Perrin rose from their seats to stand with Garat and R'chal, Kurbah and all present went down on one knee in acquiescence.

'There is work to be done,' Martyn said.

He broke the momentary spell that had come over the meeting. R'chal noted the strange look Martyn cast towards A'lek, who had stayed seated throughout the recent dissent.

'I suggest we establish a workable plan.' Martyn walked back to his chair and the others followed suit.

When R'chal took her seat, Wilder sat behind her, clearly guarding her back and displaying to all that he would always have this role.

'We will need time to bring together all that is needed,' Bren said.

R'chal was surprised by the authority in the young prince's statement. But it seemed the comment from the prince did not surprise his Gram who sat nodding with a smile of pride spreading across her features.

'Any decision we make together must protect those under the influence of the occupier. We will not relinquish our responsibility to our people,' Bren continued.

His pronouncement was met with approval and a general feeling of relief that there was now a Prince to fight for. Prince Brycen rose and continued.

'The Druids and the Apprentice will plan the defence against the Circle of Seven this may be in a form foreign to most of us. Meanwhile Garat Omholt and the Hunter plan our resistance against the soldiers of the invader and coordinate with our allies. We must utilise our strengths and support each other's weaknesses. Is there any more to be done?'

'No, your highness. I think you have the best of it,' Martyn said.

R'chal looked between the two druids Martyn was staring at the young prince, who had only just reached his majority, and then he turned to his sister. She had guided this young man over these last turns. A small smile crossed his face and he nodded in her direction with the knowledge the old witch had done good work once again. R'chal followed his gaze to A'lek, who again had a far-away look of indifference, and she vowed to follow that up as soon as possible.

Che and Boid of the Elves once again strode to stand before the dais, this time looking to the prince for acknowledgement, giving their tacit approval of his station.

'Your highness,' Che said. 'The elf tribes will only unite under the leadership of S'anie or her heir. While the Elf Nation is willing to help defend the Southlands, we cannot field an effective fighting force while the only heir is still at the breast and the Queen cannot leave her. While elves are long-lived, we do not often mate to produce young ones. The Queen can and will give all the support possible but cannot march at the head of her forces. The birth of Princess Elsi was the only event that dispelled the period of mourning after the tragic loss of Princess Aayla.'

'Aayla, the Keepers, the desolation, bring the stone,' A'lek said.

A'lek's eyes glazed over and rolled upwards until only the whites showed, and the Apprentice slid sideways in a dead faint.

CHAPTER NINETEEN
Aayla

Sacrifice gladly given, survival demands dominance
Warriors gem anchors, battle won without surrender.

A'LEK'S ANNOUNCEMENT stirred a hornet's nest and brought about the end of the meeting.

'It seems we have chosen well, Winnie,' Martyn said.

The druids stood over A'lek as a very concerned Quinn gently tried to coax some sense back into a befuddled brain. The Apprentice was slowly coming around.

'What information do you have? Why did you say those things?' Martyn asked.

'I don't understand it. During the meeting, I sensed a whisper in my mind. It was insistent; it was immense, powerful and glowing but so very far away. I could not concentrate on anything being said here. I had to follow it. I sort of went away. I don't know,' A'lek said.

'A'lek, since the invasion, the disappearance of Koiy Aayla has been the subject of discord between our two races. While she does not directly blame the people of the Southlands, Orkoiyot S'anie has always thought more should have been done to protect the heir to her throne. Che's companion, Boid, was the koiy's friend and, even as a youngster, showed bravery and resilience in bringing the news of the plight of Aayla's party to the Court of the Elves,' Winifred said.

'S'anie has never accepted the death of her beloved daughter, but with the birth of Koiy Elsi she has begun to heal and forgive,' Che said.

Martyn had cleared the cavern, and all but the principal representatives remained to discuss this perplexing announcement. Now, the two druids sat on the edge of the podium with Bren and Perrin, K'dnce, Devron, Garat, Heleana, Che, Boid, R'chal, and A'lek arrayed before them. Wilder and the two wolves sat apart from the group.

Martyn sat waiting as Lady Winifred had insisted refreshments be arranged and tea made before beginning to delve into this development. Movement brought his attention to Devron as his hands began automatically preparing his pipe. When no one seemed concerned, he lit it with a fine twig held to one of the torches lighting the cavern. Martyn, who had been deep in his own thoughts, considered the Wolf Rider and, taking out his own pipe, repeated the actions of the smaller man.

'Hurumff, excuse me, brother,' Winifred said.

Martyn looked at his sister, who had her own pipe in hand.

'If you want to pipe, you should have your own tobac,' Martyn's dismissive tone caused one eyebrow to be raised on his sister's countenance.

'I have no time to gallivant around the forest finding leaf. I know Mother taught you better manners,' Winifred's tone was no less dismissive and her brother had no choice but to hand over his pouch.

Like Devron and Martyn before her, she pinched some strands and brought them to her nose. Winifred gave a nod of approval and filled her pipe. While enjoying the first puffs of their pipes, Martyn looked over at the Apprentice and considered the trance he had experienced during the moot.

LADY WINIFRED SAT ON the edge of the dais with her pipe and cup of tea, surveying the young people before her. She had to agree with Martyn's assessment of the group. She was delighted with the quality of those who would set the current imbalance to rights and bring about the next phase in the development of Tol. While only she and her brother knew the complete histories, they were often surprised by the twists and turns the ancients put before them. Down through the turns, these types of events had tested the peoples' resilience and staved off stagnation with continual adaptation. It was seen as a necessary means to ensure the growth and prosperity of Tol. Lady Winifred did not relish being a pawn in the game, but saw the benefits to the people and their world when adversity was overcome.

'Che, it is time we hear the story of Koiy Aayla,' Lady Winifred said. 'There seems to be more to this misadventure.'

Che took a moment to collect her thoughts.

'Koiy Aayla was residing in the capital with the family of your sovereign. She was under the care and tutelage of her elven carer Beatrice, the teacher and mentor of the children of the elvish royal line. Aayla was in her fourteenth turn and was joined by Boid, her younger cousin and childhood friend, to ease the cultural transition.' Che indicated for her companion to take up the story.

'The Northern Empire invaded without warning, and there was no time to send to the Orkoiyot for an escort, so a party set out to return Aayla home. The party consisted of four guardsmen, the koiy, Beatrice and me,' Boid said. 'The South was unprepared for the incursion, so the guardsmen, although well trained, had never faced battle. The Sovereign only had news from Sudhemere and did not know the Northerners had landed all along the coast. The invaders sent out bands of skirmishers to harass the countryside, spread fear amongst the population, and hamper attempts to coordinate any form of defence.'

'Our party travelled well for a few suns with no signs to worry us. Then, we started to encounter other travellers. These people were fleeing the ravages of the invading forces, and told stories of the sudden attacks of the Northerners and the vicious nature of their soldiers.'

'We continued with increased care and decided to take to a more remote path that avoided the major settlements and trading routes. Unfortunately, our stratagem was to no avail.'

'Who was leading your party?' Garat asked

'Koiy Aayla was well able to command our group. She was educated and experienced well beyond her turns,' Boid replied. 'We stumbled upon a Northern raiding party celebrating the sacking of a large farmstead. The Northerners were toying with and torturing the women from the farm,' Boid paused and closed his eyes. 'It was horrible to see. The wife and daughters being used and treated as playthings.'

'The women's screams incensed our guardsmen, who bounded forwards in a charge without a thought to our mission. The charge was mildly successful, and a number of Northerners died, but as the guardsmen regrouped, the more experienced soldiers of the north became organised. In the second charge, a volley of flatbow bolts showered the four Southern men, felling one and injuring another.'

Boid's chin fell to his chest at the memory. 'Even though we had heard stories of the invaders atrocities it was the first time I had witnessed them for myself and seen men kill each other.'

'When the remaining guardsmen completed their second sortie through the Northern soldiers, Koiy Aayla took command and ordered them to break off the contact, reminding them of their mission,' Boid halted and poured himself a cup of water from a flask on Lady Winifred's tea tray. 'From that encounter onward, we were harried and chased sun and night, and only some little knowledge of the countryside gave us any rest as we avoided capture. We were hard pressed and occasionally within bowshot of the Northerners and suffered further losses of the guardsmen who were valiant in their rearguard actions.

'We were unable to choose our direction, just managing to stay ahead of the soldiers. The Northerners had gathered or stolen four horses, but had a way of travelling with runners being assisted and riders changing regularly. We didn't realise we were heading into the desolation until it was too late. To this sun, there is no water or sustenance to support man or beast on that rugged land. Aayla insisted I be sent forth with a spare pony to bring word of the party's plight to her mother. The koiy, Beatrice, who was suffering badly from the chase, and the remaining injured guard hoped to lose the soldiers by heading into the desolation and skirting close to the border. No word has been heard of them since.'

'Until now,' Martyn said, ominously. 'A'lek, we need to understand what you said. Were you speaking to someone?'

'No, I mean yes, I don't know. She was something more. She was in my head. At least I felt it was a she.'

'You said it was immense and glowing,' R'chal said.

'It was an impression more than an actual vision. I don't want visions.'

'A'lek, can we leave that aside for now? I will delve deeper into that with you in private. Right now, we need to understand. Is the elf heir Aayla alive?' Martyn said.

'That was the clearest part of the impression I got. She is with people called the Keepers and needs the stone. I don't understand it at all, but that was a certainty.'

'We must go. We must find her,' Boid said.

The elf hunter was ready to rush immediately into the vastness of the desolation.

'Hold on, Boid. The season of the sun is no time to be travelling in the desolation without a careful plan,' Garat said.

'I must go. She trusted me. She is my friend. She is my family. She is my Koiy.'

'Yes, you will go youngster, but there is more to this news that must be understood. Garat is correct. The heat of the season will only make any search far more difficult. My brother and I must confer with the Ancients to understand how this news was hidden from us at first, yet has been revealed now. There is also the matter of the stone A'lek mentioned,' Winifred said. 'Brother, it seems A'lek has the aptitude and is the Apprentice we need. The potential only needs refining to bring out the talent. Perhaps we should explain our part in these turbulent times and lay out the various tasks now before us.'

Lady Winifred considered those arrayed before her all looking to her for answers. She distractedly looked at her teacup, and Prince Brycen reacted to the gesture instinctively. He brought over the teapot and poured as he had been taught.

'Well, brother, perhaps you are right, for once, there is work to be done and answers to be sought.' Winifred studied her pipe before getting up and cleaning it over the fire pit, using the task as a cover to collect her thoughts.

'Have you ever wondered how this obnoxious brother of mine seems to be in more than one place at a time? Or be more than one person? In Sudhemere, he is Martyn the Miller as he owns warehouses and market stalls. In the Citadel, he is the Earl of Lotan's Rest, sometime advisor to the Duke. On the plains, he is Martyn the trader, business partner to Kimee, and dear brother, I don't understand how that girl has not gutted you yet. On the coast, he is Martyn the Chandler, and in the foothills and forests, he prefers the ruse of an itinerant tinker.'

'Dear sister, you sell me short. You have forgotten horse thief, gambler, charlatan, and sometime guide, and you know full well Kimee and I have an understanding.'

'He can achieve his mediocre feats by utilising the life forces voluntarily passed on to him through his training as a druid. We Druids harness earth magic by making requests to our ancient ones or the greater animals and plants. We are long-lived so that we may spend our lives replenishing that which we use by caring for the lands we live on and healing any injury to plant, beast or our mother Tol. Druids connect with nature and assist the Ancients in maintaining balance and harmony. You can consider us the go-betweens bringing the ancient teachings to your changing world. Of the peoples, the Dini are those most closely linked to the ancient ways and, as with the wolf riders, we druids are forbidden to kill.'

'But you are here to plan our attack on the invaders,' Garat said.

'No, Pathfinder, that will be up to you and your lady. We are here to set the right people on the right path in the defence of Tol against what is coming,' Martyn said. 'Please go on, sister.'

'The plainsmen and the elves have domesticated much of our lands, and the links between the ancients and themselves have weakened. The herds you husband no longer require the shepherding of the strong as they are bred for work and food. Only the wild herds and larger beasts still follow the ways of the ancients. Being in tune with nature gives us a resource we can use to heal others by imparting strength and health or allowing us to extend our own strength and health. Druids must always work to repay and balance that which we use.'

'Aunt Winnie, you said we were fighting the wrong enemy. Who is the Circle of Seven?' Heleana asked.

'Ah yes, the mages. When the ancients set the peoples on the path of growth and development, they may have made a tiny miscalculation. The Grove of the Ancients and she who is the centre of our world, is far to the south, and at the time the council of ancients did not consider that people could live and prosper beneath two spans of snow for half a turn. Those in Nordinium spend much of their time strengthening their holdings against others and pass their nights developing weapons, training and lusting after their neighbour's wealth. It was not until the between seas could be navigated that the northerners turned their attentions to the lands of the South.'

'Gram, who inhabits the Grove of the Ancients?' Perrin asked. 'You mentioned that she is the centre of our world.'

'Per, please be patient. Right now, the Mages are of more import.'

'It was in this environment of chaos and misery that the mages obtained a foothold in the governance of the North and now hold sway over a puppet emperor. They grow more powerful daily as they steal life force through pain and suffering. Chaos is their want, and until very recently, they could not harness their power as it is fleeting and easily evaporates. Something changed and they can now store their power in natural gemstones, creating a depository from which they can draw strength. The governance of the north has fallen under their sway as they utilise the greed of the Northern Barons to direct their subjugation of all of Tol.'

Winifred stood and looked towards the opening of the cavern. Those before her watched as her usually expressive features eased, and she seemed to enter a state much like A'lek. She walked over to Wilder and placed a hand on his head.

'There is more to the Mages efforts to be understood. We Ancient Ones sense a greater force of chaos behind them as though they, too, are being manipulated. If the darkness perceived is allowed to grow, we fear all of Tol will be rendered uninhabitable much like the desolation.' The voice emanating from the old lady was deeper and clearly male. 'She that is oldest fears the return of the eternal enemy. If the Mages machinations are not hobbled, Tol faces a far greater danger than some petty squabbles over territory. The stone must be taken to the golden one.'

Lady Winifred shook from head to toe, and her touch on Wilder was broken.

'Brother, it seems the ancients have kept vital information from us that only adds to the tasks set before us. We must define those tasks and agree to those to whom they shall fall.'

'Aunt Winnie, wait. This is becoming more confusing at every turn. Who is the oldest? Who is the Golden One? What is this stone? Moreover, how do we fight mages with the seas between us?' Heleana asked.

Garat was surprised at his wife's tone of voice. She was using her command voice, backed by her station in life. He moved closer and placed his arm around her waist, displaying his full support of her demands.

'Heleana, we will explain as much as we know. Firstly, we can deal with your question about the Mages. You are correct, we cannot thwart them from afar, and we cannot take any force north. You and your Pathfinders must force them to come to us. You must cut off their supply of riches and slaves. You need to stop their boats sailing.

'Fortunately, the season of storms limits traffic across the between seas, but we need to stop the boats in the meantime. Then, we must have a strategy in place before the resumption of sailing in the season of birth. The mages will be debilitated by the lack of victims for their vile practices and will be forced to use their stored power to maintain their chokehold on the North. The next sun solstice will be most dangerous for us, so we must be in full control of the Southlands by then. We have just under a full turn to achieve our goal.'

Winifred approached Heleana and took her hands in her own.

'Heleana, that is the task set for you, Garat and R'chal. We do not have to defeat the Brocken, only weaken them until a treaty can be negotiated.'

Winifred then turned to A'lek.

'As to she who is oldest. That is A'lek's task. The Grove of the Ancients holds the sum of the knowledge of Tol. She travelled the lands at the dawn of our world until she took root in the grove. A'lek must travel to the grove and study with her to develop the talents within. We will need the power of the Druids to support your forces and heal our lands. My brother will accompany our Apprentice and begin the training.'

'Yes, yes, I must set A'lek on the path,' Martyn said. 'But we also have the mystery of this stone and the golden one.'

'A'lek said the being in his vision was immense and glowing. Could this be the Golden One?' R'chal asked.

'Yes, likely, very likely. But we need to identify this stone before sending anyone into the desolation on an impossible quest. There are many stones mentioned in the histories, particularly in reference to the seven warriors of antiquity. I am sure you all know the song. It does not identify any single stone as being significant,' Martyn said.

'Brother dear, when was the last time you actually studied the words of the song? Mother always said you were too busy getting yourself into trouble to be entrusted with anything important. Please entertain us with your beautiful tenor voice and sing us the last verses.'

'You wound me, Winnie, but that is understandable. I always was Mother's favourite.'

Martyn coughed once or twice, then took a long breath and sang.

Lotan's ruby red as fire, bravery in battle, warrior's desire.
Mwindo's silver star does cure, intensity and honour to ensure.
Zahhak's yellow lights all shadow the glow that does inspire.

Druk diamond, white and pure, no dedication more secure.
Bazu topaz, blue for the freed, diligence others cede.
Dreq emerald to revive, ensures a world will survive.
One above all to battle and lead,
Zammok's black, an example exhorting the cohort to thrive.
A world gives up freedoms and sentience,
Endowing inner light to each defender.
Sacrifice gladly given, survival demands dominance
Warriors, gem anchors, battle won without surrender.
Seven warriors battle the horrors,
Seven warriors bring light to black,
Seven warriors are faith restorers,
Seven warriors force chaos back.

As the last strains of the song echoed around the cavern, the listeners were transfixed. They realised Martyn could stand against any bard to sing the teaching songs or the epic stories trotted out during solstice celebrations.

'Lovely, brother. Now think about the last line of the verse *Warriors, Gem anchors.*'

'Surely that is describing the gem that each of the ancient warriors were aligned with to give them the strength and inner light to defeat their foe.'

'One may think that. The song has been passed down over thousands of turns as one of the Druid's tenets. This is its current translation. The song is a remembrance of an event that happened during the darkest of times. An event that happened before the raising up of the three races of Tol.

'Are you suggesting that the song we all are taught at the knee of our mothers predates the history of the Dini, the Elves, and the Plainsmen?' Heleana asked.

'Oh, our ancestors were all running about naked in the forests at the time. They were chosen by the Ancients to be gifted with the future of our lands after this battle raged. You will note the last line of the last verse. *Battle won without surrender.* The battle was won, but was the war?' Winifred asked.

'You propose more questions than answers. So back to *Warriors, gem anchors* please,' Martyn said.

'Piqued your interest, have I? The song was not the only thing passed down by the ancients. There was an object of power passed on from one druid to another along with the oath never to share the knowledge until it is called for.'

'So, am I to assume this stone is said object?'

'Yes, brother dear.'

'And am I to assume by your smugness you know where we can find this stone.'

'Yes, brother dear.'

'Well? Where is it?'

'I assume it currently resides in Perrin's belt pouch.'

Suddenly, all eyes focused on Perrin. His complexion paled at the attention, and with his arm in a sling, it looked like he was about to collapse.

'It's alright, Per, I checked when I was healing you. Please pass me the second of your charges.'

Perrin gingerly reached with his hurt arm and untied the small pouch hanging from his belt. He tipped the contents out onto his hand. Along with some small coins and a partially whittled good luck token, there was a small blue-wrapped package bound in gold wire. Bren jumped up, took the package from Perrin, and carried over to Winifred.

'Gram, this is all very confusing. I don't know who anyone is anymore. What part am I to play?' he asked.

'Bren, my boy, you will become most important in these coming events, but please be patient until we discover the meaning of this latest conundrum.'

Winnie watched her charge return to his seat and untwisted the fine gold wire encasing the blue cloth wrappings. All eyes were upon her as the wrappings came away to reveal a polished stone. She held her hand out so each could clearly see.

'This is the warrior's gem. She who is oldest found it as she wandered Tol when she was young and supple. It has been polished over hundreds and hundreds of turns as she held it, studied it, and looked into its depths. It is a black opal, the rarest of all gems. If you look closely, you'll see it sparkles with the colours of each of the gems associated with the ancient warriors in the song. This gem was said to anchor the warriors in the defence of Tol after they were granted the life force and inner light of our world.'

'It appears that it is not just the ancients keeping secrets. Now we have this *Warrior's gem*, just who is the Golden One?' Martyn asked.

'That, brother, is the conundrum. The Golden One was never mentioned in the teachings. The Ancient Ones have kept that secret since the beginning.'

ALL EYES TURNED TO Wilder. R'chal could not be sure, but when the wolven's head dropped slightly, she wondered if the large canine was being contrite.

Hunter, I, too, have been misled.

R'chal felt her connection with the wolven weaken as he seemed to stretch out his mind. Then he was back, and her mind was almost swamped because he seemed so much more than before.

Hunter, please repeat these words to your brethren.

'Excuse me, everyone. Wilder wishes you all to hear this.'

R'chal felt a powerful presence with a strange rustling in the background.

'When I made the pact with the defenders of our land, I imbued their mother/leader with the properties of gold. As a mineral, it is more in tune with our lands and more abundant than any single gem. The warrior's leader has stood guard over the place they came since that time. She now fades and must pass on the knowledge of the warrior's pact to the next mother/leader. The Warrior's Gem must be placed in the hand of she who is next.'

R'chal almost swooned when the presence left her mind. Only Wilder giving her his strength kept her from a full faint.

Heleana rushed to her side and placed an arm about her shoulder in support.

'That was not Wilder, was it?' Heleana asked.

'No, I don't think so. I think it was her. Speaking from the grove.'

'Right, we must remember just who our first enemy is here. The Circle of Seven must act at the next high solstice, which gives us just over three full seasons to plan, train, and defeat them. All will have tasks to complete, and we must be ready,' Martyn said.

This reminded those present that they were here to plan the future, not rush in different directions.

'The Apprentice must make a pilgrimage to the Grove of the Ancients. The Hunter must oversee the preparation of these new weapons. The Pathfinders must protect the people and create evacuation and battle plans. Perrin and Boid will lead the search for the elven Koiy. Prince Brycen will learn to rule under the guidance of my dear sister, and Che must send news of this to Orkoiyot S'anie.' Martyn ticked each announcement off his fingers as he made it. 'There has been enough talk. I suggest we plan our next moves thoughtfully and well. Go now and plan for the coming confrontation. We will meet at dinner to put those plans into action. Do not act before conferring with this quorum.

R'CHAL AND A'LEK WERE relieved to be free of the confines of the large cavern as neither had much experience at caving or living with a mountain over their heads. They walked around the central lake quietly discussing their roles. Wilder paced behind them, reinforcing his support for the Hunter in the eyes of the attending Pathfinders and their allies. When they arrived at their campsite, R'chal realised her advice and guidance would be a valued commodity. The Pathfinder leaders and Che were waiting for them. R'chal took a seat on her stool, looking over the lake, and again marvelled at the crystal clear reflection it threw.

'Quinn, could you come out here, please?' R'chal asked. 'We need to make plans.'

The tent flap was opened hesitantly, revealing the green hair of the blacksmith. The young woman slowly emerged, still overawed by the company before her.

'Right, as I see it, we each have work to do. Quinn will need to set up to manufacture the new bows. She will need supplies and help from other smiths. This is a vital function. We can gain a great advantage with the new bow as long as we keep it secret. A'lek is to leave us on a quest for knowledge, and we have to find the elven Koiy. What do we know of the desolation?' R'chal asked.

'It is said that the desolation is a vast swath of land that was fought over thousands of turns ago. To this sun, it has not recovered. It is a place of sands and heat, with no life and no water. No one who enters has ever returned to tell of its interior or true size. Even those who live near the edge do not travel out of sight of safety if they traverse the border. There is no reason to cross it,' Heleana answered.

R'chal nodded thanks to the lady and then looked to the elves for input.

'Hunter, we also have no reason to travel the desolation. We are a coastal and island nation and more akin with the sea, the lowland forests, and grasslands,' Che said. 'This will not stop our search for the koiy. Aayla must be found if there is to be any hope.'

'We all agree that the search for the koiy is a high priority, but an expedition into an almost inhospitable land must be carefully planned,' R'chal said. 'Perrin and Boid must be well supplied, and a guide who knows something of the lands should be found. Let us report to the druids over dinner.'

All agreed, and the group parted to refresh themselves and look forward to the action that would unite the allies and bring closer the freedom of the Southlands.

R'chal, A'lek, and Quinn remained seated outside the tent with Wilder in close attendance. Quinn had only just heard of these plans and the need for A'lek to leave. R'chal noticed an expression of determination cross her features. Quinn stood, took a bewildered A'lek by the hand and headed towards the screened hot spring.

R'chal's own experience of sex was limited to frenzied fondling in the hayloft of the Salient Buck during solstice celebrations. Although fully aware of the particulars, neither twin had had a long-term relationship. The whole village had suspected that A'lek and Quinn would eventually unite, so R'chal was glad that some happiness could be found in this turbulent time.

The best meeting place for the leaders was the cavern, and they all enjoyed a meal served on large wooden trenchers. It had been very quickly decided that Quinn would set up several smithies in this valley to manufacture a variety of the new bows. She would need to produce them in different sizes to suit the Pathfinders, Elves and Wolf Riders. She would be protected by four trusted Pathfinder squads, who in turn would be supported by K'dnce and Selkin and their Deep forest pack. Garat and Heleana would arrange for more smiths and their apprentices to join her.

A'lek, Martyn, and Devron would travel to the Grove of the Ancients, beyond the far ranges, after traversing the deep forests. The Wolf Riders would provide protection and support as A'lek travelled through their ranges. When asked, Devron advised the group that the journey would take longer than four seven suns.

Prince Brycen and Lady Winifred would also base themselves in the valley. The prince would continue his education from his Gram, and take up weapons training with Pathfinder tutors. They would also benefit from the remoteness of the valley and a shield of Pathfinders who would maintain secrecy.

Che and Boid waited to discuss the search for Koiy Aayla, but the meeting was disrupted by a Pathfinder messenger demanding to see the commander.

A Pathfinder squad leader brought in the messenger, who had travelled hard and could barely catch her breath. The messenger was led before Garat and Prince Brycen, but before the message could be relayed, Lady Winifred ordered a stool to be brought out, and tea poured for the clearly exhausted girl. All saw the value in Winifred's approach as a clear, concise message would reduce the inevitable number of repetitions and questions.

'My Lords, my Ladies,' the messenger began. 'The inn of the Salient Buck has been razed, and the keeper and his family put to the sword. All in the village have been arrested, and the young held as slaves.' The girl could not keep the tears from flowing, even with the calming effect of the tea. 'Two Brocken squads came to the village to arrest the master smith and investigate rumours of a Pathfinder gathering. The innkeeper did as instructed and told the Brocken which way you went. Then they just killed him. Two Brocken just held his arms, and another ran him through. It happened so fast my squad could not help him. It was then my leader sent me here. As I started to run, I heard the screaming. Later, I saw the smoke.'

The messenger's resolve finally broke, and she collapsed in shock amid tears and sobs. R'chal, Garat and Heleana could not question the girl until Lady Winifred managed to get her to drink some more tea. R'chal also noticed that the druid laid her hands on the girl's shoulders and closed her eyes for a short time. After that, the messenger was calmer and gave a more concise report.

The attack on the village had happened three suns ago, and the Brocken squads were likely camping in the meadows. The Brocken usually spent time in camp, enjoying their plunder and captives. They would also continue the search for the smith. Her squad leader had four Pathfinders and was awaiting orders from Garat and Heleana.

Garat immediately sent for Kurbah, the Pathfinder who had challenged R'chal, and Aitien, who was the best woodsman and tracker. Garat sent Aitien out to scout and clear the path to the village with his squad. Kurbah was ordered to prepare their six horses for hard riding and choose two other warriors to ride with them. To give Aitien a chance to make ground, the riders would leave at first light. Che volunteered to assist as elves could travel as fast as horses. Even though horses made travel easier, they needed frequent rest periods, water, and good food to maintain their strength. The main benefit of taking a horse was the extra weight it could carry. Che would have no trouble in keeping pace.

R'chal felt guilty, as her insistence on the challenge had put the village at risk. She reflected on the choices one made and the unknown effect it could have on complete innocents. R'chal insisted on going with Garat and Heleana. She knew she had to do something and was rewarded by the presence of Wilder in her head. R'chal took this as a promise to stay near and she was imbued further with a strengthening feeling of rightness in the recesses of her mind another nudge from Wilder.

Prince Brycen and Martyn assured them that the decisions made by the group would be followed up and the arrangements for A'lek's quest and Quinn's work would be carried out.

From the meeting, each person now had an objective and a timetable to work towards. The group broke apart to begin their own preparations.

R'chal knew her skills of warfare were limited but was determined to give what assistance she could to the people who had done nothing more than host her challenge. She knew she would not sleep that night, so prepared herself for the early morning start. R'chal dressed in the uniform of a Pathfinder and inspected her bow and quiver of arrows. She chose to stick with target arrows rather than changing to a broad head, as she was still concerned that she would not be able to make a kill shot. When she took up the slim rapier Quinn had presented to her, she was reminded that she had little idea of its best use. Strapping the belt about her waist, she set off in search of Garat and Heleana in the hope that some brief instruction would be advantageous.

With the sun setting, the bowl of the crater was bathed in a ruddy glow enhanced by the reflection from the lake's waters. In her search for Garat, R'chal came across Che and Boid exercising with their own blades on the site of the knife contest. Both elves wore only boots, pants and vest allowing freedom of movement and as their swords whistled through the air the sheen of sweat on rippling muscles picked up the sky's tinge and looked much like the dark skin of their arms were covered in blood.

'Excuse me Che,' R'chal said and waited for the elf to finish her movement.

Che completed an upward thrust, followed by a quick reverse and a low knee high swipe before coming to rest with her long sword point resting on the ground. The swords pommel came to chest height on the tall elf.

'I was hoping to find someone to give me some pointers in the use of my sword. Would I be able to join you in your practice?'

'Gladly Hunter, but your weapon requires a different style of the art. Please draw your sword. Boid continue with your exercises,' Che ordered.

R'chal offered the hilt to Che who grasped it and held both swords to compare.

'As you can see my long sword is half again as long as your rapier and has a blade much thicker and heavier. The long sword is designed to fight against armoured opponents where we can shatter bones or pop out knees rather than cut. You will notice my blade is only sharpened along the business end of the blade for stabbing into weaker areas of an enemy's armour.' Che handed her sword to R'chal for inspection. R'chal nearly dropped the weapon not expecting the weight that Che so easily managed.

'Your sword is shorter and slimmer. This is a weapon for quick defence not sustained battle. While my sword can be wielded with both hands on the hilt for power and even with one hand on the hilt and another holding the blade for guidance the best use of it is based on momentum and its weight – the wielder must practice often to train their muscles so its flow becomes second nature. Your sword was forged to wield with a single handed grip. This requires greater finesse and more understanding than can be taught in an evening, so we will concentrate on only one aspect of swordsmanship – saving your life,' Che said.

'Now study Boid in his exercises, you will start there. Boid's sword is thicker and heavier than yours but is still made for single handed combat. It is not Boid's position to be at the forefront of battle. His job is to guard my back and relay my battle commands. Thus he requires speed and fleetness of foot. Now study his feet you will see he rarely places his heel on the ground. Much like the dances you will have done on solstice celebrations. Now while holding your sword at en garde, as is Boid, mimic his moves.'

R'chal noticed the muscles of Che move in unison as she watched the duo move through the exercises. With very few instructions R'chal had picked up the steps and was soon matching Boid for speed. Her grace and ability could be put down to steady practice stalking game through dense bushland.

'Good you have mastered the most important lesson never face an opponent flat footed. Move, always move. Use your sword to deflect rather than block, make your enemy swing across their body so move to their offside. Now face Boid he will strike using the the weight of his sword to add strength to the blow do not try to stop the sword - parry the stroke and allow it to follow through. The swing and the swords weight gives you time to recover. Remember your opponent is trying to kill you. There is no need to run your weapon through up to its hilt it is the first hand span of steel that does the damage so do not risk getting your blade caught up in clothing or allowing an opponent to get their hands on you. You are a leader - stick him and then run away.'

Boid and R'chal flowed backward and forward their feet moving in patterns not unlike the dances Che had mentioned. Boid was instructed to attack using a variety of clear swipes both from high point and each side. R'chal knew her job was defence only. She deflected each attack and quickly realised she could recover faster with her lighter blade. Even as Che called out each stroke for Boid to use in attack R'chal had to remember they were using real sharpened weapons. The clashing of blades echoed through the valley as the tempo of the strikes became faster and faster.

As it was R'chal had no trouble sleeping that night and woke in the early morn with welcome weariness in her arms, back and especially her calf muscles.

WHEN THE CALL TO ASSEMBLE came in the chill before dawn, the six chosen to ride to the assistance of the village were met by the entire population of the valley. It was doubtful that any had slept. Each horse had been carefully outfitted with travel rations for horse and rider, saddle knives, and extra quivers of arrows.

R'chal watched A'lek's approach as she began to stow her personal kit in the saddle bags.

I guess this is where we take separate paths on this great adventure. It is far more than the Tinker led us to believe,' she said.

A'lek smiled and gave a half shrug.

'Many lives now hang on our decisions and the future may hold many dark times,' Lack of sleep and fear for the villages kept R'chal's mood sombre.

A'lek looked at R'chal's preparations and it hit home that she was heading into danger.

'I promise to bring back knowledge from the Ancients that will shine a light on those future times,' A'lek said.

The twins came together and each hugged as fiercely as the other.

Quinn waited until A'lek had said goodbye before she took R'chal's hand.

'R'chal please be safe. I will have my forge set up and have the first of the pulleys prepared for your return. There are two pathfinders with the skill to be instructed in the making and others are being sought. We will bring the new bow to the people of the Southlands.'

R'chal was particularly moved by this because they had received the news that Quinn's village had been destroyed, and her friends killed and enslaved. Quinn began to sob and looked up at R'chal.

'Please bring them back to me,' she begged.

Only then did R'chal remember the white-haired boy who followed after Quinn as they worked in the smithy. A wave of shock came over her as she remembered Kjieran and their father had some knowledge of the new weapon. If the Brocken came to learn of the bow, many of their plans may have to change. Suddenly, their mission to assist the village had become of vital importance. R'chal did not want to add to Quinn's grief, so she hugged the girl and promised to do everything she could to reunite the smith with her family.

Prince Brycen appeared before the group, and, at his orders, R'chal and the grim-faced Pathfinders mounted and rode from the valley. It was still before dawn when the squad reached the major trade route and turned their horses for the village of the Salient Buck. As the horses began a slow canter, Che settled into a rhythm that matched the horse's pace, and R'chal was relieved to hear the message *I am near* in her mind.

The riders came to the site of Heleana's encounter with the Brocken about mid-morning and paused to rest the horses. While the Pathfinders cared for the horses, Heleana and R'chal walked Garat through the brief action. R'chal welcomed the chance to stretch her legs. Riding at the canter for any length of time was unfamiliar to her. Garat noted in his inspection of the site a small cairn of stones by the roadside. The layout and colours of the stones used told him Aitien's squad had moved through there, and all was clear. Garat was happy to have the confirmation, as he intended to walk the horses for some time to ensure they had reserves of energy if needed.

'Garat, Heleana, I have waited until we could talk in private,' R'chal said. 'We have to free the villagers. Amongst them is Kjieran, Quinn's brother. He knows of the new weapon, and the others know of the contest. We cannot let the Brocken know our secrets.'

Garat only allowed a short rest before calling the squad to continue. The mission was now more vital to the plans of the Southlands. When he called for the horses to start at a walk, Che had asked if she could move ahead and act as a scout. The elf did not to rest as much as the horses.

By mid-afternoon, the troop was almost halfway to the village and came upon Aitien and his squad of six pathfinders. Garat had known he would outstrip the squad, and when he was informed that

Che had continued on, Garat bade Aitien rest his squad and follow as soon as he could. Garat ordered up a canter to make as much ground before dark as he could. If Che ensured safe passage, Garat planned to rest until the moon rose and continue on, leading the horses well into the night.

R'chal was comforted by the knowledge that Wilder would give ample warning of danger.

Just as the shadows were lengthening towards nightfall, the six riders came upon the elf. Che reported that the Brocken had recently called in the squads that were out searching for Bartimaeus, the smith. She had found evidence of the recent passing of groups of men. Che then left to shadow those squads back to their encampment at the village. R'chal was pleased she could confirm the news when Wilder also gave the all-clear.

Garat again took the opportunity to rest the horses and riders as his intention to move through the night would leave them only a half-sun's solid ride from the village. With prisoners, the Brocken could not hope to cover any large distance, and Garat hoped he could shadow them until Aitien arrived, giving him a force of nearly twenty and the chance to choose the battleground. It would be vital for the prisoners that the attack be well planned, and surprise would be a valuable part of the strategy.

The unmistakable odour of burnt wood greeted the riders as they approached the village. Each member of the party also identified other smells they did not want to consider. The sight they beheld was of the near-total destruction of the village. Only one remote cottage still stood while the rest were smouldering ruins.

R'chal was shocked at the vista that spread before them. Houses of friends that had guested them blackened and ruined. Families of girls she had grown into womanhood with gone. Boys who she had flirted with and imagined sharing moments with were no longer. As tears fell Heleana nudged her horse closer and took R'chal by the hand providing the attachment and strength that comes with shared sorrow.

Che stood with two Pathfinders in what was once the inn's stable yard, signalling that it was safe to leave the woods and enter the remains of the village. The new pathfinders were from the squad that had witnessed the village's destruction. The squad leader showed Garat to the last remaining home and had his men care for the horses while Garat's group ate and refreshed themselves.

Lady Heleana and R'chal moved upwind of the unpleasant smells emanating from the village to find a quiet spot to eat their travel rations and check their kit as they would now have to carry it themselves. Garat had decided to leave the horses in the care of one of Kurbah's men so the squad currently bringing up the rear could rest, then catch up quickly.

R'chal watched Heleana finish up with her pack and begin to unwind the bindings on a strangely shaped bundle.

'I have seen that before. In the inn. When you returned our mother to us,' R'chal said.

'It is my bardiche. The ancient weapon of my family and the reason the Brocken have labelled me Lady Hell and added a large reward for my capture. They have never stipulated the condition I need to be in to claim the reward.'

The weapon was a long-bladed axe head mounted on a staff and would have come up to R'chal's shoulder when at rest. The blade was one-third the length of the entire weapon. As Heleana began to run a stone down the length of the blade, R'chal's skin crawled, and she understood why the Pathfinders and resistance had also adopted the moniker.

R'chal could imagine that when this weapon was combined with the Pathfinder's uniform and mask, the effect would be much like the spectre R'chal knew as the death reaper.

CHAPTER TWENTY
Du Tek

Seven warriors battle the horrors
Seven warriors bring back the light.

BARON DU TEK STORMED around the council chamber, attempting to bring his anger over his son under some control. Before him knelt three of his sergeants. Men who had been with him since the suns they had spent raiding in the north. He had elevated these men to positions of authority, wealth and property, yet none brought news of his misbegotten, wilful son.

Baron Tod Du Tek stopped pacing and looked down on the River Rayum, watching the barges transferring his plunder into the storage sheds to wait for more favourable weather and the beginning of the sailing season. He wondered how much he could hide from that fool Lothar, the supposed King-Emperor, and, more importantly, how much he could keep out of the hands of the Circle of Mages. His secret agreement with the Mages was predicated on him becoming Emperor of the South, and he was determined to keep as much wealth as possible on this side of the seas.

From Sudhemere's Citadel, he could see the vast plains stretching as far as the eye could see and, in the extreme distance, the grey smudge that was the Red Ranges. He headed the forces of the invaders, and while he had to contend with other barons trying to usurp his leadership, as long as he made them hollow promises of land for their sons in the future, he could keep them at bay. This land had plenty of room and wealth for all, but why should he have to share it?

He stopped his contemplation when he heard a groan from behind. Those men could just stay where they were. If he could not rely on them, he might as well replace them. Then he had a better idea. Turning from his view over the lands, he stormed towards the kowtowed trio.

'Come with me.'

Du Tek lined his men up along the balustrade that bordered the inner balcony, looking down into the citadel's bailey. The sergeants were well aware of the scene that would become their lesson.

'What do we learn from that fellow down there?' the baron asked. 'Let me remind you of the price of failure. That body spread-eagled by chains down there was the previous governor of our occupied lands. He failed. He put the plans of the Mages to control the Southlands back by turns.'

He looked to ensure he had the fearful and rapt attention he wanted.

'When the Mages are crossed, they can be very inventive. First, they had the man chained, as you see him now. Each arm and leg was stretched until any movement would cause the limb to dislocate. They left him like that for a sun or two, and each time his screaming stopped, they had a child throw rocks at him to wake him up. Once his screaming had the attention of the whole populace, they began carving.

'One by one, the Mages removed a digit or another body part and threw it to the curs that wander the streets. I think they even rolled dice to leave which part to chop off totally up to chance.'

The baron's conversational style and moderate tone were being used to great effect and ensured his message got through.

'When he finally succumbed to the pain and blood loss, the mages preserved his body as a reminder that failure has consequences. They did not even bother to capture his essence. They just meted out the punishment because they wanted to. So now you understand my frustration. Where is my son?'

'My Lord, your son Rankin decided to go out on a regular patrol running along the base of the Red Ranges. Sergeant Ervine was his squad leader. He is a good man and knows better than to enter the Ranges without further support. They are overdue, and we have had no report from them,' one of the sergeants said.

'You dare come to me with nothing more than what is already known. Has not my lesson penetrated your thick head yet?'

He came to stand nose to nose with the speaker and felt the man tremble.

'Did I not just say failure has consequences? You are no better than that man down there. So join him.'

The baron lashed out and the sergeant's blood-curdling scream echoed about the citadel until a sickening thud cut off any further cry.

'My Lord, our spies mentioned there was to be some sort of gathering in one of the villages in the foothills of the Red Ranges. It was something to do with the hunt, probably one of those backward rites these people observe,' the next sergeant said.

Du Tek looked the remaining two men up and down. These were good men and had been with him a long time. In an ice-cold voice he said, 'Get out of my sight and remember you serve at my behest.'

The baron looked at his two bodyguards as they helped the despondent sergeants through the doors. He turned to the departing men.

'You two, gather your squads. I will go and find him myself,' Du Tek said. 'We leave as soon as I am ready.'

Du Tek strode from the citadel into the stable yards and perused his men. His sergeants had four squads of six in formation next to the support wagons and six slaves to cook and prepare camp. He was rather proud of his personal army and pleased that every other baron had followed his lead in outfitting the men with uniforms and weapons. It would make stealing them and taking them into his service that much easier, and he would save the expense of outfitting them. Life was good.

The baron was attired in the same style as his men, with a grey quilted gambeson and cloak. The only difference was that his was quilted with gold studs instead of the cheap metal studs he gave his men. As he walked to his horse, he was comforted by the footsteps of his bodyguards as they followed three steps to the rear. Only five would be mounted on this expedition. The baron, his guards, and the sergeants. That did not stop the baron from ordering the party to march at double time. He would make sure these men knew their sergeants were not currently in his good books.

The lands around the citadel were well under his control, so he could set a punishing pace. He had his two guards ride ahead to clear the carts and beasts from the path to ensure there would be no relief for the following column of men. Du Tek would make sure these men knew who caused their misery. He rode at the head of the column, keeping up a continuous banter with the two squad leaders, all the while aware of the growing resentment behind him. The baron called a halt when the column reached the outskirts of the farmlands and allowed the men to rest. After all, it would be foolish to risk a flatbow bolt in the back by pushing them beyond endurance. He knew he had driven home his point when he looked over the men. The sergeants seemed almost scared to go amongst their men.

It was well into the afternoon, and they had outstripped the following baggage wagon and the slaves. The baron had no option but to walk the men until the wagon could catch up and camp set for the night. The men would be no trouble tonight. They would need their rest. It would take at least two more suns to reach the foothills of the Red Ranges. Once in camp, his bodyguards would protect him from any random revenge attempts.

AS THEY BROKE CAMP the next sun, Du Tek had time to reflect on his second child. The boy was the get of his second wife. After his first wife had died giving him his heir, he had taken a second one for political reasons. The only benefits he received from his union with that harpy were elevation to head of the College of Barons and a son who was almost his duplicate. Where his first son was taller, leaner and fairer, both the baron and his second son were stocky and dark with sharp features and eyes that never stopped searching for the greatest advantage in any given situation.

The baron had hoped he could train this boy to the position of Sheriff in the Southlands, leaving him in charge while he travelled between his holdings in the north and the south. The plan had been to stay well away from his wife and enjoy the company of his slave girls and warm weather all turn round. Unfortunately, the boy seemed to have picked up the habits of his mother's family. He acted as though all were his to command by right rather than through fear, strength of arm, and purpose.

His second son, the self-proclaimed Captain Rankin Du Tek, spent money like it grew in the fields and was his to take at whim. This, the baron accepted some fault for. *Could greed really be considered a fault?* he wondered.

His son's growing sense of entitlement was not a trait the baron welcomed or encouraged. It had caused any number of complaints and incidents with staff, soldiers and the populace. If his son did not have a bloody good excuse for running off and pretending to be a soldier, stern measures would have to be taken and damn any whining or recriminations from the boy's mother. The baron had heard of the beauty of Lady Heleana, and as he currently resided in her castle, perhaps a new wife and politically savvy arrangement were in his future. He must remember to increase the reward for her capture and insist that her head remain attached to the rest of her.

His thoughts were interrupted by the call to halt for the mid-sun meal. His shade tent was erected, and he lounged on his camp chair, dining on cold roast meats and pastries cooked in the citadel's kitchens. He hoped this excursion would not be so protracted that he would be forced to eat the salted pork and travel rations fed to his men. Du Tek looked towards the mountains and noted he could now begin to make out the shape of the land ahead. They were on schedule. Another sun and a half would see them approaching the foothills.

The next few suns of the journey was laborious and repetitive and the baron contemplated various explanations for the death of his son. Once the thought of marriage to Lady Heleana, the heir of Sudhemere, had crossed his mind, he had begun to picture the demise of his current wife. After all, he had to have something enjoyable to keep his mind active on a long trip like this one.

She had served her purpose. He was second only to Lothar in the Northern Empire, and until Lothar sired an heir, he had the votes to lead in both the south and the north. A hunting accident was very tempting right now. How ironic would that be? To play Lothar at his own game. Du Tek was starting to enjoy this ride. It allowed him to explore all sorts of opportunities without the constant interruptions of his court.

Baron Tod Du Tek was on the verge of turning the expedition around, returning to the comfort of his slave girls in the citadel, and leaving his son to the will of fate when his guards brought his attention back to the present. They had reached the foothills and were close to entering the forest. Du Tek ordered a camp to be made as it was late afternoon, and he was still undecided on the worth of continuing his search. He could wait another night before venturing into lands not completely brought to heel.

The best site for the camp was just beside a small stream that bubbled from the forest and crossed a small flat plateau less than one hundred paces from the forest edge. The baron toured the camp and was pleased at the neatness and conformity of his troops. Although he set a punishing pace and his men suffered from soreness and fatigue, his sergeants made sure they did nothing to inspire their lord's wrath. They were fully aware of the consequences of failure.

The baron was relaxing in his tent with a cup of good southern wine when his guards reported the approach of a column of soldiers and a wagon being pulled by civilians. It appeared to be two squads of his own men herding about thirty southern villagers. Du Tek, followed by his two silent guards, walked through the camp and came to look at the approaching column. He made out the figure of a soldier standing in the wagon waving what looked like a white cloth or kerchief.

As the wagon moved closer, the baron noticed the glint off the soldier's gambeson and recognised the reflection of gold in the dying sunlight. Baron Du Tek prided himself on being able to recognise gold from any distance. Well, at least he would not have to chase around the forest to find the boy.

Baron Du Tek returned to his tent and left orders for his son to be brought to him when he arrived. The boy was twenty-four turns and still acted like a spoiled child. Perhaps there would be an opportunity for a riding accident on their return journey. Rankin Du Tek did not even bother to ask permission to enter. He just barged in as though he had every right. Du Tek was about to explode and chastise the boy when he noticed the bandages on his hand and the strangeness of his gait. The boy only stood and held the back of one of the camp chairs even after being given permission to sit in the baron's presence.

It looked as though Captain Rankin Du Tek had learnt a lesson and now had the scars to show for it. With any luck, this might have been just the thing to mature the boy. Baron Du Tek decided to give his son a chance to explain in the hope that the telling would reveal a veteran who could see the value in experience and command.

He ordered attention to be given his son and waited until the boy was cleaned up and fed before letting him begin his explanations. The baron exerted some mighty self-control not to laugh when inspections revealed a wound in each buttock, one an arrow wound, the other from a knife. A matched set to go along with his injured hand.

Baron Du Tek was forced to endure a whining tale of misadventure and downright foolish choices as his son tried to veil his mistakes, claiming poor performances from the squads and his mishandling at the hands of Lady Hell.

'All this because you lost your horse?' the baron asked.

'That horse cost me twenty gold royales,' Rankin said.

'That horse cost *me* that sack of royales,' Du Tek countered.

At no time could his son see his own hand in his injuries, and when he reported on the village's destruction following his own humiliation, the baron could tell there was a lot his son was not revealing. Eventually, Baron Du Tek ordered his son to see to the disposition of his men.

As Baron Du Tek's own camp could not be re-struck, he ordered for the prisoners to be housed across the stream. He permitted Rankin to billet the rest of his men within the main camp, provided he left some men to guard the prisoners.

Baron Du Tek was sure he would get a truer report from Sergeant Erskine and ordered that he present himself as soon as the camps were set. The report from his son only enhanced Du Tek's resolve that the boy did not have what it took to rule and should be sent back to his mother. Preferably before the boy forced Du Tek to take more permanent action.

Baron Du Tek decided to take a stroll before Erskine arrived to see that all was done to his liking. He had not made a lesson of any individuals and thought it was high time the men were reminded who they owed allegiance to.

As the shadows of the setting sun lengthened, he walked about the camp with his ever-present guards flanking him three paces to his rear. The men were positively jubilant, an extreme counterpoint to the fatigue and fear he had hoped would be the general consensus. He then noticed the men were looking longingly at the encampment Erskine was currently overseeing and realised they were thinking about and preparing for their favourite pastime. The soldiers considered a little rape and violence was fair payment for the occupying forces, and they were currently holding lots to decide on a fair and equitable order.

Smiling inwardly, Baron Du Tek realised just the way to dampen the men's spirits and remind them of who commanded. Before sending out the order, he had better get back to his tent and have his guards doubled. This would not be popular, and he laughed at the coming consternation of his men. He almost felt the camp's mood change as the order was repeated from fire to fire. There would be no prisoners allowed in the camp, no soldiers would be allowed to visit the prisoner's camp. He would let them have their fun tomorrow after they were on their way home, but tonight, they could sleep alone.

It was just on full dark when Sergeant Erskine finally made an appearance. He had attempted to present himself in the best possible light by cleaning his uniform and boots. Erskine was one of his best men, but when an example was needed, Du Tek knew he could not be choosy. Before he announced the punishment for this man he would hear a true report of his son's misadventures and injuries.

Just as the baron ordered the sergeant to speak, the most spine-chilling, mind-bending howl went up from the plains and echoed back off the mountains.

CHAPTER TWENTY-ONE
Rescue

Seven warriors are faith restorers
Seven warriors force chaos back.

AFTER A BRIEF RESPITE, R'chal and Heleana were called in to hear the report from the squad leader, who had wisely held his men and had tried to hold the smith in check. A difficult feat as the pleading and screams from the village reverberated through the trees and tore through his and each of his men's hearts.

'My Lady Heleana, Commander Garat, my squad had accompanied Bartimaeus the smith on his journey to collect ore and black stone. He needed a particular quality ore to make his steel. On our return, my scouts reported the presence of Brocken in the village, so we went into hiding. We thought it was just the usual bullying and stealing, so many villagers sent their young ones into the forest. Then, three Brocken arrived carrying a wounded man. We could see he was not mortally wounded or even badly impaired, but he had forced his men to carry him on a rudely made stretcher,' the squad leader said. 'This was the man who had Raymond the tavern keeper questioned. Raymond pointed up the path, telling what he knew, but the officer had him held and just ran him through. He then had Raymond's family put to the sword, threw them into the inn, and set it ablaze.

Afterwards, he turned out the family from this house and took it for himself.' The Pathfinder paused to gather his thoughts.

'The next morning, he sent out patrols to look for the smith, Bartimaeus is well know as the best sword smith in the lands. Then the Brocken started to find the children hiding in the forest. We evaded the search on the first sun, but the next sun, the searchers found the smith's cart and had it dragged by the villagers to the officer. This incensed the Brocken officer, and he limped around the village, beating the prisoners with a baton, demanding to know the whereabouts of Bartimaeus. None knew, so none could tell. He kept up the beatings that sun until nightfall,' he said.

'The next morning, he changed his method. He had his men come to the edge of the forest, calling for the smith to come forth. Then, around mid-morning, he marched an old mother to the centre of the bridge and had the villagers line up and shout Bartimaeus's name. We had to hold him back. He wanted to go. The officer then held up a bandaged hand and ordered one of his men to drive a blade through the old mother's hand and pin her to the bridge. All saw her pain and heard her screams.'

R'chal and Heleana were shaken by the report and had tears brimming in their eyes, threatening to stream down their cheeks. They were intensely aware that their kindness in releasing the Brocken officer had brought about this tragedy. R'chal was even more acutely dismayed as she recognised this method of torture was directly related to her treatment of the officer. She had thought she was showing mercy in her actions. She had tried to cause the least amount of permanent damage, choosing the buttock and hand over the possibility of causing internal damage. R'chal was on the verge of breaking down until a message from Wilder entered her mind.

Hunter, there is strength in mercy.

Wilder's words brought R'chal back to the present, and she vowed to herself that she would not become as ignorant of suffering or as blasé about death as the Brocken.

'I have a further witness,' the squad leader said. He signalled and a frightened, traumatized young girl on the cusp of womanhood was brought in. 'This lass was in the village.'

Heleana stepped forwards and embraced the girl, who fell into a period of sobbing, burying her face in Lady Heleana's chest. After some soothing and a drink of watered wine, her story was finally coaxed from her.

'The officer made us call him Captain Du Tek. He was the one who ordered the inn burnt. He was the one who murdered Jainn on the bridge. He was the one who ordered the assaults, and he was the one that took my Kjieran,' she said.

'Tell us the rest, little one. I know it's hard, but if we are to help, we need to know,' Garat said gently.

'Two squads of Brocken came, and we were sent into the woods. We have hides hidden in the forest. Usually, they only stay a short while, then we can come out, but this time, they wanted our blacksmith,' she said. 'The searchers found me and made me come back to the village. We were held prisoner in the meadow, and the captain beat us and demanded to know where Bartimaeus was. Then he began pulling the women from the group one at a time and giving them to his men. They screamed and screamed. Then the next and the next,' she shuddered and gasped. 'The next morning, he had us all call Bartimaeus, and then he tortured old Jainn on the bridge. She screamed, and begged, and screamed. Just before nightfall, he dragged my Kjieran onto the bridge. No one could fail to recognise his hair and burnt hand. Without even calling out to the smith, the captain held up Kjieran's good hand and ordered his sergeant to nail his hand to the bridge using a hammer and nails made by Bartimaeus himself.'

The girl had almost swooned at the memory, and had to be revived again by Heleana. They administered more watered wine to fortify her and allow her to finish her tale.

'Bartimaeus ran from the forest screaming for his son. Kjieran screamed for his father to stop, but the smith was berserk. He attacked the Brocken barehanded. When the officer started to laugh, Kjieran pulled his hand free from the nail. He grabbed the knife that still held old Jainn's body to the bridge and attacked the officer. Kjieran was too weak with the pain and only managed to drive the knife into the captain's arse.' This memory stirred pride in the girl. 'The captain went into a fit of madness and had Kjieran dragged before his father, who was being held by some men. Without even a word, the captain took his sword and cut off Kjieran's hand. It landed right at the smith's feet. Bartimaeus bellowed, broke away from his captors, and grabbed for the man. Du Tek stabbed him.

'The captain laughed and stabbed. There was blood. He laughed and stabbed and stabbed. So much blood. I ran.'

R'chal's heart sank.

She would be unable to keep her promise to Quinn.

R'chal silently wept for her friend. Heleana sent the men out of the cottage and shook R'chal from her stupor. They had work to do. This girl needed care. She had been beaten, abused, ill-used, and seen things that could not be unseen. Any more care than cleaning her wounds and giving her wine to dull the pain would have to wait. R'chal helped Heleana and, when the girl had finally fallen asleep, took the chance to escape from the confines of the cottage.

When she stepped outside, Wilder was sitting beside the door while the Pathfinders had kept a respectable distance. R'chal hugged the canine and silently thanked him for his support.

R'chal was brought back to the present when Wilder projected, *The Red Ranges pack comes. Ten pairs have answered my summons.*

R'chal was pleased to tell Garat that he would have the support of the Wolf Riders.

Garat called for the resumption of their chase and sent Che forwards to scout. Garat led ten, with the five remaining members of the squad joining him. They took the route leading away from the village, and Wilder came in to walk with R'chal since he no longer had to worry about upsetting the horses. R'chal noticed that Wilder drew some sidelong glances from Kurbah and his man as Wilder was half again as large as the largest wolf they had ever seen.

The going became easier when the path started to drop towards the plains. Garat called for the Pathfinders to take up an easy jogging pace.

The squad leader had told Garat that the Brocken officer was being transported in the cart belonging to the smith, being pulled by the captured villagers. Garat was hopeful his group could overtake the sixteen Brocken and their prisoners before they reached the plains.

Before long, they saw clear evidence that the Brocken raiding party was not far ahead as various items of rubbish and personal property littered the route. Then, when the group rounded a bend in the road, they found several bodies left by the wayside, treated no better by the Brocken than the other items they'd discarded.

R'chal was shocked into breathlessness by the apparent cruelty of the soldiers, and while the pathfinders were also upset, it was nothing they had not experienced before. She was grateful when Garat called a stop just beyond the site. R'chal needed time to process the grisly sight, even as she was aware that Che had spent time giving the dead some dignity and had made the site look a lot better than it would have.

The thinning trees indicated to the pathfinders that they were transitioning onto the plains of the lowlands. A scout approached Garat, Heleana and R'chal at the same time the smell of campfires reached them. The scout confirmed that the Brocken had set up camp.

R'chal and Heleana awaited information as Garat climbed a tree to give him the best view of the Brocken campsite. Even in the gloaming he reported the standard square-patterned camp of the Brocken. Unfortunately, he also reported that he could see banners of Baron Du Tek.

The Brocken party now numbered more than seventy and, while the prisoners were being held separate from the soldiers, Garat's own nineteen men and ten wolf pairs would have to be used wisely. The Brocken had made an error in believing they were not being hunted and had camped within bow shot of the forest edge.

While Garat waited for Aitien to arrive on the horses, he sat in council with Heleana and R'chal. Garat had noticed that the Brocken were just completing their set-up and knew he had just missed his chance of catching the raiders. He asked his men for suggestions on how to keep the Brocken from spreading the villagers amongst their tents when each froze as a sinister howl echoed through the trees.

Will that do? came to R'chal. Garat shuddered when R'chal passed on the message. *I will lead the pack, but they cannot kill*, was the second message, which R'chal also passed on to the commander.

Garat prepared his plan. R'chal, Che and himself would see to the villagers. He would ask the Dini to line an escape route and lead the villagers to safety. The Pathfinders would use the darkness to get close enough to use their bows with some accuracy to take out the sentries, and Lady Hell would do her thing on horseback.

To gain the maximum advantage, Wilder led the wolves out across the plains and set up a cacophony of howling. Flashes of wolves running in and out of sight continued to draw the attention of the Brocken away from their prisoners. Coming from the north, the Brocken were well aware of the dangers of a hunting wolf pack. When the moon started sinking behind the mountains, Garat called for everyone to get ready and told R'chal she would signal Wilder to announce the attack.

Che led R'chal and Garat towards the prisoners. Garat and R'chal now wore the green mask of the resistance, but the elf had no need to hide a pale face. They inched forward, being passed from one wolf rider to the next along the escape route set for the prisoners.

Crouched in the darkness within reach of the prisoners, R'chal steadied her breathing. She was positive the beating of her heart would be heard by the first sentry that passed. The waiting was the hardest part. She was determined to play a significant role in saving these people who had done nothing to deserve their current predicament. Creeping through the dark and the mission had kept her focused, now the fear of failure set in. She silently begged Garat to give her the hand sign that she would pass to Wilder to signal the start of the assault. Finally, there was a flash of a hand in the night, quickly followed by a mighty howl.

Che rose ahead of R'chal and silently slipped her knife across the throat of a distracted guard. Garat moved to his left, and R'chal only saw a dark shadow rise in silhouette behind another sentry to complete the same action. She almost gagged when she saw dark blood spurt from the neck wound of the Brocken soldier.

Che moved off to take care of any inquisitive replacements. Garat and R'chal were now able to move amongst the prisoners to calm and reassure them that the wolves were here to help and rescue was at hand. They explained the Dini would guide them and they were not to look back. A wolf rider appeared as if from nowhere and took the hand of a young girl to lead her silently to the next rider in line. R'chal searched for Quinn's brother and found him delirious and in pain. She insisted that Garat carry him out while she stayed as rearguard with Che.

As the first prisoner was being led away, the night became silent and still. The wolves slowly approached the encampment. As their glowing eyes were picked up in the light of the bonfires, the Brocken's nerves snapped, and they released volley after volley of bolts. The range and their ruined night vision made accuracy impossible and a strike most improbable.

Wilder let out the loudest and longest howl yet, which was the signal for the charge. Heleana screamed her war cry as she brandished her famous axe, and four horsemen charged the camp from the opposite direction.

Lady Hell was amongst the Brocken and spreading maximum confusion and fear before they could turn and mount a coordinated defence.

Heleana's deadly axe cut a swath through the panicked men, leaving ghastly wounds and bodies separated from their heads and limbs in her wake. Kurbah had been just as effective with his long sword, and the horses were out the other side of the camp before the Brocken could mount any resistance. The baron had no time to call his men to order before the wolves dashed amongst them. The wolves rushed through the camp, ripping out hamstrings and biting arms and legs, causing injuries and great fear before they disappeared as fast as they had appeared.

R'chal and Che saw the last of the prisoners being helped away and slowly backed towards the safety of the forest, protecting the villagers. Upon Wilder's further signal, the remaining Pathfinders shot volleys of arrows into the camp to complete the overwhelming panic and deter any organised pursuit. The Brocken were now dealing with screaming wounded, fires amongst their tents and arrows flying in from the dark. Pandemonium reigned until Baron Du Tek's cry gathered his sergeants and mustered his men around the baggage cart to create a shield wall. The Brocken wounded became a counterpoint to the wolves' howls as they screamed for help or whimpered into silence.

As dawn approached, the Brocken were given a reprieve. Six archers remained within the cover of the forest to ensure the Brocken would not organise any pursuit. Heleana had taken her troop well out on the plains to swing around the battleground before making her way back so they were the last of the Pathfinders to return.

As the horsemen approached, R'chal saw that not all had gone to plan. Tied across the back of his horse was Kurbah, two Brocken bolts sticking from his back. Heleana was tearful when she reported that Kurbah had chosen to ride to protect her rear. She knew those arrows were meant for her. There were other wounded to be treated among the Pathfinders, wolves and villagers, so mercifully, R'chal and Heleana were too busy to dwell long on the events of the night.

The objective had been achieved. The villagers had been released, and Quinn's brother was now under their care. Kjieran was in shock. His pallor was almost a match for his hair. Blood loss and seeing his father murdered before him had him in delirium. He moaned and cried, and occasionally lashed out with his damaged arm. This caused great pain, and he would pass out again. R'chal and Heleana agreed his only chance of staying alive was to get him to the care of Lady Winifred.

'Can we use the horses to get him to your Aunt Winnie?' R'chal asked.

'I am sure Garat will agree,' Heleana said.

Just then, a bowman ran towards them from the forest.

'My Lady Heleana, you need to come.'

Aitien pointed to one of the walking wounded.

'You there, find the commander and send him after us.'

Aitien, R'chal and Heleana ran after the bowman. He was one of the rearguard, left to ensure the Brocken did not organise a counterattack. They dashed through the trees, dodging boles and skipping over roots, taking a direct route to the site of last night's battle. As they reached the edge of the forest, the tableau before them caused Heleana to fall to her knees and sob while R'chal rushed behind a tree and threw up the contents of her stomach.

'Report,' Aitien demanded.

'After the attack on the Brocken, we maintained watch. By the light of the fires, we could just make out the soldiers trying to reorganise their encampment. The wailing of the wounded slowly abated as they were collected and given aid or died from their injuries. The fires were also being put out, and we moved closer to see more clearly. Then, some Brocken soldiers marched two prisoners to the centre of the camp. We could only surmise one was a child or one of the Dini, and the other a Pathfinder by their sizes. There was no chance to mount a rescue. Brocken standing orders are that anyone caught wearing the Pathfinder mask is to be executed.'

The squad leader faltered in his report, knowing the telling would only get harder.

'They tied the prisoners spread-eagled to an overturned cart and began to torture them both. The screams were horrific. They had set up a rank of flatbowmen and were trying to draw us out. It was clearly an ambush. Over the screaming, we heard yelling, "Pathfinders stand!" Then, as the dawn's light allowed, we saw the Brocken withdrawing from the field. As they left, they lit the cart on fire. The child had already succumbed, but the Pathfinder was hanging on.'

The squad leader seemed to shrink into himself at this point.

'I got as close as I could. I still suspected a trap, and I was right. They had left some of the severely wounded behind with flatbows to kill any who approached. We dispatched them so we could try and reach the prisoners.'

The Pathfinder finally gave up his struggle.

'My Lady, it was Commander Garat.'

In deep gloaming chaos takes form
As blackness creeps light will cease.
Creatures stretch, stir, rumble, swarm
Time is nigh for dreads release.

Each abysmal night a battle rages,
In pitch-black the balance dips.
Evil triumph a first for ages,
Fear and doom take hold and grips.

As hope diminishes the light is lost
In deep despair a bold pact made.
Great sacrifice for each the cost
If evil to transcend is willing paid.

Seven warriors battle the horrors
Seven warriors bring light to black
Seven warriors are faith restorers
Seven warriors force chaos back.

Lotan's ruby red as fire, bravery in battle warrior's desire
Mwindo's silver star does cure, intensity and honour
ensure
Zahhak's yellow lights all shadow battle glow does inspire
Druk diamond white and pure no dedication more
secure.

Bazu topaz blue for the freed, diligence others cede.
Dreq emerald to revive ensures a world will survive.
One above all to battle and lead
Zammok's black by example extort the cohort to thrive.

RESISTANCE

A world gives up freedoms and sentience
Endowing inner light to each defender
Sacrifice gladly given survival demands dominance
Warriors gem anchors, battle won without surrender

Seven warriors battle the horrors
Seven warriors bring light to black
Seven warriors are faith restorers
Seven warriors force chaos back.